She thinks she's going crazy—the rest of the world thinks she's a hero...

After her grandson, Will, is molested and the predator released on a technicality, Martha Lavery, a practicing R. N., notices a great increase in anger, lost time periods, and things in her possession that she would never buy. Terrified that she is losing her mind, she seeks the care of a psychiatrist. Add to that, unsolicited notice from a handsome, older, male nurse, who sees her distress and wants to help, and her life rapidly becomes a hopeless, dilemma. Now she must handle what is happening—and save her sanity—while being forced to face a vile, horrendous secret about her own childhood.

I0539906

KUDOS for *The Vigilante*

The Vigilante challenges the reader to examine their values, while rooting for the vigilante! Ms. Forrest does a masterful job of introducing and building the main character, Martha, a skilled nurse and heartbroken grandmother whose young grandson's life is forever changed when he is violated by a pedophile. While Martha struggles to make sense out of her family's personal tragedy, the pedophile is struggling for his life...The Vigilante is a great read that is guaranteed to delight, especially if you are bored with the status quo. – *Mary Fuller, attorney*

All I can say about The Vigilante is "Wow!" Ramona Forest uses her in-depth knowledge of the nursing field to weave a story so intriguing and twisted that it's hard to put down. Martha Lavery, a nurse at the local hospital, struggles to try to figure out what is happening to her. I loved The Vigilante and read it in one sitting. – *Taylor, reviewer*

Forrest's knowledge of the medical field is obviously quite extensive and I thought the retribution that Serena dished out to the predators of children quite appropriate. I liked her characterization and the romance that sort of flitted between the pages of the story. The plot is solid, the writing well-done, and as Taylor points out, it is not a story you want to put down until it is finished. The Vigilante makes you examine your values while giving you a reason to do so, in other words, it's as thought-provoking as it is entertaining. – *Regan, reviewer*

Wow! What a wonderful, timely tale of suspense/mystery /psychological thriller...From my psychiatric background I find it to be accurate and intriguing. – *Dr. Walter Hoffman, forensic psychiatrist*

The man was scum and just because the police couldn't do anything about it, that didn't mean she couldn't...

She'd scoped out this house several times after following him home from The Paradisio two weeks ago. He was fastidious in his landscaping, in the clipping and trimming of his shrubbery. Yet the stuff disguising his carport, on the other hand, had been left to grow wildly. "Need the green stuff to hide something, eh, Denny, my boy?"

His dented green car sat parked in his driveway under a lattice-work car-port, hidden from the street by the heavy growth of vines, trees, and shrubs. Serena had observed him taking the city bus of late, keeping the old green sedan off the streets. "Doesn't want his car noticed by police."

She chuckled softly. "All in good time, Denny dear," she cooed. "When the cops come, they'll see it plain enough." They had the description, a bit vague, but his old green car fit what they'd broadcast on television. It had made him wary. From his conversations with Fred, Serena had learned that he wanted to take it out of town for a paint job, but feared driving it in public. "It's too late, Denny," she murmured. "Hiding your car won't help you anymore. I know the truth and, believe me, I don't give a damn about the color of your car."

Serena waited long past the hour Denny usually entered the alley, and decided that once again, this was not her day. It had gotten too bright, and though the lights glowed in the kitchen, it didn't appear he'd dump his garbage this morning. Today was garbage pick-up. Maybe he'd put it out last night like most people.

Turning to make her way back toward the street, she heard the back door open. Her pulse quickened and pounded in her breast as she quickly retraced her steps. She slunk down behind the large, black plastic garbage container and waited.

Denny opened his back gate and entered the alley carrying two large, full, white plastic bags, secured with twist ties. As he dropped the bags he carried and reached to open the container, Serena stood up and, using both arms, swung the soft, heavy sandbag against the back of his head.

ACKNOWLEDGEMENTS

I wish to extend my appreciation to Walter D. Hoffman M. D. for his kind commentary regarding my treatment of Dissociative Identity Disorder. Also, I extend thanks to Ryan Mapus, for allowing me to use his name for my detective, and to my friend and author, Pinkie Paranya for all those reference books. Add to this list all those who have overwhelmingly applauded the content of this story.

THE

VIGILANTE

By

Ramona Forrest

A BLACK OPAL BOOKS PUBLICATION

GENRE: SUSPENSE/MEDICAL THRILLER/ROMANTIC ELEMENTS

THE VIGILANTE
Copyright © 2013 by Ramona Forrest
Cover Design by Jackson Cover Designs
All cover art copyright © 2013
All Rights Reserved
Print ISBN: 978-1-626940-11-6

First Publication: APRIL 2013

Published by Black Opal Books **http://www.blackopalbooks.com**

DEDICATION

I dedicate this book it to all children forced to suffer inhumanity at the hands of those who have the care and nurturing of them, but especially, to all those little souls forced to endure life-destroying degradation at the hands of a child predator.

CHAPTER 1

Serena's heart pulsed rapidly, and her eyes narrowed. After weeks of planning and observation, her long-sought mission lay before her. Any thoughts of wrong escaped her conscience—for she had none. A small boy crying out in fear and shame had become her driving force. His deep, broken sobs—those long periods of staring into space, seeing nothing, hearing nothing—held her in a cold, calculating state of hatred.

His suffering and extreme fear of strangers, burned deeply into her soul. She was the protector—always had been. She alone possessed the strength and will to avenge the child. A heinous crime committed against his innocence had cruelly ripped his world asunder.

Serena tossed her head, as she snorted in disdain. *What have the police done? Nothing to save him from the unspeakable things that pedophile running ahead of her had done to his small body. And now unbelievably, the man is free to repeat his crimes on another child.* Unable to accept or forgive the failure of the authorities, her unrelenting anger had forged her hatred into a hard, unshakeable resolve.

She watched her breath become a fragile mist, rising to vaporize and fade away on the ice-laden, early morning air. She trotted lightly and easily, a lioness on the hunt, this frigid, crisp, March morning in the high, mountain city of Colorado Springs. She made her way silently down a sandy trail that wound in curving pathways through Leesford Green, the city's jogging park.

Passing several small wooded groves, Serena came up a gentle rise that led through a thick tangle of stunted scrub oak, and halted her run. Slinking deep into the grove, she observed the area carefully. *This'll do.* Secluded and spacious enough for her needs, she decided and solidified her plan.

Lightly panting from her run, she rested, idly noting the pattern of dirty snow scattered in shadowed patches beneath the many scrubby, stunted bushes. The graceful bend of bare twigs were starkly outlined against the snow. The little birds, mostly chickadees, scolded as they sought a scarlet seed or two from low, leafless shrubs, hidden away from the pale morning sun. It shed no warmth and barely sufficient light, as it rose behind roiling, diffuse layers of grayish clouds.

Waiting in the shadows, she narrowed her eyes into slits as she watched the running track. Her target ran ahead, but the circuitous trail would bring him close enough when he passed by again. And he would. She'd watched him many times before.

"Habitual little bastard, aren't you?" She uttered the low growl as the fierce intensity of unreasoning hatred seethed within her. Serena shrugged it away, leaving only sheer determination.

She waited, looking about the area. A few scarlet berries clung to starkly bare twigs and faded leaves lay scattered about, moldering into the few spots of bare soil. Crusted patches of old snow, hidden in the shade, resisted melting. Smiling to herself, she decided, *I'll use that.* Impressed at the cleanliness of natural things, she appreciated that creatures of nature might be brutal, even seeming cruel to human thought, but never evil or mentally sick.

She lost interest in her surroundings, other than its use in concealment, as the man's slightly rotund body chugged steadily toward her. With disgust, she noted how easily he'd become winded from his efforts. His arms flailed out, and the wispy fog of his breaths gusting on the icy air had become increasingly short and rapid. How well she knew him, both form and face. Revenge against the man hardened her purpose and fueled a burning revulsion for his destroying, pedophilic soul.

Finally, his panting and blowing alerted her he was coming close. Her plans had been carefully laid out. With the morning very cold, few joggers were out this early. *How perfect!*

She nodded. Restless, she allowed a few fleeting doubts to cross her mind but, haunted by the unspeakable outrage that drove her, she ignored them. The clenched fists of the boy's father, the heartbreak of his mother, and the utter futility of finding justice in a broken system had hardened her.

With jaw clenched in helpless anger at a system that no longer protected the innocent, she huffed, "We no longer have rights. Only the sick bastards who inflict unspeakable suffering on others, to satisfy their own sick needs, are important these days. That monster has ruined the peace and sanctity of more lives than he knows, and the authorities do nothing!"

Her heart raced. She tensed her strong, athletic body as the shuffling gait of her target sounded on the graveled pathway. Older, yet strong, supple, and totally capable, she'd been drawn into this cause unwillingly. Yet as always, it was her duty to protect her host and her loved ones. Squaring her shoulders, she muttered into the icy air, "I must do this— there's no one else." With a strong feeling of purpose, waiting in the dense thicket, she prepared to exact vengeance for an evil crime against humanity. *I can, and I will!*

The wheezing gasps of her intended target neared. Her heart hammered in her chest as she pulled a sand bag covered with thick, sturdy, tan twill from the old blue duffle bag, laid it on the gravel and gripped it firmly in both hands. Her body tensed, tight as a bowstring drawn to shoot an arrow, she prepared to spring.

The tiring man lumbered across her path. She looked about once again. Seeing no other joggers, she stepped out behind him and swung the sandbag heavily against the side of his head. He staggered and dropped soundlessly in a sodden mass on the gravel trail.

Serena tossed the bag aside. She grasped his flaccid, flabby carcass by his sweat suit top and dragged him into the depths of the thicket just off the trail. Cold hatred of this man and what he was, gave her additional strength. Moving him was no problem despite his bulk.

She reached for his neck, felt his pulse along his jugular. *It's rapid and strong. He's alive. Wouldn't want to do him in, though he might wish we had.*

Chuckling softly, she went to work, opened a pack of supplies, and laid them out. Then she grasped the elastic waistband of his joggers and under shorts and, rolling him to his side, pulled them down to his knees. Donning rubber gloves, she moved his upper leg a bit higher, neatly exposing his privates. She opened a scalpel and reached for the loose, pink, wrinkly skin over his scrotum. The flaccid skin over the soft mounds tensed in her grasp. Without a moment of hesitation, she slashed across each with the razor sharp scalpel.

"Slippery little devils!" she exclaimed softly, ignoring the oozing blood. Squeezing firmly, she expressed the testes one at a time. Burning rage overwhelmed her yet again. She threw the rounded baubles of his sex onto the ground and stomped them into bloody mush with the oversized men's hiking boots she wore. The smashed pulp of them seeped into the sand and gravel beside the man's inert body.

"They'll do you no good from now on, you filthy, destroying, monster!" She spat the words in low, deadly tones at the figure lying before her with his bare, bloodied buttocks exposed to the frigid, early morning air.

She opened a small, dark vial and splashed a brilliant violet liquid over his bleeding wounds. After picking away part of the frozen crust of a small chunk of snow, she packed it into the bleeding mess. *Wonder if it'll hurt with those icy edges.* Her eyes narrowed into slits, and she grinned, caring not at all.

Taking out two elongated, hospital-type sanitary napkins, she placed them snugly over the bleeding, melting mess, and pulled his shorts over them, struggling and rolling his flaccid, unconscious bulk. She pulled his joggers, twisted and wrinkled, up to complete the mission.

She observed his pallid features with disdain. His face, rounded and rather feminine, seemed pathetic to her way of thinking, right along with that stubby little nose. The rest of his equipment was nothing to write home about, either. She snorted her derision. "No wonder he picks on small children."

Her mission done, she enjoyed the sense of complete satisfaction.

His moaning forewarned her he was regaining consciousness. He looked pale, and though blood seeped slowly from his jogging bottoms, she believed his life lay in no immediate danger. "You won't bleed to death, you filthy, stinking, bastard, but you might wish otherwise." She laughed softly as her eyes drew into narrow slits again.

Rushing to avoid discovery and recognition, she repacked her supplies and sand bag before sprinting out onto the trail. She'd be just another casual morning jogger if anyone bothered to notice. Maintaining a soft trot, she removed the purple and blood-stained gloves. She twisted a bit and stuffed them into her back pack, and zipped it closed. Continuing on toward the entrance, Serena left the running park with an air of casual nonchalance and sauntered slowly and leisurely several blocks to her small car, an old 'ninety-five, white, Toyota Celica.

On the drive home, she smiled with a sense of satisfaction that she'd done the world a small, but needed, justice. Pulling into her garage, she pressed the button, closing the wide door.

Before entering the house, she slipped off her rough clothing and men's boots. She tossed them, along with the pack, behind a piece of unused plywood leaning against the wall near the gardening tools. A few dark spots on her jogging suit caught her attention. Were they blood? They looked more violet in color, but her thoughts, rapidly becoming cloudy and confused, faded quickly as she entered the house.

Once inside, memories of the past hours left her consciousness. Confusion and fatigue descended over her. The hiking boots, back pack, and blue bag were already gone from her memory.

Discarding her clothes, she entered the shower, scrubbed her hair and body unmercifully, seeking the feel of cleanliness.

The purple spots on her arms refused to wash off. She frowned as she examined them, but no longer knowing where they'd come from, she shrugged, dried herself, and dressed for bed. Tired, she climbed into her bed and gently slipped away into a fog of exhaustion and bewilderment as she drifted off into a deep and dreamless sleep.

CHAPTER 2

Struggling into consciousness, Fred Callahan opened his eyes. He raised his head, looked about, and saw he was lying in the underbrush amidst decaying leaves and crusting snow. "What the hell happened?" He shook his head in bewilderment. "Why am I on the ground?" Looking around, he realized he was surrounded by brush and not on the running track. Bewildered, he murmured, "I never came in here."

He rubbed his eyes to clear away the mist clouding his vision and made an effort to sit up. Something was wrong. Noticing a dull, aching pain, he reached down to his crotch and felt a wet, sticky fluid. He drew back a hand covered with blood. "God, damn! What the hell?"

The gory discovery sent gouts of alarm coursing through him, and he came fully alert. His scalp felt like ice and a terrible fear rose inside his chest. His heart hammered and his crotch burned like fire. His hands dripped blood! His face tightening, he struggled to get to his feet but couldn't find enough strength and fell back. In desperate fear, he fumbled for his cell phone and punched in a number.

"Yeah, Denny?" He heard his own voice sounding weak and tinny as he struggled to explain what had happened. "I've been attacked."

"Attacked? In the park?"

"Yeah, right here in the running park. Can you get here real quick?" He groaned. "Something's horribly wrong. I think I'm in that grove of trees and bushes on the rise. Hurry! I'll wait here till you come. I don't think I can walk." He struggled again. "Oh God! I can't get up!"

He sank down on his hip and elbow, avoiding pressure on his painful scrotal wounds and waited in a pile of faded, crusty leaves. The snow hadn't seemed to touch them to make them sodden or frozen, but in his pain and confusion, it escaped his notice.

Callahan's head ached and his vision appeared to blur. He touched his crotch area again, feeling the lump of something soft that had been placed there. "What the hell!" he groaned aloud. The area burned like fire and as his fear and conscious-ness grew, the pain increased.

"Please, Denny, hurry. Something's really wrong!"

His frenzied cries reached no one. His friend hadn't had time to arrive. Burning pain radiated down the back of his legs. Panic and fear grew in his mind and settled in his thoughts re-garding what might have happened. "Some filthy bastard has done a number on me. I need a doctor, I know it, and I need one fast!" Tears of helplessness filled his eyes. "Son of a bitch!" he sobbed.

Footfalls crunched on the graveled pathway, and the fa-miliar figure of a slight, dark-haired, older man, pushed his way through the bushes.

Hysterical with fear, Callahan cried, "Denny, Denny, somebody jumped me, and they've cut me! I need a doctor, real fast. I'm bleeding down here, Denny, look—oh, God!" He screamed out his terror as he reached for his only friend.

"Okay, okay, Fred—my God, you're bleeding, sure as hell. Let's get you to the hospital. Can you walk?" He inched a few steps closer, peered down at the man on the ground, but held no comforting hand out to him.

"Hell, no, I can't even stand up." Callahan's voice quick-ly reached a high pitched whine. "Call 911, I need an ambu-lance here, right now. I'm dying Denny, I know it." He searched his friend's face for answers.

"Okay, okay. Hold your horses. Looks like you're not bleeding enough to die." Denny whipped out his cell and punched in 911. "Man's been attacked right here in the run-

ning park. No I don't know what happened, but he's bleeding,"
he said. "Yeah, he's awake and shaking like a leaf from lying
on the ground. It's cold as hell out here!" He gave the needed
information, then, turned back to the man on the ground. Okay,
they're on the way, be here in a few." Taking another look, he
asked, "So what the hell happened, Callahan?"

"I don't know for sure. Didn't see anybody else out here.
You know I don't like to miss my training, even on a bitchin',
colder'n hell day like this. I've been trying to lose some
weight, you know, keepin' in shape. Maybe there was somebody...I can't think straight right now." Callahan held his head
in his hands, leaving a wide smear of blood across his forehead. "Oh God, Denny, I'm bleeding to death. You sure
they're coming?"

"Yeah, I'm sure." His slender, dark companion peered
closer. "Your crotch is bleeding all right, that's for damned
sure." He reached out but failed to touch Callahan.

"Tell me about it," Callahan sobbed. "Somebody's tried
to do me in, that's what. I'm real scared, Denny, scared what
they've done to me." His muscles tightened with fear and pain
as he contorted his body in misery and writhed about on the
frozen ground.

Denny's scalp felt like ice, looking at the bloody mess
congealing on his friend's jogging pants. "Better call the cops,
huh, Callahan?" He clutched his belly. "God, I feel sick!
Who'd have done a thing like this, Fred?"

"I don't know, but yeah, we'd better call 'em." Callahan
let out another whine. "After all that's happened lately, they
won't give a shit what's happened to me, you damned well
know they won't." He shook his head, "I've been assaulted. A
crime's been done to me. They'll have to take care of it, won't
they?"

The doubtful tone in his voice gave notice. After his own
brush with the law, he had little faith in his own protection,
especially from officers who knew him. "I got rights too, don't
I?" To his pleading query, Denny shrugged.

Both men lifted their heads as the scream of an ambulance neared the park. "They're coming, Denny." Callahan

breathed a sigh of relief. "About damned time, maybe they can fix this." Deep within himself, he knew they couldn't put him back together, but in his horror and disbelief, he couldn't say it. Hearing the words spoken aloud might make this nightmare real.

At the sound of heavy, running feet, Denny stepped out to meet the approaching EMT personnel and wave them into the grove. "This man's been attacked and he's bleeding." He pointed to Callahan's crotch. "Look at that! Look what some dirty bastard's done!"

The EMT leader, a big, brawny, crew-cut type, introduced himself. "I'm Jack Larson. We're here, we'll handle it." Gently, but firmly, he pulled Callahan's knit joggers down and shivered visibly while assessing his condition. "My holy God, man, what the hell happened here?" he questioned as he knelt down to the area, opened his red emergency case and, donning gloves, cleaned and dressed the wounded area with fresh, sterile dressings, before pulling the soiled knit pants up.

"How'd that purple stuff and the damned snow get in there? It's melted in the wound and made one hell of a mess," he continued. "So how'd this happen?"

Callahan cried out in terror and frustration. "I didn't see the guy. Bastard must have hidden in these bushes right here and whacked me over the head by the way it aches. I'm bleeding bad—real bad, man. Whoever did this cut me something awful. I need a doctor, and right away." His sobbing cries cut into the icy air along with his panting breath.

"We're takin' you in right now. You can answer questions on the way. You're stable enough right now—could go shocky if you lose much more blood. We'll keep an eye out." Jack exuded confidence to the patient, but as the rest of his crew pulled a stretcher up close, he queried Callahan, "I don't find any cuts or bruise marks on your head. Sure you were hit there?"

"How the hell do I know? Knocked me out colder'n a mackerel," Callahan whined out the words. Yet even with mental shock from the sudden attack, he'd gotten a very fearful idea of the seriousness of his wounds, and their permanence. "Think the docs can fix me?" he ventured, not sure he wanted an answer.

"Dunno, mister, looks kinda mutilated down there, but we'll see what the doctors have to say." Jack tried to sound upbeat, but Callahan easily read the EMT guy's real thoughts in what he hadn't said. He already knew what had been done to him, though his mind tried to refuse the knowledge.

Jack grabbed his phone and called the ER Department at Mercy Hospital, identified his unit, and said, "Man's genitalia's slashed and mutilated." He listened a minute. "He's stable but needs to see a doctor and soon. ETA's about ten minutes." After listening a moment, "Okay, yeah, we're on our way."

Several brawny EMT's loaded him on the stretcher and rolled it down the running path toward the ambulance. Once loaded, an attendant sat with him as they revved the engines, turned on the flashing lights and, with sirens blaring, sped away. Callahan caught a glimpse of Denny, hurrying to his old green sedan, and felt relief, knowing his friend would follow.

CHAPTER 3

Henry Graves, MD, completed his treatment, stitched the wounds, and stopped the bleeding. Callahan already knew what the surgeon would tell him, but he had to hear it spelled out. "Okay, let's have it, Doc. Am I gonna be all right?"

"Mr. Callahan, you'll be fine, but you must realize that an injury such as you have sustained, renders you completely sterile and impotent as well. Hormone replacement might be a possibility if that is your wish." He added, his face stern, "You were savagely attacked by someone and may still be in danger from that person. Your personal doctor will follow up with you on this injury, along with the Police Department, as far as criminality is concerned. They've been called on the case, as they are on any case of assault."

Dr. Graves shook his head. He'd seen about everything, but this extensive, totally incapacitating, genital mutilation was a first. He found it shocking enough as a doctor, even more so as a man. He shivered involuntarily.

"The police?" Heart hammering in his chest, sick, and horrified from the doctor's confirmation regarding the severity of his wounds, Callahan now faced the realization he'd have to deal with the police department—again.

After the doctor left his side, he muttered to Denny, who sat patiently nearby in a hard bottomed metal chair. "The police don't like me much, probably hate my guts." He sank down on the ER gurney and pulled up the blanket. "In fact, those bastards'll be happy as hell and dancing in the streets over this. You know they will, don't you, Denny? You damn well know it."

The doctor and nursing staff, busy attending other patients, gave them privacy. Denny stayed beside him. "Fred, you'll have to deal with them. A crime's been committed against you. They'll have to find out who did this. That's their job, isn't it?" He sighed and added, "I know how they might see this, but, God almighty, Fred, what else can you do? This whole damned thing's a nightmare, just when everything had settled down." With a twist of fear in his own gut, he mumbled, his breath escaping through tight lips. "Shit."

"You know they wanted to put me away for years for the little kid thing. God! How they'll enjoy this." Tears slid down Callahan's pale cheeks. "A man like me has got no rights according to those unfeeling bastards." He snuffled. "Could you get me a lawyer if I need one, Denny?"

"Yeah—sure, sure, but let's see how it goes. Maybe they'll know who did this," Denny replied. His voice completely lacked conviction, but that fact nearly escaped Callahan's worry-filled mind as his friend moved away several feet and sat quietly in the background.

When a shadow crossed Callahan's gurney, he looked up to see a big, sandy-haired, nicely-dressed, man wearing an open-necked, stripped shirt and slightly-wrinkled jacket. He held out a hand. "Good morning, I'm Detective Alan Harris. I'll be investigating this incident."

"Incident? This wasn't no God damned *incident*, officer." Callahan's voice reached a higher note in his panic as he shook the officer's hand. "Some asshole tried to kill me!"

Harris pulled a chair from an empty area and sat down, facing him. "So, what happened here? Take your time and tell me in your own words the best you can." He whipped out a metal covered book to take notes.

Callahan saw the officer's eyebrows rise slightly when he gave his name. Knowing the police wouldn't be on his side in this case, his fear rose. He felt sick, and additional hopelessness filled his mind.

"It was hardly an incident!" Callahan shouted, believing the assault on his person had just been belittled. His indignation raised his voice a few more notches. "Somebody jumped me in the jogging park this morning, cut me real bad, and I never even seen him. Bastard sneaked up behind me like a goddamned coward and slammed me one right over the head." His whimpering rose as he cried his tale of woe to the cool, hazel-eyed detective. "And now I'm ruined for life!"

Denny stayed out of it. In silent commiseration, he intently observed the official's attitude. *Does he remember Fred as the man they had arrested, but lost the case due to a new officer's lack of experience?* He smiled quietly to himself. *Stupid-ass rookie forgot to read him the damned Miranda thing.*

The detective scribbled his notes, asked several more questions, and took leave of Callahan with a short, "Thanks." Then he left to question the attending physician regarding the severity of the injuries.

Finding Dr. Graves, he asked, "What's your take on this? Any feelings about this sort of injury?"

The doctor replied with a shake of his head. "Plenty as a man, but on the medical side, whoever did this, used a bluish solution on the wounds. Looks like Gentian Violet or Gram's Stain." He paused then added, "I find it very unusual that someone thought to use an anti-infective if that was the intention. After all, he must have had one hell of a grudge against the guy. Why try to prevent sepsis? He shook his head again. "When we're sure what the blue substance is we'll let you know."

Harris thanked the doctor. "Save that evidence if you will. We'll have forensics on it right away. Might be our best clue since Callahan never saw his assailant."

The detective returned to the patient. Callahan lay on his gurney moaning, warm blankets over him, and a bulky dressing fixed snugly between his legs. Approaching, he heard the man cry out from behind drawn privacy curtains, "Oh God, I'll never be the same."

Harris parted the privacy curtains, and returned to Callahan's side. Beneath his blankets, the patient visibly trembled, pale from the shock of what had happened. He whined in despair as Harris said, "When you're able, come down to the station. We'll need to get a more detailed report from you. You're pretty shook up at the moment, but time may improve your recall of events or anything we might have missed in your report today." He closed his notebook with a snap and saw Callahan flinch from the sound. "We'll expect to see you in a couple of days. The doc said you'd likely be up and around by then."

Harris took his leave and Denny watched intently as he walked through the wide double doors of the ER.

Callahan wondered about Harris's feeling toward him. He'd faced this man before in a totally different situation. *Did they remember him*? He dreaded having to see these authorities again for any reason, in any capacity.

"Thanks, officer, for nothing," Callahan mumbled at the detective's departing back. His friend, Denny, sat patiently on the hard brown metal chair. "It went okay, didn't it? What'd you think?" Callahan asked his very quiet friend.

"Seemed to, but it's hard to tell about those guys." Denny frowned, remembering a certain light he'd seen flashing in the cop's eye a time or two, and the twitching of a lip. Silently, more than certain the officer remembered Fred from prior arrests or court appearances, he didn't want to douse cold water on his friend at the moment. He mumbled a bit under his breath, but voiced nothing further on the subject. *Time will tell, won't it*?

The attending nurse, Helene, came to say, "Mr. Callahan, you can go home as long as you won't be left alone. We could admit you but you might have to wait most of the night on this gurney because all our beds are full at the moment, might be one later." She shrugged. "Sorry, it'll be your choice. We've been crazy around here the past few days." She went on to say, "I have your prescriptions and follow-up care ready when you decide." With that, she left to attend someone else.

"The place looks like a damned nut house, kids crying and people in wheelchairs, moaning and groaning," Callahan muttered. "But dammit all to hell, I've got complaints, too."

He tried to understand that the staff did their best, triaging the worst of those seeking care according to the severity of their complaint. But in his mind, his immediate, personal worries took precedence over any of the others. He'd been severely injured and these other creeps sitting around meant nothing to him.

"What do you want to do, Fred? I'll stay with you if you want to go home," Denny offered.

"I want to go home. This damned cart is hard as a rock and I hurt like hell. If there's something good and strong for pain in one of those prescriptions, let's get it on the way home. I want to pass out and forget this fucking nightmare. I can't believe this! I just can't!" Callahan felt tears sliding from his eyes as he struggled to sit up. At the sudden onset of fresh pain, he cried out, "Son of a bitch, my ass hurts!" He slumped back onto the gurney, remaining on his side, tears sliding down onto the pillow.

"I'll tell the nurse we'll be leaving and go bring the car around," Denny said. "Maybe the nurse will know how to get you on your feet."

She returned in a few moments with his paperwork and, placing a sturdy four-legged stool close, instructed him gently, "Just stay on your hip and slide off the gurney," She said, steadying him as he moved carefully to the side.

Whimpering in renewed pain, he gingerly edged his way off the miserable hospital gurney and, finally, onto unsteady feet.

"Your jogging pants are not useable," the nurse said. "They were very soiled." She handed him a blue-striped, hospital issue robe to wear over his hospital gown. "You can wear this home." She held his shoulder to steady him, helped him into the garment, and carried his soiled clothes in a bag.

Callahan felt dizzy and hung tightly onto the gurney to stay upright until Denny came for him. "I hope I don't pass out," he gasped through clench teeth.

The nurse said, "I'll steady you a bit." She indicated a wheel chair. "Here, Mr. Callahan, sit in this if you can."

Callahan refused the appliance. "Hell no, I can't sit in that damned thing or anything else," he moaned loudly. "Oh God, I'll never be all right!"

Fear and misery were permanently etched on his features as Denny came up to him. "Car's right outside, Fred," he said frowning. He'd already had a belly full of Callahan's endless whining and moaning.

Together, they walked out of the hospital. Denny held Callahan's arm on the right and the nurse took his left. They assisted him onto his side in the back seat of Denny's old green Pontiac. The nurse handed him his soiled clothing and hospital paperwork. The two men drove away.

∽∾∽

The attending doctor sat at his desk. The nurse, Helene, moved close to him as he wrote his notes. "What do you suppose that man did that someone would mutilate him in that way?"

"I don't know," he replied. "But someone had him in their sights. It'd take a fiend or somebody with a damn big grudge to do that to a man. My God! I've never seen anything like that." He shuddered. "Fred Callahan sure made someone mad as a hornet. Hell of an enemy!" Somewhere in his mind he had the feeling of familiarity regarding the man, or his name— something rang a bell. He wasn't sure enough to speak of it, though it nagged the far reaches of his consciousness as he turned to the onrush of other patients.

CHAPTER 4

Martha Lavery heard the phone jangling, loud, insistent, and irritating. Her senses struggled against the depths of a drugged-like slumber. Fumbling about, she reached for the phone, lifted the receiver, and mumbled, "Hullo?"

"Mom, where were you? You were supposed to come for dinner today. It's Sunday or don't you remember?" Martha heard her daughter's insistent voice on the other end of the line. She worked her mind upward from a heavy, fatigue-induced fog, trying to regain her senses.

"Oh, what time is it then?" The encroaching darkness outside her window brought her awake with rising alarm—she'd slept the day away? "Jeannie, I must have been really tired. I think I was up earlier and fell back into bed. Slept too long I guess. How's Will doing?" she added as memory of her grandson's plight reached her consciousness.

"About the same—listless, doesn't play, or want his friends over. No change there." The pain and tenseness in Jeannie's voice revealed a mother's deep pain regarding her emotionally damaged son. "You don't know if you were up earlier or not? Mom, are you okay—you're not working too much, are you?"

Hearing tears in her daughter's voice, Martha felt her guts twist into a knot so hard and tight, she gasped for breath. "Uh, I'm okay; don't worry about me, still sleepy I guess." Fully awake now, she deftly turned the subject from herself. "Is the therapy helping him at all?"

"Maybe. I don't know. It's hard to see any real change, not yet anyway. It's been so long now, three months, isn't it?" she asked. "How can he ever be normal again? How can he? I know I'd never feel the same if that happened to me. I couldn't, oh my God, never!"

Her heart ached for her daughter and her five year old grandson, Will. "No wonder people took vengeance in the old days. At least they could, but our laws consistently favor the criminal, certainly not people like us." Saying that brought back the helpless anger at the rape and sodomy of her only grandchild. This excessive rage was entirely new to Martha, and experiencing it, she felt helpless and uncomfortable because of it.

Recalling that day so well—it burned forever in her memory and always would—she remembered replying to her daughter's frantic call. "What do you mean that man has gone free?" With tortured breath, she'd cried into the phone. "Jeannie, how can they *do* that? How can they let a monster like that loose to prey on other children?" Her mind had gone spinning into a bottomless black void that day, as she'd prayed, "Please, tell me it isn't true."

The speaker phone had rung in her ears as her daughter's tear-filled voice related the sick details. "Yes, I'm afraid it is. A detective, Ryan Mapus, said the arresting officer forgot to read the man his Miranda Rights. A new rookie, who'd just completed training, overlooked that little detail. He just forgot, Mom, and because of that mistake, the evidence is inadmissible in a court of law. They can't even use the DNA!"

"What are we to do if the law won't protect us? How are we to save our children from people like that sick pedophile, Callahan? He's out again, free to savage another child. My God, Jeannie, Will is only five years old. What horrors must haunt his little mind?" After a few more words, filled with hopelessness and despair, Jeannie hung up. Oh yes! Martha remembered that day all too well.

Her mind filled with foggy dreams of sickening content, seeing images of the things she feared Will had endured, until she'd cried out, "Oh, I can't stand it! But what the hell can I do?"

Boiling rage and helplessness tore at her mind that awful day until at the end of her strength, she'd been forced to down a sedative and seek her bed in search of the soft swirling reprieve of blissful sleep.

Forcing her thoughts away from the memory of that haunting exchange, she returned to the present. "Honey, I'm coming over. Sorry about dinner. I want to see you and Will. Is Martin home today?"

"No, he had to be out of town for another conference over the week-end so we're alone again. It makes me horribly nervous anymore. I hate being afraid like this, but some days that's all I do. I want to move away from this town—this place."

"I know, girl, I think of it, too. Like we have to uproot our whole family because the law can't put these people away. It's just not right."

After her conversation with Jeannie, Martha was fully awake. She glanced at her bedside clock. The numbers said seven. She felt puzzled. *It's dark outside. Where has my day gone?*

She stumbled into the bathroom, and looked in her mirror. Seeing purple stains on her right wrist, she stared at them. "How did I come by these?" Shaking her head, she realized she'd lost track of several hours again, beginning sometime in the night. She remembered going to bed, but not with purple stains on her wrists. That knowledge made her feel unsure of her thinking and gave her a distant, fuzzy feeling inside.

Something's happening to me. I know it, have known it for the past two or three months. Tears of fear and frustration went sliding down her cheeks. *Oh, Lord, am I going crazy?*

Martha paced about her small, snug home, looking at her things. Those comforting, solid, and real things were where they always were, but she couldn't shake her feeling of unreality. Her furnishings, her desk, sat in their normal places, but somehow, nothing was right.

She returned to her bed and lay there for a few moments, trying to put the past few hours together, and failed. "If I see a psychiatrist, everyone will think I'm crazy." She punched her pillow. "But I have to, or I'll really go mad!" Thinking about how her situation would be perceived at work, she knew she could never tell anyone about it. "Who on earth would hire a crazy nurse? They'd never give me another shift!"

Suddenly she started, heart hammering. "Have I missed my shift at the hospital?" She hastened to her heavy oaken desk and checked her work calendar. "No, thank God. I work tomorrow, but if this keeps on, I'll mess up. How could I help it?" She hit the shower, laughing at herself. "And now I'm talking to myself!"

She washed her hair, scrubbed at the purple stains on both wrists, and worried silently. *Nothing on my fingers, so how did I get these? Did I use gloves or what?* Shaking off her confusing thoughts, she dried her body and moisturized her skin. She dressed in slim-legged jeans and boots. A long-sleeved sweater in a deep green, to hide the spots, completed her outfit. She'd kept her figure trim. Being tall and athletic helped, too. Her hair, chestnut-hued with streaks of blond, was short, dried easily, and curled enough on its own. It only needed a bit of brushing.

Satisfied with her appearance, without really looking, she grabbed her purse and felt a renewed shock. *Oh Lord, when did I get this ugly purse? It's awful, so gaudy—not my style at all.* "What on earth is happening to me?" she asked as she headed to the garage and her car. "At least my car looks the same." She heaved a sigh of relief as she got in and pressed the garage door opener.

Moments later, she pulled into her daughter's driveway and headed for the door. It swung wide and her daughter, Jeanne Moulton, stood in the light of the open doorway. *What a beautiful girl she is with her big, dark-blue eyes, and, long, luscious, golden hair,* Martha thought. *It breaks my heart to see her troubled this way.*

"Mom, we really missed you earlier. What happened?"

Martha shrugged. "I slept too much, I guess. I get so tired from work and worrying. And then, I get so worked up thinking about how they let that predator get away with what he did, my blood just boils!" Thinking these things made her tense up tight inside, way too tight and she hated the feeling.

"Come on in, there's food left. No one had much of an appetite anyway, and with Martin gone, things are worse." Jeannie closed the door behind Martha and followed her to the den.

"Where is he?" Martha asked, tossing her unfamiliar purse on a nearby chair, noticing once again, it didn't look like hers and an icy tingle passed through her. *What else have I done?* She couldn't speak of her fears. *Who'd believe such a thing—not knowing I bought a purse?*

Jeannie failed to notice her mother's moment of hesitation. "Will's watching TV right now, but he isn't getting any excitement or enjoyment from it that I can see. He's never excited about *anything* anymore, not like he used to be."

Martha hurt inside, seeing the helpless tears swimming in Jeannie's wide blue eyes. She and Jeannie entered the great room, paneled in oak and furnished with a thick rug and several leather chairs scattered about. A large 60-inch Sony, flat-screen TV blared cartoons. Will sat before it, silently gazing at the action, reacting to nothing. The sandy-haired boy seemed in a trance, never noticing his mother and grandmother enter the room. They stood together looking helplessly at the sad, lost, little boy.

Shaking her head, Jeannie turned away. "Let's move into the den where we can talk." She wiped her tears with a tissue as she led the way. "He just sits there like that. I can't believe they let that man get away with what he did. I just can't. I want to kill him for what he's done to Will!" Her hands clenched in anger, her lips flattened tight across her mouth. "Sometimes I hear him crying in the night. He clams up when I go to him, becoming a zombie right before my eyes." She slumped into the large, maroon leather recliner, her husband's favorite, and curled into a defensive ball.

Martha sat in a fabric-covered chair. A cozy room—lots of books, great chairs, and soft lighting. Sitting in here usually made for quiet relaxation. That feeling was impossible to find these days. "Hon, time might help some, but I've read extensively about the effects of this. Unfortunately, it tends to stay deep inside, hidden from your consciousness." She paused. "But it's always there." Trying to think of something positive to say, Martha couldn't. "Turn on the boob tube, maybe something on there will help us forget for a moment."

Jeanie switched on the local news. The newscaster, his voice high with excitement, exclaimed, "There's been an assault on a jogger in Leesford Green, the local jogging park. The assailant apparently waited in a grove of trees and attacked the man as he jogged past. It happened early this morning. The victim is stable but the police report states that his injuries are devastating and permanent." He cleared his throat, and continued. "His name is being withheld for the time being, pending further investigation, but it appears the victim was recently involved in a sexual assault case, arrested and released. We'll continue to update our listeners on this situation as more information becomes available."

Martha no longer heard his voice. The roaring in her head blotted all else from her consciousness. She felt lost in a raging, circling windstorm and gripped the arms of her chair.

Jeannie saw her mother's knuckles turn as white as her face and hurried to kneel at Martha's side. "Mom, what's wrong with you? You look like you've seen a ghost or something!"

Martha shook her head. "I don't know, dear. I don't know what came over me, but I'm okay now." She uttered a hollow laugh. "Maybe it was hearing that news flash. Don't you wish the hideous thing that man did to our little guy would happen to him? What if that was Callahan? God, I'd be so happy—wouldn't it be just retribution?"

"Let's keep the TV on," Jeannie replied. "Maybe we'll know later, or at least by tomorrow. Hey, it did take our minds off of things for the moment, didn't it?" she said. "Oh, what if it was? Maybe he's done this before and it caught up to him in a big way. Well, if it's him..." She frowned. "How would something like that help Will? It'd please us immensely, but him? I don't know. Maybe the therapist would know how an assault feels to an assailant." She sighed. "All this on our wild suppositions."

Martha stayed with her daughter for another hour. Talking to Will appeared to achieve little, though after a time, he came to her. He looked up into her eyes with his deep blue ones, so like his mother's, and crawled up into her lap.

"I love you, Grammy." At that moment she saw excitement shinning from his eyes. "Can we go to Biggie's Burgers again? Can we, huh?"

Excited at the request, she threw a glance at Jeannie, her eyebrows raised. "You bet," she said. "How about lunch tomorrow? Soon enough?" She squeezed him, rocking him gently. "Okay, Will?"

His eyes brightened. "Yep, Grammy, I need a Bittie Meal with chicken bits and Sprite."

Martha welcomed that tiny sparkle in her grandson's red-rimmed eyes. He'd been crying too much.

"Okay, Will, how about eleven tomorrow. Will you be ready by then?"

"Yeah, Grammy, I'll be all ready."

Martha couldn't stop the flow of tears at his words, and the way he said, Biggie's Burgers. "Maybe the therapy is helping, and something has taken hold. It would be Biggie's, wouldn't it?" She sighed at the tiny ray of hope she felt in her heart and saw in Jeannie's eyes. "Okay, darling, see you tomorrow," she added. "I have to be at work at three, but we'll have lots of time together before that."

Martha got into her car and backed down the driveway, leaving the boy standing beside his mother. His babyish hands clutched her skirt and the lost sadness had returned to his face. Seeing it, anger at his plight filled Martha with burning fire. This much fury, new to her and surprising in its intensity, puzzled her, but in her turmoil and worry over Will, she'd only begun to wonder about it. She certainly had cause for anger, but so intense?

As she drove, she gave thought to her lost time periods. It had happened again today, and she had no memory of purchasing the purse she carried. *Where is my old one and when did I get this? Who put it in my house with my things in it? And why do I awake some mornings smelling like a barroom, smoke in my hair and all? Man oh man, I'm losing my mind!* Suddenly she realized she'd driven past the jogging park. *What am I doing here? It's way after dark.* Cold chills crept along her spine as she turned around and drove toward her home, her mind filled with confusion. Snapping on the radio, she heard another news flash.

"It has been confirmed. The identity of the man viciously attacked in Leesford jogging park is now known. He is identified as Frederick Callahan, age forty-two, a man, recently in the news, having been apprehended and released in a child molestation case nearly three months ago." The announcer took a breath and continued. "The police have evidence in the case and the investigation is continuing. We will keep you updated as the facts come in."

Martha couldn't help feeling a satisfied glee as she pulled into her garage and switched off the motor. "Well, well, someone besides us thought he needed to learn a lesson. Wonder what they did to him? The announcer didn't say, but anything done to that monster wouldn't be enough."

Once in the house, she turned on the news again, hoping to learn more of the case. "Same old stuff," she sniffed, after hearing the same thing again. She went to bed and tried to read a romance novel. But finding the characters unworthy of her attention, she switched off the light and lay awake in the darkness, thinking.

Her roiling mind embraced the terrifying idea that she was in danger of losing her sanity. *What happens in those blank hours and days I can't account for? There aren't that many, but what have I done besides shopping for a new purse? And the smoke I sometimes reek of? Where was I? Where did I go during those hours? What was I doing?* Jeannie hadn't seemed to know of these things, no one did. *And this wild looking purse—it's all too much!*

Sleep came finally, reluctantly, but in her tortured dreams she was chased by unidentifiable monsters and tossed about in her bed. Sometimes huge, soft, cottony clouds rolled over her, enveloping her in that massive fluffiness without end. Nothing actually hurt her, yet she continuously felt threatened by a mind-numbing fear she had no way to escape.

CHAPTER 5

It seemed like any other day to Martha, except for her nagging worry over her lost hours, the strange purse, and smelling like smoke. She drove over to Jeannie's to collect Will for their planned outing to Biggie's Burgers.

Pulling into the driveway, she didn't have to wait long. The little boy hurried out with his mother. Though Will didn't come roaring out as he usually did, he certainly seemed brighter this morning, and any tiny bit of improvement in the child helped Martha forget her personal worries. Deep inside her mind, it lightened her outlook on just about everything.

"How are you, today, Will?"

"I'm okay, Grammy." He offered no further comment as his mother placed his car seat in Martha's vehicle and buckled him in. Waving a quiet goodbye, they drove away.

Martha watched him via the rear view mirror. He took no notice of passing trees, dogs, children, or even motorcycles. Normally, he'd yell excitedly when a Harley roared past. She shook her head and felt that unreasoning anger rising within her all over again. She worried about that, too.

She pulled into Biggie's and extracted Will from his seat. Entering a familiar place, filled with good memories, she watched his expressions, hoping to see delight in those dull and darkened eyes. He'd always had fun here.

"What would you like?" Martha asked him as the young girl behind the counter waited. Will gave her a serious look and turned to the girl.

"I need a Bittie Meal with bits and a Sprite," he piped up, his voice sounding so normal that Martha's heart ached with joy hearing it. He'd spoken eagerly to the dark-haired girl, and without fear. Martha's purpose had been to get him away from his stone-like presence before the TV set, to do something familiar and fun. It seemed to be working. His interaction with the girl was a sign that things were getting better.

A deep, male voice behind them, said, "My, what a fine young lad you have there."

Hearing the strange voice, Will's body tensed. He clutched onto her jeans and, trembling, hid his face against her.

"Handsome young fellow," the man added.

The man's words had a chilling effect on Will. He clung desperately to her leg, his fingers digging into her flesh. Martha, her pulse racing in agony for Will, turned to see a kindly old gentleman. A man who appeared to genuinely like young children. But the boy's recent trauma had changed the way any encounter with an unknown male might appear to him.

"Why, thank you," Martha managed. Receiving their food, she and Will hurried away from the man's vicinity and took a seat in the children's play area.

She set out Will's lunch. "Oh, my, doesn't this look good? May I have one of your fries?" she said, trying to lure his thoughts away from the encounter.

Will, sat frozen, saying nothing, his features pale. His eyes darted about. He took none of his food. "Okay, Grammy, you can have some." His voice, tight with apprehension, made her heart ache. "Was that a bad man, Grammy?" he asked, his small face white with fear.

"No, son, I'm sure he wasn't. Most people are good and kind. Try to remember that, Will." She smiled reassuringly at the boy. "He looked like someone's nice grandfather to me. Go ahead and eat," she urged. "Then you can play for a while if you like." Hoping he wouldn't fear those of his own size, she added, "And you have to be small to enter the play place." She pointed to the measuring line. "You can't be taller than that mark."

Will ate slowly. He watched the other young children screaming, climbing, and sliding about on the large, plastic, play structures. Thankfully, the elderly man had taken his meal and left.

They quietly ate their meal and, after some time, Will slowly removed his sneakers, put them in a slot made especially for children's shoes, and almost reluctantly began playing. Subdued at first, he finally joined in, running, climbing, sliding, and yelling with the others.

Martha wanted to cry with relief at seeing Will act like a normal little boy, if only for a little while. She whipped out her cell. "Jeannie, guess what? Will's running and playing, just like always."

"Oh, thank God for that!" she heard her daughter say.

After listening to Jeannie's delighted reply, she said, "See ya later, dear," and clicked off. Will played a while longer, and nearly refused to leave when it was time.

She surmised he felt safe surrounded by those his own age. He could let loose, and relax where only small children are allowed to play. A positive, she felt delighted to be able report to his mother.

Will reluctantly departed the Biggie's Burgers play area and she took him home. Watching in the rear view mirror, she noted a bit of sparkle in his eyes as he bounced about in his safety seat. She took it as a hopeful sign. "Did you have a good lunch, Will?"

"Yep, Grammy, I sure did. But it's all gone away now." He puffed out a sigh, slumped down in his seat, no longer looking outside at passing vehicles or people walking with pets—something he'd always done before.

He's returned to his dreadful memories. Martha seethed again with hatred toward the man who'd committed that foul act upon her darling. *I hope he burns in hell for what he's done.* Silently cursing the man, she drove her grandchild home, her mind roiling in fury at their helplessness.

Leaving Will at the door, Martha told Jeannie, "Except for the old gentleman speaking to us, it went fine. He had a good time, if only for a little while."

"Thanks, Mom, for taking him." The beginning of tears glimmered in Jeannie's eyes as Martha drove away, leaving her standing there.

But Martha had to be at work at three, and while at the hospital, her mind and body were kept very busy. A blessing. And it got her out of the house.

⋐⋙⋐⋙

Chief Detective Ryan Mapus sat at his desk. A thick mop of darkly-shaded, blond hair hung over his forehead as he leaned into his work. His white, rolled-up shirt sleeves, displayed well-muscled arms, the benefit of working out daily in the police gym. He raised his head when the door opened and Officer Art Jarvis came shuffling in, a sheaf of papers clutched in his hand. Ryan heard wheezing as the overweight man puffed toward him with a glow of excitement glistening in his eyes. Ryan disliked the man and wished he could ignore him.

"Morning, Ryan, how's it going?" A sly chuckle escaped his lips. "Got something for you and, man, you'll never believe this!" He slapped the manila file on Ryan's desk, making his already overloaded desktop look even messier as a few scattered papers flew about in disarray.

"Here now, dammit, quit slopping up my desk!" he groused. "What the hell you got there?" Ryan disliked a disturbance, unless it ranked high in importance, and he couldn't help how he viewed Jarvis, either.

"Remember the case where that kiddie predator, Callahan, got off on account of that Miranda thing?" Jarvis's fleshy, tanned face bore a secretive grin. He had a protruding paunch, and his clothes were even more unkempt today. He wheezed occasionally, even without exertion, as he stood before Ryan's desk.

"Yeah, yeah, who could forget that screw-up? The entire city was ready to bring out a lynch mob and I don't blame them—damned idiot rookie!"

"Somebody took real good care of the bastard." Jarvis shoved a fleshy forefinger down on the report and tapped. "Take a look."

"No shit, you're kidding—what're you saying?" Ryan's head snapped up and his blue eyes honed in on the report. He felt his pulse begin to race as he grabbed up the papers and took a detailed look.

"Read it and weep," Jarvis wheezed. "Hey, now you've got to protect the bastard. We didn't help that poor kid worth a damn, but Callahan's got *his* rights, you know." Jarvis wheezed a laugh, belched, and his paunch jiggled beneath his thin cotton shirt. Ryan suppressed a snort of disgust. "Looks good so far. Tell me what you know about it while I check this report." Ryan spread the papers over his desk and continued reading. After a few moments, he slammed his fist on them. "Jesus, God! "Somebody sure as hell had it in for the miserable bastard." As a male, he readily appreciated the utter devastation the poor guy faced for the rest of his life. He shivered in distaste. "Now that's what I call revenge!"

"Harris saw him at the Emergency Room, and it's completely permanent according to the ER Doc. It was our dear Freddie for sure. Said he sniveled and whined all the way through the report and complained about his civil rights being violated. He was worried we wouldn't work real hard finding the guy who did it." Jarvis laughed at the idea. "Bastard won't be molesting little boys real soon, not after what somebody did to 'im." Jarvis had small children at home, too. Most of the staff did.

A lazy smile spread across Ryan's lips "He'll have to come in so we can finish this report. I imagine that'll be my pleasure. Should be real, real, interesting." He continued to read the report, not finding much that Jarvis hadn't reported. "Do they know what this purple stain is?"

"Not yet, it's in the lab. Found a few drops at the crime scene, and the ER, along with what was left of his gonads. They were little more than mush by what they picked up. The boys had 'em in a little plastic bag along with some gravel." Jarvis shuddered and wheezed at the same time. "Alan told

Callahan to come in and complete his statement as soon as he can walk and sit down, something he can't do just now." He snickered. "I'm sorry, Ryan, but it's damned hard to be professional about this case." He turned to leave, a smile across his lips. "We'll call you soon as he shows his face."

"Right, keep me in the loop, and thanks, Art. Sometimes what we get isn't all bad news." Ryan had difficulty finding pity for Fred Callahan, though he knew he'd have added legwork following the evidence in a case like this.

Do we have a vigilante coming out of the woodwork? he wondered. *Was it just this particular guy*? *Will there be others*? He shrugged again, re-read the report, wrinkled his brow, and pursed his lips in contemplation.

CHAPTER 6

A few days later, Denny assisted Callahan into his car, limping and complaining about his woeful situation as he struggled to find comfort, sitting even partially upright on the worn seats. Going to the police station had him tied in knots, dreading further interactions with those officers who knew him. Thoughts of facing them at the interview held no comfort for him, only a mountain of renewed anxiety.

A bright sunny day, the air felt cool and crisp, but the occurrence of warming spring weather brought Callahan no joy. He gave it little notice as they drove toward the station. He still hurt like hell and he hated the sick kind of fear that had invaded his life unlike anything he'd ever known.

Callahan worried constantly about how the police would handle his case and how they'd receive him, especially the ones who knew him and the crime he'd committed. "Those cops wanted to hang me out to dry with this last arrest, and they were mad as hell I got off. They'll likely pin a medal on the guy who did this goddamned, fucking thing to me."

"*Last* arrest?" Denny nearly gasped. "Are you saying you've got a long string of priors, and you're still out on the streets?" He paused then shrugged. "Well, a crime's been committed against you and it's their sworn duty to uphold the law." He almost laughed. "You have rights, same as anyone else, and don't you forget it!"

Denny's own knuckles were white enough as he gripped the steering wheel. His private life had never been discussed by the two men, yet they sensed a brotherhood, an unspoken commonality between them.

Both men were positive the police had thrown a big party after hearing about the assault committed upon Callahan.

"Vindictive bastards, the lot of them!" Shaky and uncertain, Callahan couldn't help but add, "The Miranda thing worked for me, but I hope to hell it won't work for the bastard that did this to me." He tried to feel optimistic, and found it impossible.

"Yeah, well that was a damned lucky fluke for you. Don't forget, your ass'd be in stir for years to come if they could've used all those priors you never mentioned before today."

"What about now? Won't they be celebrating what happened to me, Denny?" They pulled into the parking lot and Callahan's tension mounted. His face felt tight, his ass burned with pain, and icy chills ran rampantly through his body. "Oh, God, I wish we didn't have to come here. You don't know how much I dread this. They won't want to help me. You know they won't. I don't know why we have to haul-ass down here anyway."

"Oh, shut the hell up, Fred. Let's just go in and get it over with. I'll be there with you, and let me tell you, police stations aren't real high on my list of favorite places. You're damn lucky I've come at all." Denny stepped to Callahan's door to assist him. "Go easy, now. If you need a hand, just say so."

His face felt tight as hell, and ice water had settled into his guts. But as was nervous as he was about being at a police station, he probably couldn't match Callahan's reluctance at coming here this morning.

Together they made their way into the station. Approaching the youngish, blonde woman who managed the front desk, Callahan stated his business, hating that his voice sounded halting and weak. "We're here to complete an assault report and need to see an Officer Harris. I believe he's the one."

The young woman behind the desk stopped chewing her gum and asked for names and the complaint. After quickly making a few notes, she punched a button. "Officer Harris, someone's here to see you, gives his name as a Frederick Callahan." She listened for a moment then said to Fred and Denny, "He'll be right here. Go ahead, take a seat." She motioned to a row of chairs lined against the outside wall and turned to the next person in line.

The place crawled with people, some uniformed, some in plain clothes, and a few souls in handcuffs. They didn't know any of them and all concerned seemed intent on their own particular business. Seeing the bustling place only added to their discomfort.

"Denny, she seemed okay, didn't she?" Callahan murmured, referring to the receptionist, while teetering sideways trying to find comfort on the hard metal chair. "Damn, I can barely sit, even now." He snuffled. "No padded seats in this hell hole."

Denny said nothing as he looked at a magazine that was scruffy and ripped around the edges. "*Woman's Day*! What the hell's a thing like this doing in a police station?" He threw it down, lacerating the already torn pages further and settled to wait with Callahan. "This place looks busy as hell," he commented, watching an officer haul a manacled prisoner behind him. Even a few police dogs were on the scene.

Several moments later, Officer Harris came out. "Good morning." He motioned for them to follow. "Please come into the interrogation room and take a seat. Our Chief of Detectives will sit in on the interview with us—be here in a sec." He ushered them down a narrow hallway into a spare, austere office and more uncomfortable metal chairs.

It contained a desk and two chairs on one side for the interviewee and a couple of padded ones on the other side for the officers. None of the visitor's chairs sported any sort of padding, Callahan noticed, as his misery continued to mount. He edged onto a seat while they waited for the other detective. *Would he know the man? Would the man know him?* He already knew the answer to that question. Everyone at this station knew him and what he'd been accused of.

The door squeaked as it opened to admit Chief Detective Ryan Mapus. *Oh shit! This bastard detective was on my other case.* Callahan felt his scalp prickle. *Oh, hell yes! He knows me.* His heart sank in agony at the plight he faced dealing with this particular hard-boiled lawman as the man edged into a seat opposite him. He thought the man wore a smirk across his lips, but he couldn't be sure. Easy enough to borrow trouble these days. He already knew nothing would turn out right for him, not anymore.

Officer Harris started the interview. "All right then, Mr. Callahan, begin at the beginning. Tell us in full detail, as best you can, what occurred in Leesford Park on the morning in question. Try to remember if you saw the offending person, what he wore, his voice, his smell, anything that'd be helpful in identifying your attacker—anything at all."

"Well, officer, I didn't see anyone else on the track, but I wasn't looking to see any other joggers there so early anyway. Went around the track twice like I always do, trying to take off a few pounds, you know. When I came to this thick grove of trees on the rise, he must have jumped me." His voice had reached a high-pitched whine as Callahan put his hands over his face and doubled over. "Oh God, he's ruined me for life! I wish to hell he'd killed me!"

"You didn't catch a glimpse of the guy at all, eh?" Ryan tried to fill in the time allotted for this statement, having to fulfill his duty as a duly sworn detective, but he felt like busting a gut, seeing this sorry-ass child predator whining about his injuries and demanding his civil rights. *Could Callahan's voice have gotten higher already*, he wondered. *So soon after his injuries?*

The questioning went on for two hours before the officers called it quits. "You haven't given us much to go on here, but we're checking everything out. We've done forensics at the park and we'll keep you informed on the case." Harris and Ryan stood to usher the two men out. Both men noted Callahan's halting, limping gait.

Harris returned after he'd escorted Denny Garver and Fred Callahan to the front. "Well, we haven't a lot to go on here: men's boot tracks, purple specks on the ground, same as the ER doctor found on Callahan's wounds. And let's not forget the crushed and stomped gonads. Looks like someone wearing men's boots ground those little bastards into the gravel. Must have been mad as hell at Callahan by the looks of it, all the stomping and grinding they did on those poor damned things."

Ryan shivered just thinking about it. "Whoever did it used those long hospital-type sanitary pads on him. Are we dealing with someone who has hospital or medical exposure? And why try to prevent infection? Obviously, the perpetrator wasn't out to kill Callahan."

"Possible, very possible," Harris offered. "Definitely looks like revenge, but would a man think of using sanitary pads? I guess a hospital-trained man might. What better sterile dressing than that, easily bought at a hospital supply store, or taken home from work?"

The men sat for a time, pondering possible scenarios. Finally, Ryan said, "It could be revenge taken by some family member. The Moulton kid can't be the only child this man has gone after. With a child predator, many cases are never reported if family members are involved. Could be a lot of people hated the man, including people we don't know about. Someone sure as hell had reason enough." He laughed slightly. "Took the wind out of Callahan's sails and on a scale of one to ten, I for one, can't feel more than a minus zero for his sorrow, pain, and suffering." He paused, chuckled again. "Pain and suffering—sounds like a lawsuit. This whole damned thing tickles the living shit out of me!"

Harris let out a loud guffaw but instantly tried to tone it down. "Brother, you are not alone. I can't think of a soul around here that isn't snickering in his chops over this case."

Ryan didn't want to sound unprofessional, but after he closed the door, they both let loose for a long moment. It felt damned good—still, he could help but wonder what the hell they were dealing with.

CHAPTER 7

Martha parked in her usual spot in the employee's lot at Mercy Hospital and checked with the staffing office. The staffing officer handed her the evening's assignment with a smile. "I hope med-surg is okay with you."

"It is," Martha assured her and made her way to 3-West, a surgical floor. After greeting several of the other staff, she got a coffee and settled in the conference room. It was a quiet area away from the bustle of the busy floor. Sitting there, Martha awaited the taped report from the previous shift. It was usually recorded for the oncoming staff.

Some workers reported in person from hasty notes taken during the shift. Others made individually taped reports on their patients, then left to complete the last remaining tasks of their shift.

The oncoming staff joked and laughed, held coffee cups or sodas, and loaded up on recent gossip while they waited for the details on their own particular patients. The sounds of paper shuffling and chatter filled Martha's ears, but quieted when the charge nurse, Gracie Monahan, wearing the mien of a no-nonsense person, settled into a chair at the head of the table. Seeing who she had this evening and nodding at her crew, she pushed the button and started the tape. This evening all the reports were taped.

Martha tried to listen attentively and take intelligent notes, but she kept seeing Will's face before her. Her mind frequently seethed with frustration and helplessness at his suffering. *I hope that bastard burns in hell for what he's done, and I'm glad he's the one that got beat-up in the park, too!* She fought off, yet again, the insidious anger that dwelt within her.

"Martha, you take 360 to 366 tonight, okay?"

Shaking herself alert from her funk, Martha replied, "Okay, Gracie, fine with me." Most of the information lay before her in a print-out. She could fudge the rest, but she knew she'd better pay attention from here on. *This is no place for a screw-up, Lavery.*

"Hey, you guys hear about the pool soul who got it in Leesford Park?" a solidly built, red-headed nurse, Mary Mason, asked. "ER said whoever did it fixed the guy real good, and I mean *real* good! It's all over the hospital."

"Please, I can't talk about it!" Bob Chance, a tall, rangy RN with a touch of gray at his temples, shuddered. "It puts my knickers in a twist. I shiver all over just hearing about it."

"Why, Bob?" Jake, a youngish, blond, male, nurse's aide, asked. "Hurt you somewhere—the gonads, that it?" His dark-brown eyes twinkled, seeing Bob's discomfort at the thoughts of something like that. Jake was ready anytime to push a button or two if he saw a chance for it. Gracie gave him a withering glance and pressed the stop button.

Bob shuddered again. "Hell yes, if you want to know. Somebody fixed the guy permanently. I mean, real permanent!"

"Wasn't he the one accused of child molestation a few months ago?" Mary put in. "Bastard got off on a technicality, after he molested that kid."

Martha listened, saying nothing, but she felt the ice filling her veins and the outer aspect of her scalp. The gossip, too close to home for her, struck a cord of unease far above her norm. She wasn't sure if any of these particular staff members knew her connection with Will. Some of the hospital staff did, but as a float nurse, she frequented many wards. What had happened to Will was a subject she felt reticent to mention. It was very painful, and not open for discussion with anyone. About Callahan's attacker—her head swirled with dreadful shadows and hateful thoughts!

"All right cut the jabbering, we've got a lot to do so knock it off, all of you. We've got a full house and several post-ops to tend." Gracie Monaghan shook her head and pressed the play button again. They completed the taped report and the room emptied quickly as each took up their assignments.

Martha's shift went well enough, though her thoughts dwelt too often on Will and the predator who'd savaged him. And when she wasn't thinking about that, she was haunted by what she might have done during her blackouts and lost hours. Her mysterious purple stains were hidden with cover-stick and she hoped they went un-noticed. Where they came from and why she felt she had to hide them, she had no idea.

Bob noticed the faint purple stains on Martha's wrists, and that she'd done her best to disguise them. He knew about her grandson, too. Reticent to speak of it, he kept his interactions with her strictly on a medical level, but he'd had his masculine eye on Martha for quite some time. Having taken in her mature good looks more than once, he'd considered asking her out. They were of similar ages and he'd always been attracted to her trim figure. With those deep greenish eyes, topped with that curling rusty-blond hair, all in a solid package, she'd turned his head more than once. Healing his own wounds, he'd not dated for way too long and getting involved was still too soon for him.

Bob was the kind who never missed a detail of any sort and had all the pertinent details neatly filed away in his mind. Martha suffered acutely this evening. He'd noticed it several times before today. But this evening her distraction and lack of friendly interaction with others on the staff, gave him the feeling she was especially vulnerable. He noted the deep pain in her eyes and wanted to help. But not wishing to intrude on her personal problems, he couldn't think of a way. He merely asked, "How's it going?" when he met her in the halls.

"I'm busy enough—my hernia guy is restless, and the gall bladder bled a little from her incisions, tiny though they are." Sighing, she said, "Thanks for asking." She didn't try for a lingering conversation, didn't have the energy.

Jake had also noticed Martha's attempt at concealing the purple spots. His buddy worked in the ER and had mentioned finding purple liquid splashed over the cuts on Callahan. *Hmm, tried to cover her funny looking spots, wonder why. Vanity I suppose, women are funny that way.* But those same spots set off a tiny alarm in his mind. The busy shift buried it under several layers of other concerns. His patients kept him running and, being a male, he was always asked to help with any heavy lifting or unruly patients. He understood it, resented it, often felt used, and groused, "They get the big bucks and I get the shit!"

At eleven thirty, Martha walked to her car and to her surprise, Bob walked beside her. "You doin' okay?" he asked. "You were awfully quiet this evening, more so than usual."

She felt his hand touch her elbow and flinched. "I'm okay, but things keep happening with my grandson, Will. I wonder if he'll ever be all right. I'm sure you know what happened to him."

"Yes, I know about it, and I'm sorry to hear of it. Wasn't the guy who did that to your grandson the one who got *fixed* in the Park?"

Martha nodded. "I believe he is. If so, he sure had it coming. Do you know what happened to the man?"

Bob laughed. "Hell yes, somebody clipped his gonads for him, molested more than one kid, looks like." He grunted, "God! Somebody had it in for him alright." He left for his hunky looking four-wheel drive. "Night, Martha."

Martha looked at her watch and noticed the purple spots were faintly visible under the concealer. She felt suddenly panicky. Had anyone seen them? And why should it worry her so much if they had? Where had they come from? What had she done? By the time she reached her car, she could scarcely breathe. "What's happening to me? Something's been going on these past three months!" White knuckled, she drove home trying to understand, worrying about the missing hours, the smell of smoke in her hair some mornings. "It's all so weird. I'm losing my mind. I know it!"

Her small home lay in a suburb of Colorado Springs. "Maybe I could see someone in another city," she mused aloud. "Of course, all doctors have to respect the patient's right to privacy. If I check around, maybe the right doctor will jump out at me as the right one for my case. I have to see *someone*. These time lapses are driving me out of my mind. Where have I been? What have I been doing during those lost hours? What's happening to me? I've got to know."

Her thoughts returned to the recent attack on the child molester, Callahan. "Of course I'm glad it was him. He certainly had it coming, but why does it bother me so? Why do I feel so weird about it?" She looked out her window. "Good Lord! I'm driving past that Leesford Park again. I don't believe it!"

Martha reached home, sighed with relief and, once inside the house, snapped on the TV. She popped some kettle corn and put her feet up. An old *Jane Austen* movie came on and she settled in to watch it. Nearly falling asleep, she jerked awake as the loud blast of breaking news interrupted the sedate quiet of the film.

"This just in! A man near the Craycroft Elementary school tried to entice two young girls into his car earlier today. Terrified, the children ran home from school and told their mothers, who quickly notified the authorities." The announcer went on: "They told police they screamed real hard and ran away. The little girls provided the police with a description of the man. There is an all-points bulletin out for the arrest of a small, dark-complected male driving an older green sedan. This is the best description they have of the assailant."

Martha was upset at this latest news. Something about it haunted her until she couldn't bear thinking about it anymore. She paced about her home for a time.

Sometimes I feel like our world is crashing about our ears! Our children are no longer safe, and the authorities only seem to protect the criminal element. Exhausted from her inner turmoil and feeling suddenly dizzy, she fell onto her bed and passed out.

CHAPTER 8

Two days later Ryan sat at his desk. His thick mop of hair stood awry from sun glasses, he'd forgotten about, carelessly shoved on top of his head during a busy moment. His shirt sleeves were half way rolled up and his shirt was open enough to reveal tough blond chest hairs. He turned to Harris, his favorite detective and definitely his best investigator. "Alan, looks like we've got to check out families that have been subjected to Callahan's crimes." He thumped the desk with his fist. "But what if there are others in our area that we don't even know about?"

Harris shuffled the papers in his hands. "He did prison time in Harrisburg, Pennsylvania before he came to our fair city, and then of course, the Moulton kid—got away with that one. So far, we haven't found anything more on him. These guys just keep on, so who really knows how many little boys he's *done*?" He couldn't help the bitter chuckle. "He won't be *doing* any more. Thank God for whoever it was that took care of that for the bastard."

Frowning in distaste, Ryan nodded. "Yeah, that's right enough, but Hell's bells, now looks like we've got to check out the Moulton family. Imagine how happy they'll be to see we're diligently prosecuting this particular case.

"Everybody's a suspect, so when you're out there, take a good look around. See who might take it into their head to get revenge." He hesitated. "I hate to add to their pain, especially seeing us trying to find out who fixed the miserable bastard that molested their boy."

"You got that, right. I sure as hell know what I'd think about it," Harris snorted, making a face.

"Go check it out, Alan. Let me know what they have to say and what your gut feelings are while you interview them." Ryan sighed, his forehead furrowed. "Never know. Might be something there, but I hope to hell there isn't. That'd be tough as hell, finding justice for a criminal when we couldn't manage it for their kid."

Ryan frowned. "We need more info on this Callahan while we're at it. The man's got to have more priors than what Harrisburg gave us. I've got someone checking the national computer register on pedophiles. A man like that has to have a sizable record."

"I'll go see the Moulton's, maybe find out how the kid's doing. They won't like seeing me on this mission—don't blame 'em one damned bit." As Harris took his leave, he added, "So far, we have no strong leads, only a few bits of evidence. And I confess I've never been more reluctant to work on a case."

☙☙☙

When the doorbell rang, Jeannie answered it. Her eyebrows rose in surprise. She recognized the officer standing there from Will's case. "Inspector Harris, my goodness, how may I help you?"

"Sorry, ma'am, we have to ask a few questions. It's about the man who was attacked in Leesford Park. May I come in?"

Jeannie let him in and ushered him into the den. "I don't want Will to see an officer in this house, or any strange man. He's been through enough." She closed the door, but not before Harris caught a glimpse of the boy sitting quietly on the floor, listlessly playing with brightly colored *Legos*, building shapeless creations, using little creative imagination. *A sad little guy, one we didn't help.* He hurt inside, seeing the boy sitting like an automaton.

Jeannie saw the regret on his face, but seeing it did nothing to avert her anger and disgust at this man's presence.

"How *is* your boy? We certainly regret how that case went. You must know that. None of us wanted that to happen." He took the proffered chair as sweat broke out on his brow. "The arresting officer was a rookie."

Jeannie sat opposite him. She saw his discomfort, but had no sympathy for the officer. "What are we supposed to do now? Why are you here questioning us? What's going on?"

"Well ma'am, as you must have heard, the man who committed the crime on your son was attacked in the running park. You know, Leesford Park. We have to ask any and all people who might have had a reason to take revenge on him." He felt the heat rise in his cheeks. "We need to know your whereabouts at the time in question."

"If it happened in the morning as they said on the news, we were still in bed, or getting breakfast," she replied. Her reluctance and distaste in discussing this ugly subject made her voice short, clipped, and angry. "What time are you concerned with exactly?"

"It happened just as the sun came up. About six thirty, we believe."

"We were asleep." Tears welled in her eyes. "Since this happened to Will, he doesn't jump out of bed anymore to watch early morning cartoons, not even his favorite, Sponge Bob." She sighed. "My husband was in Denver attending a conference on cost efficiency and marketing. He works for Bonaventure Corporation, and they keep him jumping. He's gone a lot, these days, too much, in fact."

"Will he be able to prove he was there at the time in question?"

"Of course. He'll be home soon. You can ask him yourself. He won't like seeing you here, helping the man who destroyed our son. You must know our boy will never be the same!"

The anger and sorrow in her voice apparently added to his discomfort, but Jeannie didn't care. The time for politeness had passed.

Harris held his ground to complete the questioning. "It's not that we want to help the man, it's that a crime has been committed, and we have to take care of it." He sighed. "This isn't easy for us, ma'am. Believe me. We understand your feelings in this matter. We most certainly do."

Jeannie's lips tightened and her face grew rigid at his words, obviously trying valiantly to control her emotions. The man worried she might erupt at any moment.

The officer's increasing nervousness pleased Jeannie. "Yes, for him, justice for that filthy bastard, but not for our son. You had no justice for our son, and you never will have!" Her fists clenched tight, her nails dug into the flesh of her palms.

Harris noticed her body had gone rigid as she rose from her chair. "Please ma'am, we were sorrier than we can say about what happened to Will." Sweat trickled down his face. "You must know that."

She dismissed the nearly pleading tone of Harris's voice. "Maybe so, but coming here with this business about that horrid man is just too much!" Her tears started falling. "Please leave, I can't stand this."

"Okay ma'am, I will, but ask your husband to give me a call." He handed her his card. "Just ask him. I'm doing my job, and I have to say, it's not so pleasant at times, ma'am." Harris headed to his car as Jeannie slammed the door behind him.

She wanted to slam it hard enough to break the small, inset glass window, but didn't. He had a job to do. Understanding that, she went into the den, flung herself into her husband's chair and cried her heart out. A bit later, she called her mother.

"Mom, would you believe it? The cops were here questioning us about our whereabouts the other morning, wondering if any of us attacked that monster, Callahan!" She bit off the words as her anger and frustration flared.

"I don't believe it!" Martha responded. "They had the unmitigated gall to question *you*, of all people, about what happened to that sick monster? Oh, Jeannie, sometimes I just can't bear it!"

"It was that nice Officer Harris. He said they had to ask anyone remotely connected to the man. Now Martin is required to prove he was at the conference. I told him where Martin was during that time, but that wasn't good enough to satisfy him. I just can't take this anymore, Mom." Jeannie's voice broke. "Is this hideous nightmare ever going to end and our son become a normal child again? What that man did to him is almost the same as committing a murder. Our happy little boy is gone from us now, and I don't know if we'll ever get him back!"

"I'll be right over, Jeannie, just you hang on."

Martha's rage seethed within her until she thought her heart would burst. Her mind began spinning as if she were inside a wind tunnel. "I've got to hang onto myself. Jeannie needs me these days, more than ever," she muttered as she took a quick look in the mirror and headed to the car. "Oh Lordy, I hope a psychiatrist *can* help me, before I go totally off the deep end."

She drove too fast, barely avoided jumping a curb or smashing into a tree. At Jeannie's, she nearly ran to the door.

Jeannie met her at the door. "Mom, you're so pale! Come in and let me look at you. You feeling all right?"

"Yes, of course I am. Your call just put me in a tizzy." She took a deep breath. "Jeannie, these are tough times. In a case like this, the police would naturally look at people having reason to avenge themselves on a man like that. In earlier days, he'd have been hung by his balls or shot at the very least. But we are civilized now, so the police give *them* protection. Seems that way to me, anyway. It's called Miranda Rights. Do we have Miranda Rights? No, we've got nothing!"

Jeannie led her into the den. Her deep blue eyes appeared dull and lifeless, and her hair hung in a mass of rumpled, tangled curls as she slumped into a chair. "Martin will be home soon; maybe he'll get this taken care of."

Martha saw Will sitting in front of the television. "What's Will up to?" She gestured at the television and the dull-faced boy sitting there. Isn't he spending too much time doing that?"

"I think he is, but he refuses to go for walks in the park like we used to. He's not even interested in feeding the ducks." They heard the sound of a car, and Jeannie brightened visibly. "Thank God, Martin's home."

The garage door rumbled as it rolled up.

Then Martin breezed in. "Hi ya, hon, how's it going?" He hugged his wife with a bear-like embrace. Noticing Martha, he asked, "Hi, Mom, everything okay?"

"Martin, the police were here," Jeannie informed him. "You know that incident in the park?" She sniffed. "The detective came here asking if we knew anything about it! He wants you to prove you were at the conference during that time. I guess he believed I was asleep when it happened, lucky me."

"The hell you say!" He stared at her in shock. "Of course I can prove it, but I'd sure as hell like to pin a medal on the guy who fixed that bastard!" He managed a laugh. "Bring those cops on. I hope they find the guy, the whole town will celebrate what he did, and me with them." Then he sobered and his voice grew quiet. "So, how was our boy today?"

Jeannie couldn't hide her frustration. "About the same, going to Biggie's Burgers the other day seemed to perk him up. It's the only thing that does.'"

"We'll be going again," Martha said. "But even there, an older man spoke to him and it frightened him terribly. He clung so tightly to me, I knew he was petrified. I tried to convince him the man was good and after a while, he finally played like all the other kids. Anymore, when I look at a bunch of kids, I wonder how many of them hide terrible secrets. Who knows what happens in their homes? I hate it!" She paused then went in to see her grandson. "Hi, honey, when are we going out to eat again?"

He left his chair and climbed into her lap. "You know where we could go, Grammy?"

"Why no, I can't guess, Will."

"To Biggie's!" Then he spotted his father. "Daddy!" He scrambled from Martha and ran to his father who scooped him up and swung him in the air.

"Hi ya, son!" Martin hugged his small son warmly and kissed his cheeks. "What's all this about going out to eat?"

Will exuded excitement. "Grammy's takin' me to Biggie's for 'nother bittie meal!" the boy exclaimed and chattered happily for several minutes.

Tears filled Jeannie's eyes as she looked at Martha. "Thanks Mom, you'll never know how much." She leaned into her husband's big body for the strength afforded there. Martin enclosed her in his arms for a few moments.

At the door, Martin hugged Martha in a warm bear hug. "Bless you, Martha. We need all the help we can get." The pain in his eyes hurt her and that terrible inner anger over her helplessness against people like Callahan rose in her again.

"Whatever helps. Who would have thought it'd be Biggie's Burgers?" Martha replied and chuckled as she headed for her car. The sky had darkened into night, and she didn't have a hospital shift for today.

"Thank heavens, maybe I can get some rest," she mused aloud as she drove. "I have to find a shrink, maybe tomorrow. I wonder what he'll think about my problem. What if he finds me a certifiable nut case?"

She felt more relaxed after visiting at her daughter'. Any spark of normalcy in Will produced hope for his recovery and confidence in his counselor's efforts. Martha watched television before showering and going to bed. There were no further details about the Callahan case or any movies worthy of watching to take her mind away from the harsh realities of her present life.

Feeling restless, she took a mild sedative, actually a Dramamine, and fell into bed. Again, she had wild dreams, but felt nothing chasing her, though evil feelings lurked in the shadows of her mind and waited there to punish her.

CHAPTER 9

Martha woke with a jolt. Checking the clock, she realized she'd slept very late. "Ye Gods, it's almost ten. I don't believe I've slept so late. I have to be at work again at three." She realized something else, too. "I feel tired, like I've run a million miles."

Her phone rang. It was Jeannie. Listening with half an ear as Jeannie went on about Callahan, Martha's mind swirled with feelings of unreality. Her thoughts centered on the new case she'd heard about, another attempt on children, and two more little girls haunted by nightmares.

"Yes, thank God," Martha managed to answer. "He won't be molesting kids again." Laughing softly, she continued. "I heard the gory details at work last night, and I applaud whoever did it."

"I know, but God, Mom, when will it end?"

"It never ends, Jeannie. There's another devil on the loose." She broke off and shook her head. "Hon, I have to work today, so I'll see you tomorrow. Give my love to Will and we'll go to Biggie's again if he wants."

Martha hung up. Her mind made up, steeling herself to contain her apprehension, she called Dr. Michael Carton's office, a psychiatrist she'd heard good things about. She seldom worked psych, and consequently met few psychiatrists in the course of her hospital work. She was thankful she didn't know Dr. Carton personally.

His nurse asked why she was calling and Martha answered, "I don't exactly know what to tell you, but I have memory or time lapses." She went on to explain. "I have lost periods of time. I don't remember where I was or what happened at all. I'm frightened about it and I need to see someone."

"Do you have insurance?"

"Yes, I have coverage. I'm a nurse at the hospital."

"Oh, well, since you're a nurse, I'll try to squeeze you in. Let me think. I guess Dr. Carton could see you the day after tomorrow."

"I'll be there." Sighing, Martha hung up. She had an appointment in two days, and only because she was in the medical field. "This way if I'm losing my mind, at least I'll know why."

She turned on the tube, looking for news of that latest crime against children. Hearing nothing, she flipped the channel. "Maybe the soaps would be better."

The doorbell rang. Martha opened the door and, to her delight, saw Lizzie Marin, her friend of many years. Lizzie, a well-put-together woman with dark, curling hair swept back from her temples and a wide smile, was always a joy. "Oh hi, come in!" She flung the door wide and reached for her.

"Lady, what's wrong, you look like hell."

Martha laughed. "And good day to you, too. Want some lunch in a while? I just got up, had a bite of breakfast, but I could eat again if you're hungry."

Lizzie grinned. "Sure, anything—hey, I haven't heard from you for a while. Anything going on?"

Her quizzical look put Martha on guard. "No, nothing out of the ordinary. Work, of course, and there's my grandson, Will. I wonder if there's ever an end to what happened to that poor child. Do they ever recover from a thing like that? Do you know anything about those things? I may be a nurse, but this has me baffled."

"I don't know, but someone sure did a number on the dude that attacked Will. You hear about that?" Lizzie laughed in delight. "He won't be out molesting kids any time soon, or ever. We need more of that in this country, I say." She flipped her hair back as she spoke. "They ought to cut the balls off every child predator in the country!" Her bright, hazel eyes sparkled with mischief.

Martha nodded in agreement, thinking her friend was a nice looking woman for her age. In her forties, Lizzie had married very well, and no doubt had had a bit of enhancement work done. At least Martha thought so, but she had never asked. "I was glad to hear about it," she said. "He must have more enemies than us. Guys like that never stop, I'm told. Maybe you're right in your idea of a permanent cure. But that wouldn't be politically correct, now would it?" Martha uttered a deep, derisive chuckle as she pulled out the coffee pot. "Would you like a cup?"

"Sure, coffee makes my world go round." After it brewed, Lizzie took the proffered cup and cradled it in her hands. "How come you look so tired, Martha?" she questioned with narrowed eyes. "Tough night at work?"

"It's always busy on the wards these days and charting is out of hand. The government won't pay Medicare payments unless every procedure is written out in detail. So, instead of actually giving nursing care, you just write all about it in the treatment book or nurse's notes." Martha sighed. "It's a pain in the ass of nursing, I can tell you that much."

She hadn't covered her fading purple spots, and noticed Lizzie eyeing them. The instant unease of it set her heart racing.

"Martha, I worry about you sometimes. You need to get married again. Don't you ever meet any great guys on the job, business moguls, millionaires? They get sick, don't they?"

Martha laughed. Lizzie always lightened her mood. *No need to mention needing a psychiatrist. Who would understand a thing like that? I don't understand it myself, and I'm scared as hell. I wish I could tell someone, it would be a relief.*

"There's a great looking guy at work, Bob Chance, she answered. "He's a quiet one, sees things about me and wants to help. He knows about Will and offers his shoulder, so to speak. He's nice enough, but I can't get involved just now. I'm in such a whirl over everything. I couldn't handle a relationship right now and I don't know if he has leanings that way. He's just a nice guy."

"Ooh—*love* his name. You could be Martha Chance if you worked at it. You're a good lookin' gal, Martha. Don't sell yourself short." Lizzie waggled her head for emphasis, and added, "What's the purple stuff on your arm there?"

"I don't know what I got into. Looks like the gram stain solution we used in training, but I don't remember going near the lab. Whatever, it's fading now." Martha shrugged. "Sometimes when I come home, I have about every stain there is on my uniform."

"Good enough. Girl, you seem to need me just now. Why is that, Martha? You can tell me anything, you know that." Lizzie's hazel eyes darkened significantly. They delved too deeply and were too knowing for Martha's comfort level.

She drew herself up, unable to speak of her fears. She barely eked out a weak reply. "Lizzie, you are without a doubt the best friend I've ever had. But for now, I have a lot of worries on my mind, mostly about my grandson, but that's not all of it. In time, I'll get things sorted out."

She felt a tear welling up, "This latest thing on the news set me off all over again. Now two more children have learned to fear for their safety because the law can't seem to protect us anymore. Where's it all going to end?" She felt hot salty tears drip down her cheeks.

"God, Martha, you *are* upset. If I can do anything to help, you know I will. I'd like to be the one to fix those guys myself." Lizzie couldn't stop the giggle escaping her lips at the thought of what happened to Callahan.

Martha found herself caught up in it, too. "You're good for me, Lizzie. You really are."

They both laughed until tears escaped down their cheeks.

"Lizzie, you are the ever lovin' limit!" Martha dabbed at her eyes and reached over to give Lizzie a big hug. "I love you, girl. I'm so glad you came over. You've saved my life today. Don't ask me why—you just did!"

After a hasty lunch neither of them really tasted, Lizzie took her leave and Martha felt several degrees lighter for the visit.

She showered and headed to the hospital. "Another shift and I couldn't care less. I can't hide my worries, and I'm tired as hell. Hope my patients won't suffer for it." She parked her car and went to her assigned ward.

During report, she noticed Bob scoping her out more intensely than usual. Then he quickly looked away. She felt furtive for having noticed and decided she'd speak to him later if she found the time. *He seems concerned. Do I look that bad? Does it show that much?*

Her patients kept her running the entire shift and she had no chance for a supper break. Heaving a sigh of relief, and with great fatigue, Martha headed out of the hospital toward the sanctuary of her car. Keys in hand, she was about to click it open when felt a solid, warm hand on her arm.

"How about a bite of supper, Martha?"

Bob had moved so close, right next to her elbow. In her worn condition, she hadn't noticed his nearness, not even the masculine scent of him.

"Oh, hello there," she mumbled in a voice that sounded weak and thin to her own ears. Startled at how close he stood, she managed a subdued response of refusal. "I'm not hungry, Bob." She wondered how that sounded to him, but didn't care. Was he was making a move on her, perhaps a dating overture? In her present state she couldn't emotionally handle any sort of an intimate relationship. She desperately wanted to go home, go to bed and get away from everything.

"Look, I know you're worn right down to your toes, but we need to talk. Come on, a bit of dinner might do you good. I happen to know you didn't have time to eat." His soft voice held a strong note of urgency and he directed a concerned look deep into her eyes.

His tone, so gentle, yet insistent couldn't be denied. Martha saw only a look of kindness in his eyes. Realizing she sorely needed a friendly voice just now, she replied, "Okay, I'd love it, where?"

"Oh, Denny's would do, wouldn't it?"

At the sound of that name, Martha froze. "Uh—any place but there, Bob. I don't know why I feel that way, but right now, I do." She barely got the words out. *Why does the name Denny's, upset me?* She hugged herself and waited for his reply.

"Hey, we'll go to La Fiesta. They're open late. Okay then?"

Martha nodded her acceptance and they went to Bob's big GMC four-wheel drive. It was a high climb getting in, so he helped her up. She felt the heat of his hands on her body when he did, and she shivered at that unexpected sensation.

"I don't want to be nosey, girl," he said. "But something big has got a grip on you. You need to relax. Maybe a bit of down time will fix your wagon. What's going on? That is, if you'd want to spill. I'm a damned good listener."

Martha managed a smile. "A lot has happened and everything *has* kinda snowballed on me. I can't talk about it, but I appreciate your company, Bob, I really do."

His truck, big, warm, and strong, just like him, gave her the feeling of badly needed security. Basking in his gentle masculinity added to the feeling of stability. She realized she felt comfortable with him—an unexpected pleasure.

The loss of her husband Chet had left her alone. Sometimes she felt like an Eskimo woman left out on an ice floe alone to die. No family members, though they helped, had ever filled that great hole in her life. Indeed, they never knew the depths of loneliness his loss had left her to face. They had their own lives, and she wanted them to live peacefully without worrying over her problems.

She'd been more than aloof when men came near, fearing additional pain should she become entangled in a good relationship and face another loss. But now, with something as casual as a snack after work, she'd allowed a male to enter her personal sphere, if only this once. "Nice truck, Bob, rides smooth," was all she could manage to say.

"Thanks Martha." He glanced her way, his eyes warm and soft, and hesitated. "You know, I've always liked the way you look at work. You're good with your patients. The way you are makes me think you just might be good people."

"I always hoped I was." Relaxing a bit, she nearly giggled, but held it to a chuckle. No need to act the silly female. "You're one fine nurse yourself, Bob. I've watched you, too." To another nurse, being good at the profession made all the difference in how they were perceived by their peers.

They said no more until he'd ushered her to a seat in La Fiesta. It had the usual Mexican décor: sombreros, serapes, and wildly colorful *ollas* sitting around filled with brightly colored paper flowers. It wasn't busy this late—just a few patrons ordering small stuff. They received their colorful menus and ordered. By then, Martha realized she had a ravenous hunger. "This is nice, Bob, I didn't know I was so hungry."

He smiled in return, but said nothing and kept looking into her eyes as his long fingers toyed with his napkin.

Martha took a good look at him. He was approaching middle age. His hair, touched with gray, was thick with a hint of curl about it. Slim and fit, about six feet, she guessed as she wondered what his story would be. She'd never heard anything of his personal life, and asked, "How are things for you, these days?"

Sadness edged his smile as he replied, "Not so good in a lot of ways, but I'm handling it. My family's gone now. Had a bad auto accident a couple of years ago, I made it—they didn't."

"Oh Bob—I'm sorry to hear that." Martha felt tears forming and blinked them away. "We get so tied up in our own lives, we tend to forget that others have been there, too. I didn't know about your family."

He shrugged, a half smile spread across his firm mouth. "I'm learning to live with it, but I think about my two younger kids. They'll never have the chance to marry, or do the things we'd hoped for them. One girl was away at school, so I do have her, but when they leave home, they never really come back, do they?"

Martha felt his pain. She reached out and took his hand. The sorrow in his voice compelled her to offer, "Bad things happen, Bob. We all get a shot of it at one time or another, but I have to say, you've certainly had more than your share."

He squeezed her hand and his smile lightened the mood considerably. "Hey thanks, Martha. Looks like we've lots of things to share, but for now, let's relax and have a good evening. And here comes the chow."

After the waitress set their plates before them, they ate in comfortable silence. The sounds of people murmuring to each other, and the distant clink of dishes and glassware in the background, added to the warmth of their surroundings. Their booth encircled them, and Martha had greatly needed the feeling of security and comfort. The company wasn't half bad either.

She sighed and smiled at him. A tremor of excitement passed through her at his return glance. Her thoughts lightened even more as he reached out and squeezed her hand again. His touch had an unexpected effect. One she'd never experienced, not even with Chet, her lost love.

"I lost my husband four years ago," she murmured. "It was tough for me, but you have to go on. I'm sorry to mention it, but things happen, don't they?"

His eyes held hers with their warmth. "Yeah, I'd have to say they do, so you doing okay with that, these days?"

"Yes. He left me well enough monetarily. I work more to get out of the house and be with people, than for expenses." After a quiet moment, she went on. "It's the aloneness, isn't it?" She laughed. "Sorry, let's enjoy our dinner—and the company."

"Hey, it's okay, and sometime I'd like to hear everything about you." After they ate, Bob returned her to her vehicle and made sure she got it started before he waved goodnight. Martha felt enveloped in a lovely glow and for a time, forgot her oppressive worries. "How good it is to shelve all my troubles, if only for a little while. I'm off tomorrow, thank God! I'm so tired!"

CHAPTER 10

Two days later, feeling close to panic, Martha entered the office of Dr. Michael Carton. Her hands trembled so that she barely completed the required paperwork while sitting in the quiet, comfortable office, awaiting her first appointment. Not knowing what she might learn made her edgy. Her hands clenched into tight knots until she untwisted them and clamped onto the arms of her chair.

When the nurse appeared at the door to summon her into that dreaded inner sanctum, she rose tight-lipped. With fear and escalating tension, she entered the doctor's office, took the indicated chair, and sat stiffly upright, neither enjoying or caring how nice the large, soft, brown leather chair felt against her back. Heart hammering, she waited for him to begin.

After introducing himself, he asked. "How are you, Martha?"

"I'm fine." Her voice didn't sound like her own.

He nodded, indicating he understood her hesitancy. "I want to help you. Your reason for seeing me states you've had periods of time lapses. Why don't you just tell me as best you can what has occurred, when these episodes began, and what concerns you enough to seek treatment. We'll take a look at those things and see what can be done."

Fearful of his reaction, she began, "Doctor, things are happening to me, lately. I have memory lapses. I find new things lying about that I don't remember buying. I even have spots on my arm—I don't know how I got them or even what they are." She looked at him, wondering if he thought her crazy as a loon, but even with this small beginning, she felt her hands loosen their frantic grip on the arms of her chair and her insides began to warm and relax as she let her worries out.

"Humm, of course, as you know, everything has a cause, a reason, if you will, for its occurrence. Perhaps we could go back a few months to begin with and bring the events up to the present. Continue relaxing, you are safe here." He paused and took a sip of water. "I can plainly see you've been under a strain and it will help you a great deal if you tell me as much as you're comfortable with. Why don't we see if you can take me back to a time before you began noticing these things?"

Martha made it through that first fateful hour and left the office feeling she had gotten nowhere, with no real answers, though for some reason, she felt a little lighter. Telling her worries to the doctor had relieved her in some way. She hadn't been able to confide her fears to anyone else. Psychiatry usually took a long time. She knew that, too. In any case, she had nowhere else to go.

"I think it went well," she told herself. "He was nice, and he made it easy for me to talk. But am I doing the right thing?" She laughed. "Now I'm talking to myself again. Dare I tell him that?" She decided to go to Jeannie's. "No matter what, I won't burden her with this latest fiasco. That poor girl is up to her eyeballs with her own worries. All she needs is to find out her mom's seeing a shrink!"

Barely watching the road in her mental preoccupation, she arrived at her daughter's home, though this time, she did notice how well all the trees had leafed out and that summer rapidly approached.

"I hate being so preoccupied with all this mental stuff," she muttered, upset with herself and angry at the turn her life had taken. "The world is so beautiful. The weather's warming. It's wonderful outside, but with all that's happening I scarcely find the time to enjoy it."

At Jeannie's, she stood with her daughter in the hall, watching Will. He sat quietly in his small bucket chair. The TV played *Bozo and Friends.* Jeannie whispered, "He sits and watches, but I wonder what he sees, the program, or what? I don't know what's going through his mind." She choked back a sob. "Nothing's the same with him anymore, Mom."

Martha put a commiserating arm around her. "I don't know what to do, Jeannie. I get so furious at the police for letting that man go, it tears me up inside. Don't these monsters realize how many lives they ruin when they attack just one innocent young child? It's never just the child, is it? The whole family pays the price."

Martha stayed for a couple hours, held Will on her lap, and then took her leave. "I'm tired today, Jeannie, had a couple of heavy shifts. Maybe I'll take a few days off."

Jeannie stood in the doorway watching as her mother tossed her purse in the car. She'd noted the worry on Martha's face recently, maybe even more than her own. "Gosh, Mom, are you all right? You haven't been yourself lately. I'm not so messed up I can't see that."

"I'll be fine, dear. You just take care of Will. I need more sleep, that's all. Don't worry about me." Saying that, hoping to comfort her daughter, Martha stepped into her car and drove home with enough presence of mind to notice she didn't drive past the running park.

Trying to relax, she showered, had a cup of tea, watched a bit of news, and then slid into bed. Her thoughts swirled with recent events, preventing any hope of sleep. The news report she'd heard on the tube kept haunting her. She imagined those two little girls running and screaming from the nice man who'd offered them goodies with hideous evil intent. "Now we have one more devil running through our streets, another damned pedophile stalking our children! Where are our police?" She put her hand on the phone. "I wish I dared to call Bob Chance. It would be nice just to sit and talk with him—maybe get my mind off things."

She wouldn't make that call but knew he'd like it if she did. It would be a forward act to her way of thinking, and not anything she could do. But, remembering how nice and easy things were between them when she'd sat with him at the La Fiesta, she felt defeated. "I would meet a nice guy when my life is so screwed up." She sighed and reached for the sleeping aid she'd taken from the med drawer at work.

"It's just a *Tylenol* with *Dramamine,* not like it's a narc or anything," she muttered in justification. She wasn't an abuser, but she needed something at the moment. "Why am I so tired anyway?" She flipped on the radio at her bedside, but turned it so low, she could barely hear it. Sleep came at last.

ℰℱℰℱ

Martha kept her next appointment with Dr. Carton. "What do you think Doctor, am I going crazy?" She feared his answer.

"It's not that Martha, but time lapses are quite out of the ordinary, and there are definite causes for aberrant behaviors such as these. I have a few ideas, but it will take time to find out. We'll need to go as far back as you have memories, perhaps a period somewhere in your childhood."

"What are you looking for?" Something in his queries made her feel uneasy. A deep feeling of dread suddenly filled her mind. Without conscious thought, she clutched the arms of the comfortable leather chair.

Her action was not lost on the doctor. Firming his jaw, he continued. "Was there anyone you remember from your childhood who didn't behave correctly with you when you were a little girl, a male relative, or female for that matter, an uncle or brother?" Dr. Carton kept his inquiries gentle and non-threatening. Knowing he had to proceed very carefully to reach the root of her time lapses. If what he suspected lay at the heart of Martha's problems—the very thought of it made his heart race unexpectedly.

Doctor Carton's strong face, but sincere mien, aided Martha's relaxation. She tried to see in him a danger to herself, but couldn't. Relaxed, she let her memories come forth. "I grew up on a farm, Doctor." She hesitated and then went on. "We had this hired man, Pete Sykes, his name was. I'll never forget that horrible man—or his name." She shivered. "He frightened me and when I told my dad about the time Sykes tried to touch me down there, my father wouldn't believe me."

Martha indicated her pubic region and felt her face tighten. Tears began to form, "My dad said I just imagined it. Sykes was a good worker, the war had started, and dad needed him. After that, I knew I couldn't say anything else against Pete." Martha felt tears well up and she couldn't stop them. "He punched me in the chest one time and it hurt. I was too small to have breasts then, though."

"You're crying, Martha. Do you remember this man, Sykes, as being so bad, that after so long, the memory of him brings you to tears?"

"I don't remember for sure." Martha wrung her hands and twisted in her chair. "I want to leave. I have to leave now— now! I don't feel well at all!"

She'd become restless, uncomfortable, and close to panic. "Well, our time is up for this session, Doctor Carton gently replied. "We'll re-introduce this subject the next time. Trying to remember things that are painful is very upsetting." He helped Martha up. "It will be extremely helpful if you can remember even the smallest, seemingly insignificant event." He ushered her out, his hand at her elbow, and noticed how she shrank away from his touch.

Alone in his office, Dr. Carton pressed a button on the intercom. "Jennie, get me Dr. Schoenfeld, will you?" He waited, his hands tented before him, whistling through his teeth.

The phone buzzed. "Carton here," he answered, then, asked, "Herman, could you step in here for a moment? I think I've got something very unusual. I'd like to consult with you." He waited with an impatience that made him pace the floor. He only had a few spare moments before his next patient.

The door opened, admitting a small, slim, gray-haired man with thick glasses. ""He adjusted his glasses and patted his thinning hair. His bright, dark eyes brimmed with curiosity. "What you got, Mike?"

Carton noted his impeccably-fitting gray suit, thinking how well it suited the man. "It's too early to be sure, but I think I may have a case of Dissociative Identity Disorder go-ing."

"My God—you know how *rare* those cases are, Mike?" Herman shook his head and blew on his knuckles. "Take your time, be extremely cautious. You know how fragile these pa-tients can be."

Carton detailed some of the aspects of the case.

After considering the findings Carton had imparted to him, Herman smiled and shook his head slowly. "You may be correct in your diagnosis, it certainly could be." He turned to leave. "How about we meet later for lunch?"

"Sure thing, I'd like that." Carton waved Herman away and admitted his next patient. Containing his excitement took real control.

☙☙☙

Back in the familiar confines of her home, Martha paced restlessly about, feeling at loose ends. She almost wished she'd taken another shift so she'd be too busy to worry. "Am I losing it completely?"

She tried to remember her lost hours, where she bought that damned purse, or when. When had she spilled the Gram's stain on her wrists? If that was what the stuff was. She had no memory of that, either.

"Something's wrong with me," she said over and over. "And I hope that doc finds an answer real soon." But she didn't want to re-visit her childhood. For some reason, those thoughts had become very painful.

Startled by the jangling of the phone, she stopped her aimless pacing and picked it up without checking the caller ID. "Hello."

"Martha, it's Bob."

A smile crossed her tensed lips. "Bob, how'd you know my number?"

"Trade secret. How about we get together and see a movie this afternoon?"

She listened to his warm voice, her hands plucking nervously at a magazine carelessly tossed on the coffee table. "Oh, sure, I'd like that. What time?"

"An hour?"

"Perfect."

Martha hung up, shaking her head. "Like a bolt out of the blue, he calls me, just as I'm about to fall apart. He'll never know how much I needed to hear from someone. He's the best person to be with right now. I wish I could tell him everything, but I can't tell him anything!" She grimaced. "And that would be if I actually knew what was happening."

She headed for the shower. He'd come by in about one hour. "A movie, huh? I can't remember the last time I've seen one. God bless that man." *She was going on a date!*

He was quiet and smooth, as he ushered her to his truck, and said little other than okaying the movie choice with her. In the darkened theater, he supplied pop-corn and a soda. Martha felt like a teenager again. She even giggled a few times.

"So what is this about?" she asked.

"Oh, just a bit of fluff actually, but maybe we both need a little nothingness to lighten our loads." He nudged her shoulder and smiled, helping himself to a large fistful of popcorn. "Takes you back, doesn't it?"

Martha wanted to cry at his gentle masculinity. Her husband had been a good man, and she continued to suffer from that loss, but here was someone who made the memory of Chet fade away without even trying.

She smiled at him. "Thanks Bob. It's wonderful being here, the pop-corn, and the company." Her smile spread wider across her cheeks as she gazed at him.

He said nothing more. The sound blared as the coming attractions exploded across the screen. A time or two, he reached over and took her hand. The feelings his touch aroused were like nothing she'd ever known. It frightened her, but thrilled her far more, and best of all, she forgot everything else.

Later, they had a light supper at a small hide-away called Nickie's, a nicely decorated spot with a French theme. It had French scenes on the walls, dark wood, and finely wrought, iron filigreed chairs. He ordered a huge burger and she a French dip. She hadn't taken time for dinner and was hungry. More than that, she enjoyed his company and actually felt like floating when he looked into her eyes. Everything he did brought new sensations, things she'd never felt with her husband or any man she'd ever known.

Chet had been a good husband. She'd loved him dearly and mourned his loss terribly, but he'd never touched her the way Bob did without conscious effort. *But what would he think if he knew he was keeping company with a nut case?*

At her door, Bob took her in his arms and kissed her long and fully. He didn't try for more, but said, "I've wanted to kiss you for a long time, Martha. I like you, everything about you, and I had a great time tonight." Still holding her, he gazed into her eyes.

She knew he didn't want to say good night. His big body felt hard and strong against her smaller frame, and as much as she wanted to stay in that safe, warm place so much longer, she knew better. Reluctantly, she moved away. "I had a wonderful time, too, felt like a kid again, and forgot all my troubles. I like you, Bob, I really do." She reached out and hugged him. "Thanks for tonight, I enjoyed it and appreciate it."

"Well, my dear, goodnight then. We'll have to do this again."

Martha smiled into his eyes before he left her. "I'd love it." She lingered against her door, watching him walk to his truck, enjoying the masculine look of him as he moved. A longing sigh escape her lips.

Once inside, she wondered if she should have invited him in, but with so much uncertainty facing her, she couldn't handle another complication in her life. "What'll I do if he becomes serious?"

She undressed and slipped into bed, her mind swirling with the wonderful evening, His solid, masculine strength, gentle yet sturdy—all the wonderful qualities she valued and would ever want in a man. Laying there, feeling the glow from Bob's strong, searching kiss, Martha forgot her worries for once as she basked in the lovely feel of femininity he'd

aroused inside her tension-filled body. It felt so good—he felt
so good!

CHAPTER 11

Martha entered the psychiatrist's office for her next visit, nervously picking at her sleeve. She took the comfortable seat the doctor indicated. "Hi, doc." She tried to sound relaxed, but her tight grip on the arms of her chair and whitened knuckles belied the attempt.

Dr. Carton faced her, his jaw firm. "Martha, we've reached the point in your case where we need to take the next step. My colleague, Dr. Schoenfeld, is an expert in certain areas we need to continue in your treatment. May I include him in our sessions?"

Martha felt a chill creeping across her. "In what areas, Doctor?"

"In this case, I am referring to the use of hypnosis."

Her own research had told her hypnosis was frequently used. These doctors had the means to help her. Knowing she must, she nodded. As the small, unassuming Dr. Schoenfeld entered the room, she liked and trusted him instinctively, yet worried he'd be another person who knew her too intimately.

Satisfied, Dr. Carton indicated Schoenfeld to a seat and began. He'd sensed her rising fear had to do with going back to her childhood, but knew he had to force her along in order to continue his treatment. "Now then, we discussed going back to an earlier time. When did the first time lapse occur, can you tell me that?"

"I have been thinking about that, Doctor. When I was in the second grade, I remember wondering where the whole first year went. I have no memory of that first grade year, or most of it, anyway. They said I made good grades and passed, but I don't remember that, either."

Fighting his rising excitement, he began again. "When you did begin to remember?" He cleared his throat. "What was different, when you remembered again?" Noticing how she gripped her chair, her knuckles white, her jaw tightly clenched, he pushed her farther along the road of remembrance.

"One thing I remember was feeling glad our hired man had gone. My father said he joined the Army or something. We had a new man, but he was real nice. I don't remember being afraid of him at all, but I never let him get me alone, either." Martha smiled. "His name was Leonard. He worked very hard and my dad really liked him. He never could stand a lazy worker." She sighed. It was a relief to say normal things about a man. Speaking of Sykes had made her feel very uncomfortable.

"I wonder. Were you able to recall anything that happened before the other hired man, Pete, wasn't it, had left the farm?"

The doctor watched Martha's reaction carefully. Noting her increasing nervousness, her pallor, her clenched fists twisting her clothing, he now believed childhood trauma to be at the root of Martha's memory lapses. In fact, he was sure of it.

"I don't remember. I—I—have to leave now!" Martha rose from her chair. "I'm sorry, Doctor, but I can't do any more today."

"You've done very well, Martha, but we have more work to do. Make another appointment in two days. We'll have another go at this." He wrote a few notes and called the front desk to set up the appointment. "We'll see you then," he said as he ushered her out.

Back at his desk, he turned to his associate. "Well, Herman?"

Schoenfeld's flushed face betrayed his excitement as well as the way he nervously fingered his blue patterned tie. "I'm absolutely certain you've a case of Dissociative Identity Disorder on your hands. She's coming around rather rapidly I believe, perhaps too fast. I'm not sure."

Carton tented his hands and shook his head. "These things are so rare. I hope I'm up to the challenge this woman presents and can handle this case to her benefit if D.I.D. is truly what she suffers from."

"I'll sit in on a few more sessions if you like. You may want to use hypnosis at some future juncture. It frequently helps them come to terms with the causative trauma. In any case, it certainly lets *you* know what those traumas were." Dr. Schoenfeld gave a soft, uncertain chuckle. "You are one lucky man to be given a chance like this."

"I've considered that, too, Herman. We *will* try hypnosis, but she's not ready, not for a while yet. Give it a few more sessions. I'll let you know when I think she's ready." He studied his colleague. "That's a specialty of yours isn't it? I could certainly use some help with this situation if you're willing."

"I'd be happy to help in any way I could. You know that, Mike."

'"Great, sitting in on a couple of sessions with us, acquainting herself with another doctor will facilitate our level of understanding of her problems. It may seem rather drastic to her way of thinking. She is a nurse by profession, but nevertheless, an exceptionally frightened woman in need of intense therapy."

"Of course, of course, we mustn't overlook the medical-professional aspect." Unable to disguise his excitement, Schoenfeld stood to take his leave. "Thanks again for sharing this most interesting case, I appreciate it."

Carton held great respect for his fellow partner in psychiatry. Of anyone he knew, Herman was the best of the best. That he was exceptionally well-versed in hypnotherapy only added to his ability regarding this woman's therapy.

Carton eagerly awaited her next appointment, his mind deeply into Martha's case. As a doctor, he knew the excitement of treating a condition rarely seen and worried anew if he'd be equal to the challenge of helping this patient.

D.I.D. certainly wasn't his strong suit since he'd never had a patient with it prior to Martha Lavery. He planned long hours of study into this particular mental aberration, wanting to be fully prepared.

☙❧☙❧

Martha woke slowly. Rising from her bed, she noticed the heavy smell of stale smoke clinging to her hair. "Not again! What is this?" She ran to her bathroom mirror and scanned her face and body. Faint traces of heavy make-up clung to her skin. Her hair looked dull and reeked of stale smoke. "Oh my God, what have I done now? Where have I been? What on God's green earth is happening to me?"

She raced to the shower and lingered there for a long, thorough cleansing. Her hair felt dry and her body burned from the severe scrubbing. "Dare I tell this to the doctor?" She knew she should. He needed all the details she could provide.

Pulling clothes from the closet, she noticed the shiny black, high-heeled leather boots lying in the back. Aghast, she stared at the length of them—they were long enough to reach nearly to her buttocks. "I never bought these! I wouldn't be caught dead wearing slutty things like that!" Uttering a sick laugh, she shook her head. "Wonder where my fishnets have gone?" But she'd also bought a purse at some unknown time and not remembered that either. "Thank God, I'm seeing a psychiatrist. If I wasn't, I'd be hunting for one now. And I'm taking Will to Biggie's Burgers again this afternoon. Hope I can hold myself together for that."

☙❧☙❧

This time at Biggie's, Will quickly entered the play area, joining the others in normal little-boyhood. Happy to see it, Martha watched the boy climbing, sliding, and running while he yelled, screamed, and interacted with other children his age and size. But when a boy, larger and loud-voiced, begin pushing Will about on the sliding tube, he quickly ran to her side, tears shining in his eyes. "That big boy's bein' mean to me, Grammy."

Worried that Will would now be easily cowed by aggression, she wondered if this might be another outcome of the assault he'd suffered at the hands of Fred Callahan. Anger boiled within her at seeing the end result of adult aggression against a child. Would the boy take up for himself as he aged, or would he be cowed in the presence of larger males? What would this do to his ability to interact with females? Her frustration mounted anew as she pondered these new considerations.

Driving home, Will sat silently in his safety seat and Martha felt the familiar sense of sickening defeat all over again. Reporting the details to Jeannie only added to the hurt. The pain and agony over Will's assault continued and Martha fought the unusual amount of internal furor that had taken up permanent residence within her. *Where did I get this anger? It's so not like me.*

In response to Martha's worried report, Jeannie shook with renewed angst. "I'll ask his therapist what to expect down the line for Will. How many ways will this assault affect his life?"

The futility of helping Will haunted Martha. At every turn she saw how the victimization of her grandchild affected his mind, his behavior, and the devastating effects on his family. *Is this personal destruction permanent?* She feared it truly was. Could anyone, even in a lifetime, ever forget being sexually molested?

Martha left her daughter's home, facing another defeat. Her wild, unreasoning fury lingered as she drove through the sunny streets and mocked her. She did not see the clean streets, new flowers, or the freshening green of the new spring season as she drove by. She nearly hated the sight of innocent people walking by, laughing and talking, holding the hand of a little child—those souls whose lives had not been altered by an evil assault on an innocent one in their family. It left her feeling sick at the unfairness in life. She wanted answers, and there were none to be found.

ოუოუ

Dr. Carton welcomed Martha into his office. "How do you feel today?"

"Oh, about the same, Doctor." Martha felt extremely tense, but she couldn't admit that to the doctor. After several visits, she knew the next step would be hypnosis. "I guess I'm scared, Doctor. I smelled of smoke again when I woke up this morning and I'm afraid about the hypnosis thing. I'll find out things I never wanted to know. You know I will." She couldn't bring herself to mention the disgusting boots.

"Yes, you likely will, but not to worry, we do hypnosis quite often and it's a very helpful tool. It could certainly make all the difference in your case. My associate, Dr. Herman Schoenfeld is familiar with your case now, and is an expert in hypnotherapy. If you'll agree, I'd like him to do that therapy."

"Well—" Martha hesitated, fearful of what they would learn. "Are you sure all this is confidential?" she asked, her eyes on his, seeking an answer she could believe. Being a rather private person made this step all the more traumatic and she felt a heavy foreboding that something dreadful would be brought forth, something she deeply feared.

"Of course it is, Martha, we want solutions for your problems, and today, with hypnosis, perhaps we may begin to understand the basic cause of your time lapses. Dr. Schoenfeld has joined us several times now. I believe we have a good chance to help you, especially if you'll agree to undergo hypnotherapy. Many times, it's the only method open to us."

"I know I must, and I'm frightened. I admit it." Her tautly held body and white knuckled hands bore out her statement, but she fearfully nodded her head in consent.

Dr. Carton picked up his cell and dialed. "It's all set, Herman. We'll begin today if you're ready."

They waited expectantly until the man entered. Martha nodded to the small, unassuming Dr. Schoenfeld. His eyes, dark and warm, and his relaxed manner tended to instill trust in a wary patient. But then, what choice did she have if she wanted answers? Resignation filled her mind and, squaring her shoulders, she readied herself for the fearful unknown.

They began. Dr. Shoenfeld's voice, measured and soft, calmed her. After a time, Martha easily slipped into a hypnotic state. The doctor gently and slowly began the regression to her childhood, aiming for the lost year. From prior discussions, both doctors felt certain the hired man had abused Martha during the year she'd been in first grade. After careful questioning, he reached the correct point in her regression and asked her, "What do you see, Martha? Is anyone there with you?" Both doctors noted the paling of her features and the tenseness of her mouth.

Martha, her voice, higher pitched and childlike, said, "I'm coming home from first grade. My daddy is out on the tractor, but the hired man is in the barn looking out at me." Tears slipped down her cheeks and her body twisted.

"Is the hired man, Pete Sykes, there, with you, Martha?"

"Yes. He makes me come in the barn." Her voice quavered. She shuddered violently. "Mommy's in the house, but I can't go to her. He said I have to stay with him."

"What is happening to you now, Martha? You can tell me, it's all right. You are safe here and will not be hurt if you tell us what is happening." Schoenfeld kept his voice low and firm.

"No—no, I mustn't tell. He said he will stick me with a pitch fork if I do. It's real big with long, sharp, shiny things. It's awful! He said he'll hurt me real bad if I tell my mommy or daddy."

Drs. Carton and Schoenfeld listened to the voice of a small child emanating from Martha's mouth. Dr. Schoenfeld, his voice soothing and calm, said, "No, Martha, Pete Sykes can't hurt you. I won't let that happen. Is he touching you? Is he touching you in private places?"

"Yes—he's poking into me down there!" She gestured at her pubic area. "It hurts me bad! Sometimes I bleed, but I can't tell my mommy or daddy. They don't believe me anymore. Oh please—don't—don't!"

From then on, the Drs. Carton and Schoenfeld listened to evil, depraved, things they'd never wanted to hear told in the frightened, pain-filled voice of a small child in agony. Sweat broke out on Dr. Carton's brow as he heard the sickening details of this child's suffering.

Finally, Dr. Carton shook his head, saying, "We've done enough, Herman. My God! Bring her back now."

Dr. Schoenfeld called to Martha, told her it was time to come back now, and worked to help her relax as he completed the process. "At the count of three, you must wake up." He began to count and at three, Martha's eyes took on the look of present reality. She straightened in her chair.

"Well, Docs, did you help me?" she sneered softly.

Looking deeply into her eyes, Dr. Carton saw the certain look of a terrible knowledge he'd never seen in Martha. "Who am I talking to?" he asked. His heart raced, thinking of the phenomena he believed had happened.

She uttered a harsh laugh. "Guess who, Doc?" She crossed her legs. "I'm Serena. You wanted to meet me, didn't you? Well, here I am." She thrust out her breasts and gave him a highly suggestive leer, accompanied with a half-laugh.

Dr. Carton nearly stammered. "Tell me about yourself, Serena."

"Cut the crap, Doc. You already know what I'm about. That pathetic wimp, Martha, needed me. I kept her from going crackers. She needs me now too, don't you know? Or do you?" A look of slyness emanated from her eyes. Then, glancing at Dr. Schoenfeld, she sniffed, "And who's this little pip-squeak sitting in here with us?"

Carton introduced Dr. Schoenfeld. "He's here to help with the hypnosis. Looks like it worked all too well." Then, his voice firm but gentle, he asked her, "Please, I would like to speak to Martha now." He feared Martha might be submerged overly long and needed to assess her mental status after the traumatic event they'd just witnessed.

"No sweat, doc." Serena turned away, twisting in her chair.

When she turned back, both doctors easily recognized Martha. They were stunned to have seen this phenomenon. Neither doctor had ever seen that particular occurrence before today, and it took them a moment to find their voices.

Dr. Carton said, "Martha, you did very well. We will be able to help you. In time, you'll remember everything. Would you like to know what's happening, and why?"

"Of course—but, will it be something terrible? I'm not so sure..." Her face paled, her eyes deepened to a darker green, and both doctors could see the icy dread they held.

"Nothing that was your fault, but something did happen to you as a child. We need to help you put everything together. We now know you have an alternate personality. One created in childhood to help you survive some very traumatic events, none of which were your fault." Dr. Carton repeated, carefully leading Martha toward enlightenment and guilt avoidance.

"We need to end this session for today. We'll take it up again, perhaps in our next meeting." He ordered a new appointment for Martha and gently took her arm to usher her out of the office.

"Thank you both. I feel lighter somehow. Then, will I have to undergo hypnotherapy again?" The biting edge of fear had crept softly into her voice, though she managed a smile for her doctor.

"Yes, likely many more times," Dr. Carton answered.

She waved goodbye, and walked out into the brightness of a fine, spring day.

In the confines of his office, Dr. Carton clamped his hand on Dr. Shoenfeld's shoulder. "Whew! How about that? I've heard of it, of course, but never had a case of D.I.D. I've never seen anything like that in my entire career." He sat leaning back in his chair, feeling amazed, saddened, yet completely elated.

"Thanks for allowing me to participate, Michael. I've never seen anything like that in my practice either, nor met anyone who has. It's that damned rare, and I've been practicing a long, long time." Dr. Schoenfeld turned to leave. "I've a patient waiting at the moment, but I'd certainly like to sit in on your next therapy with Martha."

"Carton laughed uncertainly. "Sure thing, Herman, sure thing. I value your company on this journey, and that's the truth. Thanks again."

ℰℐℰℐ

Martha drove erratically through the streets, her thoughts spinning wildly out of control. "Ye Gods—an alter—what is that? You can bet I'll be studying that aberration." She barely saw where she drove as her mind dealt with Dr. Carton's findings. "Maybe I'll understand why these crazy things have been happening. I need to find out, but dear God, I'm afraid to know."

She swerved to miss a pedestrian. "What would Bob think if he knew what a nut case I am?" She had another date with him, too. "I'm getting in way over my head with him." Feeling helpless and frightened, she heaved a deep sigh.

She had no idea of her direction and paid little attention as she drove through the streets. Ignoring the fine weather, swaying trees, and flowering shrubs along the byways, she passed cars, busses, and nearly decked a man crossing the street. "Oh man, I've got to watch it or I won't live long enough to find out what's wrong with me!"

Martha found herself at Jeannie's, not even realizing she'd driven that way. She went in. "How's Will?" She spoke automatically, barely able to form a coherent sentence, while an inner turmoil raged inside her mind.

"He's better, a little maybe. I heard him laugh at something on TV yesterday. A cartoon, I think it was." The hopeful sound in Jeannie's voice helped Martha regain her senses. Hearing about Will helped her return to normal thought.

"So glad to hear that, even a small advance helps, doesn't it?" She hesitated. "Jeannie, I should tell you something, not to worry you—but I learned something today. As a small child, something happened to me and I'm just now finding out about it." She held up her hand to stop Jeannie's questions. "I'm seeing a really good doctor, and at least I know I'm not going crazy. For a while, I really thought I was, but I couldn't tell you. You've so much on your mind, you don't need more." She paused, wondering how far to go with her news.

"Mom!" Jeannie cried, her hands shaking. Tears filled her eyes. "What's going on to make you say such things?"

"I'll tell you everything in time. I don't know enough about it myself, yet. The doctor said I'll be just fine, once we get it out in the open. So that's a load off." Martha found she could laugh about her problems, something she'd never imagined just a few days ago. She also found being able to inform her daughter a little helped lighten the mental confusion of the past few months.

"Try not to worry, if I thought it would turn out wrong, I don't think I could have burdened you with it, but it's good to be able to talk about it now that I have a clue." Martha picked up her still strange-looking purse and, subduing her wild thoughts about that item, laughed. "I'll see you tomorrow—and I think I have a boyfriend!"

"Mother!" Jeannie gasped, her tone exasperated. "You are full of surprises!"

"See ya."

Martha took her leave without further explanation to Jeannie. Driving home, she felt the haziness overtaking her and barely made it into her bed. She felt unbelievably tired, but how good it had been to unburden herself, if only the smallest amount. "Maybe I'll be all right," she murmured as she drifted into a deep slumber. Her last thought was, *What mischief will my alter commit tonight while I sleep?*

❧❧❧

Martha had another date with Bob. Basking in the glow of the unusual sensations he sent zinging through her body, she wanted more of it, so much more. On the other hand, if he knew about her mental condition, would he want anything to do with a woman suffering from a raging case of psychic aberration?

Her tortured mind swirled with worry. *I wonder how much of this crazy stuff would be safe to tell, if I ever dare to? He's certainly known enough sorrow of his own, and he always knows when things aren't right. He's a nurse, too. Maybe he'd understand, but I can't say anything, not yet. Bob's no fool, but who on earth would understand an alter personality?*

CHAPTER 12

Martha felt like she barely knew what she was doing. "A ship without an anchor, that's me. Will I crash against the sharp rocks of insanity?" She laughed aloud at her quandary.

After extensive research about Dissociative Identity Disorder, Martha knew her past held the answers—terrible answers she dreaded to learn. An added sorrow that shocked her and hurt deeply was that her parents had not protected her. This painful heartache made her wonder how many other hapless children dared not tell their parents what was happening. Small children were often forced to suffer the horrors of abuse, alone, terribly afraid, with no one to turn to. This new knowledge made facing the next appointment a greater anxiety, unlike anything she'd ever known or imagined.

She hadn't taken a shift in two weeks fearing for the safety of her patients. They deserved a nurse who had her head screwed on straight, didn't they? The sound of the doorbell nearly made her jump out of her skin.

With racing heart, she met Bob at the door, a warm smile across her lips as she flung it open wide.

Try though she might, she knew her eyes betrayed a deeper misery she couldn't hide. Clearly unable to miss the depth of her distress, he hugged her and laughed. "All right, lady, what's going on?"

"What do you mean?"

"You're all tied in knots again, girl, have been for several weeks. Right now it's worse than ever, and I can see it. You can tell me anything, you know that." He held her out from him, looking deep into her eyes. "Does it have to do with those purple spots on your arm, a few weeks ago? It's okay if you can't tell me. Just know I'm here for you."

Martha wanted to sink through the floor. "I don't really know how I got those, Bob. I just woke up with them on my arm one morning. It really has me worried—I'd tell you if I knew."

She didn't mention the time lapses, or the psychiatrist, however, and certainly not the oversexed high-legged boots. She uttered a weak, tinny, little laugh and held her hands out in a helpless gesture. "Think I'm looney, huh?"

"No way, lady. Let's go eat, I'm starved, okay?" He ushered her to his vehicle, touching her waist as he helped her in. She felt damned good. Lately, touching her occupied a good bit of his mind. He was a patient man. In time, he'd know everything about her, and he wasn't worried. For some reason, he felt he understood her without knowing what the hell bothered the woman. He'd wait and help her when that time came. *Am I falling in love?* he often wondered.

Again, when their evening was over, he kissed her at the door, but she didn't invite him in. Bob thought she wanted to get closer, maybe wanted him, but some inner secret or sinister darkness held her back. He left her and drove away chuckling softly to himself. "Someday we'll get together. When we do, look out, lady. I'm ready, oh so damned ready!"

ᘓᘓᘓ

"How are Will's treatments going?" Martha asked. She'd come to take the boy for another lunch at Biggie's Burgers.

"I wish I knew, mom. Sometimes I believe his reaction to things, when you take him to eat, gives us a better picture. He still won't ask his regular playmates to come over and I've noticed a subtle reluctance on the part of some mothers to have their children here. For heaven's sake, being attacked by a

monster like Callahan isn't something that rubs off on anyone," Jeannie said, her pretty face tensed with frustration.

Seeing her out flung hands, Martha tried to placate her.
"Who knows how anyone will react. People are frequently put
off by someone who has suffered tragic circumstances. Perhaps they feel guilty it didn't happen to them, or maybe they
actually feel some of the evil karma might rub off. I don't
know, Jeannie."

Just then Will came rushing up to Martha's side. "Grammy, we goin' to Biggie's?" His excited face turned upward,
urging her to take him.

Martha saw with delight, the excitement in the little boy's
eyes. "Sure we are, Will. Get your red jacket and we'll go."
She raised her eyebrows in silent surprise to Jeannie. "How
about that? At least this particular outing seems to help his
mood. Thank the good Lord for that, anyway."

"Mom, thanks for taking him. It helps so much." Jeannie
helped her young son into the safety seat, fastened the straps,
and kissed him goodbye.

As they drove away, Martha asked, "How are you today,
Will?" She glimpsed her grandson in the rearview mirror, hoping for the continued excitement he'd shown.

His little face contorted in confusion. "Oh, Grammy,
sometimes I see bad things at night. A big, soft thing chases
me and I can't get away."

In that instant, Martha caught a glimpse of deep sadness
and fear on her grandson's face. The now familiar blind rage
swept over her again and she barely managed a reply. "Yes,
Will, those are dreams, and we all have them, but they are *never* real. Remember that. I had them as a child, too. Nothing is
chasing you when you wake up, is it? Your daddy and mommy
are right there waiting. You know, Will, when I was a child, a
train used to come off the tracks and chase me all over our
fields. It never caught me, though."

"I know. They don't catch me, either, Grammy, but they
make me real scared. Sometimes I don't have bad things after
me, I just think about bad stuff."

Martha thought about asking him to tell her about his frightening dreams and thoughts, but feared complicating matters with Will's therapist. What to do? She didn't know and didn't take him further into it. She breathed a sigh of relief when they arrived at the brightly colored Biggie's.

After eating Will headed toward the play area. This time, more at ease, he removed his sneakers, put them in the bin, and joined in with several others his size. They ran and played happily for a while and Martha relaxed, enjoying the happy sight of Will playing normally.

Suddenly Will came shrieking to Martha's side. "Grammy, that big boy is here again!" He looked up at her with tear-filled eyes and she hated the fear and cowardice he displayed. He looked like a whipped puppy as she reached out and took him in her arms.

"Has he hurt you, Will?"

"No, but he might hurt me. I want to go home now— please, Grammy?"

Not knowing what other course to follow, Martha helped him on with his shoes then took his hand to lead him from the play area, but she halted when they saw the bullying child shove another boy smaller than himself.

That little guy stood his ground and refused to move. He took a swing and punched the bully in the face. Will watched the incident with rapt attention. He tensed as he saw the startled bully take on an astonished mien, begin crying, and run to his mother. The boy's nose dripped blood and mucus down the front of his shirt.

Silently, Martha thanked all the luck gods in heaven that her beaten, whipped-puppy grandson, had witnessed a small boy standing up for his rights. Hoping it would influence him in the future, she muttered softly, "A bit bloody maybe, but that is a definite reality he'll have to face on his own one day. I'll let Jeannie know what happened. She can inform the psychologist about the incident if she feels it's necessary."

"Grammy, was it okay for that little boy to hit back?"

"Some people might say it wasn't, but I don't think that bully will bother that boy again." She smiled at Will via the rear view mirror. He might have internalized what he'd seen, but only time would tell what effect it might have on him.

Will entered the house and ran to his mother relating everything he'd seen. "Mommy, the little boy hit that big boy back and made blood run right out of his nose!" His eyes sparkled and shone with the telling. "That big boy won't push that little boy again, will he, Mommy?"

Jeannie couldn't miss the gleam in her young son's eyes. "He did! No, Will, he'll stay away from that boy, I'm sure of that. What did you think about that, Will?" She looked at Martha, cautious optimism lurking in her eyes at this new development.

"Well, if he gets near me again, I'm going to beat him up!" Will sounded as if he welcomed the challenge, even looked forward to it.

"Will, you know we don't look for trouble," Jeannie said. "You'll remember that, won't you?"

"Yes, but that boy needs a good fight. He does, Mommy!" With that, Will ran into the den, took his box of *Legos,* threw them all over the floor, and kicked the box they came in.

"Oh God, Mom, what next?" Jeannie's jaw tightened in anger. "Everything affects him so strangely. Will he turn to violence, now?"

"Inform his doctor about this," Martha replied. "It may be a normal reaction under the circumstances. They say violence begets violence. I'm afraid I don't know enough about these things, but I already know more than I ever wanted to know about violence against children. This nightmare just keeps on, doesn't it?"

"Yes, it does! I want to get away from this city so much! I've spoken to Martin and he isn't against the idea."

Jeannie's tears kept flowing and once again, Martha felt the raging anger come over her. "I can't blame you for wanting to leave this city where so much has happened. Of course, if you did move, I'd not be far behind. But remember, these things happen everywhere, you know that."

"Yes, I know, but with Martin gone to Denver so much, it's a natural move, or would be for us."

Martha considered Jeannie's words. "You're right about moving, I guess. And too, maybe I shouldn't keep taking Will to the same Biggie's Burgers where he'll meet that bully. But then, we can't run forever, either."

"No Mom, we can't run from everything. We never can." Jeannie seemed to shrug off her anger. She squared her shoulders and straightened her body. "If anyone knows how evil it is to suffer from child predators, it's us."

"Oh, Jeannie."

Martha hugged her daughter warmly and turned to leave. She drove home, wondering if taking her young grandson out so often was a good idea and knew instantly that was not the answer. The child needed to get out of the house. It would require more thought, and her mind felt clogged with the events of the day.

She needed time and distance to sort things out. And then, she'd see the psychiatrist again in the morning. She groaned in despair. "God, help me, I really am going out of my mind. I need to run away—I am so afraid of what I might learn!"

She drove past a strange little house on a side street. It looked familiar to her, but why? *God, where do I go, and what do I do when I'm someone else*?"

Her alter did things she knew nothing of, Martha mused, remembering the unfamiliar purse and those horrid boots!

In her driveway, she put her head against the steering wheel in despair. "All this is making me exhausted. I can't trust myself to work, and now, someone else is running my body when I don't need it! So where will all this end?" A few futile tears escaped and ran down her cheeks.

She entered her garage, her home and, tired out of her mind, showered and sought her bed. Drifting into fitful sleep, she saw someone standing over her with arms upraised. Startled awake, her heart racing, she saw no one there. "Now, I'm seeing ghosts!"

She crawled out of bed and snapped on the tube. "Hmmph, nothing to watch but Jay Leno tonight. Good for laughs, that's for sure." She fixed a bowl of *Cheerios* with milk. "Maybe the tryptophan in milk will help. That amino acid is supposed to make you drowsy." She knew it could and enjoyed the taste of the oats.

She pondered what must have happened to her as a child. "I don't want to think about it! Why didn't my folks watch out for me?" Heartsick at those thoughts, she turned her mind to a recent book she'd bought. "At least I remember buying it." She laughed at herself and began to read. Finding it dull, she tossed it across the room. "So much for that trash. Maybe my alter had something to do with my buying this crap. Can't say I care much for her taste."

Later, she helped herself to another sleep-aid and tried it again. Drifting off, she again, vaguely sensed someone standing beside the bed but slept nevertheless, her extreme fatigue finally winning out. Tossing and turning, her dreams turned to nightmares, and she awoke with a silent scream on her lips.

CHAPTER 13

Ryan entered the ER seeking more detailed information. He introduced himself to the triage nurse. "If you have a moment, I have a few questions. Perhaps you or one of your other doctors could help me out. I'd like to get more input from your staff regarding the morning they brought in a recent trauma patient, Fred Callahan."

"Okay, sir, I'll call one of the docs." Punching a button, she made a call.

In short order, a doctor appeared. "Yes, sir, I am Dr. Graves. How may I help you?"

"I'd like to speak personally to anyone who took care of the man injured in this vigilante-type attack a few weeks past. I believe you know the one I mean." Ryan cleared his throat. They all knew the man he referred to.

"Oh yes, who could forget that case? So that's what you're calling it then, a vigilante attack?" Dr. Graves grimaced. "I was on duty the morning they brought him in, sad state of affairs for that poor soul—very mutilated."

"Great, maybe you could help us out with our investigation in this case. And yes, we're leaning toward the possibility of a vigilante of sorts. Tell me what you remember, doctor, of the man, mutilated in this particular manner." Ryan frowned. "We have the gentian violet stains, large boot tracks, and some other forensic findings. We believe the perpetrator may be in the medical field since he or she used medical supplies on the victim. We consider long sanitary napkins and purple liquid to be in line with a medically trained person. Maybe an EMT, nurse, aide, or doctor. We'd like to get a medical slant on it."

"He or she?" Dr. Graves asked. "Would a woman do such a thing? Well yes, I guess she might if she had an astronomical sort of grudge." Dr. Graves scratched his head, thinking. "The cuts were fairly straight, and the attempt at anti-sepsis was made. Could be, I suppose." He thought for a moment. "When I was a boy on my grandfather's farm, he used gentian violet as an anti-infective on the male calves, sheep, and pigs when he docked them. At least it was the same looking purple stains I remember. I'm sure it's the same solution, the devil to get off, once you get it on yourself. Maybe your person has a farm background as well as medical."

"Hey, thanks for the input. Anyone else here who might have something to add?" Ryan looked around at the frenetic pace of activity in the busy ER department. He wondered how anyone could find time to talk with him. "God, this place is a zoo!"

"Yes, it's usually like that on this unit, but I'll ask around," Graves replied.

He spoke to several staff members. Ryan saw several shake their heads and rush away, maybe too busy to have a chat with the police or else they had no input.

A young man approached Ryan. "Hi officer, I'm Jake Collins. I was here the morning Fred Callahan was brought in. I didn't have him as a patient, but I heard him say he didn't see his assailant, and he sure had the blue stuff all over his wounds as you say. Whined a lot, but who could blame the man, all cut up the way he was." Jake involuntarily shivered as he spoke.

"Anything else?" Ryan asked, immediately recognizing Jake as a busy body type. Every facility had one.

"Well, he told his friend that came in with him, he believed what happened to him was an act of revenge for what he'd done. I don't think they knew I heard that, but he was the guy who got off on that child molestation thing, anyway, didn't he?"

Jake gave a knowing smirk and Ryan disliked him even more.

"That's very significant, Jake, it adds to what we suspect may be a motive on the part of the attacker. Thanks for the input. We may need you as a material witness one day." He saw the aide's chest swell with importance at the idea of being a material witness in a trial.

"Yeah, sure," Jake replied.

Ryan left the ER, feeling he'd gotten some new information. "It all adds up in some unusual way. We need a break. Strange case, this, can't get a handle on it, not yet anyway. Sounds like our perp knew what Callahan had done and took vengeance on him." His brow furrowed. "Farm background, eh? Might be important if we can find anyone that fits that particular bill. Farm and/or medical, or maybe both, might be what we're looking for. Must be an early riser, didn't mind the early hours for his grisly deed. And there must have been some intensive stalking done before that. Sure enough, the thing was well planned."

෧෨෧

Jake found a moment to take coffee in the nurse's lounge. "Something seems familiar about that purple stuff they keep going on about. Where the hell have I ever seen anything like that? I know I have, and lately, too." He tried to recall something, he'd seen, but where? His reverie, interrupted by the charge nurse, ended when she called him to attend a mother threatening to deliver, and far too soon. This new emergency filled his mind and he forgot his train of thought.

The place, filled with anxious, demanding, frightened patients and crying children, kept him running for the remainder of his shift. He had no time for thought, but in the back of his mind, knew he'd seen something, but where?

Jake worked a double, which he frequently did, having no one at home to complicate his life. After work, he often sought relaxation at a dive called The Paradisio. Though not of the gay persuasion, he found the place more entertaining than any night spot he knew. "Lots of action in the place. Never know what'll happen, and something always does. "He laughed as he pulled into the parking lot. Tired but wound up from two hectic shifts, he needed a diversion. "Lot of fancy wheels out here. Somebody in that crowd's got a few bucks."

Edging into the throng, he met a few guys he knew, but he eschewed the company of the females. He wasn't sure of the status of their sex and didn't plan to take one home and find out she wasn't a *she*. "Hey bro, what's happening?" he asked a lanky, stubble-faced dude named Joey.

"Aw, 'nuthin' much so far, unless that guy that got clipped happens to show, then we'll get some action. Can't take a joke, no how. Getting kinda late for them to come in. After midnight and all."

"Hell, it's a wonder he's brave enough to show his face anywhere after what happened to him," Jake returned, putting the frosty, foaming glass of golden brew to his lips. "Had a tough couple of shifts and need to relax a bit. This place is a real kick, huh?" A trickle of beer ran down his chin. "God, I must be wiped out, drooling like a baby."

"Hey, Jake, here he comes, tagging along with that slicky lookin', weirdo friend of his." Joey nudged Jake in the ribs to catch his attention. "Don't look real chipper, now does he?" he snickered, seeing Fred Callahan shuffle in with his companion, Denny.

He needn't have bothered pointing Callahan out. The sight of the unfortunate victim not only held Jake's attention, but everyone else's, too. Jake was enthralled at the sight of the rotund victim and his friend. He'd seen the extent of the man's injuries first hand that night and would never forget the sight of those lacerated genitals.

Jake waited to see how the mutilation had altered the man's life, wondering that the poor soul had the courage to come out at all, when he was forced to endure the snide remarks, raw jokes, and such. "He's got to feel well accepted in a place, to stick his neck in here like he does," he murmured to Joe. "Wonder who his friend is? Even a creep like Freddie boy has friends? Go figure."

"Yeah, everybody in here knows and accepts those two. Anything pretty much goes in this place. Heard some mighty rotten stuff about both of 'em, too," Joey confided. "Somebody really had it in for Callahan, and from what I hear, what he got, he well deserved. That is, if you go for the revenge thing."

"Well, if he'd done to my kid what they say he did to that nurse's grandkid, I'd have chopped his damned balls off my-self!" Jake said.

"Yeah? What nurse's kid?" Joey was surprised, he hadn't heard that.

"Grandkid. She never talks about it, but most of us know what happened anyway. That dude right there is the one who molested her grandkid and got off clean, so they say."

"Hell ya say, Jake—him?" He gestured at Callahan.

Within moments, comments flew thick and fast toward the two as Denny and Fred found a booth. "Hey, queenie, how's tricks? Gittin' any lately?"

"How's things holdin' up?"

The words floated across the room, accompanied by raucous, roaring, laughter. Jake watched Callahan's face redden in anger and embarrassment. His temper hadn't been chopped.

"Up your asses, you bastards, maybe you're next!" Fred growled. His voice approached a thin, high-pitched, whine. His face wore an ugly scowl. "Don't forget, that son-of-a-bitch's still out there. They ain't caught 'em yet, and the damned bas-tard cops don't give a damn if they do!"

"Hey man, your voice is higher'n one of them sopranos!"

Above the roaring laughter, Jake heard a woman's voice ring out. "Aw, shut up; leave the guy alone, can't you? Ain't he suffered enough for you? You can behave yerselves or git the hell out, that's what!"

Jake saw a tall, raw-boned, female, or maybe not, wearing black studded leather pants, and very high, tight fitting boots. "Jeez, Louise, all that big bitch needs is a whip!" He chuckled. He'd heard the owner dressed like that, no surprise there. Sat-isfied, Jake knew he'd found excitement. He usually did at The Paradisio.

Later on, his eye caught another woman sitting in a booth, far back, partly hidden in the deep shadows, watching, and alone. Something about her nudged his conscience. She sat there watching the action and sipping her drink. Her make-up, exotic and excessive, didn't hide her mature appearance entirely though her spare, athletic figure sported tight pants with a saucy flair, leather high-heeled boots, and a sleazy see-through blouse cut in buccaneer style. The gathered sleeves draped down, baring a good bit of smooth, creamy shoulder.

"That chick's getting on in years, but she's sure as hell a bundle of dynamite anyway, ain't she? Wonder what she's doing in a place like this? Refuses any and all close contact, females or males, reminds me vaguely of a lioness on the prowl." Jake thought she looked familiar, but he couldn't place her. "She's got too many damned miles on the clock for a hooker, but she's sure one hell of a dancer, ain't she? Can't take my eyes off her, either. What the hell! What is it about her?"

"Won't take up with any of the ones she dances with, either, always leaves alone," Joey told him.

Finally accepting a dance, she moved with passion and wild abandon. Jake noticed she chose her partners carefully because in The Paradisio you could never really be sure. That was the reason he stayed on his bar stool. Being an observer was entertaining enough.

Later, he saw the woman edge out of her booth, move to the exit, and disappear. "Humph, wonder what that's about. You never know what you'll see in this damned place." He tossed off his beer, said good night to Joey, and left. He needed some sleep. "Guess I won't be doing a double tomorrow."

CHAPTER 14

Hands clenching, then unclenching, face feeling drawn and tight, Martha entered the psychiatrist's outer office. Her nerves were on edge, stretched to the breaking point, adding to the dread of facing the new depths her doctor's hypnotic questioning would lead to. Unsettled in the extreme, she shook visibly when the nurse beckoned, but she rose from her chair and entered Dr. Carton's inner sanctum.

She couldn't run away. She needed this doctor for the sake of her mental health. Frightened beyond belief though she was, she'd have fought for the chance to be here. He was the only one who could save her sanity.

"Good day, Martha. How're you doing with all that's happened so far?" Dr. Carton said after settling her in the soft, brown leather chair.

"Not so hot, Doctor, I'm very afraid of finding out what happened to me as a child, and if I do, what's the use of it? What can be done about it now? It's too late for me." She took a deep breath. "It can't be anything I'd ever want to know, you must realize that." She gulped, holding back her tears. "I had good parents. I don't understand how these terrible things could have happened to me?"

"We'll know it all in time. Frequently parents will not believe what their child tells them. When that happens, the child has only herself to rely on and does what she must to survive. Obviously, you had to create an alter personality, one with the strength to withstand the terrible things done to you. Your 'alter' had that strength." He smiled gently. "What we're working for is called, 'fusion' or 'integration.' When that occurs, you will be one person again, and the hidden part of you will become an integral part of your consciousness. That also takes some length of time for adjustment. In some ways, you'll be a bit different. You'll have her additional strength, but you'll still be you."

Martha had done extensive reading on the subject and understood his explanation and the ramifications fully. But her heart raced. Dr. Carton wasn't talking about some patient in a medical book. It was her! It wasn't some character in a story or doctor's treatise. That made it incredibly more frightening. She decided to inform the doctor of the strange occurrences she'd faced only recently.

Hesitantly, vacillating between wonder and embarrassment, she said, "Doctor, sometimes I awaken in the morning, smelling of cigarette smoke. I find traces of make-up that I would never use on my face. I have clothes in my closet I don't remember buying or ever would. I have high-heeled leather boots, I mean, real high! Never in my life have I ever worn anything like that!" She panted. "Is that what's going on? Am I doing things I am not aware of as another part of myself?" She gulped for air and continued. "I know we've discussed some of this before but it's still happening!"

His eyes held hers. She knew instinctively he would be able to help her no matter what happened today. "It sounds like your alter has been a busy girl," he said. "The day will come when you two are integrated, and she will become a conscious part of your life." He smiled and nodded. "She'll no doubt be a rather strong personality, in the bargain."

"I'm not at all sure I want to know her." Martha sighed in futility but had to continue on. "Okay, I'm ready to try it again, but I can't help being afraid. How will I know all the strange things she has done?"

"That's all right Martha, you have every right to be apprehensive, and yes, you will know everything. We're all a bit fearful of the unknown, aren't we? Just remember, my dear, none of this was your fault, or caused by you. Though you now suffer the consequences of what happened to you as a child. During those terrible times the strength of your alter protected your sanity. She told me her name is Serena."

"Serena?" Martha asked, puzzled. "You've spoken with her? Why that name, and will I ever know? You're sure I'm not insane?" At his assurance of her sanity, she settled back and allowed them to begin.

Dr. Schoenfeld slipped quietly into the room. She smiled warmly at him, taking comfort from his presence. He was gentle. Both men knew everything about her and soon would learn more. Dr. Schoenfeld sat facing her, took her hand, and began the hypnosis in his soft, comfortable voice.

After the session ended, Martha felt lighter. She knew by her burning eyes, she had cried.

"You did very well, Martha," Dr. Schoenfeld said. "Some things will come to you quite soon; other things will take more time. We're making great progress."

She left the office and got in her car, thinking deeply about her therapy. She guessed it was a good thing. She'd begun to look forward to the time all this would be over. Preoccupied with her thoughts, she drove aimlessly until she found herself in Jeannie's driveway with no memory of driving there. "How scary, I've got to get this mess straightened out before I kill myself."

Jeannie met her at the door. "Mom, how are you?" The young women's reddened eyes gave away her anxiety. She took Martha's hand and led her to the den.

Martha quickly forgot her own troubles, seeing the pain in her daughter's eyes. "What's happening, dear? Why do you look like that?"

Jeannie frowned and pursed her lips into a straight line. "Will has been acting out. We went to the park. He threw stones at the ducks, shoved a little girl down, and tried to bully another little boy. We had to leave before he hurt someone." She took a deep breath. "Mom, I'm frightened!"

"Oh, I think he's acting out some of his anger. In some ways that's a good thing. Better than sitting like a zombie in front of the TV all day." Martha blew her breath out in a soft whistle. "What does the psychologist say about it?"

"He agrees with you to some extent. He says Will is going to undergo many phases on his road to recovery. This is an ugly one we don't want to continue. I swear, Mom, I could go out and stomp all over that bastard's balls myself for what he did to our child, and I'd like to kiss the guy who did exactly that!" She managed a smile at those words. "That filthy monster Callahan is lucky to be alive—or not. And no matter what phases Will goes through, he'll never be the same. His innocence is gone, and he's only five!" Tears slid down her face unchecked.

"Jeannie, I don't know what to say. Should I take him to Biggie's Burgers again? If I do, I'll caution him not to act the bully." She sighed. "It's easy to see why people who've been abused, become abusers. We're seeing it! It's happening right before our eyes to someone who's been traumatized. It makes me think of some of the patients I've had through the years." Her thoughts turned to an abused woman she remembered. Had her husband gone through a damaging childhood, suffering beatings, loneliness, and cruelty to then become an abuser as well?

"Maybe someday, we'll all be happy and not have these terrible feelings. I wonder if we'll ever know peace and tranquility again." Jeannie sighed and smiled at Martha. "What's happening with you, these days?"

"I wonder how to tell you. I've seen the psychiatrist again and he's hopeful that my problems are solvable."

"Mom—what problems, you're scaring me!"

"I *did* mention that I had a problem the other day. You must have forgotten about it, but then again, I didn't tell you much." Martha looked at Jeannie, "I should tell you, I suppose, but I hate mentioning it. Your load is heavy enough with all that's happening around here."

She took a deep breath. "When I was a very small child, something dreadful happened to me and it's affecting me now. All these years, it hasn't, and I knew nothing about it. But this thing with Will, and the anger we all felt when that man was released, must have pushed me over the edge. I don't know it all yet, but I will." She cleared her throat.

Jeannie sat white faced, listening to her mother. "Over the edge?"

"Yes, but only in the fact that I have an alter personality. Someone who lives inside my mind, created by the terrified, frightened child I was at that time. She came into being, to save my sanity. As by myself, I couldn't survive what was being done to me. I know her name, too, it's Serena." Martha held out her hands in wonder. "Hard to take in, isn't it, Jeannie? I can scarcely believe it myself."

"You're creeping me out!" Jeannie put her hands over her ears to shut out the dreadful things she heard her mother say. "She or it, has a name?"

"Oh God, Jeannie, maybe I should never have told you, but I wanted you to know about it. It all ties in somehow with what happened to Will. In general, it only occurs when something extremely traumatic happens to a small child. It's one way they can cope with dreadful pain and fear—a way to survive. Remember the book *Sybil*? It's something like that, but in my case nothing quite as severe. Her victimizations were very cruel and prolonged, she had many alters, twenty seven, I believe." Martha hesitated, smiling. "Hey, think of it this way— the doctor found only one for me—well, so far anyway."

"Mom, I think I'm going to be sick!" Jeannie's face paled from the shock of her mother's words. "I don't know what to say, I loved your parents—my grandparents. They'd never have allowed anything that hideous to happen to you! How could they? They loved you!" She paused. A quizzical half-smile broke out. "Only one, you say?"

"That's right, and she says her name is Serena. We don't know the why of it for now, but we will. I'm frightened, Jeannie, because in time I'm going to learn hidden horrors of my childhood I had no idea existed. I hate to burden you with this, but it's something you should know. My Chet was a fine, decent man, and a good father, but all men are not." She huffed. "We know that all too well."

"My father was a good man," Martha continued. "But he failed me, he never believed me. My mother never had much of a clue about anything. I think she lived in a dream world. Cooking, movies, books, and her soaps held most of her attention. All in all, she was never really a happy woman, married to my father. I think he may have chased around a bit, too." She sighed. "I'm sure my doctor already knows what happened to me, but thinks I'm not ready to handle that as yet. He puts me under hypnosis to find out these things."

Jeannie gasped. "Mom—hypnosis?"

"Yes, that's how they find out everything. I must have told them a lot, by the looks on their faces. Several times when I'm awakened, I'd been crying, so it must have been pretty rough."

"Whew, that really up-ends me! I had a wonderful childhood, you know that. There are no ghosts inside of me." Jeannie hugged her mother very hard. "Our lives will never be the same. They can't be after everything that's happened, and now this! I have to say, it's totally unbelievable."

"Yes, ask me, I know. And what do I do with this wonderful man I've been seeing?" Martha couldn't stifle a giggle. "How will I ever tell him about all this? What man wants to deal with a raving nut case?"

"Mom, you're no nut case. I'll never believe that!" Changing her thoughts, she asked, "Is this man really so wonderful?" Jeannie was all ears for this new item of interest and momentarily set aside her concern with Martha's mental state. "I want to meet him."

"All in good time, dear. I won't tell him anything, not yet, I couldn't. Actually, he knows something's going on. He told me that, and said he'd help if he could. I can't say I have no support, can I?" Martha shrugged and turned to leave.

"What do I tell Martin, or do you want me to wait on that?" Jeannie asked. Then she said, "Will wants to go to Biggie's again, too."

"I'll take him tomorrow, but will it be alright to warn him against being too aggressive?" Martha had a helpless smile on her lips as she said, "And you can tell Martin as much as you like."

"Certainly, Mom, I'll mention some of it to Martin. And we're not raising a potential abuser either. I don't know how we'll do it, but I couldn't bear it if Will turned out that way." Her eyes filled with tears. "I'll never find it possible to forgive that evil, destroying fiend! How can I—how could anyone?"

Martha left and drove home. When she entered her garage, she noticed the plywood leaning against the side. "Wonder whatever possessed me to buy that, I'm never going to use it. I wouldn't know where to begin and the good Lord knows I'm no carpenter." Exhausted from the emotional turmoil of the day, she went into her house. "Couldn't get any worse than today, or could it?"

She made a coffee and sat in Chet's big leather chair, hoping to relax. With the TV on she settled to watch an old movie. The phone rang and she saw on her caller ID, it was Bob. "Oh, how I'd love to see him, but seeing anyone just now would be too much. I can't tell him what's happening to me. Not now. I just want to finish the movie and go to bed."

She let it ring and listened to his voice on the answering machine.

"Hey darlin', I'm hungry. If you get this anytime soon, give me a ring. I'd really like to see you tonight. I won't be off for several afternoons after this." His soft, deep-toned voice gently cajoled her into picking up—almost.

"Darn him, oh how I wish I could. But, today's been too much." She hadn't eaten all day. "I don't feel hungry anymore, either!"

She hadn't taken a shift for more than two weeks. "I'll delay taking Will for a day and take a shift tomorrow," she promised herself. "I need to do something 'normal' for a change."

❧❧❧

Martha arrived at the hospital and received her assignment. "Oh good," she murmured quietly to herself. "Med-surg.

I couldn't hack any other floor, especially Psych. Too close to home for me."

She picked up the printed information on her patients and settled in for the report. Her heart took a turn when Bob sauntered in and sat beside her. He nudged her shoulder. The questioning look in his eyes made her feel hunted and she hated it.

"Not home last night, or were you?" His friendly, understanding grin eased her guilt for not returning his call, but she admitted nothing.

She realized he didn't blame her for being reclusive. Warmed by his understanding, she finally admitted. "I was home, Bob. Someday, I'll tell you everything and be glad of it, but not now. There's no way I can."

Gracie Monahan cleared her throat, tapped her pen on the table, and started the tape. The room became all business. They listened intently to the taped report, accompanied by the sounds of sipping coffee, soda, and scratching pens on paper.

Bob had difficulty paying attention. He noticed her arm bore no further odd stains, and she looked as though she'd actually had a good, long sleep. The mystery of Martha dug deep into his mind. He'd know everything about her one day. He felt certain about that. He'd have this woman for his own. He knew that, too. Anymore, the very sight of her excited something in him. He was sure she had feelings toward him, but that hidden something in her life held her back. Something had this woman in a vice-like grip, and it had to be something monumental.

Martha's mind was happily filled with dressings, pain control, doctor's orders, charting, and emergencies that always popped up. Troubled thoughts were buried by her hectic schedule. She reveled in the work. It healed her troubled soul, yet, down deep, everything waited in her mind until the frenetic activities, expected and unexpected, ended.

As Martha picked up her purse, Bob appeared at her elbow, now warmly familiar. "You won't put me off tonight, lady. Hungry?"

She knew he meant to spend time with her, if only for a snack after work. Martha wished to escape his company and

instantly hated the disturbing thoughts that prompted her feelings. Knowing she couldn't avoid him, and since the larger
part of her ached to be with him, she smiled, tremulously, as
her bottom lip quivered. "Yes, I could eat a bite, I guess."

"Such enthusiasm, come on then." He ushered her into his
truck. Turning to her, his eyes searching her face, he kissed
her. "It's worse, isn't it?"

She enjoyed his kiss in spite of her negative thoughts.
"Yes, I think I'm about to lose my mind. Everything is piling
up on me. I take very few shifts these days. I'm not sure I'm
able to do a decent job anymore and I fear for my patients."

Bob reached for her, enclosing her in a bear-hug. Looking
into her distraught face, his eyes, deep with understanding,
entreated her to let him help. "I wish you'd let me in, woman.
I've heard about everything, and nothing you could say would
turn me off. Nothing!"

Martha couldn't allow his help but she did relax in his
embrace, even managed a smile. "If you knew the truth about
me, you'd never say that or be so sure of yourself."

"What, you're an ax murderer now?" He laughed. "I believe you'd be the nicest ax murderer I've ever met." He kept
her in his embrace and laughed again. "I always wanted to date
one of those."

"I see you're full of nonsense this evening," she said with
a chuckle. Then she grew serious. "I'm terribly temped to tell
you the whole story, and I would if I really knew what it was."
She couldn't stop the frustration that crept into her voice and
knew she only made things worse with every word.

"Ye gods woman, the mystery deepens!"

"It's still mostly an unknown to me, too. Strange things
have happened to me over the past few months, and I'm learning it relates to some hidden, traumatic, occurrences in my
very young childhood." She puffed out an exasperated breath.
"I don't know everything as yet, and I dread finding out. It
scares me to death. They say I'm not quite ready to know everything."

"*They*, Martha? When you can, let me help. You need a
strong shoulder to rely on, and I've got just the one for you,

right here. Don't you realize how good we are together? You make me feel whole—complete somehow. I don't want to lose that. I never thought I'd find it again."

"Oh, Bob!" Martha pressed closer into his solid presence, so reassuring and safe. "I think we'd better go eat, mister." She pulled away and smiled through her tears. Touched by his words, she found it difficult to say more.

He shoved the big vehicle in gear and they sped away. Her mystery remained un-resolved, yet he knew a deepening determination to find a way to help her. *I'm falling in love with this woman*!

CHAPTER 15

Martha tried to relax after her date, wonderful though it had been. Bob aroused feelings she didn't know how to handle. Her nerves were tied in knots as she paced about her home until, in desperation, she switched on the tube and settled with a cup of hot chocolate.

With intense shock, she heard the commentator blare out his latest: "This just in! Earlier today, two young girls, age six and seven, were attacked and one of them was sexually molested by a small, dark-complexioned man who forced the other child to watch. They fought and struggled, and finally managed to get away from their abductor. He escaped, driving what the girls described as older green sedan. The police are following the case closely, looking for a potential suspect in the same area where two other small girls were accosted."

Martha was overwhelmingly enraged by the newscast. She clenched her fists and ground her teeth. "Will our children never be safe?" She jumped up and paced, wringing her hands and staring blindly at the TV. Her fingernails dug into her palms and her knuckles were white with tension. "Why can't they stop these fiends from terrorizing our children?"

Something in the newscast tore at her memory. *An older green sedan*? Why did the description of the car sound familiar? Martha's hair stood on end. Had she seen a car like that somewhere? She wracked her brain trying to remember where she'd ever seen such a car.

A fog began filling her mind. Her thoughts became muddled and feelings of familiarity dogged her until she finally sought her bed.

"Maybe I'll get it together in the morning." Turning to her side, she bunched the pillow up under her head and against her shoulder. "Maybe if I think of Bob and not another child predator, I'll get some sleep. I can't believe how wicked our snug, safe world has become!" She lay there, her heart racing, and mind whirling in agitated frustration. Finally, unable to fall asleep, she took a Dramamine. "Maybe now, I'll rest—I'm so damned tired!"

ᴄ⌁ᴐᴄ⌁ᴐ

Serena rose from the bed, shook herself and headed straight for the garage. *Time to reconnoiter.* She grinned. Hadn't she kept watch on Callahan's small home for two months or more—watching, waiting, and learning his every move? "If I remember correctly, this Denny guy owns an older green sedan. How many times have I seen it parked at Callahan's, taking him out for drinks, to The Paradisio, or to the jogging park?"

She'd watched Callahan enough to know his habits and often wondered why he avoided driving his own car. What sort of work did Denny do that he couldn't afford a decent looking car for himself? Had someone fingered Callahan's car from a previous crime, and the police were looking for it? *With his record as a pedophile, he must have been busy in other areas.*

His buddy, Denny, definitely had an attraction for little girls. More than once she'd seen him waving and offering treats to school children walking to or from school. Had he been the one who'd attacked the little girls? Ages six and seven, the newsman had said. First grade and second grade ages, the kind of small girls Serena had seen Denny waving to with his sweet little gestures.

He frequented areas where children played or walked, away from their homes. Sometimes he offered candy or toys to them, usually to small females. Why so small? She wondered.

"He'd be the kind Callahan would gravitate to. Of course, Denny would maintain an association with a child molester like Fred Callahan." She snorted in derision. "Birds of a feather—filthy, depraved, pedophilic bastards. Sure, they'd know each other. Why not?"

"That dizzy wimp, politically correct, Martha hasn't got the courage of a gnat, but I do, you damned bet I do!" Serena exclaimed into the air about her. She felt strong and enraged at the injustice of the world. "Somebody's got to stand up to these monsters. If the police haven't got the balls to take care of these bastards, I know someone who has!"

Action was required, but with caution. It had to be planned very carefully so the wrong party didn't get nicked. She giggled at her thoughts. "More work for the strong one." She laughed and plotted a course of action based on what she'd already seen.

Martha had completed a course at the Junior College, learning the art of theatrical make-up. She couldn't imagine why she'd taken it. Just a fun course, a whim, she'd decided. Learning the intricacies of some of the bizarre sorts of disguises and character building make-up had proved enlightening as well as fun. Serena knew why. Being invisible aided her in her work. A thing like that had to be learned. Serena knew Martha, but Martha did not know Serena.

In the garage, Serena pulled a black case from behind the plywood. Inside she saw what she needed for tonight's business. Setting to work, she transformed herself into a homeless man. A scruffy, half-bearded face, reddened eyes, filthy, ragged clothes, a torn old hat, and gloves completed the disguise.

"I could use a grocery cart full of old junk, but for tonight I'll have to wing it." She got into the car and drove to Callahan's area. "Maybe his buddy, Denny, will pay a visit, and I can scope out his car."

Parking two blocks away, she walked aimlessly toward her target. "I'll get close enough so if Denny shows I can hear what they're talking about." She leaned against a light pole, and waited. "I need to be sure. Wouldn't want to make any mistakes now, would I?" She grimaced at the thought. "Most men could use a bit of clipping." She never wondered why she disliked men, she just did. Well, except for that sexy Bob Chance, but she had a few reservations about him, too.

Feeling chilled from the high-mountain, night winds, she'd begun to shiver a bit when an older sedan pulled up in front of Fred's place. "Well, if it's not an old green Pontiac. Didn't know they made them anymore," she muttered softly under her breath. Denny got out and went in, not bothering to knock.

"Must feel right at home around here." It puzzled her. "Wonder why he comes here so late, long after midnight." By the shadows passing across the windows she guessed the two men went toward the back of the small frame house.

"Maybe take in a game or two while they discuss their latest crimes?" she muttered as she stepped over the sagging fence and entered the yard. She'd made certain Fred Callahan had no dog. A dog sinking its teeth into her leg—wouldn't be that nice? She quietly made her way toward a window. A sub-dued light emitted from it and the shade, raised just high enough, allowed her a partial view of the room.

Suddenly, a hand reached out and yanked the shade down tight, but through a small hole in it she saw the two men hud-dled together. Their voices were too muted for her to catch their conversation.

She placed her ear to the icy glass. "I should have taken lip-reading, too. It's hard to tell what they are saying. Denny looks scared. I wonder what about. I may need a lot more time with his case." She waited and listened, her ear freezing cold against the window, and felt chilled to the bone.

"You damned fool!" Serena heard that comment clear enough. Callahan's voice was a thin, high-pitched wail. "Wasn't what happened to me bad enough? What the hell's wrong with you, Denny? Now what'll you do? They'll be looking for an old green car. Why not drive that thing to Den-ver and have it painted? Better yet, drive the dammed thing off a cliff!"

"Jeez, tell the world, will you, Fred? And stop your inces-sant whining. I'm the one under the gun now. I'm trying to think what to do. I wish I'd shut both those damned kids up. The one got loose and screamed her goddamned head off. I had to get out of there, and fast!" He glared at Callahan. "Hiding your own car? You never take it anywhere. Why not, Freddie Boy? Police looking for it?"

"Never you mind about *my* car. It's yours they're after. Mind your own business, you damned fool!" Callahan changed his tone, becoming conciliatory, "Shit, Denny, I know how badly you needed *it*, but now, what'll you do?" Serena saw Callahan's hand reach out in sympathy, touching Denny's shoulder. "I hope to hell it was worth it!" The two men stood together, commiserating, trying to figure a way out of Denny's dilemma.

"Filthy, damned, birds of a feather!" Serena breathed. "He *is* the one! That evil, sorry little bastard raped and molested that poor little girl!" She gnashed her teeth while she made her way around the side of the house. She wanted a look at Fred's unused automobile. She saw it parked close against the back of the house, a dark blue sedan, partially hidden by heavy growths of shrubbery.

"So, Freddie, boy, you've got yourself a sordid history all tucked away back here behind the bushes, just like your dear friend, Denny. Bet the police would like to know your past a little better." Hmmm," she mused. "Must be a reason Fred never drives his car, fool should have traded it in if it was hot."

Serena turned away from that house of evil, made her way from the yard, and slipped down the street to her vehicle. She chuckled as she drove the darkened streets. "This will take a bit of putting together. I hope Martha isn't planning to work a lot in the next few weeks." Once in the garage, Serena shucked off her disguise, shoved the materials behind the sheet of plywood, and entered the house.

Scrubbing at her heavy make-up, she snorted. "No need to drive poor Martha any crazier than she already thinks she is." Smiling, she added, "That Bob Chance is worth a look-see. Martha, you dizzy milk-sop, go for it!"

⌇⌇⌇

Struggling awake, Martha stumbled to the bathroom. At a casual glance in the mirror, she jerked in alarm. "God in heaven! What *is* this stuff on my face?" Peering closely, she saw the remnants of scraggly hair and smears of heavy make-up clinging in several places. Martha scrubbed vigorously to clean away the strange stuff. Her cheeks were reddened from whatever her alter had used. "It looks like rouge or something. What's going *on*?" Her face appeared pale with dark circles beneath her eyes. "I look like I never get any sleep, and I feel like it, too."

Fretting over this newer aberration and her inability to remember, she knew for certain that once again something had happened. "How could she have gotten all that make-up or whatever it was on me without my knowledge? And I can't believe how tired I feel this morning. Morning? It's after ten o'clock!"

In her heart, she knew the reason was her other self. But what had that unknown person been up to? Feeling very uneasy and puzzled, she stepped into the shower and scrubbed herself clean. Toweling off, she checked again and thought her appearance, though reddened, had improved.

Martha wanted to call her daughter but refused to add to Jeannie's already overwhelming troubles. "I can't put this nonsense on her."

She'd wait and see how she felt. "I'm taking Will to Biggie's Burgers again, I'll see her then." She sighed in frustration. "Oh, how I long to confide in someone! Worrying about an alter's aberrant behavior is taxing me no end. I'm frightened and completely alone with it. Who'd believe it if I told them?"

But she knew her doctors would, and she planned to tell them.

CHAPTER 16

Jake took some time from watching TV to think about the purple spots he'd seen. "When that detective, Mapus, came into the ER, asking about the creep who got cut, and mentioned seeing spots, I couldn't remember where I'd seen them at the time." He frowned. "He said purple spots were found on the ground at the crime scene. But I've seen someone with funny spots, too—at work, I think. Could a thing like that be a connection to a crime or just a coincidence?"

He jumped up suddenly remembering. "I saw those spots on that older nurse, Lavery. She'd tried to hide them with make-up, but I saw 'em, at least the one time." Excited, he paced the floor of his tiny apartment. The walls seemed too close and he felt closed in. *My God*! *I wonder what this means*?

He worked to remember when she'd had the damning marks. "I'll keep an eye out. Maybe I'll remember it better if I see her at work again. I don't want to call that detective until I know what I'm talking about." Unable to rest in his excitement, he switched on the TV. Finding nothing of interest, he hoisted a few beers and went to bed.

Lying there, he listed the possibilities. "I've seen blue spots on AIDS patients, too, but they look furry, and are symptomatic of *Kaposi's Sarcoma*. But on a nurse, I wouldn't think so. Of course, it's not politically correct to test for AIDS when you apply for a position in health care, or a restaurant either, for that matter. You must test for TB, but are not required to test for AIDS—how strange is that?" He continued grumbling until, finally, he slept.

ᚲᚱᚲᚱ

Will jumped with excitement when he heard Martha's car pull up. "Mommy, she's here! Grammy's here!"

His wild-eyed frenzy caught at Jeannie's heart. *What's next? He certainly isn't himself in this way either.* "Settle down, Will. Give her a chance to come in for a minute."

Since his last visit to Biggie's, she'd watched the wildness steadily building in him—his eyes and voice, his movements, were jerky and barely controlled. The helplessness, of ever getting her innocent little son back, had crept insidiously into her soul. *Has my boy changed into a total stranger, a monster in the making?*

She eagerly met Martha at the door. "Hi, Mom, Will's all excited, in fact, too excited. I'm worried sick about him. He hasn't settled down at all since the incident in the park. He doesn't sleep well, thrashes and moans in his sleep at night." She frowned, blinking back tears. "I don't feel right spanking him after all that's happened, but maybe I need to consider stronger measures, or some way to get his attention."

"Let's see how it goes today," Martha said. "I'd like to be able to correct his behavior if I need to. You may be right about a stronger hand, but you'd best see what his therapist says about that, too." She felt Will's small hands clutching tightly at her jeans, his face upturned to hers, and his feet nearly jumping on the floor.

"Hi darlin', ready for Biggie's today?" she asked. "Maybe you'd like to go to another place, would you?"

"Nope, Grammy, I like my old one with the slides, and I'm not afraid of nobody, no more!" His voice, strong and belligerent, sent a pang through her.

"Wow, Will! I hope we won't meet any dinosaurs or dragons today." She took his hand and led him to her car. "If we do, let's talk about it, okay?"

Will chattered on, his speech excited and aimless. He sat restlessly in his safety seat, occasionally letting out a shrill shriek. Martha couldn't believe the changes in his behavior compared to their last visit to Biggie's Burgers. "Grammy, will the bad boy be there?"

His voice was so shrill, it made her sick to hear it. "I don't know, Will. Why?"

"I'm going to punch his nose and make blood come out, Grammy."

Nonplussed at Will's attitude, Martha cautioned, her voice stern. "You'll not be a bully at Biggie's today, Will, I *won't* have it. If he's there, we'll see how he acts. If he's nice, you must be nice too. Got that?"

She knew her firm voice made no difference to Will, or even got through to his overly excited mind. With his belligerent new attitude, she wondered how the day would play out.

At the counter, they ordered. Will took no interest in his choices. He searched about for the bully.

"He's here, Grammy! That mean old boy's here!" He could barely wait until they were seated before he pulled off his shoes in readiness to play.

"Not until you've eaten, Will." She made him sit and finish his Bittie Meal. "Now you may play, Will, but I won't have you being a bully, and don't you forget it!"

Will approached the bully, a larger, freckle faced, red headed child. "Wanna play?" he asked, standing straight and strong, face to face with the larger child.

"Yeah, with you and who else!" The boy raised his chin at Will and sneered. "Get away from me, you snotty nosed brat!" He reached out and shoved the flat of his hand against Will's chest, making him step backward.

Will doubled up his fist, took a good swing, and hit the larger boy square on the nose. Seeing the blood spurting out of the child's nostrils, Will stood there, just staring. Suddenly, the boy screamed and tore into him with both fists, pummeling, heavy and fast.

Martha swung into action, pulling the boys apart. "Here now, stop this. Where is your mother?" she asked the red-headed boy, holding him away from Will. Out of the corner of her eye, she saw a thin, dark haired woman approach, her face clouded with anger.

"You leave my boy alone, and mind your own business!" The woman grabbed the boy and held him. "Lester, you okay! Did that boy hit you?"

"Yeah, Momma, he busted me right in my nose. He's a meany, he is!" He sniffed tears while his mother blotted at the blood dripping down his shirt.

"Just wait until your father hears of this. You know he'll tan your hide again, and real hard, too." She lowered her voice to a soft menacing whisper as she spoke. The boy stopped crying and became silent. His face took on an ashen glow that Martha knew was terror.

At the haunting look of fear in the boy's eyes, and his tightly drawn face, Martha knew instantly this little fellow was one more small child who suffered abuse at his father's hands, most likely severe and often. Her shoulders slumped in a deepening sense of futility "Must you tell his father if the punishment will be so severe?"

"Lady, you just mind your own damned business. We know how to raise our boy, and don't need 'nuthin' from the likes of you." She yanked her son sharply by his arm, and as they left the play area together, she warned, "You'll be lucky if we don't sue!"

Sickened, Martha gathered her grandson into her arms. "Will, I know why that poor boy is mean to others. It sounds like his parents are very harsh with him. I wouldn't want what happened to you to make you a mean person. Do you see how the bad punishment at his home makes him behave? We don't want you to be that way. Stand up for yourself, but *never* be mean, *never*! Do you understand?"

"Yes Grammy, I think so. Maybe I shouldn't hit first, huh?"

"That's right, Will. Stick up for your rights, but watch out for the rights of others, too."

She hoped he heard her. He was quieter and seemed lost in his own world as they drove home. *What's going through that boy's mind now*? Will remained silent and took no interest in any sights passing by their car. *What now*? Martha thought in despair.

She told Jeannie the things that had taken place. "Somehow, today might be a good thing. Will knows why the boy acted so violently. And sorry as it is to say, he knows it's because that boy's parents are very severe with him. Cruelty begets cruelty, and while I don't want to say the boy's parents are abusive, I saw a very real look of fear in that boy's eyes." Martha held out her hands in frustration. "Are we to be surrounded by abuse everywhere we turn?"

"It looks that way right now. Maybe that's why I want to move from here. But if these things happen everywhere, would a new place be any better?"

Martha had no answer. "See what Martin has to say. I wish he wasn't gone so much. You need him home, more. He's very good for Will and you, too."

"He realizes that. We may need to move to Denver since he spends so much time there." Jeannie paused then added, "Would you move there, too?"

"Probably, but not until I get myself straightened out."

"How's that going?"

"I see the doctor again in a couple of days. I dread going anymore, but I know I have to. Else I'll never get rid of this thing."

"This thing? It sounds so weird." Jeannie shuddered. "Let me know what happens, okay Mom?"

"You know I will. You can tell Martin whatever you feel is necessary. He might want to know what a kook his mother-in-law is. Or would he?"

"He loves you, and your troubles are ours, you know that."

"Thanks Jeannie, that means more than you could ever imagine. I wonder how you'll feel when we learn all of it," Martha said. "I wonder how I'll feel, too."

She took her leave, wondering what would happen next. Her hope that young Will would be influenced positively by what he'd experienced today held her attention.

But under all her other concerns, lay the dreaded knowledge of what had happened to her as a child. "It must have been horrendous, if I needed another part of me to withstand it." She shuddered as a sick chill passed through her.

As she arrived at her driveway, she saw with delight that Lizzie Marin's Caddy was sitting there in all its glistening glory. When Martha pulled in, her friend hopped out, slammed the door, and came striding over.

She leaned into the car window with her hazel eyes fixed on Martha. "Hey, girlfriend, haven't heard a word from you. What's happening?"

"Come in, Lizzie. Soon as I park this thing, I'll make tea and we can talk." Martha wanted to tell Lizzie everything, but couldn't, not just yet. Same with Bob, I can't tell him these insane things, either. *If this dreadful thing isn't taken off me soon, I think I'll explode from it.*

Once inside, Martha gestured to the couch. "Have a seat. I'll just be a minute." She went to her bedroom, tossed her purse on the bed, and returned to the living room where Lizzie sat, with an expectant look on her upturned face.

"Well, what's going on?" Lizzie asked. "You wouldn't tell me anything the last time we talked, but you're not getting off so easily this time."

Martha put the kettle on and brought out a few bite-sized cookies. "I don't know where to begin. Have you ever had a dream where huge, bulky, soft things are tumbling and rolling at you and you can't get out of the way?"

"I think we've all had that dream at one time or another. Things building up on you—is that it?"

Martha sipped her coffee, tasting nothing. "Like you'd never believe. I can tell you some of it, but I don't know it all, not yet."

"You're kidding! Can I help? What can I do?"

"Liz, I'm seeing a doctor." Martha hesitated. "A psychiatrist, he's trying to sort out what's been bothering me these past few months. He says I had a very bad experience when I was small, and now, it's causing memory lapses. When I know more, I'll tell you." Martha squared her shoulders and added,

"It's wonderful to see you. I don't want to waste a bit of time on dark things. What have you been up to?"

They drank tea, chatted, and watched another *Jane Austen* movie. Enjoying a movie about another time, where only income and status were of major importance, created several relaxed, enchanted hours for them both.

Martha enjoyed this friend like no other. Basking in the glow of their camaraderie, she finally confided, "Now about this male nurse, Bob Chance." She nearly giggled. "I've been seeing him and it could become serious between us, maybe it already has."

"You mentioned him the last time we met. So things heating up, eh?" Lizzie's curiosity roared into full gear, her probing eyes demanding more details. "So?"

"I have unbelievably intense feelings for him, but with all my worries, I'm afraid to let things go any farther. I just can't! I never thought anything like this could happen to me. It's not fairy tales, Lizzie, it's real. I know that now. He's wonderful, he really is!" Martha let out a smothered squeal, like a high school girl. It felt so good to speak of Bob this way!

"You go, girl. I know you had a hard time of it when you lost Chet. If a good man comes along, go for it!" Lizzie lingered a bit longer, then took her leave, waving goodbye with a knowing twinkle in her eyes.

Martha heaved a sigh and headed for the bedroom. "Hope I can catch a few zzz's. I sure must have been busy last night. God, I'm so tired!"

CHAPTER 17

Serena rose from the bed and stretched herself, much like a large, tawny cat. "I have business tonight, someone to find, and a great idea where to start looking. The Paradisio is a fun place. Fred hangs out there along with his best bud, Denny, our latest resident child predator. From there, I'll suss out where this wart on the ass of humanity lives. I have business with that dude.

"Denny boy will soon be out offering toys or cookies again, maybe saying he needs help finding his lost puppy, as he hunts his next victim. That man is in need of a real permanent lesson!"

She felt especially strong tonight as she entered the garage and reached behind the plywood. Satisfied all her supplies were there, she pulled out the box of disguises and applied the heavy make-up of a hooker to her face until she was satisfied she looked like one. "Tight leather pants, boots up to my ass, and not a helluva lot on top—something glitzy and see-through."

Appraising the heavy make-up, she laughed, ready for a night at her favorite sleazy bar. "I'll find the rat's hole, if he's there with Freddie boy," she said, her voice nearly a growl of hatred. "I heard his remark about hoisting a few at The Paradisio. I've seen them there before. They love that disgusting place—they fit right in.

"I go there for kicks, though it's really closer to *their* speed, not a place for a good girl like me." She snickered.

"Martha would hate this make-up and she'd have a coronary if she saw herself in this outfit! But a girl's gotta have a bit of fun now and then, don't she?"

Her outfit complete, her make-up applied, Serena stepped into the car and pulled out onto the street. "If he shows up with Freddie boy again tonight, I'll follow the rat and see where he holes up." Her jaw tight and firm with resolve, she smiled. "If I can take care of one, I can fix another one, too.

Arriving at the sleazy nightclub, Serena edged furtively into the smoke-clouded room. Odors of heavily-scented perfume, sweat, and booze lay thick over the crowded throng. Serena wound her way sinuously through the fuggy atmosphere in those high-legged boots and, reaching the back, slipped into a booth, edging far enough back to provide cover as well as a wide view of the patrons.

The bar was filled with mostly men. There were a few females hanging about, though gender confusion reigned supreme in the majority of this crowd. Some females took more interest in each other than in the males present. "What a place," she murmured. It's gender-bender around here all the way, with both sexes playing their parts. A good, anything goes, sort of spot for a sick bastard like Fred, and his friend Denny, too. No wonder they come here. They feel right at home."

She didn't see Fred or Denny, but ordered from the leather and chain-garbed waitress, or was she a he? Serena wasn't sure about the waiter-waitress's sex, nor did she care. Sipping her favorite drink, a stinger, she fended off offers from females and the occasional male wanting to take a turn about the psycho-frenetic dance floor.

The colored lights flashing under the floor gave the dancers a surreal look that made for entertaining surveillance. Women kissing and groping each other, males doing the same with other men were a turn off for Serena, but nothing unusual for this place. She had no plans to dance tonight, in any case.

It was after midnight before she saw Denny, quietly slinking in, Fred in tow behind him. She had a great view of their booth and giggled to herself at the sight of Fred wincing as he gingerly edged into his seat.

Ass still hurts a little, does it, eh, Freddie boy?

Denny ordered drinks as the two huddled together taking in the crowd.

Well-known and accepted in the place, the two men still created a bit of a stir. Serena heard laughing, and a man asked in a friendly voice, "How you doin' there, Fred?"

"Shit, man, what do you think?" he answered.

Another piped up, "How're they hangin', Fred? Loose—a little limp?"

Fred's face grew red. "You son-of-bitch, mind your own business!"

Serena chuckled to herself. Poor Fred had heard it all before, but couldn't stop his flush at the howl of laughter the remark evoked. She heard him whine to Denny, and she stifled a giggle because his voice had reached an even higher than usual pitch. "Let's get the hell out of here." Fred tried to get up from the booth.

Denny wiped the smile off his face. "Aw, let it go, Fred, it'll die down in time. Everybody knows about it. Forget it." The evening had definitely lost its glow for Fred, but they hung on. Several tried to express sympathy for him, but he obviously didn't care anymore. His spirit lay in ruins, as crushed as his gonads had been after she'd stomped them into the ground.

Serena watched them with glee. That the man suffered and bore the brunt of his shame in a public place had no effect on her. "Denny, my boy, wait your turn. It's coming," she growled quietly into her glass of booze.

One of the guys from the hospital glanced her way frequently, and she recognized that nosey aide Jake. It made her nervous, but she made no move to leave. *This place is too much even for the likes of him. Wonder why he comes here.*

As Martha, she knew him to be a dreadful busybody. His presence made her feel increasingly uncomfortable. She worried at the possibility of him recognizing her, though she felt certain her costume was good enough to put him off. But, seeing no chance for action this night, she decided to slip quietly away. "As Scarlet O'Hara would say, '*Tomorrow is another day.*'"

Chuckling to herself, she drove home and pulled into the garage. She carefully removed her sexy costume, folded the stuff, and placed it behind the plywood. Entering the house, she casually tossed the boots into the closet, laughing. "She freaks every time she spots these!"

She showered thoroughly, scrubbing the heavy make-up off her face and washing the smoke fumes from her hair as best she could before the familiar fuzziness came over her again. It was not all fatigue as she slipped into the bed and fell into a deep, exhausted, sleep.

ℰↃℰↃ

Martha awakened feeling tired. "I feel all dragged out again this morning, and I think I slept well. Or did I?" Finding it difficult to pull her body out of bed, she lay there, considering her day.

She had another appointment with the psychiatrist, but couldn't bear to think about it. It frightened her more each visit, while she tried not to imagine the hideous trash from a screwed up childhood of which she had no memory.

In the bathroom, seeing the remnants of heavy make-up, she knew her other self had been busy in the night. On edge and upset, she scrubbed at her face. Unable to face the day on her own, she called her friend. "Liz, could you come over for a minute?"

"Sure. I'll be right there."

"Thanks. I'll put the pot on."

Lizzie appeared in a just a few minutes. "What's wrong, Martha, you look like hell!"

"Feel like it too, Liz."

"What's that stuff on your face?"

"Thought I got it off." She frowned, "I just can't be alone right now. I think something happened last night, but I don't know what."

"Like what, then?" Lizzie asked.

"I woke up this morning with this god-awful, sticky make-up on my face. I took a course in theatrical make-up several months ago. I don't know why, but look what I'm doing!"

"Just what *are* you doing?"

"That's the thing, I really don't know. I've seen a psychiatrist because of lost periods of time. I can't remember events. I buy things, but don't know when or where." She pointed. "See that purse? It just appeared one day. I have no idea where I bought it." Martha flung out her hands in helplessness. "That's what I mean, Liz. I think I'm losing my mind."

"So what does your doctor say?"

"He says I'll be fine when we get it all out in the open."

"Well, he's the professional now isn't he? Let's get the coffee." Lizzie laughed. "You worry too much, girl."

"Now you know why I called you, Liz. What a voice of sanity you are!" Martha got the coffee and they both relaxed. Martha giggled like a school girl, basking in the warmth of her friend's acceptance. "Think I'm nuts, huh, don't ya?"

Liz giggled a bit, too, but her eyes were somber. "You'll be rabidly out of your mind if you don't pay more attention to this Bob Chance."

"I'll get serious if I ever get out from under this evil cloud. I can't put this on him, even as much as he wants to help." Martha shrugged. "I must wait until the doctors bring me together with this Serena, who inhabits my body. I don't know her—but she knows me." She gasped. "Oh God! Now I've said too much!" Her cheeks felt like ice and her palms were sweaty as she searched Lizzie's face for signs of shock.

"Martha, you astound me! That thing you just said—is this what's going on with you?" Liz moved closer. "Please I'll never tell anyone about this. You know I won't, but it might be good for you to let things out. I can take it. We've been friends for a long time."

"Actually, what I've already said is all I really know. I wake up some mornings smelling like booze and cigarettes.

The doctors tell me they believe my alter has been a very busy girl. The thing is—at what? She hasn't told them."

"Oh wow! This is better than a movie!"

Martha relaxed. "Well, that's it Liz. You know it all now, or as much as I do. She helped herself to a cookie and urged one on Liz. They spent the rest of the time discussing clothes and men while Martha hid her deep foreboding under a cloak of casual chatter and gossip.

৩৩৩

Martha kept her afternoon appointment with the psychiatrist. The session left her feeling drained and she'd learned nothing new. *They* had, she could see it on their faces, but they didn't tell her what they knew and it made her feel increasingly uneasy.

CHAPTER 18

Three weeks later, as the first flush of dawn lightened the sky, Serena waited quietly in the darkened alley behind Denny's home. She wore thick, figure-disguising garments, heavy men's boots, a pasted-on, scraggly beard, a pulled-down, woven cap, and plastic gloves—prepared and ready in case he decided to empty his garbage once again in the early morning air. She'd waited many mornings in this dismal alley to learn Denny's habits. He'd proven to be a well-scheduled type, a creature of habit like most humans. And today—was garbage day.

Waiting and watching, she struggled to calm herself. If not today, then another day, but she'd rid the world of one more sadistic pedophile. Knowing this one preyed on helpless little girls, her hatred crept close to the danger mark. "Cool it girl, rage won't help you in this important work."

In the trees, birds stirred and began their songs. A lizard scurried about leaving faint trails in the sandy soil. But nothing much moved in the slowly lightening alley. "Not even a stray cat out. Nice and quiet. Good for my work—come on out, Denny darlin'. I'm here for you," she crooned softly under her breath as she hid behind a large dumpster.

She'd scoped out this house several times after following him home from The Paradisio two weeks ago. He was fastidious in his landscaping, in the clipping and trimming of his shrubbery. Yet, the stuff disguising his carport, on the other hand, had been left to grow wildly. "Need the green stuff to hide something, eh, Denny, my boy?"

His dented green car sat parked in his driveway under a lattice-work car-port, hidden from the street by the heavy growth of vines, trees, and shrubs. Serena had observed him taking the city bus of late, keeping the old green sedan off the streets. "Doesn't want his car noticed by police."

She chuckled softly. "All in good time, Denny dear," she cooed. "When the cops come, they'll see it plain enough." They had the description, a bit vague, but his old green car fit what they'd broadcast on television. It had made him wary. From his conversations with Fred, Serena had learned that he wanted to take it out of town for a paint job, but feared driving it in public. "It's too late, Denny," she murmured. "Hiding your car won't help you anymore. I know the truth and, believe me, I don't give a damn about the color of your car."

Serena waited long past the hour Denny usually entered the alley, and decided that once again, this was not her day. It had gotten too bright, and though the lights glowed in the kitchen, it didn't appear he'd dump his garbage this morning. Today was garbage pick-up. Maybe he'd put it out last night like most people.

Turning to make her way back toward the street, she heard the back door open. Her pulse quickened and pounded in her breast as she quickly retraced her steps. She slunk down behind the large, black plastic garbage container and waited.

Denny opened his back gate and entered the alley carrying two large, full, white plastic bags, secured with twist ties. As he dropped the bags he carried and reached to open the container, Serena stood up and, using both arms, swung the soft, heavy sandbag against the back of his head.

He fell like a pole-axed beef onto the sandy soil of the alley, scraping his face. Sand entered his nose and drooling mouth, and Serena saw a line of spittle draining onto the ground. He'd be unconscious for only a few moments, but time enough for completion of her task.

A sand bag easily knocks a man senseless and leaves no identifiable marks. She'd chosen it for that reason. As his inert body lay before her, she whipped out her bag and set out her equipment: gloves, a sharp scalpel, bottle of violet liquid, and a couple of long sanitary dressings.

Thankfully, he still wore his pajamas. Pulling down his drawers, she turned him to his side and went to work, deftly slicing through the soft wrinkly scrotal tissue and expelling the offending testes onto the ground. Quickly, she doused his wounds with the purple liquid she carried in a small vial, applied two large sanitary napkins to the wounds, and pulled his pajama bottoms up as best she could.

"Thanks for not getting dressed this morning, Denny my boy, I'd have hated to fiddle with belts and stuff this late in the morning. You've made it so much easier for me. Thanks a bunch." Serena chuckled as she finished, collected, and repacked her equipment.

Noticing the testes lying on the ground, she picked them up and tossed them into the trash. *These babies are right where they belong, you filthy, molesting bastard*! Her intense anger made her feel destructive, but she quelled it and crooned, "You won't be using those little zingers any more to molest little girls, you sick bastard!" She aimed a solid kick to his backside. "Ooh, hope it didn't hurt—too much!"

Blood stains marked her gloves, but she didn't want to leave them so near the scene. She stuffed them into another glove and shoved them into her pack. She'd chuck them later.

Serena slipped quietly out the end of the alley and sauntered several leisurely blocks to her car, a satisfied smile across her lips.

ᕮᔕᕮᔕ

Denny heard his own moaning as his mind stirred into wakefulness. "Oh, damn! What the hell's happened? Oh Lord! Have I been attacked?" He checked his scrotal area and felt his hair stand on end. "Oh God, oh God, please no—not the same as Freddie!" His hand came away bloodied.

"Fuck. He got me, too. Why me? How could someone, anyone, know who did that little brat?" He tried to get up. "I need help here," he screamed. "Help me, help. I've been at-tacked!" He scanned frantically about, but the alley appeared completely empty. No one came. A few birds chirped brightly up in the gently swaying tree branches, a mockingly happy, normal sound. A lone tom cat watched from atop the fence.

"My cell—oh hell, I left it lying on the kitchen table!" Sobbing with shock and blood loss, he felt new aching pains, burning and crawling downward from his crotch toward his lower legs. He struggled to his feet and fought a wave of nau-sea as he slowly, painfully, limped away.

Bleeding and crying, he crawled up the back steps and in-to his house. He felt dizzy and faint. "I'm going into shock, for Christ's sake!"

Grabbing his cell off the table, he punched Fred's num-ber. "Fred! Fred, I've been attacked, just like you! Get over here quick. Drive that damned old car of yours, and hurry. I'm bleeding like hell, here! I don't give a major fucking shit if somebody sees you in it!"

"Want me to call nine-one-one?"

"Yes, call them, Fred. I need the ER too, same as you. I'm bleeding like a stuck hog, hurry!" He hung up and sunk down onto the floor moaning. "Damned fool, keeping possession of his car when they most likely have an all points out on it, and he thinks I'm stupid!"

His head swirled with pain and fear. "Somebody's done me in. How would they know what I did to that kid? How could they? My car's hidden the best I could. Haven't had time to get it painted yet." He groaned. "A man's got his needs. I'll never be the same—not anymore. I know that, I know it!" His voice sounded far away as he squealed in terror and sick ac-ceptance. Finally, he heard Fred stumbling up the back steps.

"Damn, Denny, somebody had it in for you!" Fred ex-claimed upon seeing him. "Did you see who did it? And in broad daylight, too." Fred stood there, his hands spread out, yakking uselessly while Denny lay bleeding on the floor.

Finally the EMT's arrived, sirens blaring loudly as they roared up the street. He hurriedly opened the door for them. "He's right in here." Filled with importance at the moment, he beckoned them in and showed them the way. He pointed to Denny, writhing in blood and misery on the linoleum clad kitchen floor. "He's been hurt real bad." He tried to keep the satisfaction from his voice, but deep inside, he knew he wasn't alone in his misery any more.

The paramedics recognized Fred. "How're *you* doing, guy? What's the problem here? Same as what happened to you, is it?" Jack, the same EMT leader asked in disbelief after seeing the bloody drainage from Denny's stained pajamas. "By holy hell I believe it is! Let's have a look." He knelt down at Denny's side, finding it difficult to believe this could have happened to another man, not this type of injury. Never!

"Yeah, same guy has attacked Denny here and left him lying out in the alley," Fred informed them.

The EMT's checked Denny and redressed his wounds. Jack shivered involuntarily when he surveyed the slashed privates of this new victim. "Better call the police on this, guys—apparently, we've got another assault case here." He took up his cell and dialed. He needn't have bothered, because the police siren sounded as it neared Denny's home.

The medical team ushered two officers into the house to see Denny as he lay on the kitchen floor. Officers Ben Figueroa and Charles Manning introduced themselves and questioned the victim as well as the EMT's.

"This one's got that blue stuff splashed on him like the other guy," Jack, the head EMT informed them. "Sure looks like the same thing all the way around, to me."

"We'll decide that matter, son," Sergeant Charles Manning said, wearing his best official scowl. "Better get this man to the ER. We'll have an officer meet him there to take his statement."

To Sergeant Figueroa, he said, "We best check out the alley and have a good look around the place." They didn't see Denny's face whiten when he heard them saying they'd check his place over thoroughly, but Fred did.

Denny was taken out via stretcher, while the two officers headed to the alley where the crime had occurred. Fred, wondering what the detectives would find, followed the ambulance in his own car, a dark blue Olds cutlass.

"Jeez, Louise," exclaimed Officer Figueroa, examining the scene in the alley. "Look at the blood here." The perpetrator must have used a dull knife for this hit." Figueroa bent closer. "Look, it's these same purple spots. Isn't that what they found when Callahan was attacked?"

Then he noticed large boot imprints. "Check these. We've got some nice boot prints here. We'll need a cast for evidence. Didn't notice any in the park, but there was the gravel surface, didn't leave a decent track like this one. Someone must have tossed a bit of garden soil or sand out in the alley here."

"This job looks like the same MO. Whoever did this must think this guy is a child molester, too. Wonder why. Maybe he knows something we don't." Manning took careful samples, placing them in clear plastic specimen bags. "Find the missing parts?" he asked, his eyebrows raised.

"Nothing yet, but we have this garbage can here, and oh shit! Here comes the damned garbage truck!" Figueroa waved the truck on past, ignoring the craning heads nosing out the windows. A few neighbors, who'd heard the sirens and seen the police, had gotten curious. He waved them away, as well.

"Clear on out, this is a crime scene! Avoid this area for the time being," he commanded, using his best police officer voice.

Manning raised the lid on the trash receptacle. "Oh, oh, here we go." He reached a gloved hand in to retrieve two bloody rounded bits of flesh. "Whoo-wee, poor bastard! No chance for re-implantation here. These babies are gone, gone, gone." He placed his findings into a plastic bag and labeled them. "Thank God for rubber gloves," he murmured. The two white bags of trash still lay where Denny had dropped them.

"Let's check out the house, inside and out." The two officers walked around the outer perimeter of Denny's house, checking for tracks, or signs of trespassers. "Well, what's this now?" Figueroa said. "Here's an old green sedan. Weren't we looking for a vehicle along these lines?"

"You mean the one the two little girls described as the car their attacker drove?" Manning smiled and nodded as he stepped closer to the old Pontiac. "Best we call forensics to go over car, eh? Could our perpetrator know something about this Denny person that we don't? The little girls said the man had driven past them several times before he grabbed them. They sounded pretty sure about it, small as they were." He chuckled. "Maybe we *do* have a vigilante working here. If so, he knows a hell of a lot more than we seem to.

"Makes for a real interesting report, now don't it? Wait'll Ryan gets a look at this one." Manning grinned, imagining Mapus with another vigilante case on his desk. "Now he'll have two. Whoo-ee!" He whooped again. He had small children at home, too.

CHAPTER 19

"ere we go again," Jake commented to the nurse as they examined Denny in the ER. "Isn't this like the other guy you had in here not so long ago?" Jake had ER tonight and hated it, but as a floating aide, he went where they assigned him. "God, he's even got that purple shit you guys were talking about."

He remembered seeing spots like that on Martha. He was sure of it. He didn't want to make trouble for her for no real cause, but the importance of imparting this bit of information to the cops filled his mind.

"Knock it off, Jake, and get his vitals. You can take a look at his chart later, that is, if you have the time." The charge nurse, Mary Carver, had never liked having Jake around, since he tended to be lazy and he talked too much. She had no time to waste prodding the man to get things done. If her tone was sharp, she didn't really care. "The appy needs to be taken to a surgical waiting room right now. She'll be prepped for OR up there. Get on it, they're waiting for her."

"Right on it, Mary." Jake took Denny's vital signs again then carefully wheeled the young girl with the hot abdomen out the door.

"Sorry miss, I hit that bump a bit fast. I'll go a little slower." He turned his attention to the pain-filled young girl as he trundled her into the nearby elevator.

Later, as Jake passed near the new assault admission, he heard part of the whispered conversation between the men.

"How could somebody have known what I did to that little girl, and how in the hell did he know where to find me—how?" Denny asked, his voice, low and nearly pleading. "Something damned freaky's going on if you ask me."

"He sure as hell knew where to find me, Denny." Fred, his voice equally low, but with a sly hint of humor.

Jake knew he'd just heard an admission of guilt from Denny Garver. "Whew! They don't know I overheard that," he said under his breath. "The police will need to know about this, that's for dammed sure." His chest swelled with the importance of his newly learned knowledge.

ഗ∽ഗ∽

Ryan saw his door open and a grinning Officer Harris shuffling in, a sheaf of papers clutched in his big paw. "Hey Ryan, I swear if history don't repeat itself, but it's happened again." Harris dropped the papers on his desk.

"What you got there?" Ryan asked.

"After this morning, looks like for damned sure we've got a vigilante working in our fair city." Harris pawed the papers. "Here take a look. He's struck again! This time, he permanently fixed the perp who attacked those girls. You know the ones I mean, the little Mercer girl and a friend of hers."

Ryan looked the report over in detail. "Hell's bells, the same MO, right down to the blue stuff, which is Gentian Violet, by the way, or medically, Gram's stain. We got the lab report several weeks back. Use the stuff in medical labs and such. Looks like our vigilante's for sure in the medical field, used those long maternity pads again, and gentian violet is used in the labs." He shifted in his chair and pointed to the papers. "The doc I spoke with about this, said it is or has been used on farms when male animals are docked, you know, clipped." He shivered. "Whoever did this sure as hell knows how to use a knife, where to use it, and no doubt has a rural background to boot."

"According to Deputies Figueroa and Manning, this new guy, Denny Garver by name, has an old, beat up green sedan,"

Harris informed him. "A ''92 Pontiac, I believe the report said. We'll have those girls come down and see if it's the one their attacker had," he added with a twinge of excitement in his voice. "They said he kept the thing half-hidden behind a lot of bushes, hard to spot from the street." He paused and shook his head. "His buddy is none other than Fred Callahan, our resident pedophile and child molester—or was." He couldn't stop his grin from spreading as he said it. "Hell Ryan, I've got small kids, and I'm glad as hell to know at least one or two of these pedophilic bastards are off the streets, for good."

"Birds of a feather, eh?" Ryan said. "Hard to get serious hunting for this perp, but we have to take a stab at it, now don't we?" He sighed long and deep. "Can't have a for real vigilante running the streets. He may not always get the right man, you know." He grimaced at the thought.

"How do we know it's a man?" Harris queried.

"Hell, we don't, do we?" Ryan looked at the report again. "Could be a lot of people, couldn't it? These pedophiles never quit with one victim. I wonder about this new bird. Does this Denny Garver own a computer?"

"I'll order a search warrant," Ryan said. "Could send out Manning and Figueroa again. They're already familiar with the surroundings. But you know what? I'd like to take a look myself, a good nosing about around for my own sense of what's what. I hate to think what's on his computer. Those things too often tell very sordid, sick stories, ones we don't ever want to see. We'll see what the house search turns up." He scratched his head. "How in hell did the perpetrator know about this man?" he demanded. "Lots of questions and damned few answers. This is one hell of a case, Harris."

"I'll ask the ER personnel a few more questions—never know what may turn up." Harris shrugged. "I'm almost afraid to see this guy's computer. There's a huge network of child porn floating around out there, and no doubt this Denny Garver has a shit-load of it on his."

"You're right. We don't know enough about this dude, do we?" Ryan scanned the papers in front of him, over and over. "We'll need to check the medical backgrounds of anyone remotely connected with either of these two men. There might be a connection, and why the perp used Gentian Violet? Why would he even bother with an anti-infective? Why in hell would he care if his victim got an infection?" Ryan laughed. "Docking, huh, get it, docking? There's a new word for you."

Harris laughed. "It's real new to Garver."

Ryan had never had a case like this, but then, no case was ever quite the same. Crimes were as different as the humans who caused them. "Looks like our vigilante is not out to kill, just maim a little." He uttered a soft half-laugh. "Get some people on that and ask around the ER if anyone has seen anything else of significance. Sometimes the oddest detail is the tip off." Ryan paused and then scratched his head. "They used that purple stuff in the past. Along with a farming background, our busy clipper could be older, too."

Harris turned to leave Ryan's office, his face etched with curiosity. "Funny sort of case—this one—isn't it?"

"Yeah, it's funny alright," Ryan replied, as he re-read the reports again. Nothing on the Moulton family. They came out clean. No other recent cases from Callahan. He'd had a rather busy past—these kind always do—but in another location. Could be someone tailed him here, but he wouldn't know about Denny. Or would he? If the two hung out together? Yeah, they just might. His thoughts covered many areas as he mulled the case in his mind.

❧

Martha slept late—very late, but now lying awake, her thoughts swirled with worry. *Where on earth have I been, or what have I done? I'm sick of being tired all the time!* Heading for the shower, she noticed a couple of those purple spots on her left arm. "My God, another one—two! I've been somewhere, and done something—I know it! I have a bad feeling about these stains. Why? I can't tell anyone about them. Should I tell Dr. Carton? Dare I?"

She scrubbed herself thoroughly, but the blue spots did not come off, though they seemed less bright. "Have to use cover stick on this when I go to work this afternoon, or maybe Band-Aids, they'd cover these things," she murmured, upset at finding the new spots. "I want to call Bob. He always makes me feel safe. I hate to burden Lizzie any further and he'd be wonderful to talk to. I'd like to confide in him, but what reason could I use when I've kept it to myself for so long?" She frowned. "He said I could tell him anything. But could I? Would I dare to tell him what I am going through?" She knew she wouldn't.

His solid presence was something she needed right now, and badly. Her heart cried out for the security of his arms. *I shouldn't be seeing anyone, with all the mental problems facing me. Who needs a psycho for a girl friend?*

In two days she'd see Dr. Carton again. Icy chills filled her body as she wondered what new horrors he'd drag up from her past. Every visit revealed more from her childhood, and though they never let her know the details, she knew it had to be hideous by the expressions they bore when she awakened. They'd heard unspeakable things while she'd been under.

They felt she couldn't withstand the truth and kept it from her. She feared they were terribly right about that. There were times, when happenings she remembered nothing about lurked within her mind, ever nearer to the surface. She felt those hidden things coming closer to her, too.

Her own research had proven to her the undeniable probability that she had been subjected to severe sexual tortures as a small child. Those things were known to be almost entirely the cause for a person's creation of an alter personality.

It was true, it had to be! I have an alternate personality—Dr. Carton said none of it was my fault. Does that help? What happened to me that I needed that sort of help? If the usual causes are sexual abuses of a small child, and those things happened to me, why wouldn't my parents have protected me—why didn't they?

Martha broke into deep wrenching sobs and fell on her bed, praying for the release of sleep.

CHAPTER 20

At work, Martha, discovered her assignment was the Psych Unit. The thought of dealing with crazies tonight brought her near to a state of hysteria, but stifling those feelings, she took the assignment. Stepping into the elevator, she punched the button much too hard for the fifth floor and Psych.

It was a small ward, and an effort had been made to create a more homelike atmosphere. She stowed her purse, got a coffee, and settled for report. "Maybe I'll learn something working here that will help me," she murmured while she read the reports and took information from Susan Dempsey, RN. They enjoyed a cozy one on one type report in this area, which she took along with Jake. He'd been assigned to this unit, she noted without enthusiasm.

Susan began the oral report. "Now, this new woman, Jean M—came in suffering from hysteria, related to the severe trauma she has suffered at the hands of her husband. Well, that's according to the police report. She has multiple bruising, fractured ribs, and facial lacerations in addition to the loss of several teeth and some of her hair." Susan sighed then went on. "She's heavily sedated and has been for three days. They're bringing her out of it, starting this morning.

"So far, she has awakened enough to cry continually, but hasn't said anything against her husband, at least, not yet—the bastard. The police would like a statement from her so they can arrest him for assault and battery." She turned to Martha.

"Watch her especially close, tonight, Martha. Maybe she'll awaken enough to tell the police what happened. They really need her testimony to put that man away."

"Sure—I'll see what I can do." Martha tried to sound brave and sure, but already, she seethed inwardly at a man who'd treat his wife or any woman so despicably. She scribbled her notes and counted off narcotics from Susan while she mentally prepared herself to deal with a battered patient.

"It's hard to be emotionally detached from battery cases like these, and I haven't even seen this woman yet," she said to Jake.

"Hon, don't get so worked up over it. She'll go back for more. They always do, you know."

He shrugged and, noting his assignment, walked away. Jake had little or no empathy for the battered woman in their care.

"Unfeeling guy to work in the medical field," Martha muttered under her breath. She took up the chart and entered Jean's room. "Hi, Jean, I see you're waking up for us." She saw deep blue eyes, with heavily blood-tinged sclera, appearing from beneath swollen, discolored lids. Martha shuddered inwardly at the pain of the battered woman lying there.

"I'm getting awake. You guys really snowed me. I want to go home now. I have to get home." Her voice lisped, sounding muffled as a result of the injuries to her mouth and teeth. Her tone revealed deep seated anxiety. Or was it fear?

Martha barely concealed her shock. "I don't believe your doctor feels you are quite ready for discharge home. Your ribs are broken, some of your teeth are missing, and you have other injuries. You need a few more days."

"I didn't ask to be here. They just came and got me. My husband will be worried if I'm gone too long. He won't like that at all. Neighbors must have ratted on us when it was none of their damned business. Jimmy hates stuff like that. He's had several run-ins with those nosey people before. They refuse to mind their own damned business."

Sick fear shot through Martha for the life of this patient. Yet she was not surprised that Jean wanted to go back to her batterer. Even in the face of the terrible disfiguring wounds this woman had just suffered, she'd go back and suffer more abuse from her darling Jimmy. There'd be another return to the hospital and likely there'd be a time she wouldn't survive.

"Have the police spoken to you about this?"

"Oh no, I could never say anything against Jimmy. He loves me so much and for sure he wouldn't like me doing that. He wouldn't. That'd *really* make him angry!"

Martha saw her face tighten as she spoke, but her eyes held a sly, vague look, unfathomable to Martha. To her, that strange, off beat look meant she'd go back and be beaten, to return again, likely in worse condition, or dead. Could it be possible this woman, or any woman, actually relished their beatings? Did they get some sort of satisfaction from it? Perhaps in some perverted way, Jean believed she deserved the brutality heaped upon her by her husband.

"Has my Jimmie been here?"

"No, dear, not that I know of." Martha figured the man feared showing his face where people understood what a batterer he was after seeing and treating the damning evidence of his violence and rage.

She re-dressed Jean's wounds, helped her rinse her bloodied mouth, and medicated her for pain. Returning to the desk, she felt defeated and placed her head in her hands. "How can you help someone when they willingly suffer the abuse? She won't tell the police a thing," she said to Jake. "Won't speak against her husband, not one word and one day we'll see her in the ER, nearly dead, I'm sure of it."

"Hey, that's her problem. Maybe she asked for it. Who knows, anyway?"

Shocked at the lack of feeling in Jake's voice, Martha countered, "Jake, that man nearly killed his wife!"

"So? Happens all the time. You work here. You've seen it all before. Nothing we can do about it." He shrugged, his indifference so obvious, it made Martha gasp for breath. She didn't know how to counteract an attitude like Jake's.

She walked away. "What a guy! He doesn't give a rip about these people. It's just another job to him. God help the

patients in his care!" She resolved to put his behavior in a report, but did anyone care as long as staffing filled all the posi-
tions for the shift? Did administration know what kind of man
they'd hired to care for their patients? Martha had no real answers for these baffling questions.

Her other two patients slept quietly and needed little care
during the shift. Martha charted their care leisurely, all the
while pondering why some people allowed continual, brutal,
physical violence to be committed against them.

She knew her reaction to what she'd seen had been over
the top. As a professional, she should be able to handle things
like this without getting personally or emotionally involved in
cruel events that were not her fault.

Everything affects me in a crazy way these days! she
thought and kept on charting.

Jake wondered at Martha, getting her knickers in a twist
over something she couldn't change. This couldn't have been
the first case of brutality she'd ever seen. He'd worked closely
with Martha before but never had the habit of paying attention
to the older broads. He concentrated on the younger nursing
staff. He'd found enough friendly females for casual dating,
and that was his major concern for the present. In fact, he kept
a really busy social calendar, though he always went to The
Paradisio alone.

He was only vaguely aware of the older women, but
something about Martha caught his attention tonight. When
she reached high for a stack of forms, he noticed the blue spots
on her left arm, and that she'd carefully covered them with
make-up.

"Here, let me help you with that," he said. He reached
high to take the forms and caught a closer glimpse of the spots.
Wonder why she tries to hide them? Female vanity—I wonder.

Martha gave him a tight, thin smile. "Thanks, Jake."

"What the hell are those blue spots, Martha?"

"Oh, I don't remember where I got them. I only noticed
them this morning. Must be part of my make-up, I guess. Or
else I picked up something in the lab." She hadn't been in the
lab, and she knew it, but something in his voice gave her cause

for alarm. Unable to pinpoint her reason for feeling that way, she passed it off.

"Just wondering, that's all. You had a few like that on your arm a while back if I remember." He felt a rise of excitement. Was this something the police needed to know about? It gave him pause. He wouldn't feel right in bringing suspicion on a woman like Martha—hell no, not Saint Martha, the wonder nurse! *This may be something for the police but I'd better wait on it. Can't imagine why she'd have those crazy spots.*

Martha shrugged off Jake's nosy questions. Still upset at his lack of feeling regarding the battered female patient, she considered Jean's plight and Jake's lack of concern. Her role as a nurse had its limitations. She could only do so much and felt helpless and frustrated because of it.

Night came on and the shift ended for Martha. As she reached her car, Bob stepped up to catch her elbow.

"Hey, girl, I hoped I'd see you tonight, but you were on another ward. Care for a bite? Come on, I'm a starving man."

Delighted to see him again, Martha couldn't wait to say yes. He ushered her into his big GMC, looked into her eyes, and said, "All right, what is it, now? You're going to tell me about this one day, so why not now?"

"I don't know. I had Psych tonight, and battered and beaten though she is, this crazy woman can't wait to return to her abusive husband. Do you ever get the feeling of hopelessness dealing with these things?"

"Sure, don't we all?" He smiled softly and nudged her shoulder. "It's hard to understand people who tolerate brutality that way."

Feeling relieved of her anger and despair about things she couldn't change, she smiled back at Bob. "You're the easiest guy in the world to be with, you know that? Here I was, all twisted into knots and you are untying them at a miraculous rate. I needed this so much, Bob."

"Hey, let go of things. You can't change the world and you can't change people. You can help in your own little corner and that's about it." They pulled into a small, cozy-looking place Martha hadn't been to before. Mickie's Coffee Shop. "How about here?" he asked.

She nodded. "Sounds good to me, and I *am* hungry."

They ordered and sat looking at each other across the table until Bob broke the silence. "Listen, lady, let me in. Maybe I can help. You're having a rough patch and it's no good going it alone. How bad can it be anyway?"

"I'd like to. I don't know everything yet, but enough that I'm embarrassed, ashamed, and scared to death." She shuddered and looked into his warm, receptive face. "I've recently discovered that something bad happened to me as a child and it's just now catching up with me. Dare I tell you? I'm seeing a doctor about some of it—uh—just lately, that is." Martha's face burned and her scalp turned to ice all at the same time. But oh, it felt so good to finally say something to another human soul, especially this all-important man.

"You don't need to tell anything you don't want to, but when you're ready, I'll listen." He smiled. "Martha, I really care about you, more than I thought I could care for anyone after losing my family. It feels so damned good. It's like I'm alive again." He reached for her hand and she felt the solid strength of those long fingers.

"Oh, Bob!" Martha wanted to protest this feeling from him. At the moment, she felt herself unworthy of this good man's affection. He didn't need her screwed up life to complicate his, but it felt so good to hear his words she barely managed, "I don't know what to say," and fought back her tears.

"Better get to your sandwich, then." He laughed, winked at her, and took a big bite of his Reuben. "Hey, this is mighty good."

She watched the muscles of his masculine jaw work as he chewed and a deep thrill passed through her, seeing him take so much enjoyment from a simple sandwich. "Mine's good, too." She smiled at him, forgetting all her worries during this magical moment in time.

He drove her back to her vehicle and at the door of her car, he kissed her deeply. The wild sensations it brought made her long desperately to ask him home for the night. She admitted as much. "Bob, I want more than anything to spend the night with you. I need you and have the most wonderful feelings for you." She kissed him, softly and gently. "But the time is not right." She felt a deep sense of desolation as she watched him drive away.

ↄↄↄↄ

He left her sitting in her car, and while driving home, he delved into what he knew of Martha. "What are your terrible secrets, girl? You know I'll find out. Knowing the kind of woman you are, they couldn't be as serious as you believe. I'll be invited in one day, and that will be it for you." He whistled a tuneless melody as he pulled into his lonely home. He'd made one woman very happy and knew he could do that for Martha as well. Thinking about her slim waist, fine features, and slender body made him anxious for that day.

CHAPTER 21

Harris accompanied Ryan on their mission to Denny's small home. They walked past the vine covered portico where Denny had kept his vehicle.

"So here's where he hid his car," Ryan said, checking out the secluded area.

"The little girls were sure this was the car they remembered," Harris replied. "A good bit of evidence right there. It's being impounded as we speak." Walking around the side of the house, he scuffed a few leaves away and stooped down. "Hey, check this," he called to Ryan.

"What you got?" Ryan leaned over to examine the dim boot tracks outside Denny's window. "Not much left of them after that last rain, but we'll take casts. They could match up with the ones found in the alley. Size looks about the same."

"These tracks are old. Looks like the perp scoped this place out a while before doing the deed," Harris offered. "Get Al on this and let's check out the house."

Ryan gave orders to the officer with them, and then he and Harris entered Denny Garver's home.

Ryan opened the computer. He didn't need a password. It booted up nicely on Denny's "remembered" one. Flipping to past entries, he shuddered. "God damn, Harris, look at this stuff! Bastard's got this computer loaded with the most disgusting kiddie porn you'll ever hate to see!" Beads of sweat broke out across his forehead. "Son of a bitch!"

"Not really surprised, are you?" Harris scoffed, scanning page after page of things he'd known would be there. In his line of work, he'd already seen too much. "This guy sickens me to the core. I want to vomit just looking at this stuff. I find it difficult investigating this. I'd do the same as our vigilante friend, if I caught one of these predatory monsters even looking at one of my kids."

They confiscated the computer and, upon further investigation, found a small collection of ribbons tucked away in the back of Denny's closet. "Now what do you suppose these mean?" Ryan asked, holding out the colorful strips of ribbon, some soiled with dark material that could easily be blood stains, some with strands of hair clinging to them. "Oh Lord above! Some of them have hair attached. You don't suppose..."

"My God, I hope it isn't what it looks like. Has he made a collection of his victim's hair ribbons?" Harris felt sick. "You don't suppose he tied them with..." He couldn't finish his thoughts as his mind whirled with mental pictures of the many little girls the man must have encountered, molested, and murdered over the years.

"Put out an arrest warrant on this bird. We'll have enough DNA evidence right here to put him away for a long time. Why in hell hasn't someone caught up with Garver before this? Prosecution is so damned lax about these monsters. I sure as hell understand why people take it into their heads to fix the bastards on their own."

Ryan frowned. "Must be a connection between these two cases." He spat into the trashcan, trying to remove the bitter taste in his mouth. "Hell of it is, we don't know a damn thing for sure, do we?"

"We'll go on line to every police department in the country, asking for cases relating to what we've discovered here. Garver must have a long history somewhere, likely many places. What we're seeing here may be the tip of the iceberg— right here in front of us." Harris wrote himself a note. "I'll get his arrest in the works. He's still hospitalized, isn't he?"

"Better be. I couldn't take the scandal if this one slips past us. Fred Callahan looks like an amateur compared to this bird." Ryan cleared his throat. "We can't search Callahan's property, since he was acquitted, but I'll bet it's a gold mine of garbage, too." He frowned. "Too damned bad—I'd bet my life on his history being long and sordid, too." Most child predators had a long and hellish history, some more than others.

"Likely it is. Anyway, the fire's out of his furnace, eh?" Harris managed a quiet chuckle remembering Callahan's day in their office. "Miserable assholes. Glad our vigilante fixed the both of them, you damned bet I am. You can't imagine how often I've wished we could give these bastards some real justice. Looks like we needed a vigilante to do it for us."

"Harris, you're a vindictive son-of-a-gun, now aren't you?" But Ryan silently agreed. His inborn reluctance at hunting the vigilante down and making an arrest haunted him— bitterly—although he knew it was his sworn duty. "They always go too far, you know that. As justified as these cases may be, there will be one that isn't, and we have to prevent that unhappy event from taking place."

"You're right about that, man, and if he makes a mistake, I hope it won't be one of us." Harris uttered a soft laugh, finding a modicum of relief after the horrors they'd seen today.

"Funny as hell, aren't you?" Emotionally worn, Ryan joined him in humor and release. "Let's catch us some lunch. How about it?"

They drove away with what they'd found and confiscated, heading for the nearest diner.

e⁄∂e⁄∂

Martha entered the psychiatrist's office as scheduled. Her apprehension soared sky high today. Her hands shook. Tightly strung, she fought for control. The answers were close, too close. Soon she'd find herself face to face with the hidden terrors of her childhood. "Will today be the day?" she worried in a whispered breath. She took a seat after signing in, picked up a magazine, but couldn't focus on anything or even read the print.

The nurse beckoned and she rose to enter Dr. Carton's office. He greeted her, sat her in the familiar chair, and began the session. "So, Martha, tell me about it, anything new or different, happening in your life?"

"Yes, something has happened again. I know I've been roaming around at night lately. I smell of cigarettes when I awaken. And two days ago, I found these crazy spots on my arms again. I'm sure that's why I'm so tired. She held out an arm for his inspection. "Why wouldn't I know what this Serena does? 'It's my body, isn't it?"

"We're hoping to remedy that situation fairly soon, when we believe you'll be able to withstand what you'll learn." His voice, soft and comforting, soothed her shattered nerves and apprehensions. He knew his work and she felt confident that he would complete her treatment successfully. But knowing the certainty of it made her tremble. The day was very close!

She needed his skills and she knew it. But the final resolution already haunted her. "I'm a strong woman, always have been," Martha said. "But how can knowing these things possibly be so dreadful that a mature, grounded woman like myself wouldn't be able to cope with knowing?"

"We're waiting to be sure you're ready," he told her, his dark eyes full of concern. "The time is coming fairly soon for the fusion or integration of your alter with yourself. What are your feelings on the matter?"

"Uh—maybe another session or two of hypnosis would be a good idea, doctor. Maybe you'll know then if I'm really ready or not." Martha knew she'd just copped out, putting off the inevitable. *I'm a sniveling coward for having asked for more time.*

"We'll do that, of course. You'll be unable to heal this affliction until everything is out on the table and the connection between you and Serena is complete. You remember we talked about that?"

Martha saw the compassion in Dr. Carton's eyes, and it gave her the courage to continue on as before. She'd face her monsters soon enough. "Thanks, Doc, let's keep going. I admit I'm a coward, but it's also very hard to find that, as a little child, you hadn't been safe in your parents care. I find that unbelievable! It shatters all the good things I remember of my childhood, of my father, and mother." Tears slid unbidden down her cheeks.

"You'll be fine, Martha. You really will. But you're right in having those feelings about your parents. It is hard to see them in another light. Remember, I'm quite certain they never knew what was happening. They'd have taken action if they'd known." He turned to call Dr. Schoenfeld, who'd managed not to have patients of his own during Martha's visits to Dr. Carton. They continued on with her treatment together.

෴

Later, feeling exhilarated, as though a big part of her burdens had suddenly, mysteriously lifted, she visited Jeannie, wondering how Will's recent change of mood had affected his behavior. Had he internalized his recent bout of anger and lashing out? Hopeful they could counteract this new and aggressive persona, Martha felt ready for another trip to the children's play area at Biggie's Burgers.

When she entered the home, Will came running to her. "Grammy! I been waitin' for you. When we goin' again?"

"My, my, aren't you full of vim and vigor today?" She looked at Jeannie. "How's he been these past few days?"

"I'm good! Been to the park, too, an' I didn't hurt the ducks, neither. I just played, Grammy."

"He's been much brighter, taking interest in things again," Jeannie confirmed. "I'm wondering if it's a phase or if he's turned a corner. I don't know, but what a welcome change!" Her bright hair looked freshly washed and her make-up well applied. The sparkle in her deep blue eyes had returned as well. Martha felt a rush of well-being at this change in her daughter. It made a difference in her, too.

"Are you going out, Jeannie?"

"Why—because I'm put together for a change?" Jeannie patted her hair. "See, my hair is combed and everything."

She laughed and Martha's heart filled to bursting at this positive change.

"Well, it's nice to see. I'd begun worrying about you, too."

"It's been tough. Martin is in a quandary, thinking of relocating and going through all we have these past months."

"Any good news is welcome, you know that. Don't let your moving be influenced by me in any way. Of course as a nurse, I can work anywhere so I wouldn't be far behind. I need to see my grandson. I could never live far away from him, or you and Martin, either."

"What about this boyfriend, or should I say—man friend?"

"I don't know yet, and I can't worry about it now. Things are moving pretty fast with the doctors, too, so maybe all this mental stuff will be over with before I have to make a decision about moving or getting too heavily involved."

Certain that Bob had fallen in love with her, Martha feared her mental problems would turn him away, despite his protestations of understanding. "He doesn't need to be burdened with a mental case." She laughed, refusing to relinquish that sense of lightness she felt.

"Mom, you sound almost giddy today, you all right?" Jeannie frowned, until she saw her son waiting eagerly, his red coat pulled on.

He couldn't stand still. "I'm ready, now!"

Will took Martha's hand and they left for his favorite eating place. Martha wondered what would happen today. Every visit had become a major event in Will's progression toward either regression or normalcy.

After ordering, they took a seat in the play area. Will craned his neck looking for the bully. "That bad boy's not here, Grammy." He dug into his nuggets and fries. Even his appetite seemed improved.

After eating, he removed his shoes and ran into the play area. Martha watched intently. She saw him climb, slide, scream with joy, and help a small toddler girl who had fallen "You were a real gentleman helping that little girl," she told Will. "That's what a big boy does, when someone needs help."

Driving back to Will's home, with him sitting in his safety seat, she looked at him in the rear view mirror.

"She was soft and nice, Grammy. I wanted to look at her down below, but I knew you wouldn't want me to."

With sinking heart, Martha saw a sly look in his eyes she'd never seen before. "That's right, Will. *Her* mother wouldn't have liked it either."

She tried to hide her shock at his words. But with this new concern, she worried he might have become overly interested in sexual things. *Is this another aberration we have to work out?*

"Girls are different down there, aren't they Grammy?" "Of course they are, Will. One day, you will learn all about how different boys and girls are. Your father will be the one to help you with that, when you are ready to know these things." But she knew he'd also learned the ugly side of sex from the violence committed upon him, more than any little boy needed to know at age five. And the evil way he'd learned it made her shudder.

She imparted this new bit of news to Jeannie. "I don't know what this means, but his doctor needs to know this new wrinkle on his road to recovery."

"At least he isn't sitting in front of the TV or kicking his toys all over the place." Jeannie hesitated. "Mom, I have decided to go visit the Mercer family and I'm taking Will with me. After what we've suffered, they might appreciate a visit from someone who's been there." Her look of determination told Martha not to object. And Jeannie was right. It could be helpful for both families.

Still, she had to ask, "Are you sure it's good for Will? Won't it bring back bad memories or visions for him to face all over again?"

"I'll call the doctor first and see if it's okay, but think of what they must be suffering now. I believe a visit from someone in a similar situation will help. I know a visit from someone who'd been through the same thing would have helped us, but no one came."

"Let me know how it turns out. Poor little girl, her life is changed forever, too." Martha felt that raging, deep anger again. Wondering where her towering rages came from, she put it toward her feelings about Will's assault. She couldn't remember ever feeling anything like this in past years. Why now? Where did it come from? *That is not like me at all, or, the person I used to be. Could my new self be a part of this?*

CHAPTER 22

Ryan read the reports coming up on the computer. "This Denny Garver has a history spanning nearly twenty years, from what these reports say." He picked up his phone. "Hey, Harris, could you come in here for a minute?"

Harris entered quickly, his questioning eyes on Ryan. "Yeah, what've you got?"

"Look at this damned stuff. Why wasn't this monster put away years ago? Apparently, he's a nice, unassuming little fellow, who quietly goes about abducting and torturing little girls. His MO in these files suggests he ties them with pretty hair ribbons before he sexually molests them, shaves their heads, stuffs objects into just about any orifice—oh God! Damn it, anyhow!

"Most have been found dead. Only a very few have escaped to tell the tale. The descriptions they give fit Denny Garver to a tee, and we've got DNA this time. We got that off the little Mercer girl. I hate to do it, but we need her to ID him in a line-up as well. I guess we know how those ribbons tie in." He looked at Harris in disgust, a tear lurking in the corner of his eye, and shook his head. "Son of a bitch!"

"The reports fit with the ribbons we found," Harris confirmed. "Man, it'll be hell to put that little child through the line-up process, but what else is there? Her parents are very cooperative, that's lucky." He heaved a sigh of regret. "We'll have to have them bring both little girls in to take a look." Harris grimaced. His job held many such unsavory moments. "Shit!"

"How'd Denny Garver take his arrest?" Ryan asked.

"Wanted to fight, but most of his fight's been cut out of him if you get my drift." Harris laughed. "He's real popular down in his cell. Gets catcalls and suggestive remarks all day long. Worries he'll be deprived of his civil rights. Got himself a shyster lawyer already, plans on fighting the case and suing the city for allowing predators in jail to prey on the likes of him."

Ryan laughed. "I'm impressed!" He spread out the damning evidence displayed on the copy sheets from the computer. "Wonder how Garver will fight this stuff we've found in his home."

Harris looked over the sheets with Ryan. "He'll deny everything, of course, but some of those other cases will have DNA as well. When we put this together, he'll get the death penalty. He won't have such a nice time in the lock-up while he awaits trial. Most prisoners hate guys like him. On Death Row, he'll want his own private cell, won't he?" Harris couldn't find a modicum of sympathy for the fiendish pedophile.

"We need more information on this Callahan dude. No doubt he's got damned near as big a backlog of cases, too. Anything come in on him yet?"

"Not specifically, but reports from Harrisburg say they're on the lookout for a dark blue sedan, ID'd by a six year old boy who barely escaped being lured into a car of that description. Do we know what Callahan drives?"

Harris got excited. "Good question. We'll have a look. Don't need a warrant to look from the street. We'll get one if we need to. Maybe we'll get both these bastards off the street, though in reality, both are rendered useless anyway. Oh how it pains my aching heart!"

Ryan chuckled. Justice, though illegally committed, was still justice in his eyes. "I'll send a man out, take a look at Callahan's car, and if it looks remotely suspicious, get full forensics on it. If it's a wanted vehicle, get full forensics on the house, and his computer, too."

"It won't be pretty, getting into Freddie boy's computer." Harris shuddered, "God, I hope his car is wanted. Maybe they've paid for their crimes via our vigilante. Won't those two have a hellish good time being incarcerated?"

"Scares the hell out of me just thinking on it. Let's get some lunch," Ryan suggested.

"Hell yes," Harris replied, and the two men left the station.

☙❧☙

Jake, already late for work, looked at the clock and decided he could squeeze in a shower before getting ready for another shift. His thoughts centered on Martha. Those purple spots he'd seen on her arm at least twice stayed on his mind. "She came to work with the stuff on her arms. Claims she didn't know where it came from. Wouldn't she have tried harder to cover them up if they were related to a crime?" he said, talking it through with himself while deciding what he ought to do about it. "If I tell the cops and they arrest her, she could lose her license. They might even try to tie her in with the crime on those two kid predators. She's not the sort for anything like that." He frowned. "No, couldn't be, probably just a coincidence—got to be."

Shrugging his indecision away, he decided to sit on his information for the present. But his curiosity was aroused. He hoped to work with Martha again, wanting to scope her out. "An overly intense old broad, good nurse, though," he said as he grabbed a towel.

He couldn't stop thinking about it as he drove to work. "Her face has a familiar look. I swear I've seen her somewhere, but not the way she looks at the hospital, all business and overly sentimental like she is. Must have been somewhere else, but where? Maybe the mystery woman will work tonight," he said and chuckled, pleased with the quality of his own wit.

☙❧

Martha took a shift against her better judgment. "I hope I'm up to working this afternoon. It's one place I can forget my crazy problems. I'll be too busy to worry about things. It's never dull on med-surg." Her major worry lay in giving her patients her full attention. How could she when somewhere in her mind, another being lived and had a life unknown to her? That mysterious being obviously did things Martha knew nothing of. "If this shift goes well, and I don't kill anyone, maybe I should work more to get my mind off things."

Assigned to med-surg again, she felt a wave of relief. Bob was off and she'd not be going to the psych ward again. Somehow, that night had caused her even more pain and anger. She had enough of her own problems to handle without the mental debacles of other people. She entered the report room. Jake was on duty and she shrugged. *He's a lazy ass, an unfeeling lout, for a health-care worker but pleasant enough, otherwise.*

Gracie Monaghan began the taped report and Martha listened attentively. Out of the corner of her eye, she noticed Jake eyeing her and wondered about it. He'd ignored her on other occasions when they'd worked together. *Maybe he thinks I overreacted that night over Jean M.*

Jake, trying not to be too overt in his observation of Martha, noted the frown and squinted look that came over her face when she noticed him checking her every move. He took up his duties and left the area, feeling slightly confused about the woman. Her arms were clear this evening and she didn't look like a predatory person. He was unclear what one looked like, but not her. "Must be a coincidence, no other explanation could be possible," he mused half aloud.

Focusing on one of the new grads fresh out of nursing school, he put Martha from his mind. Unsure of themselves, the newer nurses hadn't passed their boards as yet, and he found them willing to learn from him as well as the others. They weren't above giggling at his slim, blond good looks, either, especially the little blonde chick. She'd just made her

BSN in Nursing and he saw her as a possible. *She'll pull down a bundle when she gets going.*

Martha had had a quiet shift and enjoyed it. After her report, she glanced idly over the list of patients. Ice crawled insidiously into her midsection at a name she'd missed earlier, Peter William Sykes, 74-year-old male. Room 372, bed A. Whispering in horror, she gasped, "Could it be possible he's the same man who worked on our farm so long ago?"

Unwilling, yet compelled, Martha walked in the direction of his room. She had to know who lay in bed A. With leaden feet, she moved down the corridor toward the back areas of the Med-Surg Ward while the off-going personnel moved toward the bank of elevators and their cars.

"Hey Martha, you're heading the wrong way," someone called, but moving as if in a trance, she continued on. Nervous tension mounted until she felt tight as a stretched rubber band. With each step, her scalp burned and the coldness within her veins froze her until she could scarcely catch her breath.

She reached the room. Her skin burned like a bonfire as she opened the door and slipped in. In the bed lay a scrawny, withered, corpse of a man, far advanced into his cancerous disease. His admitting diagnosis: Prostatic Carcinoma with metastasis to lungs, brain, and spine.

She stood over his bed. He *was* the same man. She felt certain of it, though no vestige of his youth remained for her to recall. Yet, to her mind, an aura of evil hung over him like an invisible cloud.

Seeing the man now, she felt nothing of the fear she'd had as a child and felt no sympathy for that wasted form on the narrow hospital bed. Sickened at seeing him, she felt that burning fury rise within her and willfully wished the man untold amounts of pain and suffering.

Why do I feel like this? Why do I have such hatred of this poor wasted man? What the hell's going on, here?

This sudden appearance of a ghost from her past, made her guts twist into a painful knot. She'd tell Doctor Carton of this occurrence. In some vague way, she knew this man held the key to her recovery.

Standing at his bedside, knowing who he was, she felt no mercy for the pitiable thing he'd become. Did he feel the intensity of her burning hatred? Occasional moaning escaped his withered lips, but he never opened his eyes.

❧❧❧

Jake had noticed Martha's retreat into the back reaches of the ward instead of heading to her car. "What the Hell?" he murmured. He slunk back into a recessed area to watch her. Others left the ward but he fixated on Martha's leaden, sluggish, movements and whitened features as she walked slowly toward one of the rooms at the back. *God! She looks like she's in a trance!* He slipped closer and followed.

When she entered room 372, he stood outside the door and listened. For long moments, he heard no sounds emanating from within. He peeked in to see Martha standing over Pete Sykes aged, emaciated form for several moments. She said nothing, just stood there.

Martha couldn't leave. The familiar foggy feeling came stealing over her body and mind. *What's happening to me? Why now? Is this something to do with my other person?* Panic shortened her breathing. *I've got to get out of this place before I do something I shouldn't. I can't let this crazy mood overtake me.*

She felt her face drawing into a nasty snarl. She leaned over the crumpled soul on the bed, uttering a menacing, vicious growl. "You filthy devil, I hope you suffer the tortures of the damned! I hope you burn in hell, and your pain-filled death is long in coming!"

Shocked at her vicious outburst, Martha turned and fled from the bedside. *What on earth came over me to say such things?* In her hurry to exit the ward, she nearly knocked Jake off his feet. Her glazed eyes neither saw him, nor recognized him.

Jake pulled back in shock, steadying himself after her hasty departure. "God, she nearly decked me!" He'd overheard most of what she'd said to the luckless soul in room 372. The patient must have been in bed A, because she'd stood close to the door.

"Must have a grudge against that poor old man, but how would she even know the guy?" For Jake, the mystery of Martha had just deepened dramatically.

Although he was absolutely sure she wouldn't have done the two mutilations, the woman certainly managed to mount a hell of a raging temper on short notice. He'd seen it and heard it—and on a dying man, at that!

"Whew! I'd hate for her to have it in for me. That woman's got one hell of a temper. You'd never know it to work with her, all sentimental and touchy-feely the way she is." Jake walked slowly from the hospital, his mind in a whirl of confusion. "I'll never go to sleep right away after this. Might as well go check out The Paradisio, just for the hell of it."

೮つ೮つ

Shaken by the sight of that old wreck of a man, Martha drove madly home and immediately sought the comfort of her bed. Why did that pathetic creature cause her such terrible unease and dread? Seeing him had set her on edge to the point she couldn't sleep. She rose from her bed and wandered her home, seeking something, anything, to ease her mind.

My life is a series of horrible shocks any more, and I want the end of it! Why now? Why did I have to look on that man's face once again? She wondered why she hated the sight of Sykes so deeply. *He was an ugly part of my childhood and I was afraid of him. Must I assume he is part of what is wrong with me? What else?*

She suddenly realized she eagerly awaited her next visit with Dr. Carton. *Well, that's a new one!*

Heading back to bed, she swayed and steadied herself on the dresser. She felt faint all of a sudden. Not again! She barely made it to the bed before she blacked out.

೮つ೮つ

Serena did not want or need sleep. Her time to meet Martha edged closer. "That lady has a lot to learn, but all in good time." She uttered a loud, raucous laugh. "I need a night out of this stuffy little shit-hole."

She applied her usual heavy, over the top make-up then pulled on the high leather boots and a very short skirt with flimsy, nearly see-through top with hanky-hemmed edging. Fishnet stockings added a final touch. Checking herself in the mirror, she thought she made a very fetching picture.

"This is sleazy enough to fit right in at The Paradisio. It's late, but so much the better. I wouldn't want to see Jake sitting there eyeing me again. I get the idea, he thinks he knows me. He doesn't really. He'd better be careful; I'd hate to nick someone not a predator!" She giggled at the thought of it, got in her car, and drove to the dive.

Entering the crowded, smoke-filled atmosphere, she moved quietly toward the back where the booths were more concealing. Knowing she attracted attention, she shrugged all comments and invites away, as she edged along. Brushing off one offer, she snarled, "I'm not here for a pick-up, buster, get lost!"

I could take on some of these guys, but who knows who they are, or what they are. She laughed softly. Taking a quiet, dark booth, she ordered a stinger, sat back, and relaxed, surveying the scene. The two boys she'd clipped were absent, but she spotted Jake sitting at the bar. He hadn't noticed her arrive, and she wanted to keep it that way.

A wild, rousing dance number began, and the participants whirled around over the rotating, intermittent, flashing, psychedelic lights under the dance floor. Serena enjoyed this event most of all. The dancers looked surreal as they moved sensuously about, like puppets jerking rhythmically on strings. Men with men, women with women, and couples of both sexes danced to the frenetic tempo.

"Care to have this dance, lady?" A soft, low, and commanding voice broke into her quiet observations, along with the heady aroma of an expensive, exotic cologne.

Serena looked up to see a tall, handsomely-mature man dressed in a finely cut, silk business suit—a big, solid gent with graying temples, a hawk-like nose, and extra-pale blue eyes. He was definitely of the male persuasion, but something about him set her on edge. With her nose tilted into the air, she declined his offer. "Sorry, mister. I'm not into dancing to-night." She slid farther into her booth to emphasize her nega-tive response.

"Sorry, don't cut it for me. I'm asking and what I ask for, I always get, baby." He reached in and grasped her arm to pull her up, his expression, a sly one of self-assurance and power. His entire demeanor exuded confidence, magnetism, and pow-er. This was a man who ran things his way.

She jerked her arm away. "Excuse me, sir, but I don't plan on dancing with you or anyone else."

She edged to the far reaches of the booth and the man slid in next to her, pushing himself far too close. She caught anoth-er whiff of his cologne, unusually seductive and enough to lull her senses. If anything would cause her to get up and dance with a man, it might be that. *Whew. That stuff could make a girl do just about anything.*

"You're a damned fine looking woman, and I don't plan on taking a no from you. Got that?" He bent a darkened blue-eyed gaze into her eyes, and his brute strength sent a message she couldn't ignore. He looked menacing in a cold, unfeeling way. Serena, definitely not wanting to create a scene with Jake in the place, decided she'd best dance with the man.

Only his size and power kept her temper in hand. She didn't like being forced into doing anything, but an attention-grabbing scene with that nosy-ass aide at the bar was some-thing she had to avoid. Lately, Jake tended to watch Martha at the hospital for some crazy reason. It had begun to make her feel hunted and she resented it.

Trapped, she decided to accommodate the big man. "Okay. Have it your way, mister, but don't whine if I walk all over your feet."

"Not a chance, lady. I've seen you in here before. You move with the slinking grace of a damned cat. I peg you as a very fine dancer. And I'll damn bet you're all of that, and—oh baby—a hell of a lot more."

The suggestive way he uttered *more* chilled her deeply as he pulled her out of the booth and led her to the floor. A new round of wild music had just begun, and he swung her along to the beat.

"Lady, I knew you'd be good, and you sure as hell are!" He caught her closer attempting a kiss. "Come on now. Don't play coy with me, sister. I've seen your kind before."

"I'd have to doubt that all to hell, mister." Serena leaned away from his body as far as possible. Resisting the man's advances without creating a scene was not easy and she felt his growing anger in the vigorous way he spun her around.

During a pass around the floor, she caught Jake's prying eyes watching. She'd hoped to avoid that, but the hard-ass she was dancing with wouldn't give up. Knowing what she had to do to allay any suspicions, she turned her attentions to the big man. She shot him a sultry, burning look from beneath lowered lids. "Hey, mister, you're damned good yourself," she crooned as she leaned against him, portraying a more than cooperative partner, maybe for the night. She swung wildly across the dance floor with him, the absolute picture of a more than willing participant.

"Now that's more like it, my little hell-cat," he responded with a sparkle in his eye. "We might just have a real wild night of it. I've got a few tricks up my sleeve that'll knock your socks off. What'd ya' say, baby?" He raised his eyebrows in a very suggestive manner and pressed his hard male body closer to her. He'd had more than a few drinks and Serena saw that as an advantage.

She waited for the right moment. When whirling close to the entrance, she leaned into him, beguiling him into thinking he'd won the sexual game he played. And then, leaning far back, smiling into his eyes, she brought her leather-clad knee up hard into his groin.

Serena watched him crumple onto the bustling dance floor, groaning in pain, his face ashen and sweating. Standing over him, she snarled, "Told you, I didn't want to dance, you pushy bastard!"

Spinning around on her spike-heeled boots, she stormed out the door without a backward glance. The dancers stopped in stunned silence while the wild music ground on.

Completely startled by the action the woman had taken against her dance partner, Jake looked at a guy called Mike. "Man, did you see that? That foxy old gal just decked that guy she was dancing with. Wonder what the hell brought that on? Look at him, layin' out there, groaning like a bastard."

"Well you might ask. That lady'll be lucky to see another few hours if that guy gets his hands on her." He looked at Jake, his eyes wide. "That fool woman just gave the knee to Charles Imperato, the biggest drug lord in this whole damned area... well, from what I hear, anyway." Mike shuddered. "God, hate to have that bastard on my tail. They say he's a bad one—likes to play rough with the ladies too, so they say."

"Ran out of here like ten devils was after her," Jake muttered. "Wonder if she knows who her dance partner was?" He shrugged. People made stupid moves every day. This was none of his mix and, in this case, he was doubly glad. "I'd hate to have that man after me."

℘﹠℘﹠

Serena ran swiftly out into the night, leaving the nicely dressed man in his natty business suit, doubled up on the floor, groaning in pain. Laughing carelessly, she leaped into her car and sped away. "Whew, close call tonight! I won't frequent that place anytime soon. That fancy cologne of his nearly made me change my mind, though. Some stuff that was! Whoo-ee!"

CHAPTER 23

Safely in her garage, with the door closed, Serena slipped out of her sexy duds. She tossed them behind the plywood then took another look. "If Martha ever pulls this plywood out from the wall, she'll get the shock of her life, seeing that stuff." She paused, thinking. *Don't know why I feel this way, but I'd better junk anything with blood on it, gloves, scalpels, those bloody dressings, and that half used bottle of Gram's as well. It's damning evidence, that's what it is.*

She gathered the offending articles, except the racy clothing—and the sand bag. She couldn't part with that, not knowing when she'd have the opportunity to obtain another one. Donning jeans and a sweat shirt, she put the stuff in the trunk. "I'll slip over to a big dumpster and toss it." With the evidence in a garbage bag, tied hurriedly at the top, she drove away as her garage door swung down behind her.

In another part of Denver, she slipped behind a Safeway store to several huge metal dumpsters. Seeing no one about, Serena stepped out, opened the trunk, and grabbed the trash bag. She tossed it into one that looked the emptiest. "When they finish filling this thing, they'll never see what's in the bottom."

Driving away, she felt the usual fatigue settling into her body. The fog came creeping softly over her mind as she pulled into the garage. She sought her bed immediately, tossing the jeans and sweatshirt into a corner of her bedroom.

Jackie Pitcher, snugly ensconced on a pile of rags near the bottom of the empty dumpster, heard the car pull up and the hurried footsteps. Without warning, garbage cascaded down onto him and his cozy sleeping quarters. His main concern that he'd be caught sleeping in the dumpster, he shoved the mess aside, hurriedly stood up, and looked up over the edge.

He'd had a hard time finding a dumpster clean enough to sleep in and now someone had ruined his resting place by tossing refuse onto him and his clothing. In the dim light of early morning, he noticed the bag had come untied. As he pushed the garbage aside, a small glass bottle fell out, hit the bottom of the dumpster, and shattered. Drops of some dark fluid splattered the sides of the dumpster. He felt the liquid hit his face.

"Damn, man cain't find no place to rest his head, no how." He didn't see anything or anyone lurking about and, homeless or not, he had an inborn disdain of filth. "Cleanest place I had in ages, too." He felt the rumblings of hunger stirring in the pit of his stomach. "Best head for the soup kitchen. Maybe they'll let me peel a couple 'taters this morning. I like to pay for what I eat, I do."

Using a box he'd kept handy he slowly climbed out of the dumpster and shambled along the dark and deserted streets. It was coming light and the morning feed would be in the works. Thoughts of fresh coffee and maybe a nice fresh donut made his mouth water and his stomach grumble as he headed for the only friendly place he knew in his lonely, homeless world.

"Some damned fool, dumpin' trash at this unholy hour, anyway." Fearful of contamination from the garbage, he was eager to get to the shelter and wash off. The sky paled and the gnawing discomfort of hunger in his gut kept him moving. "Sure hope the guard'll let me in."

Martha had scheduled a shift for that afternoon. She'd slept until eight, felt exhausted, and smelled of smoke again.

Alarm and confusion regarding her condition made her glad she was to see Dr. Carton at ten. She showered, dressed, ate a few bites of toast with her coffee, and squared herself for the visit.

"I'll have to tell him about everything that's happened, though I wish I knew more about it. Seeing Sykes nearly did me in. He's a broken wreck of a man now, but looking into that face made me crazy." She rambled on in the privacy of her home where speaking aloud was a comfort to her. "I felt such horrendous anger at the sight of him. That's not like me, though lately it has *become* like me, and that frightens me even more. I don't get it." She hoped the doctor could enlighten her about her feelings upon seeing that poor old wreck of a man.

෧෨෧

Once in the doctor's office, she responded to his initial questioning. "I've been alright, but..." She related the latest incidents in her life, including smelling of smoke again, and named that hapless patient, then asked, "Why do I feel such terrible hatred for that broken down old man? I told him I hoped he suffers the tortures of holy hell before he dies. And he *is* dying. I know it's cruel of me, but it happened so fast, it just slipped out!"

"There's a very good reason for that, Martha. He figures deeply in what happened to you. When you're ready, we'll delve into that time of your life in full detail. How about another hypnotic session? It might prove helpful in getting these things out where we can look at them."

"See if you can find out why I smell of smoke. I worry about that, too. I don't smoke, never have. And why am I so horribly tired some mornings?"

"We'll have to see what Serena will tell us. She hasn't mentioned much of what she does when she's out. She thinks you're a bit of a wimp, though." He chuckled. "That's common enough in these cases. She had to be the stronger one, as you know."

Dr. Carton worked unaided by Schoenfeld today. He proceeded to place her under hypnosis and when Martha had gone under, he asked for Serena.

"I'm here, Doc, like always. What can I do ya' for?" She giggled seductively and added, "She wants to know what I've been up to, eh?" Turning serious, she said, her voice low and confidential, "You wouldn't want to know, Doc, and neither would the wimp. I'm here to tell ya, she couldn't handle it."

"Why the cigarette smoke? Can you tell us that?"

"Sure thing, Doc. I need a night out sometimes, and nothing too tame. Sometimes I go to The Paradisio. It's a real jumpin' dive. Lot's to see around that place." She laughed, and the sound rang harshly in his ears.

"Anything else of interest?" he asked casually, masking his intense curiosity as best he could.

"Now you're getting nosy, Doc. I'm leavin'." She withdrew her presence, leaving Martha, who sat quietly, her eyes closed, unresponsive—waiting.

Obtaining no further verbal intercourse with Serena, Dr. Carton awakened Martha.

"So, find out anything?" she queried. Her eyes weren't burning, no crying, and no emotional workout under hypnosis this time.

He passed on to her what he'd heard from Serena. "Ever been to that place, The Paradisio? Serena has, and often, I'd guess. She wouldn't go further into her activities." He hesitated. "I have the feeling they may not be something you'd approve of." He cleared his throat. "Eventually we'll get you and Serena integrated, and the sooner, the better, for your own protection, perhaps."

"Are you saying I may be doing something illegal as Serena?"

"It's possible. She was very evasive about what she does, other than mentioning the night club. It seems she likes to frequent The Paradisio. Often personalities like Serena have their own set of rules. Be very attentive to anything you hear or see. Not that you could ever guess what she does, but who'd be better than you to keep an eye out."

"Do you know why the sight of that old man is so upsetting for me?"

He nodded. "Yes I do, but the time is not right to tell you everything. Neither Dr. Schoenfeld or I feel you're quite ready to handle it emotionally." He smiled gently. "Give us a bit more time, Martha.

She nodded slowly, knowing he must be right in his summation of what he'd learned and suspected. "I guess I understand and I'll try to be aware of what Serena does, but I don't know that I can. A place called The Paradisio? My God! Sounds sleazy. What kind of hell-hole is it?"

The doctor merely shrugged, a half-smile on his face. "I have no idea, but apparently, Serena likes it."

Feeling tense and fearful for a new reason, Martha took her leave. "Now I have to watch my other self—what is she, some kind of slut?" The futility of it struck her deeply. "The Paradisio—no way!" This was another worry, a big one, but she was determined to find out what sort of place it was.

Though extremely tired, she'd be unable to rest if she stayed at home so she worked the shift she'd taken. Entering the staffing office, she received med-surg again. "Okay, that's fine," she told the smiling young staffing clerk, all the while wondering if the young woman knew much about the people she sent to various floors. Jake came to mind, efficient perhaps, but caring? She wondered if he'd ever been.

Bob walked onto the floor, and Martha felt a surge of excitement as she greeted him. "Hi. On again, huh?"

He sat beside her as the taped report began. "Hey, lady, good to lay eyes on you, but unless I'm mistaken, you are more tired tonight than ever. You need me, don't you? You know you do," he said, keeping his voice low and confidential.

His nearness warmed her and the way he let his leg touch her below the table, excited her. If only she could confide her situation. It would be such a relief to tell this good man everything. *If I knew what the hell that was!*

She took in the fine male scent of him, and her fatigue seemed to melt magically away. After report, she felt a great sense of relief, knowing she didn't have Sykes. That assignment, she'd have refused, and knew she could never explain her reasons. She waited to find out those reasons herself.

Jake worked the ER, for this evening shift, but came to med-surg on his break. Martha had the uneasy feeling he sought her personally, though he did no more than nod in acquaintance. He chatted with Bob, and she overheard his gossipy commentary. Jake loved the importance of imparting gossip.

"Hey, man, you should'a caught the action at The Paradisio last night. This overdressed dame rammed her knee right in the crotch of the biggest drug lord in the whole damned area. Dropped him like a rock. When he got back on his feet, I swear I've never seen such fury in a man's eyes—nothing like that, not ever. He shuddered slightly with the telling. "God, they dripped cold, deadly murder!"

Martha felt icy chills run rampantly throughout her body. Hadn't she awakened smelling of smoke? She wanted to ask Jake more about the woman, what she looked like, but she couldn't open her mouth. Could it have been Serena? Of course, it could have, she corrected herself. It all sounded right, somehow. She lingered around, hoping to hear more.

Full of himself, Jake mouthed off to anybody who'd take the time to listen. "You ought to get a load of this chick! Dresses like a hooker, but won't take up with any guy, or gal, who comes near. I've seen her in there before. Looks like a cougar on the prowl, watching everybody all the time—well, until she took up with Imperato. You could see she didn't want to dance with him by the sour expression on her face. I think he forced her into it, dragging her around the floor that way. And then, my God, she decked the dude and left him moaning on the floor." He laughed. "She ran out of there in a damned big hurry. You could hear her tires squealing clear inside the place."

He hunched his shoulders and lowered his voice. "If this Imperato dude ever gets hold of her, she'll be wearing cement shoes in short order. I tell you, that man was mad as hell and damned embarrassed, too. You just don't give the knee to a guy like him in public...well, not if you want to live, anyway."

He got up to leave. "Better get back, or they'll be sending a guard after me. That big red head, Mary Mason, is the boss from hell." He left the unit, his gait even slower than usual.

Shaken, Martha struggled to get herself under control. She attended to her patients, and completed her charting. Her eyes burned with the fatigue that finally overcame her. She wanted to go home and sleep forever.

Walking with her to her car, Bob stayed at her elbow. "Come with me, Martha. Let's get a bite to eat. You don't want to be alone. I know it. God, I wish you'd let me help you."

He crushed her in his arms. She held herself stiff and board-like until she suddenly gave way and crumpled against him, bursting into tears.

"Oh Bob. I'm scared to death and there's nothing I can do. I'm not getting myself together, and I feel like I haven't slept in a month!"

He held her for long moments then ushered her into his truck. "You're coming home with me. You can't be alone, not tonight, not the way you are."

His jaw, tight and firm, let her know she couldn't fight his resolve, and since she had none of her own, she let him settle her into his big truck. He said nothing as he drove away.

She didn't even look out the window. Having no fight left, she only wanted to hide away in some safe place and forget everything.

Reaching his small home, Bob led her inside. Taking her in his arms, he said, "Martha, I love you. I don't care what your problems are, and just for tonight, I'm going to hold you close and keep you safe all night. I ask nothing more than that. Have no fear of me, you don't need to." He led her to his bed and helped her remove some of her clothing. "Here, have a T-shirt to sleep in." He motioned toward the bathroom. "Go wash up, or whatever you do, and let's get some rest."

As if in a dream, she complied. When she returned to him, he settled her into the bedding and slipped in beside her, embracing her. All stiff and trembling, she gave no dissent.

She slowly relaxed against his solid, warm body, nestling ever closer into his quiet strength.

"Oh, thank you, Bob, it feels wonderful, and safe, so heavenly it must be wrong—but it feels so right," she murmured softly as she pressed herself into his big body soaking in all the warmth and security she found there as she drifted slowly off.

Together with her, in his king-sized bed, Bob held her snug against him until she relaxed and let go. He heard her soft, deep breathing. "Now, my darling, sleep close to me. I won't let anything happen to you, not tonight, not any night." He felt hot tears flowing, and his chest swelled tight with emotion. It had been a lifetime since he'd held a woman he loved so dearly in his arms. He uttered a soft, earnest prayer, "Please, oh God, please, let me keep this one."

CHAPTER 24

Ryan sat at his desk, frowning, his hands frequently shoving the unruly mop of thick blond hair off his forehead. Grabbing his intercom, he barked, "Harris, got a minute?"

Harris shoved the door open. "What's up?"

"Have we checked around the flop houses with our information? Who knows what we'd turn up? We can't overlook any possibilities. Clues come from many sources. That is, if you can get any of those people to talk. They're not too open with police." Ryan grimaced. "They don't have much truck with us, these days—worried we'll get them on vagrancy charges."

"I'll get someone on it right away. Don't know why I didn't think of it myself. Could it be I'm finding it difficult to apprehend and prosecute this vigilante?" Harris half-laughed his answer. "It's got to be someone who hates any and all child predators, molesters, pedophiles, or whatever." He paused, added, "And you know in this crazy world that could include a hell of a lot of people."

"True enough, but we have a job to do, Harris, and like it or not we have to arrest this suspect and prosecute the hell out of him, or her. I can tell you, I don't care much for the prospect of facing an angry public if we do just that. People are fed up with the leniency handed to child predators. Hell, in some states, they're practically given a free ride." He sighed.

"In this state, it often looks the same damned way. Just ask the Moulton's."

ᘓᗐᘓᗐ

Sgt. Figueroa made the rounds of the flop houses asking if anyone had information on the recent vigilante attacks. In his query about finding blue, indelible marks on the victims, or if any of them had any truck with child predators, he was met with cold stares and a few reticent replies. One elderly man hesitantly raised his hand.

"Yes sir?" Figueroa queried.

"Well, officer, one morning a couple days past, I was sleepin' real good. Found me a nice place." Jackie decided not to mention the dumpster. "Someone tossed a bag of garbage on top of me. Later, when I got a look in a mirror, I seen this here blue spot right on my forehead. I scrubbed like hell, and the damned thing wouldn't come off." He gestured at his forehead. "It's faded now and sort of gone, but I don't like being dirty, no siree, an' don't like no spots on me neither."

Figueroa stepped closer and took a look. "Sure appears to be a similar spot. Can you tell me just where you received this stain?"

Reluctantly, and wishing he'd kept his mouth shut in the first place, Jackie nodded. "Well sir, I found this nice clean dumpster and nearly had a good night's sleep down in there, until a car pulled up and somebody threw a bag of trash in on top of me. I never seen 'em, though. They drove off right after. 'Course, I didn't want to show myself till they'd left."

"Will you take me to that dumpster?" Figueroa asked. He took Jackie's name and what information was available. By not making an issue of his sleeping in the thing, he hoped to win the man's co-operation.

"Yes sir, I sure will," Jackie complied, not willingly, but he'd opened his big mouth and had to go along with the rest of the investigation. "I need to get back to peel more 'taters, officer."

"Just take me there and I'll see you get back real soon, Jackie." Figueroa opened his squad car door for the vagrant to enter.

∾∾∾

Figueroa found that the dumpster in question had been emptied earlier that morning. He ordered it off limits and sent forensics to check it out. Later that day, he took the report to Ryan. "So far, nothing at the flop houses except what this homeless man told us. Someone dumped trash over him and it included this." He held out the report.

"Stains found in dumpster prove to be Gram's stain, or Gentian Violet." He looked at Figueroa. "Good work, Ben. Our 'vigilante' is getting nervous, getting rid of evidence that way. We can't warrant spending thousands of dollars digging in the city dump for a few stains, but this tells us a little bit anyway. What part of the city did this find take place?"

Figueroa told him. Ryan scowled. "Not too far from either family. Have we run a thorough check on every family member of both the Mercer, as well as the Moulton families?" He gave the officer a stern look and added, "I want the aunts, uncles, grandparents—all of them—questioned, too." He dismissed Figueroa, and grabbed the intercom. "Harris, got a minute?"

∾∾∾

Martha awakened slowly, stretched luxuriously, feeling elated and rested. But the feeling of warmth, and the sound of the deep breathing of another soul in bed beside her, startled her into vivid awareness. Realizing her situation, her eyes flew open and, not wanting to disturb her sleeping partner, she slithered carefully out of the bed to find the bathroom.

Returning, she looked at Bob's sleeping form and listened to his soft breathing and occasional sigh. She remembered some of the night. She'd entered into a new dimension in their relationship and wondered, *What asinine thing have I done, now?*

He stirred, raised his head, and smiled at her, his eyes shining, with a devilish twitch at the corners of his mouth. "Good morning, darling."

"Good morning yourself, Bob," Martha murmured. She felt her face flush red. "Lord, I'm blushing like a school girl!"

"Look like one, too, hair all mussed up that way. Did you sleep well?" He stretched his arms and she saw his long, smooth muscles, moving beneath his slightly tanned skin, and the thick, bunched hair under his arms. He stayed that way, hands beneath his head, watching her, saying nothing.

That sight of him lying there like that had an erotic effect on her. He wasn't in his nurse's uniform now and his masculinity struck a cord deep inside her in a way she'd never known. "Y—yes, I slept very well," she stammered. "But, Bob, what happened last night? I have to know."

"Nothing happened," he assured her with a slight nod of his head as he gazed longingly at the long, finely sculpted legs displayed below the T-shirt she'd slept in. "You needed rest and security. I could do that for you and I did."

With a sly grin, he added, "When you come to me, I want all of you, not the poor, fractured soul you were last night. I won't take advantage of a woman that way. Our day will come and I'll wait for it. But you're in some kind of trouble, lady," he went on. "I've watched this happening to you over the past several months. I'll help if I can, and if I did last night in a small way, I can hardly say it was a great sacrifice. I loved every minute of it. It's been a long time since I held a woman in my arms all night, especially like that."

He smiled, mischievously, devilishly, and in response, she was thrilled inside. *Oh Man! What a charming, devastating, wonderful hunk of a guy!* "I don't know what to say, but I do feel well rested this morning. Thank you, Bob. I think you saved my life last night." She hid the erotic way he affected her, not daring to admit it to him, and barely to herself. Her worries were missing this morning, as well, she noticed.

"Hungry?" He slid out of the bed. "I'll be just a minute, go ahead into the kitchen. It's to the left, off the living room." He ducked into the bathroom and she noted he'd worn only skimpy shorts last night. She also caught a glimpse of a well-put-together male body—tall, strong, and finely proportioned. Just now, he looked an ancient god, and those touches of gray only added to the appeal of the man she knew he was.

Martha hurriedly dressed and left the bedroom. As she moved through his home, she noted the masculine furnishings, leather chairs, a wide screen TV, magazines lying about, but no plants or figurines. A man's digs, no doubt of that, and she felt the comfort of being there with him. From all she'd seen of Bob, he was totally a man a woman could trust. He'd certainly proved it during the night. Not even a wayward touch that she was aware of, though she did wonder about that more than once, with a smile tugging at her lips.

He came into the kitchen, put on a pot of coffee, took out a pitcher of orange juice, and turned to her. "So, my lady, bacon and eggs?" His eyebrows twitched with humor. "Doing okay with all this?" He wore snug jeans and an old T-shirt, but no shoes. His feet, long and slender, had crisp dark hairs on the toes.

"I'd have to say yes to that, Bob. This is all so bizarre. I can't believe any of it!" She found herself laughing and completely relaxed. It felt so good to feel normal, just plain normal. No other words could describe her feelings.

But, with all the wonder and security of the present moments, outside this haven lay her confusing world of unknowns, waiting, just waiting—she had to let him know what she faced on a daily basis. Now, after the goodness and caring he'd lavished upon her, she had to ruin it all with the truth as she knew it. *He won't love me so much when he knows what's going on with me.* The thought of telling him about her other personality, made her physically ill for a moment. *I'll wait until we've eaten,* she decided.

They had a merry breakfast. He did a fine job of cooking and told jokes and made funny comments while she ate. But finally, she opened the discussion. "Bob, I want to tell you what's happening with me. I see now, that you have a right to know all about me. I don't know everything yet, but I hope to soon."

"You don't have to tell me anything, Martha."

"I realize that, but with what we have between us now, I do need to tell you. I care more deeply for you than you know, and it's only right." She squared her shoulders and began. "It started about six or more months ago..." And she told him her story.

When she finished, he looked puzzled. "Aside from the fact that you know you *have* an alternate personality, you have no idea what it, or she, does? That's incredulous! It could also be criminal, have you thought of that, Martha?"

"No, not really. I smell smoke in my hair some mornings, but I'll never believe I'd commit a criminal act, even as someone else." She clenched her hands. "I have noticed an unusual amount of anger in myself, though, and that's not like me at all." Remembering the towering rage she felt toward the patient, Sykes, she couldn't bring herself to mention the man's name. Not to Bob, even now after she'd aired what she knew of her mental problems to him. *Now, another secret on my part. It just keeps going!*

⋐⋑⋐⋑

Ryan sat at his desk talking to Harris. "Let's run a complete check on every family member associated with the two most recent victims of child assault." "Look for medical or rural backgrounds as well," he emphasized. "Might find something that fits. Sure hate going after those people. They've suffered so much." He shook his head at that.

"Yeah, sometimes this is a tough business. We'll get right on it, Ryan."

"I'll take the Moulton's myself. I've got to get out of this damned office more, need some sun on my face. We've got all we can off the computer from other cities. Our friend Callahan has been busy in several places. I've asked the locals there to do some questioning along these lines as well. We'll get that poor, cut up bastard, on something, yet."

☙❧

Martha drove home from the hospital parking lot. Her cozy, well-furnished home, once a warm, secure haven, seemed cheerless and empty to her as she remembered the warmth, security, and closeness of her night in Bob's arms. As she was floating about her house in a romantic trance, the phone jarred her reverie. She picked it up.

"Hello." Her voice sounded soft and heavy in her ears.

"Where were you all last night?" Jeannie's insistent voice rang in her ear, filled with worry. "I called and called you!"

"I'll tell you, but not over the phone. Don't worry, child, I'm just fine. In fact, never better. And just why were you calling me all night?"

"I needed to talk to you. But I couldn't reach you. Where were you?"

"Hey, I'm on my way over. I want to see Will, anyway." She hung up, got in her car, and drove over to her daughter's.

At Jeannie's, she couldn't hide her exuberant smile. "Okay, okay. I spent the night with a friend."

"There's more to it than that, now spill!" Jeannie pushed, having some very strong suspicions at seeing her mother's rosy face.

"Yesterday, so much happened to me, I was an absolute mess and Bob wouldn't let me go home. He took me to his house and took care of me all night long." Martha felt the flush of heat crawling over her face.

"Whoa! Getting warm around here, is it?" Jeannie giggled. "It's serious, isn't it? You can tell me all about it later, and I want to hear everything!"

She quickly changed the subject to her son, her voice filled with cautious hope. "Will's in his room, playing *Legos*, and so far hasn't broken anything or slammed them into the walls." She led Martha through the house. "Look at him. Maybe he's turning a corner, but we aren't sure, yet."

Martha saw the little boy sitting quietly building a crooked structure. His childish voice muttering words as he toiled away. She took heart, feeling a ray of hope seeing him quietly at play, using his imagination, and building constructively. Maybe with good therapy and parenting, he'd survive this ugly thing that happened to him. The positive thoughts heartened her and gave her hope for Will.

"So, tell me about your visit with the Mercer's. How'd that go?" Martha asked, more than curious.

"It was painful. Their little girl Emily sits like Will did for so long. She's in therapy, of course. She has soft wavy, blonde hair, and her eyes are blue, but they were clouded. I don't know how else to describe them. It broke my heart seeing her like that and knowing their pain. Brings back how it was for us in the beginning."

Jeannie wiped a tear and continued. "I told them how things had gone with Will. You can't believe how grateful they were for the visit. No one understands how drastically that kind of trauma affects the entire family. They've also felt the drawing away of casual friends, not their real friends, of course." She looked at Martha. "Mom, when I see little children playing or going to school, I wonder what terrible secrets some of them hide. And you know some of them are molested repeatedly, just read the statistics!"

"I do the same thing, Jeannie. It's ugly giving thought to a thing like that, but how can you escape it?" Martha paused then added quickly, "Did you see where they arrested a man in the Mercer case?"

"Yes I did." Jeannie replied. "Isn't he the other one that Vigilante fixed good and proper?"

At that news, Martha felt strange, distant, and she suddenly had to leave Jeannie's home. "Well, I should go."

Interrupted by the ringing door bell, Jeannie opened it to see a man dressed in a suit standing there. "Yes, may we help you?" Her eyes narrowed at seeing him there, waiting, briefcase in hand.

Ryan identified himself. "I'm Detective Ryan Mapus, one of the investigators in the Callahan case—the Garver case, too, actually. May I come in and ask a couple of questions."

"Certainly, but we've already been through all that. Your officer Harris came here asking questions, too. Haven't we had enough? Why us again?" Jeannie couldn't keep the anger from her voice. But she opened the door farther to admit him.

"We have some information and we need to follow up on it." After settling in the den, he cleared his throat. "Can you tell me about your existing extended family?"

Puzzled, Jeannie stared at him. "My mom's here now, but Dad passed away some time ago. Martin's family lives in Connecticut. They haven't visited here for two years."

"I'd like to speak to your mother then, since she's here."

Jeannie called Martha in from Will's room. Will came along and his eyes widened in fear, seeing a strange male presence in their home. He clutched tightly to Martha's leg, his little face a mask of uncertainty.

"Now you've frightened our son." Jeannie couldn't suppress her anger and exasperation at this latest intrusion. *Not for justice in Will's assault, but to benefit the criminal!* "Why can't you just leave us alone?"

CHAPTER 25

I'm very sorry," Ryan replied. "I realize why you feel the way you do, but we have a case to solve. I'm sure it won't take long," To Martha, he asked, "May I speak with you in private? The sight of me upsets the child. I'm sorry for that, but I have a couple of questions. It's our job and we have to do things that aren't always our choice. I can say that Denny Garver will never draw a free breath again, if that is helpful in any way."

Martha sniffed. "I don't believe I know the man, officer, nor do I care. Our concern is with Will's attack and that was screwed up beyond belief." She motioned him to follow her. "We'll go into Martin's den." She led the way, bade Ryan to a seat, and took one herself. "So what's this all about, officer. Just why *are* you here?"

"We are checking several issues regarding the families of the victims, looking for corroboration concerning information we've come across." The woman in front of him appeared a solid citizen, loving grandparent, and a strong, intelligent, older female. One who'd certainly kept her fine looks. Clearing his throat again, he began with, "How long have you lived in Colorado Springs?"

Martha answered his questions, but soon felt the insidious sensation of being hunted. She didn't like it or understand it and his questions regarding her rural background made the blood in her veins turn cold. It also made her very angry, but biding her time and holding her anger, she kept up a serene demeanor. "Are there any other questions?"

"You say you had a farm type upbringing. I wonder, do you remember anyone, your father maybe using a bright blue-violet solution on anything? We had a question come up about that and I wonder if you might know anything about the use of it. It could be helpful."

"A blue solution? What possible correlation does that have with what happened to those men? What are you talking about?" This question had Martha's pulse pounding. Not knowing why, she felt threatened. *Why didn't the man come right out and ask me if I know about my father using Gentian Violet on the freshly-castrated male calves, lambs, and baby pigs*? Somehow, she knew exactly what the detective wanted to know *and* that she dared not answer his query.

"Just thought I'd ask. I don't know a lot about farming myself. It could be one of our clues, you might say." Ryan instinctively knew she wasn't going to mention knowing about the purple solution, but in her eyes, he saw the knowledge. His years on the force told him that much.

His excitement rose at this new discovery. It didn't fit with the woman sitting before him, except possibly for the excessive rage seething beneath her barely controlled mien. That was not lost on him, either.

"Well, ma'am, that about does it. You work at Mercy Hospital, you said?" He had to ask, partly to modify his other questions, but to hear the way she answered this question as well. They looked for someone with a medical background.

"I take a shift now and then, yes," Martha said. "I mostly work to keep my hand in. My husband Chet left me fairly well off—enough anyway. I believe I mentioned being a widow."

"Yes, well thank you, Martha, I appreciate your help. We have to look everywhere to solve our cases."

Her face flushed and her grip tightened. "For the child predators, yes, but you did nothing at all to help our poor, little Will, did you?" She couldn't hide her rising disdain for the competency of the local police force.

"I know how this looks. We've all got kids and deeply regret what happened in your grandson's case. You have to know that." He quickly realized his apology meant nothing to Martha. "We've done a lot of checking on Callahan. He's been busy in other areas as well as here. We'll get him on one of these other cases sooner or later. In fact, it will most likely be sooner."

"If he came here to prey on our children, it was because some other law enforcement professionals didn't stop him where he came from. Maybe they had him and let him go so he could come here and destroy our little boy." Martha bit off the words in her fury. "He'll never be the same—how could any child be?" She flung the last words at Mapus, her rage flaring nearly out of control.

Ryan caught a healthy glimpse of her deeply-held anger. He nodded. "I'm sure you're right about that and I'm very sorry." He rose from his chair. "I'll be going now, ma'am, and thanks again." He made his way to the door and Martha saw him out.

After he left, she paced the floor, fuming inwardly. "That nosey detective—just why is he delving into our lives like that?" she asked Jeannie. "Why are they looking at us—at me?"

"Oh, Mom, he isn't looking at you in particular, he couldn't be." She frowned in thought. "He was looking for something, though. I felt it. What could he be looking for?"

"I don't know, but I have a funny feeling about it. He was digging into my farm background and curious about my nursing profession, too." A heavy pressure building inside her made her gasp for breath. Some fateful knowledge nagged at her consciousness, but she couldn't quite bring it to the surface.

"Well, I must get home, Jeannie. I'll take Will to Biggie's Burger's in the next day or two."

"What's the hurry? Got a date?"

Jeannie giggled and followed her mother out to her car. Martha felt a heated flush rising up her neck as she waved Jeannie away and drove off.

e/ɔe/ɔ

Ryan sat at his desk, thinking about the visit to the Moulton's. "Something about that woman tells me she knows more than she's saying. Could she have something to do with all of this? Why was she so evasive when I got into the farm area?" He picked up the phone. "Harris, got a minute?"

"Be right there." True to his word, he hurried over to Ryan's desk. "What ya got?" By the look on Ryan's face, he realized something happened. "Come on, what's going on?"

"I don't know for sure, but we need a tail on a woman I spoke with today. Something about her..." His voice trailed off as he gave more thought to his interview with Martha Lavery. He shook his head. "Naw, couldn't be, a woman like her, a grandmother and all. But then again, she has a hell of a lot of anger pent up inside her. Makes you wonder how much and why. She's like a damned volcano, or could be—I had that feeling."

"What the hell you going on about, man?" His curiosity vividly aroused, Harris stood in front of Ryan's desk, staring at him expectantly. "What woman?" '

Ryan went into detail about his interview with Martha Lavery then asked, "How about your interviews, anything?"

"Nothing to get my shorts knotted up like yours." Harris replied. "Are you saying you've got a suspect or an idea about one, or what?"

"Not sure yet, but this woman is hiding an unusual amount of deeply-held anger. On the other hand, she's a professional nurse, with an unblemished record, far as we know. It wouldn't do to make a misstep with someone like her. She's a widow and a grandmother to boot. I plan to order a *very* discrete surveillance on her for a while."

"He grimaced, his gut churning with worry. "It'd be pure disaster for our department to have our perp be someone like her, driven to malignant violence because we can't keep our kids safe from bastards like Callahan and Garver. We wouldn't get any sympathy, but we'd sure as hell be vilified by the public for prosecuting their heroine. You know damned well, they'd hold her up as a hero, and a long overdue one." He winced. "Hell, so would I."

"You're right. I'd agree with them, too, but we have our duties, don't we? She'd be a real life superwoman to a whole lot of folks, not just around here, but all over the damned country." Harris broke into a grin and stuck his chin out. "So, Ryan, how you planning to handle this one?"

"Dunno. Let's go for coffee." The men left the office, heading to the nearest coffee shop.

⌘⌘⌘

Martha had been looking forward to her next appointment with Dr. Carton. She entered his inner office and sat down, feeling stronger than usual and less fearful of learning more nasty details of her early childhood.

"All this hypnosis has to come to an end," she told him. "I'd like to ask you to move this along a bit faster." Anxiously awaiting his reply, she believed she'd crossed a barrier of sorts and was ready for the next steps, whatever that might entail.

"I think you may be ready enough. Your willingness to face what happened to you as a child is the real key here." His tone became increasingly serious as he explained.   "You must realize it takes time for complete integration with an alternate personality. It won't be like switching on a light. In so many ways, she is stronger than you, though that part has remained quiescent for all this time. What we don't know is what brought Serena out just a few months ago. It had to be a recent, severe trauma, but you haven't mentioned anything like that in this office."

"The most recent trauma in my life has been the attack upon my grandson, Will. I've been incredibly angry about that, Doctor, in fact, extremely so. That isn't like me at all. Would that bring about anger of this magnitude, nearly a state of rage?" At that moment, Martha realized it had to be related to Will's attack by a sexual predator. "It happened more than six months ago."

"Will's attack was of a sexual nature, and as you know, so was your own childhood trauma. There's almost certainly a strong connection. Serena is the one who knows—if she'll tell us." Dr. Carton smiled at that. "She's been reticent, to say the least, of telling us about her activities or feelings."

"We must give it a try." Martha took a deep breath. "I am as ready as I'll ever be, Doctor Carton." She realized her renewed inner strength had come about partly because of Bob's caring and love, and partly from the wearing nature of her affliction. She looked her doctor in the eye. "I want an end to it. The mystery, the lost time periods, cigarette smoke in my hair and clothes, and the extreme fatigue. And those damned, sexy high-heeled boots lying in the closet that I don't remember buying, and never would!" She shrugged in hopeless confusion and disgust. "But they've definitely been worn!"

Dr. Carton asked Dr. Schoenfeld to join them. As they had previously discussed with Martha, the two doctors had awaited this particular time, a time when she felt ready to know her other self.

The three of them sat in Carton's quiet, dimly-lit office and began. When Martha was under, Dr. Schoenfeld requested, "Serena, come out please." They waited.

Serena wore a suggestive half-smile across her lips. She sat, posed, ready for anything. "Yeah, Docs, what ya need from me?"

"Martha would like to meet you, Serena. Would you care to do that?"

"No sweat, doc."

They heard a slight hesitation in her voice.

"Just wait, stay here with us," Dr. Schoenfeld turned slightly to Martha's sleeping form, sitting upright in her chair. "Martha, do you hear me?"

"Yes," her lips barely moved as she replied in a low voice.

"Serena is here. Come and meet her." He saw Martha twitch.

"How can I do that?" An anxious, fearful look, moved across her face. "She knows everything that happened to me! I can't face her!"

Serena scoffed, her voice slightly harsh. "Yes, you can, you ninny, I handled that business, not you! And I've taken care of a few more things for you lately, too," she added quietly. "Had a bit of fun while I did."

"I see you now, Serena. Come together with me. I want to handle things for myself and with your help, I know I can. I have to. You must let me try," Martha said with a plaintive note in her voice.

The men waited for a while. Martha moved about, made expressions of distaste, even disdain, smiled grimly at something, and then sat quietly for several moments.

"I think we can bring her out now," Dr. Schoenfeld said. "We may have succeeded in beginning the integration. Time will tell. It's hard to know in these cases—they differ so widely." His heart raced in his excitement at dealing with the rarity of this type case.

Martha came awake. "What happened?"

"We believe we've begun your fusion, or integration with Serena. You'll know better about that than we will. You'll learn about the lost year, and we believe you will be able to face what happened then. It takes some time to fully integrate, but we hope you have begun that process."

"I think—I know she's with me. How do I explain that feeling? I just know. Will I suddenly know what things I've been doing as Serena recently, and will I know why I smell of smoke some mornings?"

"Let us know everything you feel, know, learn, or experience. We confess we are learning from you, from this case. Dissociative Identity Disorder is very rare, and few psychiatrists ever have the good fortune to see it or treat it," Dr. Schoenfeld explained.

Dr. Carton nodded. "That's right, Martha."

"Okay, Docs, I'll give it a go." Martha thought her voice sounded a bit flippant. *Is that you talking, Serena*? She picked up her purse and started for the exit door. Her movements felt stronger and more certain.

Dr. Carton looked at his compatriot, his eyes narrowed slightly. "I think she's begun. Didn't we hear Serena, just then?" Schoenfeld smiled and nodded.

Leaving the doctor's office, Martha had no reason to notice a non-descript old maroon sedan parked across the street as she hopped blithely into her car and drove over to see Will. "Time to take the little tiger out for lunch again—sick to hell of those damned, greasy burgers, though."

Martha felt lighter, and no longer alone. "Is my imagination working overtime?" She knew it wasn't. Her heart rate increased. She tried to worry about this new situation, but found at the moment, she could not.

Jeannie came to the door. "Hi, Mom, Will's ready and waiting."

"Great! I'll just pop in and visit a bit before we go. What did you think of that detective, Mapus, coming here?"

"It burned me and I hated it! That's how I felt about it. Haven't we suffered enough over this mess? It's like rubbing their failures in our faces. Imagine, his coming here to solve their vigilante mess." She huffed. "Like we'd know anything about it."

Martha realized she did know! Deep inside of herself the acts her alter, Serena, had committed had already insidiously seeped into her consciousness. Some of the same activities had crossed her mind, and more than once. At this moment she realized that as Serena, she had the ability to act upon those thoughts, but as Martha, she did not.

She needed to have an in depth conversation with Serena, but didn't know how. *I think I've done things! Terrible things!* No way could she let Jeannie know about them. Could she tell Bob?

"Mom, you're so quiet. What are you thinking?" A look of alarm crossed Jeannie's pretty face. "What's going on in that mixed up mind of yours?"

"Jeannie, I've had a big breakthrough in my treatment. I can't spell it out, but I am dealing with my alternate personality now—Strange? Oh yes, it's so very, very strange. They told me it takes a good while to complete the process. Let me have the time I need and I'll tell you everything—maybe." She managed a short chuckle. "What I learn may be too hard to tell anyone. I'll have to let you know on that." Martha looked around and changed the painful subject. "Where is the little guy, anyway? We need to get going."

Jeannie called Will, and he came running. Martha settled him into the safety seat. "So, my little man, what's happening with you?" she asked in a chirpy voice that sounded nothing like her.

Jeannie wrinkled her brow in a frown. "Mom, you don't sound quite the same today. Is this part of what's going on?"

"I suppose so—but I'm still me, Jeannie, don't ever lose sight of that." Mumbling under her breath, she added, "I think."

She drove blithely away with Will, and several cars behind her an old maroon sedan followed.

CHAPTER 26

Ryan sat across from Officer Art Jarvis. "Anything on the Lavery woman yet? How's Sammy doing with the surveillance?"

"She sees a doctor," Jarvis replied. "We don't know which one, yet, several specialties are located in that complex. She took her grandson to Biggie's Burgers. Sammy Gill had that stake out, had a burger himself while in there. Said it all looked routine to him. The kid played and ran around for quite a while before she took him back to his mother and went home. Her activities look normal in every way. We haven't done a wiretap. You want that?"

"Hell no. If that ever got out we'd be cooked, you know—up shit creek a whole damned mile." Ryan scratched his thick mop of hair. "These things take time. Let's see where the surveillance takes us before we do anything more. Patience, Jarvis, it'll take us a while and she's not going anywhere."

"Yeah, if she did the deeds, she's got a damned good reason anyway, at least in Callahan's case." Jarvis grinned. "Made her fuming mad at you, eh? I'd like to get a look at this woman, myself. Works at Mercy, you say?"

Ryan smiled. "Why? Going to check her out? Might be a good idea, just to get a close up look. How you planning that?"

"Not sure yet. I'll run it past you when I sort it out. I know one of the aides, Jake Collins. He's too big a talker for confidences. Might drop around to see if he wants to hit a

night spot after he gets off—think I will." Jarvis looked relieved with his idea. "I'll ask the tail to tell me if she goes to
work. Might just hit it lucky if they're working together."

He left Ryan's office, his paunch shoving his shirt apart in
the front. Jarvis always looked rumpled that way.

"Damn, what a dilemma if she turns out to be implicated
some way. Hell, there's only one way anyone could be guilty!"
Ryan shoved his hand into his hair, pushed his sleeves higher
on his arms, and reached for the phone.

"Hey, Dick, get me everything on a woman of interest.
Go way back and dig deep. We need everything on her." He
gave the info he had on Martha Lavery. "And what do we have
on Callahan? He came here for a reason. We've only scratched
the surface on that dude. Find out. Okay?"

❧❧❧

Martha took a shift, hoping to work with Bob. She wanted
to see him later, and realized all too well that a part of her had
the major *hots* for the man. With a bit of disgust, she knew it
had to be her other self in addition to her own feelings.

"I'll not give into that. She'll just have to live with it!"
Martha said, talking to Serena. *Is this the way I'll get to know
who and what she is and what she's done*? She wondered.
"Maybe I'm stronger than her now, though she must have been
strong for me back then. What a dilemma!" She shrugged, and
got ready for work, wondering when she'd know what had
happened to her as a child.

"Ye Gods, I don't wear that much make-up!" Martha
carefully re-adjusted her make-up to reflect her nurse persona
and went to work.

When she got to the desk, Angelina, the staffing clerk for
the evening, looked up from her paperwork with her lovely
dark, expressive eyes. "I put you in med-surg this evening,
okay? You wanna sign up for a few more?"

"Thank you. I'll be glad to work there this evening," Martha replied. "But let's leave it at that for now. I never know
when I'll have enough time."

She entered the staff room, stowed her stuff, and took up a report paper. As she headed for the report room she saw Bob putting his jacket in his locker. She smiled and felt the heat of a flush when he gave her a lazy grin.

"Hi, lady, how you doing?" What he really wanted to ask was, *Now what's going on in your crazy mixed up life*? And she knew it.

Martha nodded and saw his interest spark. He'd be close behind when she left the hospital at eleven. She knew that, and was eager for it. She wanted to tell him the latest developments, hoping the information wouldn't scare him away. She felt sure it wouldn't. After all Bob was a nurse. He'd understand these things. *Wouldn't he*?

The evening wore on, and during that time she noticed a new presence on the floor chatting with Jake. He was an officer she'd met once. She knew him by his unkempt appearance and big protruding paunch. Sergeant Art Jarvis had suddenly appeared on the floor, and though no overt action on his part told her, she knew it was her they discussed.

She gave no sign of her knowledge, but suddenly realized her interview with Ryan Mapus had gone against her, and part of that was because of her reluctance to discuss her farm background. The Serena part of her knew they looked for evidence regarding the emasculation of two pedophiles. *Why me*? She asked herself.

Smiling, she went on her casual way, attending to her nursing duties, charting, calling doctors, and tending the sick. "I refuse to fear those fools who protect child predators but never the young innocents destroyed by them."

She talked to calm herself, sorting things out in her mind. "If I had to spend the rest of my life behind bars, I would bear no regrets for what I've had to do." She shook her head. Where had that come from? Suddenly, Martha became cognizant of her acts as Serena. *Holy Mother of God, what have I done*?

Reeling from this most recent shock, she disappeared into the nearest room. Looking at the patient, she realized it was Sykes, lying in his bed, groaning with pain, writhing in his dying misery.

The form of this miserable wretch stretched out before her, brought back the memory of him pulling her into the barn when she was six years old. Her past was now laid bare to her completely—in all its ghastly horror—every hideous detail of the tortures this ugly man had inflicted upon her as an innocent little girl.

Martha suffered again the pain, fear, and agony of those dreadful hours. Gasping in pain and disbelief, she understood what this man had done to her, not once or twice, but repeatedly over the course of a year. She ran to the sink and vomited forcefully all she'd eaten during the day, though it seemed to contain every bite of food she'd eaten in her entire lifetime!

"Hey, what's going on in here?" Dimly, she heard Bob's voice calling. "Darling, what's happened in here? What on earth has made you this sick?" Worry tensed his fine features as he grasped her shoulders, held her out from him to look into her face—a face, she knew, had to look as stricken as she felt.

"Oh Bob, I've got to get out of this place—and now! I know everything. I've just realized...oh God! See that man lying on the bed? I'll tell you all about him when we're alone. I'm integrating with this other person inside of me, and it's almost too much to bear.

"I'll tell you everything, though, you'll never want to hold me in your arms again." Martha bit her lip, hoping the pain would stop her tears. "You won't believe what I'm about to tell you."

He grasped her shoulders. "Listen, Martha, can you make it to the end of the shift? It's only another hour. Darling, I have the feeling you wouldn't want to let anyone else in on what's happening." He shook her gently. "Here now, get hold of yourself. You can fall apart later. I'll be there to catch you. I won't let you down. I said that, and I meant it."

"I'll hold you to that," Martha said, but she planned to let him exit gracefully if he chose to leave her when he knew of her crimes. She slowly straightened her spine until she felt brave enough to ask, "Do I look okay, enough not to frighten my patients, or arouse the suspicion of Officer Jarvis skulking around out there?"

"What the hell, the police?" Bob stared at her. "Martha, we'll get out of here and get this business out on the table. Pull yourself together and get this shift over with." He looked at the man lying on the bed. "What's all this about an officer, and this poor wreck of a man?" He waved a hand at Sykes and looked at her in disbelief, his face tight and grim.

"He wasn't always a wreck, Bob. It'll wait until later, and I'll tell you more than you ever wanted to know." She looked in the mirror and saw her pallor, but otherwise appeared decent enough not to cause alarm. "Bob, you just saved me again. I was rapidly coming apart at the seams." She dabbed a few tears from her face "Thank you."

Martha returned to the floor, mechanically completed her work, and gave a detailed report for the oncoming shift. She regretted not being emotionally competent in giving care, and prayed she'd made no mistakes.

After the shift, she met Bob at his truck. Officer Jarvis wasn't anywhere around, or at least they didn't see anything of him. They left together in Bob's vehicle. Hanging back several car lengths, an old maroon sedan followed.

They went to Bob's home. He didn't want a discussion of this nature in a public place. When they arrived, he settled her in a big leather chair and got her a drink.

"So, tell me what's happening with you, Martha? I'm interested on so many levels, even clinically." He looked worried, even fearful of what she would say. "This is all extremely rare."

She looked him in the eye. "I've begun the process of integration. I couldn't go on the way I was any longer and asked the doctors to get it started. It was time. This crazy business has gone on long enough. If I don't see the end of it, I'll go completely mad." She felt her face tighten with apprehension, fearing the loss of this new and wonderful relationship, and with good reason. *What man could put up with this kind of insanity?*

His eyes were warm and filled with compassion for her dilemma. "I'm listening. I've read up on alternate personalities, or D.I.D. I have some understanding of the situation."

Seeing that, Martha relaxed a bit and began. "At first, I felt a slight difference, even in applying my make-up. My daughter noticed a difference in my speech patterns, and attitude. Tonight, seeing the police—actually it was Officer Art Jarvis at the hospital—even as innocent as it may have looked, I knew it was me he was interested in." She looked into his eyes, hoping to see continued understanding. "He supposedly came to see Jake Collins, like they were close friends, but instinctively I knew it was me he observed. I'm not just being paranoid—maybe it sounds that way, but my alternate, Serena, knew. She knew because of what she's done, Bob."

"You actually know her?" Bob looked incredulous. "You say you've met her? How?"

"I'm not sure. And maybe I'll never know how this works. But she's with me. I feel her trying to influence me in certain ways. She thinks you're a real hunk by the way." Martha smiled and shrugged. I have to agree with her on that."

"Aw come on. You've spoken with her?"

"Yes, more than once. Can you believe it?" She shook her head slowly, trying to put it all in coherent form. "They said it takes time to get everything together. But tonight when I walked into Sykes room—and I did that to get away from the prying eyes of Jarvis—those terrible memories of the distant past came pouring into my mind. Those memories contained horrors long suppressed, hideous things, evil things that happened to me I'll never tell a living soul about—not you, not anyone!"

Martha gasped in pain and broke into deep sobs. "It was that man, Sykes, lying on his deathbed, writhing in pain that brought some of it back to me. If there's more than what I've remembered tonight, I'm not sure I can handle knowing it."

She took a sip of her drink, before going on. "He used to work for my father. He was a predator, Bob, a pedophile. I know now what he was, but as a small child, I didn't. I couldn't have. My father didn't believe me when I tried to tell him that Sykes touched me in bad places." She paused to cry a moment. "The doctors told me Serena came into being to withstand the unspeakable things that man did to me."

"My God! And now we have Pete Sykes in our care, to treat and make comfortable? I'd like to choke the hell out of the sick bastard. How strange it is. No wonder people believe in a higher power. We believe that God will bring justice if no one else can." Tears sprang into his eyes. "Martha, I don't know what to say, except I'd like to string the bastard up by his balls!"

"You won't need to, Bob. He's suffering now, maybe that's part of God's way. I don't know. But there's more to tell you, and it's not good. It's not even legal, but the way things are between us, I must tell you. But I wished to God I never had to. I don't want to speak of those terrible things."

"What is it, girl? You've done something as Serena?"

"'Fraid so. It began after the terrible rape and sodomy of little Will. Because that man got off on a silly technicality, Serena re-appeared after all these years due to my frustration at the injustice to our child. I didn't know it of course, but from then on, weird things began happening." Martha looked in his eyes, searching for signs of disgust or shock.

Seeing none, she continued. "I had memory lapses, found things I couldn't remember buying. I'd wake up some mornings smelling of smoke. I found horrid, slutty boots in my closet. All these things had me so worried that I sought medical attention.

"Unbeknownst to me, Serena stalked Callahan until she caught him that morning on the jogging track. You know the rest of that story."

"Oh my God, Martha!" The look of shock over Bob's ashen features filled her with dread. Her chance for happiness with him was slipping rapidly from her grasp. She saw it on his face. "I find it impossible to believe you could have done that, Martha—or are you even Martha?"

"A good part of me is. There's more to the story. There's Denny Garver, too." She squared her shoulders. "That's about it. Oh yes, and I went to The Paradisio several times. What a dive that is!" Martha was certain she sounded like Serena when she said that. She almost laughed at her own distress as she sat there losing the best man she'd ever met, and that included Chet.

His stunned silence spoke volumes and her heart sank into the blackest of depths, as she helplessly faced his shock and disgust at what she'd done. Facing the loss of Bob's solid support from now on, she muttered, "Well, it seems my nasty little chickens have just come home to roost, haven't they?"

She got up to leave. "Take me back to my car, would you, please?" she asked, nearly begging. She wanted away from his stony silence. She wanted to die.

He sat in a state of shock, disbelief in his eyes, but conviction was there, too. "I have to think about this. I have to think it through. I hardly know what to say. I know about these things, but I've never seen dissociative disorder or knew anyone who had it. My God, you've committed *crimes*, Martha." He shook his head. "And now you believe the police are after you? Could they possibly implicate you?"

"I'm sure they suspect me. I don't know what they know, but they see me as a person of interest, I know that much." She gave thought to several things in the recent past. "Do you remember when I came to work with those purple spots on my arms?" She looked at him intently, no longer seeing in him a man who loved her but, hopefully, still a friend. "My father used that solution, Gentian Violet, on our young bull calves, male pigs, and lambs, when he docked them. I suppose that's where I got the idea to use it on those men. I guess I didn't want to infect them. Now it comes back to incriminate me."

Jake had seen them, too. *Wouldn't he be blabbing that to the police? He loves to impart information to expand his sense of self importance. Was that why Jarvis was there at the hospital, this evening?* Martha stayed lost in her thoughts until Bob spoke.

"What will you do, now?" he asked. His eyes no longer held the gentleness and comforting look she loved so much. The warmth once found there had turned cold as an ice floe, the frost in his eyes invading her heart.

"I don't know. I want to run away maybe, but I can't really regret what I did, when I think of it. Those men have doubtless ruined more lives than the two children we know of. They never stop, Bob. As Martha, I might think of doing something like that, but I would never do it. Alters usually have no conscious thoughts about the laws of the land. That's what I've read, and I believe it's true."

Bob sighed. "What a dilemma. You know I'll never divulge what you've told me Martha."

She believed him. Even if she found no warmth or caring in his eyes, there was still sincerity.

"Take me to my car, please, Bob. I just want to go home now. I'm so tired I want to sleep for a week. I'm glad I've told you everything and, for whatever it's worth to you, I've loved our time together. I can't blame you for any adverse feelings you have toward me. How could I?" She couldn't stop the tears from forming. "I'll always appreciate your kindness. You've saved my life several times over." Barely able to speak, she turned away from him and headed toward the door. "Thank you."

He helped her into his truck. Even the touch of his hand no longer felt warm. Seemingly lost in thought, he said nothing as they drove through the streets. Martha sat beside him, alone and numb with the new things she'd learned tonight, plus knowing she'd lost the love of a good man, a wonderful, caring man. Unable to feel anything at the moment, she sat beside his big warm body and forced all thought from her mind.

CHAPTER 27

I'll be calling you, Martha," Bob told her as he helped her down from the height of his big truck. She bumped against him. But his touch wasn't the same now and never would be again.

His voice had sounded deep and sincere but she couldn't place hope in that anymore. "Yes, but I won't be holding my breath until you do." She couldn't keep the painful sarcasm from her voice.

Her heart pained her to the point she feared it might tear and break apart within her chest as she left him without further comment. She heard only a soft mumbled goodbye from Bob, but no lingering kiss or words of solace. Her mind in a sick turmoil, she noticed little of the sights on the streets. But driving home, she caught a glimpse out of the corner of her eye of an old maroon vehicle keeping a steady, but discreet distance, behind her.

When she got home, she undressed and sought her bed. "Serena, or whoever you are, no tricks tonight. I've had enough for this day, and enough of you, too!" Amidst her despair, Martha felt incredibly angry. She punched her pillow in helpless frustration and collapsed in tears. "What am I to do? Just sit here like a fool and accept this kind of treatment from someone I thought loved me? He can go to hell in a damned hand basket for all I care."

ⅇↃⅇↃ

"Well, how'd it go at the hospital, last night?" Ryan asked Jarvis.

"Martha Lavery was there, but nothing out of the ordinary. The aide, Jake Collins did a lot of talking, but he talked all around anything I could use. She saw me, and I got the feeling she knew I was watching her."

He chuckled softly. "She avoided any contact with me. I hope she thought I was there to visit Jake." He laid his report on the desk. "She hasn't a very high opinion of any of us and I can't blame her. Funny thing, though, she looked damned pale near the last of the shift, in fact, she looked haunted or something. She left with a big, older guy, a male nurse named Bob Chance. The tail said she went with him to his house and then after a couple of hours, he drove her back to her own car, and she went on home. Maybe there's trouble in paradise. I couldn't tell. That's it as far as last night goes."

"Not much there. Looked pale, you say? Concerning what?" Ryan wondered aloud. "See anything to cause that?"

"No, not really—say, you hungry? I haven't had breakfast yet. How about you?" Art was always ready to fill his generous gut.

"Oh hell, let's get a bite. This case is driving me loco. If she's guilty, she's a damned heroine anyway. She sure as hell is to me." Ryan laughed. "Maybe she'll start a trend."

ⅇↃⅇↃ

Jake had the night off and decided to check out The Paradisio again. "Maybe that hot older chick will show up. Sure added a nice flip to that last visit I made. Wonder if Imperato had gotten hold of her yet? Wouldn't want to be in her shoes when he does." He checked his look in the mirror and laughed. "Don't pay to look too hot in that place, never know who might take an interest!"

Arriving late, Jake sidled up to the bar where his friend Joey sat alone, head drooping low, nearly in his beer. "Hey, Joey, how they hangin'? Any action tonight?"

"Naw, too late for any action now, unless that guy, Callahan comes in. You remember the one I mean. He does some nights, but his friend, Denny's in the slammer now. You know, he's the *last* one that got cut. Hear the police got him dead to rights for molesting that little girl—DNA, the whole shootin' match."

Jake straightened up. "Cops finally got one, handed to 'em on a silver platter, you might say." He lowered his voice. "See anything of that big guy that got the knee in here the other night?"

"I've been wondering about that. Hate to be that poor woman when he nabs her. They say he's a bad hombre, and what she did to him, set him off big time. He left here lookin' about to erupt or somethin'. If he comes in, I plan to sip my beer and keep my head down."

Jake grinned in anticipation. "Wouldn't that be a sight? She just might get him again. That dame looked pretty damned tough herself."

A bit later, Fred Callahan came sideling in, alone, long-faced, and appearing at loose ends. Head drooping, he kept himself aloof and said little. He endured a few cutting barbs of other patrons in silence. There were those who had no sympathy for his devastated condition. But for the most part, even that much attention went missing. He stayed a short while then faded away.

Joey shook his head. "Damn, I almost feel sorry for that Fred. I said *almost*, when I remember his idea of a fun night out. Little boys—sick son of a bitch!"

Jake nodded his agreement with Joey's assessment. "Got what he deserved, I say." He wondered if Joey'd heard anything new. "Any news on that vigilante?"

"Seems to have gone underground or maybe he's waiting for the next predator to raise his filthy head. Lots of people want to thank that guy, so I've heard. Regular hero around here, he is," Joey replied, sipping deeply on his dark, amber draft. "Hey, barkeep, how's about another, here?" He held out his empty glass to the leather-and-chain garbed barkeep.

No one appeared to miss Fred after he'd gone. The music pounded on and on, the drinks flowed, and the low murmur of conversation hung constantly in the smoke-filled atmosphere.

"Whoa-a-a, here comes Mr. Big. I'll bet he's still looking for that fool woman. Sure as hell he is!" Jake kept his voice low. His heart rate had increased considerably with this added excitement. "Look at 'im, looking around. She ain't here mister, hasn't been back since she fixed your wagon," he murmured then snickered very softly, while looking down into his beer.

After an hour of no action, Charles Imperato left. His face bore the same wild, dark and stormy, hostile glare. Jake shuddered inside. The man held a mighty rage in check as he hunted for the flashy female who dared to ram him in the crotch with her neatly leather-clad knee.

"Whew! I wouldn't be a stand-in for that lady for all the money on Wall Street!" Jake declared. "She won't live another day if he finds her. Wonder if she even knows who she slammed in the gonads that night." He blew out his breath, realizing he'd been holding it. "I wonder who in the hell she is? Looked damned familiar to me, I've seen her somewhere but I can't place her."

The excitement over, Jake took his leave, deep in thought. He'd seen that over-dressed chick with the high topped leather boots before, but where?

ℰℐℰℐ

Martha awakened. She'd slept fitfully and felt like the cold ashes in her fireplace this morning. She needed the solace of a friend and grabbed her cell. "Hi Lizzie, if you're not busy, why not come over for breakfast?"

"Sure. Why not? I'd like that."

"Oh, good, see ya in a few." Martha hung up and ducked into the shower. The hot water cascading over her body brought her back to some semblance of life. Toweling off, she dressed quickly in jeans, a bright blue sweatshirt, and managed a bit of make up before the doorbell rang.

"Hi Lizzie, I needed to see you." Martha nearly pulled her in off the front porch. "Come on in here."

"I knew by your tone that something was up. So spill, lady, you've got something biting you in the ass this morning. Things coming unglued are they?"

Lizzie stood ready to help if there was any way she could. Trouble excited her, and a few enticing details from Martha's mad life made her dull, high-society world go round.

"I have so much to tell you, I don't know where to start. Everything isn't coming unglued—it's already unglued. I don't want to dump all these terrible things on my daughter, so how about you? Strong enough this morning?"

"You bet I am." Lizzie's eyes sparkled with excitement. "Go make some strong coffee and let's get this business out on the table." The eagerness in her voice reminded Martha that Lizzie was no turncoat coward. But could she handle the truth about what she'd done as Serena? *I'm about to find that one out. I'm not sure I could stand to lose this friend, too.*

"Okay, you gave me the go ahead, so here goes, Liz. It's not a pretty story I have to tell." Martha set the coffee on to perk, and got out some biscotti's. Her stomach felt like a fire had been set in it, but she paid it no mind.

Ulcers be damned, she thought as she sat across from her friend and began. "I've had a big break through and I am beginning to merge with my alternate personality now. I know almost everything, but it sickens me to tell it, and I fear it will sicken you, too." She hesitated. "Lizzie, I've told you I had to see a psychiatrist. I have been for some time now. Remember what I said about something that happened in my childhood, causing problems for me now? Well, it seems something so severe happened to me during my first grade year that my mind created an alter personality, one that could withstand the horrible things that were happening."

Lizzie nodded, reached out, and placed her hand on her friend's shoulder to lend what support she could.

Martha went on to bring her friend up to date. "Actually, I am a criminal in some ways, though I feel no regret for my actions as Serena." She uttered a small, tinny laugh, shrugged helplessly, and continued. "She was driven to do what she did! Actually she did what any of us would have liked to do, but can't, as we are too civilized." She clenched her fists and the knuckle bones shone white through her skin.

"Whoa, girl! Relax a bit. This stuff isn't going away, so take your time in telling it." Lizzie reached out to pat Martha's hand before she went for the coffee.

She poured them each a cup and Martha took a sip. She couldn't taste that or anything else with this weight upon her soul. Overwhelming though it was, in telling these bizarre things to Lizzie, she felt herself lighten a bit.

"How about Bob? Does he know what's happening to you?" Seeing the pallor on Martha's face, she exclaimed, "My God, Martha, what have you told him—how much?"

Tears sprang into Martha's eyes. "He knows everything, Lizzie, and it's the end for us. He couldn't handle knowing the awful things I've done. The man was shocked beyond words. He said nothing—*nothing* Liz. He said he'd call, and I said I wouldn't hold my breath until he did." She uttered a weak laugh. "Look where I'd be if I did that—bluer than I feel right now."

"Somehow, that doesn't sound like the man you told me about. You don't really know what he thinks. He never said, now did he?"

Martha shook her head. Her friend hadn't been around last night to see the look of utter desolation in Bob's eyes, or to hear the dull tones of his voice. He'd spoken to her, but in reality had said nothing, and even that had been forced. She knew their relationship was finished, and it felt like her insides were being torn to pieces. "Maybe I don't know what he thinks, but what man wants anything to do with a woman who goes around castrating guys?"

"You didn't see him last night. He was so quiet, Lizzie. He said no words of comfort. Not even a nice, 'don't worry, it'll be okay.' I've come away with empty arms and a broken heart from the best relationship of my life." Martha let go then and sobbed for a long time.

Her friend waited patiently until the storm passed before saying more. "So, what else happened while you were Serena?"

How callous and nosey! Lizzie had long been a true friend but, right now, Martha had her doubts. "How can you ask that? Here I am suffering rejection, humiliation, and you want to know about *her*!" She couldn't help herself, she suddenly broke into a laugh, and it felt good. "You brat! You know how to bring me around, don't you?"

"Yes I do. You've wallowed in self-pity long enough. So now, what did you do as Serena that you haven't mentioned yet?"

"If I tell you, you might go the way of Bob. But I'll tell you anyway. Remember an alternate personality doesn't usually think in legal terms as we do so she took an action or two that I'd have wanted to take, but would never consider. Remember the two child predators that got their gonads chopped?"

"Martha! Are you saying Serena did the deeds?" Reading the painful truth on Martha's face, Lizzie gasped. "Are you kidding me? You—she—did that!"

"Yes, I'm afraid she did. I know they're criminal acts, but I think it has to be the *best* thing I've ever done, even if it wasn't really me." Martha held her head up high, "I truly believe all pedophiles should be castrated. That's the only way to stop them. You can talk about education, your mental aberration blathering, and all the rest of the modern politically correct psychobabble garbage, but those sick bastards never change their ways, and everybody knows it!"

She knew she was going too far but couldn't stop herself. "They're let loose to molest over and over again, until they torture and kill some poor little child. Then, maybe the authorities will decide to get serious. But it's too late for that child and all the other poor kids who'll never be the same."

"Well dear girl, I had to ask. You sure laid it on me. Wow!"

Martha sighed. "Now you'll turn your back on me and I'll never see you again, either." Her head spun with the sinking feeling she'd soon be all alone in her misery.

But Lizzie was grinning from ear to ear. "Don't you worry about scaring me off. A man might find you a bit threatening, knowing what you're capable of. I know you couldn't help what you did and I'm one person who applauds you in that." Lizzie had a sparkle in her eye. "Any more guys in your sights?"

"Lizzie!" Martha laughed. "Here you are—so good for me, and look at me, I'm so wrapped up in myself I haven't even asked how things are going for you these days."

"Same ol, same ol. Boring. If I didn't have you to liven things up, Martha, I'd go rat-traps, these days. Haven't even got a guy on the string, but then, if I did, my husband might object." She giggled. "Martha, you mentioned this place, The Paradisio. Why don't we go there some night, you know, just for a look-see? We can sit way in the back where we won't be noticed and watch the action. You make it sound like a crazy, kind of fun place. We'd have lots to look at. I'd like to go, just to see what goes on in there. My husband wouldn't be caught dead in a place like that and might want to divorce me for going, but what the hell? We'd be together."

"I don't know, Lizzie, those days are over for me. I refuse to let the Serena part of me out like that, now that I know what's she's like."

"Aw come on, what's the harm in going just this once?"

Lizzie nearly begged, and Martha found she was a little curious herself.

What she remembered of the place seemed rather hazy. Maybe it would take her mind off things for a while. She shrugged. "Well, okay, Liz. We can go, I suppose. It's a really sleazy dive. I remember that much about it in a hazy sort of way. Remember, I was Serena when I was there, and we aren't all the way integrated yet. But, if you want to take a look-see at the place, just say when. I don't have any more shifts this week."

"Okay then, what does a person wear to a dive like that?"

"I used to wear high heeled boots up to here." Martha pointed to her bottom. "Lots of garish make-up, and black leather, but no more, that's not *me*." She thought a moment. "Come to think of it, I have that stuff stashed around here somewhere. Some of it is in my closet, but there's more stuff around here, I know it," she said, realizing she had much more to discover about her other self.

"Why *not* dress that way, then? It'd be a blast, come on!" Lizzie's eyes snapped and shone with excitement. "We'd fit right in."

"I couldn't dress like that. I'm a professional woman, Lizzie," Martha murmured. "Of course, we wouldn't want to stand out like a couple of church matrons either. We'll have to work on our outfits."

Her friend had the ability to bring out the fun in every situation, even one as dire as the one she was now embroiled in, and Martha treasured that quality in Lizzie. She felt her pulse race with a keen sense of excitement that she hadn't experienced in a long while.

"So where are some of those oversexed outfits of Serena's?"

"Maybe in the garage, that seems familiar, somehow. Let's check it out." Martha led the way. In the garage her eyes lit upon the large, flat, plywood leaning near the neatly hung gardening tools. "Maybe behind this, I never knew why I bought this wood or when I bought it! I guess Serena did." Martha gingerly pulled the heavy wood away from the wall and they peeked behind it.

"Look at this stuff!" Lizzie said as she grabbed up a blue duffle bag. "Man, this weighs a ton. What's in here, anyway?" As she turned it up, the long beige colored sand bag fell to the floor.

"Oh no!" Martha gasped. "It's really true—all of it! Look, here's the sand bag I used to knock them out before I clipped them." As this concrete proof of reality struck her, Martha looked at her friend. "Oh, Lizzie, I knew it was true, but this is so real. It's actual proof of my guilt! What should I do now?" she asked, holding out her hands in appeal.

"Nothing, dear heart, nothing! What you did, you had to do. Those devils deserved everything they got. I'm so sick of being politically correct and worrying about the civil rights of people like Callahan and Garver! I'm glad you did what you did and protected how many more innocent kids? Don't you ever wonder how many others you've saved by putting those two out of commission?" Lizzie huffed in anger. "Remember, they never stop. You know that!"

"Yes, I do know it, and for that reason, and whenever I see my poor, devastated grandson, Will, I cannot feel sorry for what I've done," Martha said sadly. "That's what I said to Bob, too, but he couldn't handle it. He turned to stone before my eyes, Lizzie." Tears streamed down her cheeks.

Lizzie hugged her. "Too bad about him, I kind of had the idea you had a good chance for happiness with that guy. Chalk up another one for the bad guys." She turned back and dug into the rest of the contents behind the plywood. "Wow! A tramp wig, torn clothes, huge boots, and a regular theatrical make-up kit. You could be anyone with this stuff. How'd you learn all this, anyway?"

"I took a course in theatrical make-up and dress. At the time, I couldn't imagine why I chose a crazy subject like that, but I guess Serena knew exactly why. Strange isn't it, what happens to us?"

"Extreme stress can make almost anything happen. We know that well enough, don't we?" Lizzie laughed. "You're amazing Martha, you know that?"

"In what sick way are you suggesting I'm amazing?"

"How many people would like to do what you've done, but because of laws and convention, dare not? You dared. It's the best thing ever and criminal or not, you have to come to terms with it."

"If I come to terms with it, I'll keep doing it." Martha shoved the board back against the wall. "I should get rid of all this stuff. It's incriminating to say the least. How can I do it? If the police were watching me at work, why aren't they lurking around here, too?" She looked thoughtfully at Lizzie. "I might have someone following me. In fact, I'll bet I am being tailed."

Her memory of the old maroon car came into her mind. "The next move I make, I'll be on the alert. I'm taking Will to Biggie's Burgers again. I'll see then, if they're watching me."

They returned to the kitchen and Lizzie grabbed her bag to depart. "We'll go out and have some fun, you just name the night." She hugged Martha tightly. "Call me anytime, girl. I don't know when anything this exciting has ever happened in my life."

"Hey, how about *my* life!" Martha shot back.

Lizzie laughed as she hopped into her Caddy and drove away. After she left, Martha slumped into a chair, wishing Bob would call like he said. "Good thing I didn't really hold my breath!" Depression and anger settled in as she thought about her untenable situation.

CHAPTER 28

Martha drove slowly to Jeannie's home, all the while, carefully observing if anything or anyone followed. Eventually, she noticed the older maroon sedan a few cars back. *I've seen a lot of that car the past day or two. If it's the police, they could at least change cars now and then.* When she turned into Jeannie's, the car rolled past the house, too slow not to raise suspicion. "I'm not that stupid, you jerk!" She flung the words at the passing car and heard Serena's voice in them.

Jeannie greeted her at the door. "Hi, Mom, anything, new?"

"Not really Jeannie. How's Will?" Martha had had a bellyful of confessions and couldn't face another round. "Is he ready to venture forth to Biggie's Burgers again?"

"It comes and goes, moody, fits of temper, but he does play a little now and then. Maybe things are settling in too deep for us to see. I don't know. And yes, he's more than ready." Jeannie looked closely at Martha. "What's going on with you, Mom? Don't play games with me. I see something dark and sad in your eyes."

"Well, that's more than I see. I'm fine, really, just trying to get a handle on being two people at the same time. It's a bit of a tussle, working things out with someone who isn't real, yet stronger than me, so they say. She likes too much make-up, that's for sure." Martha laughed, hoping to divert Jeannie's prying attention. It came to an end when Will stormed onto the scene.

"Grammy, you ready? I am, let's go!" His eyes shone with his eagerness to have yet another Bittie Meal thing.

Martha rolled her eyes at Jeannie. "Okay, get in the car. We'll go to Biggie's. Want to go to the same one, again?" Martha asked, wondering if he wanted to see the bully again.

"Yup, Grammy, I like it there." Will sounded so normal, Martha wanted to cry with joy. Aside from that, she kept a lookout for the surveillance she knew would be close behind and snarled under her breath, "Now while I'm driving, I have to watch behind me too, so much for traffic safety—nosey bastards!"

They pulled in and ordered. The older maroon sedan she kept seeing had tailed her to the place. Watching out of the corner of her eye, she watched a portly man, dressed in jeans and dark sweater, come in and wait in line to order. She hurried Will to the play area, but had difficulty keeping her mind on him.

The anxiety of constant surveillance made her edgy and unsure of her next move. When Will ran off to play, she furtively glanced at the man. He didn't look like a cop, but of course, he wouldn't. It made her overly angry and the Serena part of her easily moved closer to the surface. Understanding the reason behind the venomous nature of her rage, she found relief in the knowledge that it wasn't really her, now was it?

"No wonder I could do the things I did, if I felt that way. Serena, knock off the temper, okay?" she mused then wondered, *Does talking to an alternate personality constitute talking to one's self?*

Martha's mind turned to methods of eluding her tail. Will seemed very normal today, and she paid little attention to his behavior. Her thoughts were rudely interrupted, however, when an aggressive little blonde girl shoved Will and pushed him headlong down the slide. Martha heard his terrified screaming as he slid downward through the tunnel, before he shot out into the open. Crying hysterically, he searched for her and ran, crying, into her arms.

"Grammy, I want to hit her and bloody her nose. I want to—can I?" His face red with rage, Will stamped his small feet on the softly-textured matting that covered the play area.

"No, Will, we don't ever, ever hit girls. You remember that?" An image of Joan M. flashed into her mind. They'd never allow Will to grow into a sadistic monster like that husband, Jimmy.

"But she needs it, Grammy." He clenched his fists. "She does!"

"Maybe she does, but boys grow much bigger than girls, and a gentleman never hits a woman. Can you remember that, Will?" Martha watched Will to see if he planned to act aggressively toward the little girl in spite of her admonishments. She'd never allow it.

"I'll try, Grammy. Can we go home, now?" His eyes filled with tears, which helped Martha see this episode as basically normal. He'd faced a lesson of life—one of many.

"Sure, Will, we'll go right now."

They started for the exit.

"Excuse me please." A pretty blonde woman held the offending child by the hand. "My daughter wants to speak to your little boy."

Martha turned Will to face them. "This little girl wants to say something, Will."

He cast his eyes downward and silently held his ground, his lower lip stuck out in a stubborn pose.

"I didn't mean to puth you, little boy. I thorry, din't mean it." The little blonde girl held out her hand, and Will took it. He only nodded, and Martha thought he was ashamed of the tears that had formed in his eyes.

Later, as they drove home, Will said, "She's cute, Grammy. But I wonder what she looks like down there?"

Martha saw him grinning as he said it and heard a sly giggle. Feeling sick and defeated, she hated the leering look she saw in his eyes.

Worried her grandson had formed an appetite too mature for one so young; she wondered how Jeannie would take hearing this latest report on Will. Anger shook her violently once again, but she calmed herself. "Will, you shouldn't spend time thinking about things like that. She *was* a very pretty girl, wasn't she?"

Will only nodded, but Martha felt a chill at the curious gleam in his eyes. "Callahan I'd *do* you all over again if I had the chance!" she muttered and gave no thought to the car following.

She ushered Will into the house, then turned to her daughter, barely able to control the anger she felt toward Callahan. "Jeannie, Will seems to have developed quite a curiosity about looking at the intimate parts of little girls. Would you let his therapist know about this latest concern? It worries me no end. God! I hate all this and I despise that evil molesting fiend more every damned day!"

"Mom, take it easy. The doctor said we might expect just about anything from him. We have to meet each event as it occurs."

Her tone indicated she felt ready to handle whatever came up, and Martha took relief and comfort from seeing it. Had Jeannie found a new strength in her battle for Will's future? Martha certainly hoped and prayed she had.

"I suppose so. It's just one more thing we face in this battle for our little guy's return to normalcy."

"How's Bob? We haven't met him yet. When's that going to happen?"

"Later on maybe, no rushing things, Jeannie," Martha couldn't bring herself to tell Jeannie the sad story of how she'd lost him. *Time enough for that. I'm being followed like a criminal, and I've committed crimes. What could I possibly tell her that wouldn't drag her down with me?*

She shrugged, "Well, I have to get back. I see my doctor again tomorrow."

"Okay, Mom, you're not telling me much. Something's happening, and you're keeping me in the dark." Jeannie's frustration seeped through in the tone of her voice. Her daughter was no fool.

"Sometimes that's the best place to be, my daughter. All in good time. See you later." She turned to leave then added,

"Maybe you're better off not knowing how rapidly my life is going down the toilet!" She left Jeannie standing there, mouth agape.

While fuming with anger at her untenable situation, Martha saw the little maroon sedan behind her. She stopped her car and got out. As the surveillance person drove by, passing her, she shook her fist at him, and laughed. "Not so good at your job are you? Get lost, you snoopy bastard."

Then she realized it easily might have been her other self who had spoken those ugly words.

芝芝芝

Martha entered Dr. Carton's office in a quandary. Trying to get together with her alternate personality, Serena, had succeeded in bringing untold troubles, even danger into her life. "How do I stop worrying about what Serena may have done, when it was really me? What do I do?" She studied the doctor with eyes that were burning and red from crying and frustration. "What should I expect? I know I'll be considered a criminal if the police ever find out what I've done," she said, wondering how much the doctor knew about what she'd done as Serena.

"You will experience all sorts of strange things, getting acquainted with another part of yourself," Dr. Carton answered. "Exactly what sort of criminal acts are you worried about?"

"I don't wish to go into that just now, Doctor. But suffice it to say, I might have done a few things I wouldn't normally do."

The evasiveness of her answer did not escape the doctor, but he didn't press her on it. Time would change her forthrightness about her alter, he felt certain of it. He also had read of cases where criminal behavior had occurred. Actually, they were not that unusual, but no alter could make the host person do those things considered especially heinous or deadly, according to his understanding of the subject. Martha's worries were important, but he felt certain her actions were not overly criminal.

After an hour of counseling, she left the doctor's office feeling no less confused and shaking her head in frustration. She hurried to her car, longing for Bob's solid presence, but had to face the fact she'd lost that comfort. "I guess I'm on my own in this. I've never felt so alone. Lizzie is the only soul who didn't freak out at what I've done as Serena. I couldn't bring myself to tell those things to Jeannie, and I don't even care if the cops are following me, not anymore."

Feeling lost and depressed she drove home and pulled into the garage. "I've got to get rid of what's left of that weird collection behind the plywood. If the cops ever find those things, I'll be in jail longer than any criminal." She stowed the offending articles in the trunk of her car and slammed it shut.

Since I'm under surveillance, I'll have to give that nosey cop the slip to get rid of this stuff. Deep inside, she had the help she needed to achieve her goal and she allowed it. With Serena's help, she'd make it happen and, for the first time, she welcomed the confidence of knowing it.

She turned the lights off about 10 p.m., hoping anyone watching the house would suppose she'd retired. Waiting until well after midnight, Martha slunk out the back way to scout the streets around her home. The surveillance car sat a block away. She carefully drew near enough to watch the man until she saw an avenue of escape.

"He's drowsy for sure, that head bobs way too often." She chuckled softly as his head jerked upright again. How often had she done the same on long night shifts when things were too quiet? She could almost hear the occasional snort, as sleep overcame him. He fought it until finally his head hit his chest and she knew he'd dozed off.

She opened the tip-up-style garage door manually after unhooking the electric motor. Pushing her car out into the street, she rolled it down a-ways then went back to close the garage door. She left out the small side door, got in her car and drove away. In her rear view mirror, the surveillance car sat in its place, lights off, the driver's head nodding in sleep. "Thank God this car wasn't too heavy to push!"

Laughing at her victory, Martha drove several miles out toward the edge of the city. Spotting a large industrial dumpster, she stopped and tossed her incriminating clothes, big men's boots, and most of the theatrical make-up. Regretting her very poor ethics regarding the care of sharps, she tossed in the few remaining scalpels right along with the other things. "Good riddance, you incriminating garbage!" She'd kept the things contained and felt certain no fingerprints could be found on any of the stuff tossed into the dumpster. She'd always been very careful of that, never knowing why.

"I can't go home. He'd see me and know I'd been up to something. I'll find a place to wait out the night and visit Jeannie in the morning. Since she was wearing suitable clothing, she decided to seek an open all night diner.

She remembered Mickie's Coffee Shop stayed open all night. She'd been there with Bob in better times. She couldn't go home until after the morning rush hour and made the decision to sit there and nurse a cup of coffee. It would use up time and help her stay awake. Taking a booth far in the back, she surveyed the people, sitting, eating, talking, and some, nearly copulating in their booths. She easily ignored it all.

Her mind in a flurry of hopelessness, loneliness, and distress, she felt a bit of relief as a few stray tears escaped. Putting her head down on the table, she murmured softly, "Oh God, will this nightmare of mine never end?"

The blood froze in her veins when she heard a deep voice behind her. "Yes, Martha, how will it all end? I'd like to know that, too."

"Bob?" She breathed his name softly and turned to peek behind her at the man in the next booth. Without further comment, he slid out of his booth, shoved his coffee cup across the table, and slipped into the opposite seat, joining her. He fixed his eyes on hers with a look, close to desperation. "You got things sorted out, yet? You're out so late, anything wrong?" Deep concern lay in his eyes, and the warmth glowing from them set her pulses racing. The heat of him radiated toward her like a furnace. Her body quivered with weakness at seeing that look on Bob's face again.

"No, just couldn't sleep, is all," she murmured weakly. It was all she could' manage. The sexual heat that emanated from his darkened eyes filled her with a desperate need to crawl into his arms and forget about everything. "How about you? No sleep either?"

"Yeah, same here—Martha, can we go somewhere and just talk? That's all, just talk." His soft tone convinced her of his need. "Come on, my lady," he insisted, his voice the low growl of an impassioned man.

"About what—haven't we said everything?" Her despair lay deep in her voice. She could hear it and knew he could, also.

He'd never even called her, not once. She held her anger over that. But his presence here, and the concern radiating from him just now, confused her. *What was happening?*

He readily took advantage of her weakness. Somehow, he knew she had no strength left. "Come on, let's go—come on," he urged.

When he rose and took her arm, Martha had no will of her own. She stood and walked meekly beside him, holding to his strong arm as he led her to his vehicle. She struggled to ignore the heat of his hands on her body when he ushered her inside.

She knew he headed for his home, and made no move to stop him. She had no strength to stop anything he might do to her this night. She'd never felt so weak and vulnerable in her life.

Deep down, she trusted the kind of man Bob was and knew he wouldn't intentionally hurt her—though his silences had. And plenty. She said nothing as he drove without speaking through the darkened streets until he reached his home. Then he led her inside and sat her in his big leather chair.

"I'll get you something to drink. Looks like you need it." She heard the clink of glasses and ice, then a pop as he opened a bottle. Returning to her side, he handed her a stiff shot of whiskey. "Here you go."

She drank a good slug of it. Scalding her throat like fire, it warmed her down to her toes. She really didn't care what she drank as she waited for him to speak. It seemed impossible to care about anything. *What's wrong with me?*

"Martha, I've tried to sort out how I feel about the things you've told me," Bob finally said. "In spite of illegalities, criminal acts, and alternate personalities—try though I might, I can't get along without you and I can't get you out of my mind. God knows I've tried to put this in perspective, but I can't. I only know I need the sight of you, the smell of you, and for damned sure, the feel of you!"

He reached for her then, crushing her tight against his big body. He held her close, nuzzling into her hair, kissing her lips so long and deep she almost fainted. His lips raced over her face then began to travel down the front of her shirt. "Oh God, Martha," he cried, his voice muffled, broken, and trembling. "I love you so!"

CHAPTER 29

Martha gasped as tears of disbelief formed in her eyes. "I don't believe this. I'd lost all hope. My world is all messed up, and losing you was the last straw for me. I thought you despised me!"

He said nothing more as he kissed her tears away and started opening her blouse. She struggled and jerked out of his arms. "Bob, I can't. I don't know what you're—I can't believe this is happening."

He reached for her again, crushed her tight, and kissed her long and hard. Her breath came in panting gasps as she clutched onto him. Her blood raced, only partly in fear, but more because it was him. She wanted him, she burned for him, and she knew at last she loved him, truly loved him.

"Shush, it's all right. Everything's all right," he murmured. He wanted her, and he'd have her tonight. No tears or recriminations would stand in his way, and no thoughts of guilt.

Martha, unable to resist his advances, did nothing to stop him and became more than willing. In shock at this turn of events, she let his passionate, burning kisses quietly turn her frozen soul into a mass of molten longing. A desperate fire burned within her and she had no will or desire to stop what was happening.

Nothing mattered now, not anymore. Lost in the heated madness he'd created in her, she forgot her despair. Her heart soared inside her chest until she nearly fainted.

He lifted her lightly into his arms as if she were a feather-weight, and took her to his bed. "No Mr. Nice Guy tonight, my love. It's been too long."

He unfastened her clothes, pulled them off. At this, Martha came alive and, fired by her own passion, began to help him divest himself of his things.

He gasped in delight at finding a fiery and willing partner in his arms, closed her mouth with his, and went deep as he sought it all from her.

Helpless to stop his assault and filled with fire, she met him fully, kiss for kiss, touch for touch. She'd never known anyone like this man and if it only lasted this one night, so be it. She didn't believe in his love. She knew better than that after his long, painful, silences, but she had no doubt of his passion.

Go for it, girl! Martha heard the words, felt the sentiment, and realized how well she'd become fused with that other part of herself. She returned Bob's kisses with unbridled lust, leading him on a wild, hot-blooded adventure that lasted through the few hours left of their night together and into the softness of the morning light. He drove her to heights of passion she'd never imagined possible. His skill and desire tore all her worries asunder.

◌◌◌

Sammy Gill entered Ryan's office. Shamed faced, he related the details of his surveillance of Martha Lavery. "Well, she must be seeing a psychiatrist. I saw her enter the offices of Doctors Michael Carton and Herman Schoenfeld, both of 'em psychiatrists." His face reddened. "She knows she's being tailed, too, because she stopped suddenly and when I passed her, she shook her fist at me to let me know she'd made me. That and her angry glare told me what she thought about it.

"But worse yet, she gave me the slip last night. I think I must have dozed off—long hours you know. All the lights were off, so I figured she'd retired." Embarrassed at the admission, he apologized. "Jeez, Ryan, I'm sorry. It was way late and I was exhausted. But anyway, it was nearly noon today when she breezed into her driveway, got out, and entered her house with a key. So she'd unplugged her garage door last night, opened it by hand, and slipped away."

"Cagey character, isn't she?" Ryan grinned. "Don't feel too bad, your relief called off, slip-up on our part." He frowned "Wonder where she went? Why'd she need to sneak off like that? Why the evasive behavior? Maybe she resents being tailed. Hell's bells, I know I would." He took a deep breath and patted Sammy on the shoulder. "We'll have to be less obvious in her case." "Submit your overtime. We'll get another guy for a while, maybe a woman. I've got one in mind that she won't spot so easily."

He dismissed Sammy and called Harris. "Good morning, Alan," he said with a grin. "Our lady gave Sammy the slip last night. She's no dummy. Cagey as hell and getting mighty damned suspicious."

"Well, if she's our perp, she's done the world a couple of favors anyway. What's next?"

"They're picking Callahan up as we speak. Harrisburg sent us a laundry list of his activities. He drives an old dark blue sedan. We took the information off it from the street. It matches one the police in Harrisburg have been looking for. I've sent Charlie and Ben out to pick him up, confiscate the car, and do forensics on it and the house. I hate to think what rot they'll find on Freddie's computer—damn that bastard!"

"Whew! Things are moving along, eh?" Harris commented. "So where are we with the Lavery woman? She'll be a real hero if you try to arrest her. Down in Australia, a woman shot the balls off the guy that raped her granddaughter, and she became a national hero. The police didn't dare prosecute her." He chuckled. "That could happen with this case, and you know it. People are damned fed up."

"Don't I know it?" Ryan shuffled a few papers. "As far as surveillance goes, we'll have a female do the tailing from now on. Lavery's wise to us now and we need another tail—how about Carla? She's a slick one and she'll be less obvious if I know anything about that dame." He laughed. "I wouldn't mind tailing this suspect myself. Who knows what we'd find, psychiatrist and all?"

"Psychiatrist? She's really seeing one?" Harris asked. "A nut case, huh? Is that it?" He shook his head. "It don't fit, Ryan."

"Not at all. She's a very together person. Maybe with a problem we know nothing about. We'll see how it goes." Ryan stuffed the papers in a file. "The doctor won't tell us anything. He can't. You know how it is, patient confidentiality and all that. Only makes our work harder." He stretched his arms over his head. "Hell, man, had breakfast yet?"

"Nope. Where you want to go?"

The detective and the sergeant left together. Coffee and donuts always made their day go better.

ↃↃↃ

Lizzie came knocking on Martha's door. Exhausted from her heavy night with Bob, Martha slowly dragged it open to admit her. "Hi. Come on in."

"Where have you been?" Lizzie demanded. "You weren't home last night. I called several times." You look tired as hell, but there's something else, too. What is it? Spill! Come on, girl, tell."

Martha sighed. "Oh, I don't know where to begin, Lizzie. How do I even start with this?" But over a fresh cup of coffee she did, telling her friend everything, including her night with Bob, how she got rid of the incriminating evidence, and her evasive maneuvering to evade the surveillance officer.

"Speaking of Bob," Lizzie exclaimed, ignoring the rest of the story, "and here you thought it was over! How did you leave him this morning?"

"He made us a great breakfast, though it was after ten or so before we woke up. Later, he took me to my car. When I drove home, you should have seen the guy that'd been tailing me." Martha giggled. "Oh, Lizzie, the look on his face." She sighed again. "Getting back to Bob, I wonder about that myself. As far as our relationship goes, I don't know if we have one or not. You know, he's never called me since I told him about my activities. I waited in agony for days! He may never call me again, either. I think some part of me went a bit wild last night, probably scared him off. It's strange to speak of my other self that way, when she's really me. But this integration business takes some time and it's very, very strange—actually it's damned weird." She looked intently at Lizzie. "I am so glad I can tell this stuff to you. Who else would even believe it?"

"So, when do we visit the infamous, Paradisio?" Lizzie changed the subject without a comment on her story and Martha realized their outing to the infamous nightclub was the real reason for Lizzie's visit.

"Oh, whenever." Martha shrugged, too tired to care. She really wanted to sleep—and see Bob again as soon as possible. "I'm too wiped out for tonight. How about tomorrow night? I haven't taken any shifts for a while. Now that Bob is speaking to me again, maybe I should." Martha mumbled the words, musing aloud and forgetting Lizzie for the moment.

"Hey, get with it, you wildcat woman! You're worn out from your activities last night, and I'm jealous as a scalded cat, you sexy vixen." Lizzie hugged Martha. "Okay, tomorrow night, it is, and I'll get in touch in the morning about what to wear. Get some sleep now, okay?"

Martha saw her out, enjoying all over again the warm glow of their close friendship. "How good it is to feel this way, it's been so long!" She noticed her body aching with the subtle discomforts gained from her passionate night with Bob. And again, a million pleasurable sensations filled her mind. Exotic feelings, something she hadn't experienced for many long, lonely, years.

She sought her bed and collapsed into deep slumber. Over her, a dark shadow, a troubled one of her own making, loomed and threatened. She couldn't wake up to dispel the dread sensation of doom that seemed to hover like a dark storm cloud. Twisting and turning, she awakened enough to hear herself moaning, "Oh, please, please, don't touch me. I can't bear it!"

ɛɔɛɔ

In spite of her wild dreams, Martha slept well for a good part of the day and on into the night. She woke up feeling at loose ends. Bob hadn't called and that fact kept her nervous and pacing about her home. She finally decided her encounter with him was merely some wild fluke, something that just happened, because for both of them, their emotions had run so high they had no other outlet for their tensions. She almost laughed. "Well, I hope it wasn't that tawdry."

She threw on some clothes and went out for a drive. "I've got to get out of the house before I go stir crazy. I can't call him. I don't know what he thinks or how he really feels about things. We discussed nothing, just tore at each other like a pair of wildcats."

She laughed at that but kept an eye out for a tail. The old maroon sedan was gone. She'd made sure of that. "It could very well be another vehicle I haven't spotted yet. I'm becoming completely paranoid, and it all stems from seeing that fiend, Sykes. I hope he suffers all the tortures he deserves. I'm sure I wasn't the only child to suffer at his hands." *Justice comes in many forms,* she realized at last, *though it was terribly long delayed in Sykes case.* Looking about, she realized she'd arrived at Jeannie's.

"Lord, I must be driving on auto-pilot. These mind-boggling thoughts do terrible things to a person. I'll be lucky to live through this maddening chapter of my life." She went in to see how things were with the Moulton's.

Jeannie met her at the door and took her into the den before she opened her mouth. "Mom, we've decided to move to the north side of Denver. Martin spends more time there with his company than here, so it'll be a good move for us." Imparting her news to Martha, Jeannie subdued her excitement at leaving the city where a terrible evil had happened to their family. "Will you be okay with it?"

"Yes, of course I will, but don't be surprised if I make a move, myself." Martha made her statement, partially for nearness to her family, but also for the fact of her criminality looming in her future as well. She'd already read that patients with Dissociative Identity Disorder, frequently did move to new locations after integration with their alternate personalities. They stated various reasons. Most declaring they didn't want it known to the people in their lives that they'd had mental aberrations, and frequently because of criminal, or near criminal acts they'd committed. It allowed them a new beginning.

Martha readily understood that, but she had qualms about being away from the closeness she enjoyed with Lizzie. That would be the real hardship. And Bob. She didn't know how to think about him anymore.

"Why are you so quiet?" Jeannie asked. "What are you thinking? You haven't told me much recently—you haven't, Mom." She laid on the guilt. "At least let me in on how your treatment is going. What's happening?" Jeannie implored with concern in her deep-blue eyes. "I need to know!"

Martha decided to tell her only enough to satisfy her for the moment. "Jeannie, I've had a real break-through. I'm in the process of integration as we speak. I can't tell all of it, but last week, I saw the man who worked for my father during the time my alternate personality was created, a sick, dying man, no longer a threat. But it wrung me out to see that old devil lying there. Yet, seeing that evil man, Sykes, helped me face the things he'd done to me, not all of them so far, but enough to send me off into a panic."

"I can't fully integrate until I face everything, the doctor said. I even have conversations with Serena sometimes, but it's weird, sort of like talking to myself. I'm not sure it's real, but it has happened. Bob helped me make it through that shift, Jeannie." Martha managed a laugh as she tried to help her daughter understand that she hadn't been totally devastated by the unrealistic things occurring in her life.

"Good, Mom, then you're working it out. When we have a new place and get this one on the market, we'll drive up and see it, okay?" Jeannie's interest had quickly turned to her own sphere of concern and Martha applauded it.

After spending time with Will, Martha drove home. Looking about for a police tail, she failed to see anyone, though if a tail had her in his sights, Martha felt certain they'd use one whose skill far outpaced the first one. If so, Martha never saw anything obvious, and felt certain she'd gained expertise in checking for police surveillance the past few days.

Reaching the security of her home, she called Lizzie. "Hey girl, come over so we can figure out what to wear tonight for our foray to The Paradisio."

"On my way, lady."

Martha hung up, measured out the coffee, and turned it on. Wonder why Bob hasn't called," she mused. "After the scorching night we spent in his bed, he can't ignore me for long—unless Serena did him in." She emitted an uncertain giggle, remembering particular events.

Lizzie bombed in with her usual upbeat attitude. "So what's the right get-up for this fancy dive?" Her eyes sparkled with excitement as she poured herself a cup of coffee.

Martha laughed. "If I recollect from my friend, it's boots nearly up to here, and I've got a pair." She held her hand to the bottom of her buttocks. "Way too much make-up, and a lot of stretchy, too tight, shiny, glittery, stuff on top—hooker clothes, basically." She flung out her hands. "Go figure."

"I don't think I'd want to go that far." Lizzie giggled with joy at this adventure, playing charades of sorts. "I have some spike heeled boots. How about a pair of tight jeans, and skinny top, maybe a glittery belt to set it all off?"

"Sounds about right. Now, if someone asks you to dance, remember, it could be him, or maybe her. 'It's too hard to tell and be sure." Martha let out a giggle as she said it, and a memory of her other self's wild night at The Paradisio popped into her head, clear as daylight. She felt a flush creeping up her neck.

Lizzie ignored Martha's discomfort. "I don't plan to do any dancing. Just walking in that place will take more nerve than I usually have and that's quite a bit. And, believe me, I'd never consider it if you weren't going along with me." She shivered with excitement. "Can we amble in quietly and take a secluded booth? They have some, don't they?"

"They do, and you wouldn't believe what goes on in those!" Martha turned serious. "Are you really sure about doing this, Lizzie? Your husband is rather well known. Wouldn't he be upset if word got around?"

"He's a pretty hip guy. I don't think he would. I hadn't planned to tell him about it, though I don't usually keep secrets from him." She frowned. "Maybe he'd think we'd be in danger. Would—will we be, Martha?"

"No, not really. It's just a sleazy dive. Not one that a society maven like you would ever frequent, however. Or a respectable professional nurse either, for that matter."

They settled to enjoy the rest of the afternoon, choosing, or rejecting, items of suggestive clothing to wear.

CHAPTER 30

About ten, dressed in the outfits they'd discussed previously, the two women ventured out. Lizzie, literally poured into skinny jeans and slinky black low-necked top, drove her black and shiny new Porsche, while Martha, in a skirt that barely covered the essentials, wore her slutty boots, topped off by a raging red buccaneer style loose flowing blouse. She felt the absolute picture of sleaze.

The two laughing, fun-seeking women pulled into the parking lot of the infamous Paradisio and edged into the smoke-filled night club with mounting tenseness and trepidation. The music blared loudly, and dancers gyrated about the dance floor with the ever present strobe lights transforming then into comic, riveting figures.

"Liz, I feel like an absolute slut, dressed this way!"

Unable to take her eyes off the dancers, Lizzie had to be pulled into their booth. "I know for sure now, I've been here before this, and more than once," Martha said into her ear. "This place looks and smells way too familiar."

"What a dive it is to be sure, Martha. And what dancers! Ye Gods, this is better than the movies." Lizzie giggled. "And by the way, dear, you are dressed rather appropriately."

A waiter-waitress moved up to take their order.

Later, sipping their drinks, Lizzie asked, "What was our waiter?"

"Who knows, could be anything or anybody in this place."

After about an hour of smoke, noise and intently watching the dancers, Martha saw Jake come in and take a seat at the bar. She nudged Lizzie. "Oh, Lordy, there's that guy from work, the biggest mouth around. It'll get out, I was in here. But why do I get the feeling he's seen me in here before, but not dressed the same? Not only that, but seeing him in here makes me nervous. He'll blab it all over the hospital if he spots us."

Lizzie was too absorbed in the scene and didn't answer. Martha slid back further into the shadows of the booth, trying to remember, and hoping Jake hadn't spotted her. He did appear to search for someone. His gaze traveled over the entire scene frequently as he sipped a pale golden beer. The icy suds dripped down the sides of the frosty glass as well as from the corners of his mouth. It was just after 11:30 p.m. He wore his work uniform so she knew he'd come off an evening shift.

Moments later, a big, tall, older man entered, accompanied by a motley clutch of low-life-appearing men resembling a scene from a mobster movie. Shivering as a sudden chill passed through her, Martha knew she'd seen that man before. Handsome in a heavy, sinister way, he exuded power in his walk and commanding manner. He wore an expensive, well cut, dark charcoal, almost black, silk suit. Pale blue eyes, startling in a man so darkly tanned, searched the place with furtive glances. An angry, scowl seemed permanently etched across his features. Before selecting a table for the group, he moved about, cruising through the crowd and looking into booths as he passed.

"See that big man, Lizzie. I know him! I know him somehow." Martha pressed her body as far back into the booth as possible. "I don't know why, but he's looking for me!"

Lizzie's face had gone white "He's one fascinating dude, Martha, but God, he looks *dangerous*! What makes you think he's hunting for you? What have you done, now?"

"Well, I'm not completely sure, but I ran into him in here before, and it didn't go well, to say the least."

Memories of the man crowded into her consciousness. Involuntarily, she shrank back, put her elbows on the table, and held her arms up to conceal her face as the man passed their booth. When she inhaled his cologne, the scent of it sank into her consciousness and she remembered him fully.

He stopped, looked intently past Martha's arms and fully into her face. "Haven't I seen you in here before, lady?"

Martha shook her head and shrugged slightly in answer to his query. "I don't believe so. I've never been here before tonight."

Inwardly, the blood in her veins had turned cold. She knew him. His forcefulness, his deadly temper, and that she'd rammed her knee into the man's groin and left him in a crumpled heap, lying on the dance floor.

She knew her life lay in mortal danger if he recognized her. Waiting, outwardly calm, she hoped and prayed he'd pass them by.

"Well, you look damned familiar to me. Who are you?" His voice commanded, his gaze intensified, as he faced her.

"I'm Martha Lavery, and I've never seen you before, sir." She held her tone even and clipped, hoping her terror didn't show. Her clenched fists, hidden beneath the table, shook and trembled. She kept them out of sight, praying he wouldn't notice how stricken she was.

Lizzie sat in frozen silence, her lips pale and tight. Her face wore the pallor of a ghost.

Scowling, he nevertheless appeared to be satisfied with her answer. "You remind me of someone I'd like to meet again. Pardon the intrusion, ma'am."

He nodded and walked on. Martha watched to see if he left The Paradisio. He didn't. She saw him join his men at one of the tables near the dance floor.

She remembered him, and the fine quality of his cologne, that seductive essence. What was it? Like that made any difference. This evil man wanted her dead for what she'd done to him.

Lizzie, seeing Martha's ashen features, whispered, "Who was that? And what's happening? He's one scary dude. You *know* that man?"

"Lizzie, that man wants to kill me for what I did to him as Serena. He made her get up and dance when she didn't want to, and she gave him the knee right on the dance floor. I, Serena, or whoever the hell I was, left him lying, there groaning like a baby, and escaped out the door. Ran out of here like a scalded cat. Didn't know who he was, only that he was bad news. "She hid her face in her trembling hands. "God help me."

Lizzie looked frightened as she glanced furtively about the bustling establishment. "Martha, we've got to get out of here!"

"We can't just cut and run, Lizzie. He'll be watching. He may yet realize I'm the woman he's after, and if he does, I'm dead. He'd as soon kill me as look at me if he believes I'm the one." Martha looked at Lizzie. "Now, just sit tight and pretend we are relaxed and enjoying ourselves. Maybe that'll throw him off. I don't know what else we can do." She forced a tight laugh and raised her glass.

Lizzie did the same. "Okay Martha, or is it Serena? We wanted excitement, but this much? What a night! Just tell me what to do. I'm beginning to think you're definitely the right person to handle this mess. Who are you, really?"

"I don't know who I am just now, but instinct is all we have to go on tonight." She tried to laugh. "I still won't dance with that man if he comes over and asks, and he might." Her face burned yet felt like it was packed in ice. She sat up straight and squared her shoulders, a newly-found strength and determination had crept in.

Jake spotted them and sauntered over. "Maybe I should sit here with you two, for a spell. You seem to have attracted some unwelcome attention with Imperato over there." He indicated the man with a slight nod, and added, "Martha, have you ever been in here before?"

"Why no, Jake, we just came out of curiosity. Come and join us for a while, if you like." Martha hoped she'd played it cool. "Meet my friend, Lizzie. We just wanted to see what goes on in a sleazy dive like this." She gave a tight laugh and moved farther back to make room for him. "Do you know that man who stopped here a minute ago?"

"Hi ya, Lizzie," Jake stuck out his hand. "Yeah, that's Charles Imperato, the guy who got it in the balls big time from some overdressed chick in here a while back. He's madder'n hell and he's been in here several times looking for her. I'd hate to be in her shoes if he ever gets hold of her. They say he's a mean son-of-a-gun to deal with, especially for a woman." His chest swelled with importance as he filled them in. "Likes to play rough with the ladies,"

"How scary," Martha said. "What a horrible guy! I'd sure hate to be in that woman's shoes."

She relaxed a bit, even began to enjoy herself, and Lizzie loosened up as well. The music suddenly blared wildly again, and the dancers went at it full bore. The three of them sat in fascination, watching the jerky, rhythmic, effects of the strobe lights on the tight, rhinestone studded clothing, skin-tight shiny pants, and loose flowing skimpy tops, adding flair to the snaky movements as they moved to the music. The flashing lights beneath the dance floor added an insane magic to the spectacle. The music was catchy, but Martha pretended she'd never heard it before. "Must be a genre I've never listened to."

Lizzie laughed. "Wow, look at them go at it. It's all worth it, just to see something like that. Makes the country club set look like sleep walkers." She'd forgotten her fears and gotten into the wild, erotic, flow of The Paradisio.

Martha saw her body moving to the rhythm of the music and heard her laughing in joy. But Martha forgot nothing. When she heard the heavy sounds of men moving into the booth just next to them, her sense of alarm rose to astronomical heights. Their conversation was muffled, but as the odor of *his* special cologne wafted into her senses, her heart nearly stopped in her chest. She had to figure her next move. *He's right behind me! That monster's not giving up and I'm right here in his sights! Serena, what have you done to me?*

"So, Martha, when you working again?" Jake asked, not realizing her paralyzing terror. He finished his beer and signaled to the waiter for another round for all of them.

"Maybe I'll take a couple shifts this weekend. I've been so busy these days it seems hard to find the time." She tried to sound normal, hoping Jake saw nothing unusual in her behavior. "I need to work enough to keep my hand in—makes for good practice."

"Worked any more psych, lately?"

"Not if I can help it. The last time was too much for me. We'll see that poor woman again though, married to her wonderful, Jimmy. Can you believe it? She couldn't wait to get home to him!" She shuddered, thinking of Jean M.'s severe injuries. "I'll never understand that, never!"

"You take things too much to heart, Martha. Can't let stuff bother you that way." Jake remembered the purple spots on her arms that night, but decided not to mention them. Maybe when he worked with her, he would. He remembered the exotically clad woman he'd seen before, tried to see Martha that way, but couldn't. Who the woman had been, remained a mystery. Jake stayed a few more minutes, finished his next beer, and said good night. "See you at work, Martha."

After a time, Martha whispered to Lizzie, "When it gets busy and really noisy again, say it out loud so they can hear you, how you need to visit the little girl's room. It's near the door, so move outside from there and get into your car. When you don't come back, I'll come looking for you and we'll make our get-a-way. I can't take any more of this place."

Lizzie nodded. Shortly after that, she chatted up a storm and then said, "Oops, gotta visit the powder room, back in a few." She edged out and sailed toward the flower decked, *'Le Femme'* sign, as it was called.

Martha watched her go and finished a bit more of her drink. Lizzie edged slowly out of the place. If Imperato watched, Martha had no idea, but she prayed he hadn't. The men in that booth had kept rather silent, which only added to her fears. *What'll I do if he tries to dance with me again?*

After about fifteen minutes, she decided to look for her friend. Getting up, she sauntered toward the *'Le Femme' sign.* Entering, she found a good spot to take a look at the booth behind hers. The men, including Imperato, seemed to be in deep conversation at the moment. "Good, I'll slip out. Hope they're not talking about me." The thought added to her caution as she slipped to the door.

Outside, in the fresh, cold night air, Martha hurried to Lizzie's car idling nearby and hopped in. "Thanks, girl, I think you just saved my life!"

"Well, we've had our exciting night out! One I could forgo doing again for the rest of my life!" Lizzie's agitation and fear made her reckless. She swerved to get back in her lane. "That alter of yours will get us killed, woman! Look how I'm driving!"

Martha finally noticed. "Take it easy, Lizzie. Maybe we gave him the slip, but thanks to Jake's big mouth, the man knows where I work. I'm afraid I haven't seen the last of him." Martha looked behind them. Nothing followed that she could see. "If I have a police detail on me, right now, I wouldn't mind it. I don't see anyone, so maybe not."

During what remained of the night, Martha found she couldn't sleep. Instead, she wandered about her snug home, that safe and secure haven, realizing with cold reality that she'd never be safe again with a man like Charles Imperato trying to find her. *I should hop the next plane out of here, that's the only chance I've got to stay alive!*

CHAPTER 31

Martha shivered uncontrollably. *Oh Bob, I need you as never before!*

He hadn't phoned or said anything that would let her know where she stood with him. It left her feeling lost. Pacing past the phone, she saw the insistent light blinking. "Oh, maybe he called me after all!" She grabbed up the receiver and pressed the play-back button. Jeannie had called, saying they'd found a house north of Denver in a great neighborhood. She tried to be excited for her daughter but, in her own despair, couldn't manage it.

Then, she heard Bob's deep, resonant voice, reaching out to her in her despair. "Martha, I must see you again, we need to talk." He chuckled softly. "Yes, Martha, *just* talk. Give me a call. Believe me, I don't care what time it is."

She needed no further encouragement, and with numbed, excited fingers, pressed the numbers. "Hello, Bob."

"You're home. Finally. Stay there. I am on my way over."

Martha hung up and did a happy dance. "He's on his way over!" She ran to the bathroom, showered, and hurriedly changed her overdone make-up and clothes. "His opinion of me wouldn't improve a bit seeing me in that sleazy get-up." Smoothing her drying hair and lounging clothes, she waited with a heart racing so hard it made her breathless.

At the sound of his truck, she ran to the door and let him in. He said nothing, just reached for her, crushed her in his arms and covered her face with wild, passionate kisses. He bent her backwards and ravished her mouth with a hot, passionate fever that quickly turned her into a frantic mass of wanting.

"Is this your idea of talk?" she gasped, trying to catch her breath.

"Yeah, it is." He reached for her again. "I can't help this." He clutched onto her like a drowning man. "I need you, girl."

Nothing verbal would be settled, not just now anyway. The effect of his advances took its toll on her, and with her own passions madly aflame, she was powerless. She did nothing to stop his wild love making, nor did she want to.

Bob had cast some sort of spell over her, a wonderful, magical aura of passion she'd never known in her life or even imagined possible. She forgot everything and let herself go. If there existed anywhere a cure for her problems, this wasn't it, but somehow, the wild ecstasy of it seemed to help immensely. She pulled him into her bedroom. "Let's talk in here."

Later, lolling in the soft languor of fully satisfied passions, Bob raised his head and laughed out loud, an exalting, joyous, crowing sound. "Woman, what have you done to me?" He looked into her eyes. "Never in my life have I known what we have together." He cleared his throat. "Martha, I don't give a damn in hell what you've done, or who you've done it to. I only know I can't let you go. I'll never let you go!"

"Oh, Bob, I feel that way, too. I loved Chet and mourned the loss of him for a very long time, but we had nothing like this."

"Maybe we ought to get married—wouldn't you think?" Grinning broadly, he grabbed her and crushed her warm body against his. "So, what do you say, girl?"

"I'd love to marry you. But I think I should get my mental mess cleared up first, don't you?" She looked into his eyes. "Bob, I love you like I never dreamed I would ever love any man. I never thought I could." She shook her head to clear her thoughts. "You're a miracle in my life."

"That settles it then." He lay back, gazing around at her bedroom. "You have a nice home here," he mused, his voice dreamy soft. "Where would we live? It'll be your choice all the way."

Martha knew she should mention her newest debacle of Imperato. *What if it was the last straw for him?* Fear of losing him all over again held her back. She could only answer, "Anywhere with you would do for me, but I just found out my daughter and family, are moving north of Denver. I had thought to relocate somewhere within an easy distance so I can see them and Will. He's not doing so well in some areas. I take him to Biggie's Burgers and, little as that seems, it has helped in several ways."

She didn't want to get into Will's problems and couldn't bring herself to speak of the Charles Imperato threat. She should let him know of that, but the magic of tonight was too wonderful to be destroyed by such a subject.

"If you want to move close to them, I have no objections. My daughter will visit me wherever I live." He snuggled close against her and, holding her in his arms, dropped off into a deep sleep.

Martha lay awake. *Just when real happiness is within reach, I'm hunted by the police and now, an overbearing criminal who wants me dead!* Hot, burning tears flowed down her cheeks as she lay beside the best man she'd ever known, contemplating her own cruel death at the hands of a man she'd never heard of until a few weeks ago. *How on earth can I tell Bob this new threat?*

Spending long, miserable, years behind bars for clipping the *cajones* off a couple of pedophiles had become a definite possibility. She gritted her teeth. "After his silences when I told him the things I had done as Serena? I can't," she whispered into the darkness of her room. She needed to tell him everything, but she couldn't, not yet. *Oh God, please, not yet!* She wanted and needed this bit of happiness, stolen or not.

❧❧❧

Ryan called his newest surveillance officer in for a conference. Carla Martino entered quietly. Her small, slim figure, and dark features appeared wraith-like as she took a seat opposite Ryan. "Yes sir, you wanted to see me?"

"How's it going in the Martha Lavery case?"

"Puzzling, to say the least. She hasn't *made* me, not yet anyway, but the things she does are contrary to the type person we believe she is, a model citizen, grandmother, and educated practicing nurse."

"How do you mean? What are you seeing? Where does she go?" Ryan already knew the woman under surveillance to be a very real puzzle. One he'd like to unravel. If Martha Lavery was his *vigilante*, what would cause a woman like her to take that kind of vengeance?

"I saw her and a friend dressed like a couple of street walkers visit The Paradisio for one thing. That's not the sort of place one would expect a woman like her to frequent. Not a professional nurse, certainly. But as a suspect, her conduct could be almost anything, couldn't it?" Carla wore a quizzical expression across her small, petite features. "A point of interest, sir, this big dude went past her booth and came back to question her. I saw real fear come over her and her friend. In time they managed to slip out. It was an escape, plain as day." She frowned. "I asked a couple of questions. That big dude was Charles Imperato. What do you make of that?"

"Damn it all to hell! That *is* news, Carla. I'll get that sorted out ASAP. She's not the type to associate with a man like that. I'm damned sure of that. I don't know enough about her, but he isn't the sort to be in her radar."

"She's got a male friend, too," Carla added. "And things seem very active in that area, as well." She smiled. "The guy spent last night with her, anyway."

Ryan knew if she was his *vigilante*, an assault against a child might have to take place before she'd take action again. Now her personal life had taken on a whole new dimension with the addition of Imperato. *What's that all about?* "What the hell's going on with that woman? No other criminal activity so far?"

"Nothing at all. I've only been on her tail for a couple of days, but I'll keep you posted. I am alternating with Helen

Markham, so she doesn't get a line on us. Helen's very good, Ryan."

"You bet she is. Okay, thanks. Good work." He motioned for her to leave and, as Carla slipped out, the light on his intercom lit up. "Yeah?"

"Jake Collins is here to see you, sir."

"Really? Okay, send him in."

Jake sauntered in and took a seat. In spite of the self-important look on his face, he looked uncomfortable and kept his head a bit too low for Ryan's liking. *I get the feeling 'that he's a damned snitch.* He'd never held that type in high esteem. *But maybe he'll say something worthwhile.*

"Well, Jake, the receptionist said you might have some information for us, that right?" The man squirmed a bit. *Feeling guilty for ratting out an acquaintance, are we*? Ryan wondered.

"Well, maybe. I work at the hospital, Mercy, as you know. I met you there in the ER one time. You asked for any information about those purple stains, if anybody knew anything about that." His chest expanded noticeably. "I've seen those stains on one of our nurses, twice, in fact."

Ryan's gut instinct told him he'd mention Martha. "So, tell me everything you can about the circumstances and definitely the timing. Who you saw the spots on? Could be something."

Jake immediately puffed up with his own importance. Ryan actually saw him relax and become comfortable as he began his story.

"There's this nurse, Martha Lavery, by name, an older broad. Usually don't pay the older ones much mind, but twice I saw her with these spots on her arms. She'd used some kind of make-up to disguise them, but you could see them plain as day. The second time was when we were working in psyche. She reached for some stuff and when I noticed them, I asked her how she got 'em. She said she didn't know, maybe from work, or the lab. Seemed kinda fuzzy about it, like she really didn't remember. But she hadn't been around any lab stuff that I saw."

"Anything else about this Martha Lavery you thought unusual?"

"Well, one night, I saw her go ballistic at a shriveled up old man dying of cancer. That's not like her either. She's usually a real kind nurse, you know, all touchy-feely." He drew a deep breath. "Anyway, this one night, she ran out of that room and nearly knocked me over. Never even saw me—I know she didn't." He straightened in his chair. "Then I thought I saw her in The Paradisio one night dressed like a hooker. She wore leather, spike-heeled boots nearly up to her ass, skin tight leather clothes, and enough make-up for three women. I wasn't sure it was Martha back then, or even now, but I wasn't the only one who questioned that."

Ryan felt unreality creeping in at how clearly Jake described Martha's activities. After what Carla had just told him, he knew it was true.

"Well, anyway," Jake continued. "It was that same night this overdressed broad gives the knee to Charles Imperato. I'm sure you know who that dude is. Looked like he forced her out on the dance floor against her will and she got ticked off. She decked him and left him doubled up and groaning on the floor. Ran out of the place like a scalded cat."

Jake shook his head. "Damn sure wouldn't want to be in that woman's fancy high-heeled boots! Imperato's been in there several times since that night, looking for her. He's after her for what she did to him, especially in public, that way. He wouldn't be one to tolerate being made a laughing stock." Jake blew out his breath. "If it *was* Martha, she's in one hell of a mess!"

He sighed. "She came in there the other night with a friend, and I knew for sure it was her this time. Both were dressed up some, but not the way I saw her the other time. Imperato came in and looked around like he has a lot of other nights. He spotted Martha, stopped at her table, and must have asked her something. I saw her shaking her head. I don't think Imperato was convinced because he kept looking at her, even moved into the next booth. If she knows who he is, she outta be scared shitless of him. A guy I know was there and saw it, too. The gals managed to sneak out and left in a hurry. We heard tires squealing as they drove away."

"You say you believe Imperato may be looking for her?" Ryan frowned. "That's not good news. She'll be in a hell of a lot of trouble if that's true." He shifted in his chair. "He knows where she works, you say?"

"Yeah, I guess that's my fault. I sat with them for a while and we talked about it. I told her a little about him, but I'm not sure she understands the danger. Should I warn her? What do you think?"

"We'll take care of that. I've recorded all you've said here today, and when it's ready, we'll have you sign the write up. We might need you as a material witness, and your testimony in court one of these days." Ryan indicated it was time for Jake to leave. As the door closed behind him, he picked up the phone and punched a number. "Yeah, Harris, got a minute?"

"What you got, Ryan? You sound a little worried."

"Just get your ass in here."

Harris was quick to reach Ryan's desk.

"That fool woman has got herself in a real mess, now." Ryan quickly told Harris what he'd heard about Martha and the drug lord. "She needs *protective* surveillance now. If Imperato finds out where she lives, she'll be in deep shit. He isn't sure she's the woman who decked him, but he's sniffing around."

Ryan sobered considerably as he changed his subject. "Harris, we have positive DNA evidence taken from those hair ribbons we found at the Denny Garver place. That bastard murdered a young girl, six years old, in Memphis about five years ago, and we just got another positive ID from Dallas. He's got a deadly record and it spans about twenty years or more. He must have started in his late teens. He's what? About forty-five now? I wonder how many more there'll be. We got a lot of it from the trophy ribbons the man couldn't bring himself to part with." He shook his head. "Damn it to hell, Harris, we needed this *vigilante*, years ago!"

"God, Ryan, it makes me sick to hear that, but he's headed for death row with what we've got on him now. I wonder how his lawyer will plead this case. Got himself a hotshot law-yer right off. I suppose they'll beg for mercy in his case be-cause poor Denny had an abusive father, a mean dog, or what-ever the hell else they can drum up to save a pig like that. And he'll only face an easy, painless shot in the arm twenty years from now after all the hearings, appeals, and other bullshit."

"Bitter, are we?" Ryan knew the situation as well as any man on the force. "Hell, Harris, what do we do about Martha? Even if she is our *vigilante*, we'll need to protect her. How do you suppose we go about that without telling her what we know?" He held his hands out in question. "We'll double our tail on her, that's for sure. Have Carla alerted about what we know of Imperato's bunch, just in case. She could be in dan-ger, too, just doing the tail."

"Gotcha. We're going to be busy from now on."

Harris left the office and Ryan thought seriously of call-ing on Martha for an in depth interview. He knew damned well she wouldn't talk and he didn't have enough concrete evidence to force the truth from her.

CHAPTER 32

Again, Bob hadn't called for a couple of days. Unable to understand his reasons for not contacting her, Martha felt alone, isolated, and threatened. The feeling came over her much too easily, anymore. But then the phone rang and caution took over. She carefully glanced at her caller ID before daring to answer. Seeing it was Lizzie, she picked up.

"Yes, Liz, what's up?" she said, trying to sound upbeat. Lizzie had her own life to live and Martha had burdened her too much already.

"Not much. I just called to see how you were."

"I have to tell you the latest. Guess who proposed?"

"Who? What? Bob proposed? Spill, girl!"

Martha laughed. "Okay, just come on over, and keep a look out.

"A what?"

"Oh never mind, just get over here. I'm not working this afternoon and my time's my own."

She couldn't mention being watched, wanting to enjoy her afternoon with Lizzie. She needed this friend now more than ever in her overburdened stress.

She met Lizzie at the door, and glanced hurriedly about the streets before closing it. A woman rode past on a motor cycle, but nothing else moved.

"Hey, Liz, good to see you."

"What's the big news? You're saying Bob wants to marry you now, after his long silences. Have you talked any of this out?"

"That's the real trouble. We haven't. We've hardly said a word. He doesn't take time for talking, just grabs me and heads for the bedroom, saying he can't live without me. The man's hardly in the door before he goes into action!" Martha flushed. "Not only that, he hasn't a clue about that big guy, the one who wants me dead. I just can't tell him. I'll lose him all over again. Liz, what'll I do?"

"I don't know what to tell you, but I wonder how much deeper you're going to dig that hole for yourself?" Lizzie queried. "You'll be very lucky to pull out of this with your life, if that big guy's after you."

"It's not a hole I dug for myself. It's what that scrawny, dying monster, lying there in our hospital did to me years ago that started it all, and of course, that damned Fred Callahan."

"Dying monster? What are you talking about, now?"

"I didn't tell you that part. I've seen the predator that ruined a year of my life, the actual pedophilic monster from my childhood. Lizzie, he's a patient in my hospital!"

"No, you didn't tell me that! You've seen him?" Lizzie's fine features twisted with revulsion. "What'd you do? Fix him, too?"

"No need. He's an old, withered, dying wretch now. He's got cancer, and for him, even that's not good enough. He's terminal, and his dying can't come soon enough or hard enough." Martha took a deep breath. "I was in shock at first, but then this terrible rage came over me. It's never been like me to feel such anger generally. But toward him, why not? I don't know if he heard me, but I told him I hoped he suffered every kind of torture there was. Then I ran out of the room and nearly knocked that blabber-mouth Jake right off his feet. Never even saw the guy." Martha shook uncontrollably by the time she finished speaking. "Oh, God, I can't stop this shaking!"

"My God, Martha! You poor woman, no one could blame you for feeling that way!"

"Not if they knew the terrible reasons behind my rage, but they never will, Lizzie. I'd never let that out, never."

"Here, have a coffee. I don't know what else I can do." Lizzie got her a cup and held out a sweet. "Here, have a biscotti, too." She saw Martha loosen up and start to laugh. "Good, I knew that'd help."

"You are a dear, Lizzie. I don't how I'd have made it these past few weeks without you." Martha threw up her hands. "So what do I do about Bob?"

"You've got to let him know if you think someone is out to put cement overshoes on you, don't you think?" Lizzie burst out laughing then suddenly sobered. "Here we are laughing like idiots when your life's in jeopardy."

Martha shrugged and they laughed together. "Like Scarlett, I can't worry about that now. I'm sick of thinking about it. I'll think about that tomorrow."

Later in the day as Lizzie prepared to depart, Martha ushered her out and quickly checked about for unusual vehicles on her street. She saw nothing.

Restless, unable to settle down and relax even for a few moments, she picked up the phone, punched in the number for Mercy and took a shift.

త్రిత్రి

Later, Martha pulled into the hospital parking lot and walked into the staffing office.

"Will med-surg be okay this evening?" Angelina asked. Her upturned face, framed by black, curling hair, directed a friendly smile toward Martha. "You haven't been in much lately, glad to have you on tonight."

"That'll be fine, Angelina, thanks." She smiled back at the girl and took the elevator to third. A man entered with her, said nothing, and went on to the third floor. A visitor, she guessed idly, without real thought. Many people populated a busy hospital like Mercy, though mostly during the daylight hours.

She saw Bob's big solid body immediately. He flashed a knowing and friendly grin in her direction. "Hey, girl, working tonight? Not busy enough?"

"Good to see you, Bob." Martha played it cool, refusing to broadcast their affair. Hospitals constantly reeked with personal gossip, and she wanted to avoid it. Time enough if things went right, she thought as she settled in the report room. Bob sat next to her, blissfully unaware that the underworld had been added to her list of terrors.

"So, how's about a snack after?" He asked the question, all cool and casual, but she felt the heat lying beneath that calm exterior. Thinking and remembering the way he could be, set her heart pounding.

Gracie tapped her pen in a rapid staccato right then and started the taped report. As the information hummed along, Martha felt Bob's leg against hers, and her blood raced wildly thinking of their bodies meeting in the dark. He'd never settle for less than he'd had already. She knew that and was grateful for it.

"No rest for you tonight, girl!" he crooned low in her ear.

She flushed and hoped no one noticed. But then she heard the words…"Jean M., room 209, admitted with a fractured pelvis, abdominal hemorrhaging, now under control. Her neuros are poor. She doesn't arouse, pupils not equally reactive. An MRI of her brain has been ordered. If it proves a brain injury, she'll be admitted directly to ICU. She hasn't been taken up there so far as they didn't have a bed," Gracie added. "She doesn't belong on a med-surg ward with her injuries, but ER was so packed, they placed her here for the present. We'll have to watch her closely."

The shock hearing of Jean's admission struck Martha deeply, though she'd expected it to happen again. Jean, her assigned patient, had suffered devastating brutality at the hands of her "darling Jimmy" once again. Martha no longer felt the heat of Bob's presence. Her heart raced, and her anger soared at another cruel act committed against the helpless.

She plotted revenge against Jimmy. But, catching those thoughts, she realized she wasn't like that anymore. *I know better now. I cannot avenge all wrongs.* As she spoke silently to herself, she recognized that other force within her, new, and strange. *Down girl, you're not running my life.* She grinned at her own emerging power, even over Serena. It gave her courage. *I can handle this, I know I can.*

Reaching Jean's room, she saw the patient's violent mate lingering at her bedside, portraying the role of concerned husband. *You phony, battering bastard*! Martha had no time to give Jean any care. She'd arrived as they were loading her on a gurney. Fleeting glimpses of blood-matted hair and a swollen face was all she saw. Jean was barely recognizable. Knotting her fists, Martha watched Jimmy slink along behind the cart containing the pitiable figure of his wife.

Surprising to Martha, his face wore a mask of deep concern. *Why look so sad, Jimmy, you sadistic bastard, afraid of arrest for the assault on your wife?*

Getting a firm hold of herself, she visited the rest of her patients. The figure of a small, casually dressed man, somewhere in his thirties, lingering about the halls, did not worry her. She just figured he was visiting a relative. The shift kept her running, and Jean never returned.

Gracie told her the patient had been transferred to ICU, her condition extremely critical.

"I'm very glad I never trained for those units," Martha replied. "I have enough stress in my life without that place."

Later on, the evening ground to a halt and they moved out of the hospital and into the cool night air. Bob took her elbow and they headed for his truck. "Was that the battered woman you mentioned before?"

"Yes Bob. We knew she'd be back, and she is, fighting for her life. If I were her I wouldn't want to live. But then if I was married to Jimmy, he'd be the one worried. I'd never put up with abuse like that."

"Remind me never to raise a hand to you, woman. No telling what could happen, hey?" He helped her into his truck. "Where shall we go, my darling, where?"

His voice made her forget the trauma she'd seen this evening. Weak with longing, she whispered, "Anywhere with you is okay with me, you handsome devil. What a strong person I am," she added, feeling like a shameless floozy, although she hoped he didn't see her that way. "It's what you do to me."

They entered Bob's home and never left until long after dawn. Outside, Carla kept watch, sitting alone. A long black car cruised past, more than once. She'd set herself for a long, dreary night but the sight of the black car told her that Martha was definitely being stalked by Imperato.

Ryan had forewarned her of this eventuality. In detail, he'd explained how Martha had inadvertently made an enemy of the man and was blissfully unaware of it. Carla had already seen Martha's contact with Imperato during her night out with Lizzie at The Paradisio.

She punched a number on her cell. "Hey, Figueroa, glad you're on tonight."

"Hey there, Carla. What can I do for you?

"Ben, this woman I'm tailing has a suspicious car driving by at intervals. I don't like the feel of it. Got someone available?"

"Sure. I'll send someone right away. Where are you?"

She told him her placement and hung up.

Sure she hadn't been made by the drug people or by Martha, she stayed low. She was known for her competence. People rarely caught on to her surveillance, and she knew when to call for re-enforcements. No heroics for Carla. She remained in the shadows, her motorcycle beside her.

Hours later, Bob drove Martha away in his truck. He dropped her at the hospital to pick up her own car. Martha drove away and Carla saw no other surveillance. "Maybe they've given it up for now."

Martha entered her garage and Carla called for relief. She'd about had it for this segment. Seeing a cycle pass near and move on down the street, she accepted his slight nod, and left.

CHAPTER 33

Martha felt rested, her spirits higher than any time in recent memory. Real happiness seemed within reach. The nights spent with Bob made her feel she'd found something precious. She had a handle on her mental status, too. Even Will seemed to be doing better these days.

"I can't wait to see Dr. Carton. He's really helped me, and I want him to know how well everything is going." She floated about, her feet barely touching the floor as she picked up her phone and called Jeannie.

"Hi Jeannie, I'm coming over."

"What's wrong, Mom?"

"Oh, everything is great. I just want to talk." She hung up, showered, and pulled on jeans and a sweatshirt, the bright green one that always heightened the vivid color of her eyes. Looking in the mirror, she was sure she'd never looked better. "Bob, you wonderful man."

Paying only passing attention to the motorcycle moving along behind her and on down the street, she slowed and turned into the Moulton's driveway. Jeannie met her at the door.

"Mom, what's going on? You're so different this morning."

"Everything is different, Jeannie. I'm in love, for one thing. Bob is coming over to meet you later on today if we can agree on a time." She couldn't stop the elation seeping out in her voice.

"How about dinner, then?" Jeannie hugged her mother. "So, tell me, what else has' got you so up in the air, anyway?" Her deep blue eyes intensified in color as she studied her mother. "I have to say, I'm glad to see it."

"Bob and I are going to be married, Jeannie. And we'll move away from here, too. He said he doesn't care, as long as we're together. We won't be too far from you, I know that much. I have to see your family, especially my dearest little Will." She went on to tell Jeannie something of Bob's losses.

"He sounds really good, Mom. He's known sorrow, too." She grinned. "I can't wait to meet him. Do you realize you've planned marriage with a man none of us have met?" She looked serious for a moment. "And how are you doing with your treatment? Any progress there? Does Bob know about it?"

"He knows everything, which is way more than I've told you. I find it difficult to tell you the rest of it. I know just about all there is to know by now and I'm working on integration. You'll be shocked when I do tell you."

"You'd better do it now, then. I've waited long enough to find out what happened to you as a child, and all the rest of it. Or do I even want to know about it? What do you think, Mom?"

Martha saw doubt and pain cross Jeannie's face, and quickly decided to go slowly with the details. She was so happy within herself, telling sordid details from the past would only dampen everyone's spirits. "All in good time, Jeannie. Bringing up garbage now won't help anyone. So where's Will?"

Martha felt such happiness today, she refused to think of any negatives. In her advanced state of euphoria, there were no clouds on her horizons or troubles waiting.

❧❧❧

Ryan sat at his desk. Carla's detailed report had left him feeling chilled all over. He called Harris. When he appeared, Ryan said. "Our lady is in a hell of a spot and has no idea about it. She's managed to attract Imperato and his crowd. A man came in here and told me some things about Martha that, if true, explain it in part. He thought the woman who decked Imperato looked like Martha, yet he wasn't really sure it was her. Seems Imperato thinks Martha may be that person. In any case, he's got people trailing her. That fool woman can't seem to stay out of trouble."

"They didn't tag Carla, but she called Figueroa in case she needed back-up." Then Ryan remembered another item Jake had mentioned. "Oh yeah, this same guy made a report about finding purple stains on Martha, not once, but twice. I thought that to be very incriminating. Our investigative reports on her indicate a rural background as well." He sighed. "That ties her in with the attacks on the two child molesters, but how does that tie up with Imperato? She'd have had to frequent that sleazy dive, The Paradisio, fairly often and that's not like the Martha we know...Or is it"

"What do you want to do?" Harris asked, worried. "We can't let her get sucked into that mess. It's got to be a case of mistaken identity. She couldn't possibly know a man like Imperato."

"You're right as hell, but unless those thugs move against her, we can only keep watch. One slip and it could be too late if he believes she's the one that gave him the knee in front of God and everybody." Ryan flung his papers off the desk. "Damn it all to hell. We've got to protect our little lady perp. We've got to get ahead of Imperato on this. Find out what's going on with that situation if you can." He laughed. "I'd like to have been there to see Imperato get it, being such a bastard with the ladies and all. Left him groaning right on the dance floor, too."

Harris laughed. "Good for her, if she did it. We'll get extra detail on it and see where it goes from here. We have a guy or two on the inside of that organization. Maybe that'll tell us something."

Harris left the office, and Ryan sat tight for a while before muttering, "I'd sure like to have an in depth conversation with that lady. She despises us and I don't blame her for that, but we may be the best friends that woman has ever had."

సంఘ

Bob and Martha knocked on Jeannie's door. Excitement exuding from Jeannie's glowing, deep blue eyes, she bade them enter.

Martha introduced him around and took him to meet Will. "Will honey, here's a good friend of mine, a very nice man who wants to meet you."

Will looked up at a very big man. His eyes grew large, his face paled, and they both saw the little features tighten with fear at the sight of a strange adult male. His father had shaken hands with this man and welcomed him, but still, the boy hesitated.

Seeing the boy's distress, Bob knelt down to him. "Hi, Will, your Grammy and I are very good friends. She tells me you like to go to Biggie's Burgers. I like those Bittie Meal Bits, myself." He took in Will's Legos and books. "I see you like to build things and read books, too. That's great!"

Will looked up at Martha. "Grammy, is he good, like my daddy?" She heard the tremor of fear in his voice and saw the tight set of his jaw as the little boy tried so hard to be brave.

"Yes, he is. You never need to be afraid of this man, not ever." She punched Bob playfully, and the boy saw Bob's laughing response. "See, he's a big guy, just like your daddy, and a good man like him, too." She stood close to Bob. "He's really nice, Will."

Will shyly held out his hand to Bob, and as he enfolded the little guy's hand in his big paw, she saw the boy relax a bit. It was a beginning.

Jeannie stood back, her eyes shining with unshed tears. "I like him, Mom," she whispered it to Martha then winked at Martin.

The evening went well, and Martha enjoyed a glow of happiness denied her for so long. Bob chatted with Martin, finding enough manly topics to suit them both. The women frequently heard a roar of masculine laughter during the evening. Bob kept his eye on Martha, too. It gave her the warm feeling of his acceptance in every way, and her family as well.

The pleasant evening ended. It was late when they left, and Bob had only one place in mind. Martha had no objections and noticing nothing but each other, they blissfully moved through the darkened streets. A slight breeze ruffled the shadowed greenery, and intermittent street lights left puddles of light as they passed. Caught up in what seemed an eternity of waiting, in their anticipation of having each other, they failed to notice the long, shiny limo, sliding along, far behind them. In her happiness, Martha didn't care anymore, and Bob had no reason to suspect an evil surveillance or the protective shield of the police.

Their night together passed without incident, and Martha returned home later the next morning. As Bob left her off, she noticed a long, black car sliding around the corner. Alarm bells rang in her mind and her face paled as memories of the big man at The Paradisio came flooding into her mind.

"Martha, what's wrong? You're very pale all of a sudden." Bob nudged her. "I wasn't that bad, was I?"

"Oh it's nothing. I just wondered about something. I just saw a car around here I've never seen before, and I'm still jumpy about everything, in spite of the fine care you take of me." Martha blushed at her own thoughts. But she still felt a guilty reluctance in telling him about her mix-up with a man like Charles Imperato.

She feared Bob would misunderstand something like that, and she'd lose him all over again. He'd overlooked a monumental amount of faults in her already. Remembering his initial shock when he'd learned of Serena's activities, she feared he couldn't handle knowing one more thing. Besides, what did she know for sure? She'd told the man, Imperato, she wasn't the woman he sought.

"Well, sweetheart, I'm on duty tomorrow afternoon. Are you working?"

"Could be. Might be fun. Maybe I'll call in and take a shift. Are you in med-surg?" Satisfied by his affirmative nod, they kissed a long goodbye and she let him go with a soft, throaty, "I love you, Bob."

CHAPTER 34

The next afternoon, Martha sang beneath her breath as she showered. Dressed in her latest scrubs, the ones with baby elephants tumbling about over each other, she readied herself for another shift. She was careful with her make-up. She didn't want to look too racy for the workplace and consciously quelled her more outrageous instincts as they arose—the ones she attributed to Serena, understanding this as part of the integration process.

Daydreaming as she drove to the hospital and listening to pop music on her radio, she slammed on her brakes to avoid the big black car that suddenly swerved in front of her. Just as she was about to open her door to get out and give that inconsiderate jerk a piece of her mind, a darkly dressed man slid up to her car and tapped on the window.

Martha slid it down and asked, "Yes, what's wrong?" She decided to hold her tongue. He didn't look like just any man. He had narrow eyes and a twisted sort of mouth. His frame, scrawny and thin, had the wiry look of a jockey.

He growled at her. "Someone wants ta see ya'. Come on, get out." He motioned for her to get out of her car. He repeated the request, his mouth set in a firm line. "C'mon, lady, get outta the car."

"Sorry mister, I'm due at the hospital. My shift starts in twenty minutes, and you're holding me up. I have to get going." She knew instinctively this bird cared nothing for her wishes or any plans she might have. He had his own agenda, and his determination to see it through was evident on his face. She took a deep breath. "Please sir, move your car, if you will. You're making me late!"

Behind her, an older blue car had pulled snugly against hers. They had her trapped! If she put her car in reverse, it would go nowhere. Puzzled, she asked, "What's going on here?"

"Do as I say, ma'am, and no one's gittin' hurt, got it?" He jerked her car door open, and grabbed her elbow. "Come on, no fuss now." Small he might be, but his strength made up for any other lack he might have had. He jerked her to her feet, rudely pulled her to the long, black limo, and shoved her into the back. Parked in front of her car, it had effectively blocked any other escape route. Martha slid over into the middle rear seat and Mr. Skinny sat across from her.

"Where—where, are you taking me?" Her voice, tremulous at best, choked with fear as she realized without a doubt, who wanted to talk to her. Jake had said enough about the man's appetites to forewarn her of what she faced.

The lingering odor of that exotic male cologne, at once familiar, yet strange to her, entered her senses. This was *his* limo! It bore his essence and cologne. *He still believes I'm the one who did him dirty on the dance floor at* The Paradisio. *Can I play this scenario well enough to convince him it wasn't me? My very life depends on what I do now.* She shivered all over as she mulled over what she faced. But by now she'd integrated with Serena enough to know she was the guilty party the man sought.

"You'll know soon enough where you're going, lady. Just keep quiet and sit tight. Better yet, relax and enjoy the ride. There's every kind of drink back here. Help yourself. The boss won't mind a bit if you have a few, likes 'em softened up a bit."

She felt like vomiting.

Another man was sitting in the front passenger seat. His sallow, pock marked face almost had a look of sympathy on it as he watched her sitting in the back, her hands clenched tight together. "Chuck's been huntin' all over for you. Wants a word with you, lady."

Do all criminals look like these low-life misfits? she wondered idly. *What a pair of losers.* She didn't get a look at the driver. These two miserable miscreants were all she'd seen so far.

Martha declined the drink offer and sat stiffly looking out the darkened windows. No one could see her if she pounded on the windows for help. She could see out, but no one could see inside the huge limo. It purred along smoothly, passing city streets with trees, flowers, and clipped lawns. Normal everyday events went on outside this insidious car, while inside it she faced an unknown, fearful peril. It boggled her mind.

The big auto edged upward and upward until finally, she heard massive iron gates creak open to admit the sleek machine. The heavy, confining sound of them clanging shut brought additional fears flooding into her midsection. Icy terror chilled the blood in her veins.

I'll never live to get out of this place. My sins have come home to roost now, big time. I wonder what this dude wants besides my skin in little pieces tossed to those black shiny Dobermans I saw on the way in here. What an isolated, haunting place.

She felt like a character in a dark, brooding, murder mystery, but this was no fictional thing you could walk out of when the scene was finished. It was horribly real and happening to her. *Oh Bob, I'll never feel your wonderful, loving, arms around me again*! A tear escaped and ran down her cheek.

The smooth action of the big limo came to a halt and the pockmarked driver opened the door. He stood there, waiting. "Okay, lady, we're here. Come on, get out."

Martha had no choice but to comply and exited the limo. Standing in front of a massive stone faced mansion, with large windows soaring upward toward many levels of red tiled roofs, she took stock of her surroundings. The landscaping looked lush, with manicured lawns. She saw fountains, and a glimpse of naked statuary caught her eye.

She snorted her disgust at the scrawny, wiry man beside her. "They say crime doesn't pay, but in this case, looks like it does, and very well!"

"Knock it off, lady. He's waitin' inside for you." He took her arm and she walked along, not wishing to be dragged. They mounted two flights of wide flat stone steps and entered between two eight- or ten-foot-tall, heavy, oaken doors. They swung easily, which surprised her. She entered a large foyer with circles of dazzling tiled insets creating a magical pattern before her. *How many people's lives were ruined by the drugs that paid for this palace*, she wondered, her fury rising. *What a lovely, spacious, monument to criminality*!

Her escort ushered her into a large paneled room, with a fireplace glowing and soft rock music emanating from hidden recesses. He left her, exited, and closed the thick, heavy, mahogany door behind him.

Charles Imperato rose from a black leather chair and moved close—uncomfortably close. He folded her hand in his large, cool, long-fingered ones. "Ah, Mrs. Lavery, we meet once again. Welcome to my humble home." He smiled down at her, but she saw no warmth in those very pale blue, glistening orbs. Her blood turned to ice all over again.

Catching his cologne-laden scent, her knees buckled momentarily, but she caught hold of herself and managed to stiffen her body. She answered his welcome, concealing the anger from her voice. "Not by choice, I assure you." "I demand to know what I'm here for, and why!" She wore her best puzzled expression, but she knew full well why she was standing in front of this man. Her dander rose at her situation, and by the intensity of her temper, she knew it came from a source other than her conscious self.

"You demand?" He sniffed. "Lady, I believe you've deliberately lied to me about that night at The Paradisio. I plan to get at the truth, and frankly, I don't care how I do that." He drilled his forefinger into her chest, right up against the ridiculous dancing baby elephants cavorting about on her uniform. His icy blue eyes, so startling in his dark and swarthy face, tended to freeze her thoughts. Her heart nearly stopped its frantic pulsating. The touch of his finger on her chest burned deeply.

"I'm supposed to be on duty at Mercy, sir. I don't know you, or what you're going on about. Speaking of that sleazy place, I'd never been there or seen you before that night when I went there with my friend! We were merely curious about the place, that's all." Martha managed to work up a good bit of anger considering the level of terror she suppressed. She clenched her fists in helpless fury.

"Sounds damned convincing, but I watched the way you walked that night when you made your get-away, same as before, sinuous, like a damned cat slinking along. I'd never forget that. I saw you, lady, I saw you! Don't lie to me about it." He pressed closer. "I don't like lies. What silly game do you play? I'm not a man to be toyed with, especially by a slippery chick like you! Dressed like a damned hooker! What's a man supposed to think?"

Flushed with anger, he shoved her into a nearby chair. Martha knew he planned to make her pay, and pay dearly, for the pain and humiliation of that night. But she saw hesitation in him, too. He wasn't quite as sure as he sounded. *I can use that, somehow.*

She held fast to the chair and scoffed. "I wouldn't think a man like you'd need a hooker anyway. Was that the kind of woman were you looking for?" "You don't look the type to me. With this big house and fancy cars, women must be all over you." Had she gone too far? Something or someone within her had found enough guts to come across belligerent and sassy. "You and you're damned cologne!"

"Say now!" His eyes lit up. "You're not the quiet, mousy chick you pretend to be, are you?" He stood over her, put a hand on her shoulder. "Maybe you've got something I've been looking for." He pulled her up and held her out to face him. "What the hell's your game, lady? There's more to this than what you're giving me here. I knew it when I saw you the first time. You're that same damned cat that decked me that night." He tightened his grip. "Admit it, you bitch, you miserable, fucking, bitch!" A raging anger consumed him, took over and shook him, tightened and filled his mind. It left him trembling and nearly unable to control his actions.

Suddenly, he took a hefty swing at Martha's face. "I'll show you, you goddamned bitch!"

Martha side-stepped his punch and in turn, aimed a solid kick into his midsection with the study work shoes she wore.

He slumped down and doubled over, groaning. "You dirty bitch, that's two times you've kicked me, and don't try to deny it! He spit his scathing words at her. "You did it, didn't you?"

Martha knew, with that kick to his midsection, she'd entered into a fight for her very life. From now on she faced an evil, unimaginable kind of anger.

He was a big man and could easily overpower her. She tightened her resolve, knowing her chance of survival was exceedingly small. *I'm not going down without a fight*!

Groaning, he crawled upright, pulling his gun from a shoulder holster as he moved. Martha aimed a kick at Imperato's gun hand, hitting it with a glancing blow, but somehow, the weapon spun away and landed on the floor. She leaped for it and, grabbing it, quickly turned it on his midsection. "Stay right there, you murdering bastard."

She panted in fear but her hands were steady. "I know you want me dead, but you have no reason. It's not right. I told you that. I don't know you—whoever you are. I don't want to die for some mistaken idea of yours. I want to leave here. Right now!"

Terrified, Martha realized she'd had inner help so far. She silently thanked her other half, for this small, fighting chance. Her eyes searched about wildly. *How can I ever get out of this place*?

൲ഗ൲ഗ

Bob arrived on the med-surg floor and looked for Martha among the staff, but he failed to see her. The others collected report sheets, coffee, sodas, and gossiped while awaiting report. She'd been assigned here, he'd checked on it. Why hadn't she arrived on the floor? Waiting, he got a coffee. A feeling of unease nagged at him until it became a growing concern. Time passed and she still didn't show.

Marcie Bell, the charge nurse this evening, sat ready to begin the taped report, and Bob interrupted her as she started. "Just a moment, Marcie, Martha Lavery isn't here. Shouldn't we wait a bit for her?"

"She'll have to catch up when she gets here. We can't wait around for someone who may or may not show." Her clipped voice told Bob, she had no patience with late arrivals. "If she doesn't show, I'll call staffing for a replacement. We'll have to pick up Martha's load until they send us someone."

The ice in her voice, told Bob he was alone in his concern. "Excuse me, Marcie," he replied. "But I'm worried she may have had an accident. She's never late and never misses an assignment." He stood up. "I'm sorry but I have to make a few calls. I need to know if she's okay." He couldn't hide his worried face from the rest of the staff, nor did he try.

Jake was on this evening as well. He laughed. "Wow, ol' Bob's got it bad for that dame. You know, I've been keeping an eye on those two, knew it all the time." He turned his attention back to his notes, a smug grin on his know-it-all face.

Marcie saw her staff disintegrating before her eyes and stood up. "If you leave this floor now, I'll have to put you on report," she informed Bob.

She obviously meant it, but Bob never bothered with her words in his concern for Martha. He didn't know why he felt so strongly about this, but cold chills of worry had already seeped into his gut. With all she had going on in her life, she was in some kind of trouble. He knew it! "Sorry, Marcie, do what you have to do. Something's very wrong about this and I have to straighten it out. If I can't find out what's happening, I won't be worth having here in any case. I'll let you know."

Bob left the report room and called the police station. He asked the clerk if there'd been an accident. Informed there had been no such report, he felt better, but phoning Martha gave no results either. He called the station again and asked to speak to Ryan Mapus. He knew of him because of Martha's complaints about his questioning her in such detail.

Mapus came on the line. Bob identified himself and said, "I'm worried that Martha Lavery may be missing. She's never late for work and she didn't show for her shift, or call in. She doesn't answer her phone either. I've called her several times with no answer."

"We know," Mapus said. "We had someone tailing her."

Bob felt his face tighten and his hands turn to ice. "Oh God, what are you saying, sir?"

"I'll explain it when I see you. Can I meet you somewhere?"

"Yes, I'll meet you out front of Mercy."

He hung up and returned to the report room. "I hate to have to say it, but Martha may have met with some sort of foul play. She's missing!" In answer to the flurry of hurried questions, he replied. "The detective I talked with is coming to pick me up. I'll see you later. Sorry, Marcie, really!" He ran out and down the stairs, taking no time for the elevator.

Shortly, Mapus pulled up. Bob hurried to the car and got in. They quickly appraised each. "So what do you know, Sir," Bob demanded. "And how do you know it?"

"Actually, those questions are on my mind for you, as well, but I'll go first. Okay, we've had surveillance on your lady, and we know she's had another party tailing her for a couple of days. Somehow she's managed to run afoul of some really bad people." He looked worried, which didn't help Bob's outlook on Martha's situation.

"What do you mean you were tailing her? Another party, the mob, is after her? Why, for God's sake?" Bob felt raw shock hearing Martha had the underworld after her. What more hadn't she told him? He realized she might love him, but she obviously didn't trust him enough to reveal everything. But he really couldn't blame her after his behavior toward her when she'd told him of Serena's activities.

Ryan easily saw that Martha had kept a few secrets from her boyfriend, too. Bob apparently knew nothing of the Imperato deal. "The woman is full of surprises, isn't she?" He hoped he wasn't making personal trouble for Martha, but it was no time to worry over non-essentials. "It seems she's attracted the attention of a rather unsavory character. That happened the other night, when she and a friend of hers, had a night out at The Paradisio, of all places. Ever hear of a man named Charles Imperato?"

"No, can't say I ever heard of him," Bob answered slowly, his gut turned to ice, wondering what else he might learn about his lady love. "What the hell has she gotten herself into, now?" He flung the question at Mapus, afraid to hear his answer.

"It seems a woman looking a lot like your Martha, but dressed like a hooker, as a witness tells it, shoved her knee into this man's groin at The Paradisio one night and ran out leaving him flat out on the floor. She embarrassed the hell out of him and he's been hunting for the poor woman ever since. This crazy fool, whoever she was, had the misfortune to pick on one of our resident drug mobsters, a man without pity and one who likes to play rough with the ladies."

Ryan hesitated then continued. "The other night, she and a friend of hers were in that sleazy dump, just looking the place over, and this mobster comes in looking for that other woman, like he's done several other nights. He went over to Martha and asked her who she was, and had she ever been in there before?"

CHAPTER 35

"My God, that crazy woman!" Bob figured he had known much more than Mapus and now he knew it all. Indeed, he knew the woman who kneed the gangster must have been Martha, but as Serena, out on a prowl. In effect, she'd been both of them. He couldn't tell this story to the police. Martha would have to do that.

He shook his head in wonder at how he'd ever gotten mixed up in this crazy, unbelievable fantasy. That's what it had to be. An insanity. What the hell else could it be? Yet, he felt a bond with her, one he couldn't break, nor did he want to. Martha did it all for him. She was the woman for him, without question.

Mapus looked sick. "I was told she denied ever seeing him before, and eventually the two ladies slipped out without being caught. But, I guess he wasn't satisfied with that. He's been tailing her. Now he's got her, Bob. I'm damned sure of it! That poor woman can't stay out of trouble. I hope to hell we can save her life. Imperato's a devil with the women."

Bob sat there, numb. His hands shook and clenched in helpless frustration. *Damn that crazy woman!* Couldn't trust him enough to believe in him all the way, and tell him the whole truth. No way would he abandon her now. *But if I ever get the chance again, I'll find some kind of lovely torture for that lady!* His mind and heart racing with fear, he asked. "What do we do now? What *can* we do?"

"Our surveillance officer, Carla, was right on her tail. We haven't heard from her, not yet. If she's been made, we're in deep shit!" Mapus looked distraught. "I want to sit that Martha down and have a good heart to heart with her. She's a damned good woman in spite of the things we believe she's done. We want to protect her and we've been trying." He shook his head in frustration. "Now this bastard's gotten in our way. Otherwise, it's a helluva dilemma for our department. The public will be on her side. Do you know what I am referring to, Bob?"

"Like what? What the hell are you running on about?" Bob played dumb on the vigilante subject. No way would he give the police a clue about Martha's mental aberrations. "We've got to find her, that's what I'm worried about." He huffed in desperation. "Her life is in danger, you tell me, yet you're blathering about protecting her! What the hell are you talking about? Let's see some action, for Christ's sakes. I love that woman to death. I've lost one woman and I can't lose another. Certainly not this one, I love her more than my life."

"Okay, I see your point." The radio blared for Mapus. He listened, and then said, "Wish we'd get a blip from Carla. She's our best hope right now." His lips pulled tight. The grimace across his face told of the futility they faced. "Haven't heard a word from her since noon. She knew Imperato had his people tracking Martha. Slick as a cat, Carla is, but these are devils we're dealing with. I'll admit this deal has me worried all to hell, to say the least."

His words did nothing to soothe Bob's sick fear for Martha. Angry at her, yet worried to a standstill, he had to appreciate Mapus asking him along. "Man, I'm glad you asked me to come. Sorry I haven't much to tell you about Martha, except she's damned good people." Peering anxiously out the car windows, he saw that it had grown dark, and his fears only increased. *God, let me find her. Help her through this. I need her.* A tear escaped, but it mattered no longer. She was all he wanted. *Martha, where are you, out in the dark?*

享受

Instinctively, Martha knew, even if she managed to escape him, this evil-minded devil would dog her steps until one of them died. Though desperate, that realization gave her strength. Her mind whirled with wild, panicky thoughts of survival. At the moment, she saw no way out.

Imperato was hurt—and enraged far beyond his control. He now regretted asking his men to stay clear while he dealt with *this* particular woman. What a damned wildcat he'd tangled with. This crazy bitch had the strength of ten and he didn't want to confirm to anyone, especially her, that he couldn't handle the situation.

"Well, well, aren't you something," he said. Looking at the woman spitting fire as she sat before him, he rapidly conceived ideas that filled his mind with sexual heat and, against his will, he felt a grudging respect for her.

In spite of his rage, he admired her gutsy spirit. Cloying, mewling females he'd had a plenty. But one like this was a rare specimen, and she incited his sexual appetite like none other had ever done. His pride demanded that he punish her for the acts she'd taken against him, but he hated having to kill a woman this exciting.

Imagining her spread out in his big, wide bed, he felt himself responding to those thoughts, planning a real nice treat for her. The blood surged into his loins. Now he had a new agenda—an urgent sexual one!

He changed his tone. "Listen, lady, let's not get ourselves in an uproar, here. Why don't we have a friendly chat? You aren't going to make it to work anyway. Sit down and let me fix you a nice cool drink." He smiled at her. "I'm not such a bad guy. A lot of women think real well of me." He turned to a fancy gold emblazoned cart filled with bottles of every kind. "What's your pleasure?"

"I don't care for a drink. I only want to leave this place. Will you please let me go?" she entreated, her voice strong and even. She held the gun steady, still aimed at his midsection.

Then as a whim of curiosity overcame her, she couldn't help asking. "What is the cologne you wear? It's quite good, rather exotic, I've wondered about it."

"Like my *Eroticano,* do you? Comes from Columbia, very rare, very expensive. Got other stuff from there, too, strong stuff, makes women go crazy, hot—wild! How about you come upstairs with me, we'll use it. I've got plenty of time." He moved closer. "Christ! You're the most exciting and entertaining female I've ever met, lady. Our night has just begun, if you catch my drift."

His heavily suggestive overtones sickened Martha and she couldn't miss the massive bulging tumescence expanding in his lower regions.

Sickened to the point of nausea, she glared at him in disgust. "I catch it alright, and I'm not interested," she snarled. "Sir, you scare me to death and you sicken my soul. Those are the only feelings you arouse in me. I'll admit that much." Spitting like an ally cat, she added. "I want to leave your home, castle or whatever to hell you call it. My place is *not* here."

A sick desperation settled over her. If she killed him, she'd never make it past his clutch of henchmen. They were stationed all around his grounds, and she didn't know where she was in any case. But, she decided, being out of Imperato's sick presence would be a start.

Martha longed to see the stars and breathe the clean, fresh air flowing sweetly from the mountains. Would she ever draw a free breath again? How could this have happened? Trapped in this luxurious, opulent, overblown monument to crime with a lecherous beast planning to take erotic delight in her body with all the evil, sexual intentions his criminal mind could envision. When he'd finished with her, he'd have her body casually thrown off the edge of his property, or to the bottom of some deep lake wearing cement overshoes.

Her fearful thoughts filled her with a deadly resolve. When he moved toward her, she brought the gun up and aimed at his gut. "Not so fast. I don't know what to do, but I do *not* plan on further dealings with you!" Staring into his pale, eerie, eyes, she was certain that her own held a deadly glare. "I want out of here!"

In truth, she faced an impasse. The man before her believed she didn't have the guts to kill, and she didn't. But inside herself, she did have what it took. And Imperato had no earthly way of knowing about Martha's inner helper, or the way extreme stress brought that wild creature into action.

CHAPTER 36

Ryan heard a static-filled crackle on his radio. "Yeah?" He got no return voice, nothing. "Yeah, come in. Carla?" He waited. In time, he heard a thin, whispery, voice crackling over his receiver.

"Ryan, sorry to call so late—my radio is acting up. I'm inside their compound. Get a lot of back up; we're going to need it. They have Mrs. Lavery. She's alive for now, but hurry it up. I don't know how long I can escape detection here."

"Carla, you all right for now?" He listened intently, but heard nothing further. Ryan punched his mike. "Get the SWAT team out to the Imperato compound. You know the place, fortress on the hill, and all that," he added. "We've got an agent inside so use extreme caution. They keep several vicious dogs on the loose. You'll need to take care of those, too." He went on to apprise them of Martha's situation, and Carla's as well then he turned to Bob. "This could get damned ugly. Sure you want to be here for it?"

Bob nodded. "Hell yes, and if I get the chance, I'll work that Imperato bastard over with these." He balled his fists and held them out. "I'd count myself lucky to paste that sick son-of-a-bitch." His voice was quiet but full of meaning. "I hope she's okay, Ryan. Your agent said she was?"

"Yeah, me, too. And yes, she's okay for now." Ryan, impressed with Martha's ability to inspire love and loyalty in her friends, said nothing more. Talk would add nothing for either of them as they advanced into position. In their fight to save

Martha, he drove closer to the compound and pulled over. He'd ordered no flashing lights, no blaring sirens.

"The SWAT team is deploying as we speak. They'll knock the dogs out quick enough with tranquillizer bullets, using silencers, so no problem there." He got out of the cruiser to consult with several men dressed in dark clothing. He waved his hand toward the mansion and came back to the car. "All set, we're going in."

They left their vehicles and slowly moved out, working closer to the great stone edifice soaring above them, so beautifully covered with interlacing vines, and shining with soft lighting. It gave off a rather ethereal glow. "Nice place, eh?" Ryan whispered. "Crime sure as hell pays for some of these big mobsters. We've never pinned as much as a parking ticket on that slippery devil up there. Not a damned thing!"

"That drug bastard has over stepped himself, tonight. Kidnapping my woman is the last straw! If you guys don't get him, I may have to," Bob replied, keeping his voice quiet and barely believing the crazy bravado in it. "After all that's happened in our world, I understand the need for these vigilante types. After tonight, I think more people need to take care of these fiends on their own. I feel that way, Ryan, and I never thought I would." He paused then added. "I see how your hands are tied with all the lawyers and political correctness, and such, but it really hurts and angers the ones who lose protection because of it. And lately too many of those people are us."

"Jeez, Bob, down boy! We aren't that bad, are we?" Ryan grimaced. "Looks like this case has got you tied up in a thousand ways. Settle down man, or I'll have to send you back to the patrol car. We can't have a mad man running loose," he added softly. "But, you're damned right about a lot of it."

"Okay, I get it." Bob winced at his own outburst, knowing he'd been greatly influenced by Martha's frequent tirades against the injustices to her family regarding the crime against her grandson, Will.

Ryan called a halt to their advance and listened to his small radio a moment. "Carla called again. She's close to the action and will give a whistle if all hell breaks loose." He turned to Bob. "Really man, you need to head back down. I should never have allowed you to get this far. We can't endanger civilians like this. They'll have my hide as it is."

"I'll have your hide if you try to send me anywhere," Bob hissed and kept moving upward. "I'll be responsible for myself. Just get her the hell out of that bastard's place!" Nearing the fence, they saw two black Dobermans, stretched motionless on the grass. Bob whistled softly, but the dogs didn't stir. "They've been immobilized, thank God for that little favor," he muttered, thoughts of Doberman teeth tearing into his leg filling his mind.

"The fencing's been cut. Let's go, but easy does it." Ryan worked his way through the jagged edges of the severed chain-link fencing and edged slowly toward the house. Bob followed closely behind.

They heard nothing, and that made him uneasy. The place had an eerie atmosphere to it and the feeling sank into his mind. He hated knowing Martha was held a captive somewhere in the frightening recesses of a place so threatening and sinister, and with a man known for his cruel ways with women. He feared for her, and prayed for God to look after her because he couldn't. Fretting about it tore him apart.

Suddenly, they heard popping sounds within the huge mansion. The sound, dulled behind thick, ornate masonry and stone walls, meant some kind of action had occurred, and they feared the worst. They saw men running headlong into the front entrance, guns drawn, to disappear through the massive door that stood hanging agape. After that, Bob saw some of the SWAT team running into the building. They heard more muffled shots and saw men surrounding the outside. Ryan, his gun drawn, entered the gaping maw of the mansion, with Bob right behind him.

~∽∾~

In the ornate library, Martha's heart pounded as Imperato moved toward her. His purposeful mien meant he'd reached the end of his patience and was closing in. He grabbed her arm. "Come, my dear, we have the night ahead, and I'm sure as hell not letting something like you get away from me again."

Roughly, he grabbed onto her and pulled her into his embrace, crushing her against his handsomely-dressed, finely scented body. His head went down to hers and he sought her lips as if they were a feast laid out before him. He laughed as he nuzzled her hair, across her cheeks, searching for her mouth. He pressed her close against him, rubbing his swollen member suggestively against her.

Revulsion overwhelmed her. She twisted her face away from his kiss, jerked back and found within herself the strength to resist his heated onslaught of her body. She pulled away from him and struggled desperately to bring the gun up against his side. The over sexed fool had forgotten about the gun. She pressed it against him and aimed slightly upward. Squeezing her eyes shut tight and gritting her teeth, she pulled the trigger.

She heard his gasping breath, and felt a shock go through his big body. In horror she watched him jerk, lose his evil grasp on her, and slump down onto the thick, carpet, clutching his belly. "You bitch, you dirty, fucking bitch!" he hissed. "You've done for me, and with my own gun!" He gasped in pain as Martha stood watching him in shock.

The door burst open and two men rushed in. "Get her," the sallow faced man cried. They grabbed her arms from behind, twisted them up against her back, and shoved her to the floor.

Forcing her face down, one of them yelled. "Hey, Morrie, quick, call a doc. Chaz's been shot for Christ's sake!" He sent a withering look toward Martha. "You filthy, fuckin' bitch, you shot him! I'll fix you! I'll fix you good!"

Martha saw his pock-marked face filled with a deadly rage just before she felt a sharp blow to the side of her head and was lost in darkness.

She slowly drifted upward, regaining her senses. Her head pounded with a dull, thudding pain. Opening her eyes, she lay close to Imperato, face to face. He appeared unconscious. She heard his rasping and labored breathing. The henchmen seemed to have gone. She didn't see or hear them and guessed they'd run for help.

She looked at Imperato's face—sallow, waxy, and sweating.

His eyes opened and saw nothing at first, until finally, they fastened on her. Focusing, he saw her and she heard him struggle to speak. "You've done for me—I have to know—please—are you that woman?" he asked, his voice soft and rasping.

His look of appeal touched her, making her wonder why something like that would matter now to a dying man. Amazed, that this vile man, who lay dying before her eyes, had only that small thing on his mind. Blood oozed from his mouth. His pallor increased to a yellowish sheen and his respirations were shallow and moist. The blood bubbles coming from his mouth meant she'd hit his lungs, likely a fatal injury. She said. "I'm sorry I had to shoot you, but you wouldn't let me go. I had to do it."

"You are that woman, aren't you?" To Martha, he seemed to hold no other interest as his voice weakened and faded.

She wondered again why it had seemed so important to him. Shots rang out somewhere beyond the room and in the outer areas of the huge, mansion as well. "What now? What's happening?" She tried to raise her head. "Something is going on. Are they trying to rescue me?" She fell back, the dark, the blackness overtaking her momentarily. When she came to again, Imperato had gripped tightly onto her arm, his nails biting deep. Fear clutched her and in her weakness, she couldn't dislodge his grasp on her.

"Tell me, bitch! You're the one. You are her. I knew it!" His pale eyes blazed wildly for a bit, then his grip loosened and he laid still, his eyes closed. She no longer heard his labored breathing.

Martha whispered. "Yes, you sick, evil, bastard, it *was* me that decked you on the dance floor. And I'd do it again, too." She thought him dead then, but his eyes fluttered once more, and she believed he'd heard her last words.

A few moments later, more shots exploded outside. She wondered helplessly who it was and what was happening. Slowly raising her head, and seeing no one about, she managed to crawl enough to reach a chair and slowly pull her trembling body into it.

A small female form slipped into the room and squatted in front of her. "Are you all right?" "You're not shot?" She looked Martha steadily in the eyes. "I'm Officer Carla Martino. I've been keeping an eye on you for the past several days." She glanced around. "Say, nice looking shack here, huh? Don't worry about those other two thugs. I took them out a while back. I've checked around pretty good. I think we've gotten most of them" She assisted Martha to move enough to ascertain she had no wounds or other debilitating injuries.

At the sounds of scuffling feet, Martha looked up and saw Bob entering with another man. He looked vaguely familiar to her, too, but she felt too sick and fuzzy to care. In the foggy distance, she heard sirens blaring and noticed the room filling with the voices of men. Bob reached her side.

Looking at his dear face once again, tears formed in her eyes. "Oh Bob, I thought I'd never lay eyes on you again." The sight of his face faded away and she knew no more.

Bob slid close and held her. "Martha, come on, it's all over. You're safe now." He nudged her and felt no response. "Martha, you okay?" He searched about for medical help. "Hey, she's passed out. Get a medic here, hurry, she's been shot!"

"No she's not, Carla put in. She told me she wasn't. They cracked her over the head and she's passed out from that. She'll need to be checked out, though." She pointed to Imperato. "He may need some medical attention, looks real bad." She took a closer look. "My God, I think he's dead!" Then she sighed. "Oh well, good riddance, that's what I say."

Ryan took a look. Finding no pulse, no signs of respirations, and seeing the grayish pallor with tinges of waxy yellowing creeping over his face, he concurred with Carla's reading. "Yeah, he is." He shrugged. "What a helluva night this has been."

He studied Carla. "Two more lying out in the hall. You get them?" When she nodded, he patted her on the shoulder. "The SWAT guys got a few more out in the shrubbery. All in all, this has worked out damned good. In fact, it's a whole hell of a lot like stomping on a nest of cockroaches!" Ryan felt good right now. A lot of unexpected things got put right tonight, except the mystery of Martha Lavery. He hadn't sorted that one out, yet. And right now, he didn't care.

The ambulance came, and after careful examination, took Martha away. Bob never left her side. They made room in the ambulance for his big frame.

They called the coroner's wagon for the dead. Two other wounded suspects went in a separate police ambulance. Neither Ryan nor Bob wanted Martha in the same vehicle with any of the Imperato bunch. She'd had enough of those people. But Ryan held out hope for a chat with the woman as soon as possible. There were so many issues he needed to discuss with Martha Lavery.

At Mercy, Martha underwent extensive testing and was admitted to ICU for close observation. "She's had a rather severe head trauma, said the doctor, a neurologist called in for this case. "We'll need to keep her for a few days." He wrote extensive orders and followed her to the unit, excited at having a staff member involved in such a newsworthy trauma.

Bob was strung out and worried about Martha. He stayed at her side as much as they'd allow. She regained consciousness and smiled up at him before lapsing back into a deep slumber, if that's what it was. Jeannie and Martin were there, as well as Lizzie.

Martin took Bob out of the room. "Listen Bob, let's go get a coffee. She's in good hands now, and we've got a long wait ahead of us. No need killing yourself here. She's a tough lady, she'll make it." He put an arm over Bob's shoulder as they walked along the corridor, looking for the elevators.

"It's been kinda tough for her the past several days," Bob told him. "She's told me a lot of things, but what I don't know is how much she's told you folks." He didn't plan to tell the things Martha had told him. He couldn't.

"We know she'd been seeing a psychiatrist," Martin replied. "But she hasn't told us everything. We've been waiting on that until she's ready to let us in." They entered the elevators and pressed the button for the basement cafeteria. "I guess she'll tell us everything when she's ready."

"That'll be her call. I love that woman, and I'll stand behind her in every way. I want you and Jeannie to know that."

"Man, you're making it sound kind of serious—is it?"

"We'll be getting married, one day soon," Bob admitted.

They walked into the coffee area, took cups, and filled them. Martin looked at Bob. "Anything else going on between you two besides getting married?" He laughed. "Jeannie's been all excited about that."

"Nothing I can discuss with you. It's her call," Bob replied. Walking around the cafeteria, he grabbed a hero sandwich, wilted around the edges, but edible enough for hospital chow. "Let's sit here," he said, laying his stuff on the table.

"Say, what's happening around here?" Jake walked up to their table and waited to be asked to join them. "Wasn't that Martha they brought in a few hours ago? Know what's going on with her?"

"Yeah, she's had a bit of trouble. Didn't make it in to work this afternoon, but you already knew that." Bob didn't plan to enlighten this blabber-mouth any further. "We'll be heading back up in just a minute." He figured that would pass for a 'get lost' request.

Jake got the hint and left the table saying, "Well, best get back. Got an old geezer dying up there tonight, they were going to call a code just before I left, but I think the doc said to make him a 'no code.'"

"So who's dying up there?" Bob asked. "I thought we had 'em all stabilized. As if we ever could," he added.

"It's that scrawny old guy, Sykes. He's been working on it for a while. It'll be a mercy if he does die. He's had a ton of pain these past few days, extra bad, they said. Nothing seems to relieve it, either. Oh well, as they say." Jake tossed the info off with no more feeling than usual. He quickly turned his attention toward a couple of young nurses.

He walked away and Bob saw him cozying up to a young ICU nurse who'd come for her supper break. He knew that most of the details about Martha would be spread far and wide in short order, and with the death of Sykes, another chapter of Martha's past would be put to rest. He was glad about that.

CHAPTER 37

Martha stayed in the unit for three days until cleared of a serious head injury. As she ambulated about the unit on one of her first days allowed out of bed, she saw Jean M.'s cubicle and asked her nurse, "How's that patient doing? I know her."

"She's so brain damaged, she'll spend the rest of her life being fed by a naso-gastric tube or better yet, a PEG tube. They'll transfer her to long term in a few more days," the nurse, Shelly, replied. "Sad case, the police questioned her husband. He said she'd fallen down the stairs."

"I wonder, do they even have stairs at their home?" Martha said then she added, "She's been in here before, and severely battered." She said nothing more. Both nurses knew the score, and the helplessness of ever changing things.

෴

When Martha went home from the hospital, Bob remained in constant attention. Loving and attentive, he cared for her in every way. He never demanded or even hinted at physical intimacies. Lurking in the shadows of their minds, unspoken questions haunted them both. Under it all, she knew he carried lingering doubts. Why did she not tell him about her dangerous entanglement with Imperato? Did she not fully trust him? She knew that he felt the pain and hurt of her lack of trust, yet she never doubted he loved her.

Does he love me enough to overcome this last hurdle? She had to speak finally. "Bob, we must talk. I know what question lies between us, and we have to have it out in the open. I can't stand this tension any more. I just can't."

"I'm ready, love," was all he said as he sat against her cradling her in his arms. "Say it, Martha, go ahead and tell me about it."

"Okay. I know I should have said something about Imperato. After all the rest that had happened, I was afraid I'd lose you all over again, and I couldn't find the courage. Those were the worst days of my life, when you never called me and I knew I'd lost your love."

She nestled against him. "And then, when we came together again, I still couldn't believe it, but I had hope. In fact, quite a bit of hope, the way you are with me."

She giggled, shrugged helplessly, and continued. "One night when I was Serena, Imperato saw me in there and made me dance with him. I didn't want to get out on the dance floor because Jake was in there. He'd seen me in there before and it made me nervous that he might think he knew me. I waited until I was near the door, decked Imperato, and ran away.

"Later, Jake went on about the man who was in the Paradisio several times looking for the woman who decked him. That's when I realized what I'd done and what a dangerous man he was." She gulped. "Later on, when he saw me there with Lizzie, he asked me if I was her. I denied ever knowing him, but he believed I was that woman anyway."

"I'd never heard of Imperato, or his reputation. What happened was done as another part of me, you know that. But when I realized the situation I'd gotten into, it was too much to ask any man to live with. How could I tell you something as sleazy as that?"

She gave him a hopeless smile. "I never knew he had me watched, even at the hospital, but I guess he did. Later on, I believe he actually wanted a relationship with me. Not as the over-dressed hooker type, Serena, but as *me*. You wouldn't want to know all his ideas of a great night together. And he wasn't the kind to take no for an answer. I had no choice but to defend myself. He made me physically ill, Bob."

Bob cracked the biggest grin she'd ever seen. "Wow! A gun moll! Martha, I can't say I blame that man for wanting you, and it fits right in with every other crazy thing that's happened in this saga of yours. Hey! I'm just along for the ride, and what a hell of a ride it is." He reached for her and crushed her so tight, she gasped for breath. "I love you to death, lady!"

"Oh, Bob! I wish we'd had this out sooner. We've missed out on so much, and I for one am sick to death of this damned nervous tension!" Martha felt giddy and happy. She couldn't think of another incident that could dampen things for her from now on. She melted into Bob's arms and stayed there.

❦❦❦

Ryan sat in his office contemplating his next move. He didn't have enough evidence on Martha to arrest her, but he had inner convictions from his years of police experience. "I've got to know!" He frowned, trying to figure a way to get at Martha. "How in the hell can I get her to level with me? And why would she anyway?"

Making a decision, he picked up the phone and called information for her home phone number. When he had her on the line, he asked, "Mrs. Lavery, I'd like a meeting with you."

Without hemming, hawing, or trying to avoid it, she agreed to meet him at the scene of the first crime.

❦❦❦

Martha met Ryan on a sunny knoll in Leesford Park. "Yes officer, what do you want with me?" She was calm, cool, and unafraid, sitting on a bench in the shade surveying the place where her vigilante adventures had begun. The wind sent a few leaves sailing and lifted flitting birds on feathered wings. A few clouds drifted leisurely across the bright blue, high mountain skies.

"Well, my lady, you have done more for law enforcement here in our fair city than all our people combined. That is, if what we believe about you is correct. We could never prosecute your actions against those two, and I speak of Callahan and Garver. The public would lynch us if we did, but we truly believe you are, or were, The Vigilante. What I want to ask you is if you will tell me what the hell happened? I'll go to my grave with your secrets, but if I don't find out what in hell happened, I believe I will go to my grave much sooner."

His imploring gaze moved her to feel safe in speaking. "Are you wearing any sort of listening device?"

"You can search me if you like," Ryan offered.

Martha paled, but she made her decision. "Yes, I will tell you. It will be a relief to get it off me for the last time." She took a deep breath and started. "It began after my grandson was attacked. Because of all the crazy things that kept happening after that, I sought the help of a psychiatrist. He found out some things." Tears formed in her eyes. "As a child, I was a helpless victim of abuse from a pedophile who worked on our farm. It began from that."

Martha's story was long, and Ryan listened intently, occasionally whistling at some detail, shaking his head at others. She ended by saying, "You see, a child predator, or pedophile, began this story for me, and I became a helpless victim as much as the two little ones you are concerned with. I cannot ever regret my actions, though I did not consciously commit those two deeds."

She shrugged. "Imperato was a casual incident, if you will. That just happened. I really had no part in causing that aside from shooting him to save myself." She allowed herself a half-laugh with that statement.

"Martha, I thank you, and every parent in Colorado Springs thanks you, too," Ryan said, his voice shaking. "As for Imperato, more men like him spring up every day, but it's one for our side anyway. But permit me a couple more questions. Why use a sand bag, and the purple stuff? Where did you find those ideas?"

"I learned the sand bag thing in a movie called Hospital, a long time ago. It starred George C. Scott. He said it leaves no mark, but does a good job and doesn't kill. Well, unless you hit too hard. The Gentian Violet, my father used it when he docked the male calves, pigs, and lambs."

"Interesting. Martha, you're a wonder, you know that?" He reached over and hugged her. "Thanks again, lady. I'm glad you were able to tell me about it. I'll treasure having known you. And I'm sorry for what happened to you as a child." He paused a moment then went on. "I have two small ones at home, and they are safer today because of you. Thank you."

"I didn't think I would actually have the courage to tell you these things, but confession really is good for the soul. I feel wonderful." She became thoughtful. "You might like to know that I appreciate your attitude in this, and thank you for not destroying my nursing career. Oh yes, you might also remember, you haven't read me my Miranda rights. So you can't arrest me anyway, now can you?"

Ryan laughed. "Right again, lady. I sure can't."

"Bob and I are getting married, and we'll be moving to a new location."

"Congratulations, Martha. I hope for your every happiness and would like to know how it turns out for Will. I'm afraid it'll be a very long road for that little guy. These things really hurt a child."

They parted amicably and Ryan drove away chuckling. "I wonder what'll happen if a pedophile rears his ugly head in her new community?"

THE END

About the Author

Ramona Forrest is a retired RN. She keeps busy writing novels—and traveling whenever possible. Forrest has resided in the back country of Arizona, assisted in round-ups, worked in Saudi Arabia, and has had the pleasure of traveling extensively. She now resides in Phoenix and spends much time in gardening, writing, entertaining friends, and family.